CRITICAL ACCLAIM FOR MORNING STAR

"Sandra Bregman's wit and intelligence have charmed presidents, senators, ambassadors, and anchormen. She's been there. She's lived it—all the time with her eyes open. Now we see what she saw: a kaleidoscope of colors and authentic detail, of unending action. If you are reading one political romance this year, make this the one."

>—BESS ABELL, former White House Social Secretary for President Lyndon Johnson

"As diplomatic aide, political campaigner, television personality and society hostess, Sandra Bregman has seen Washington in all its tinsel glitter and all its true grandeur. MORNING STAR gleams brilliantly with the insights and thrilling events she has eyewitnessed in Washington and the world."

>—LES WHITTEN, Washington novelist and investigative reporter, author of CONFLICT OF INTEREST, THE LOST DISCIPLE, and other thrillers

**EXPOSING THE SECRETS OF
WASHINGTON'S HIGH SOCIETY,
SHE DESPERATELY HID HER OWN!**

Cover posed by professional model.

D1594582

ABOUT THE AUTHOR

Sandra Bregman, a former fashion model and an Embassy Social Secretary in Washington during the Kennedy-Johnson era, intimately knows the world she writes about. Executive Producer of a political affairs series on PBS-TV, and a frequent White House guest, Sandra Bregman resides in the Capital City with her Washington-lawyer husband. She is presently at work on her next novel.

Morning Star

SANDRA BREGMAN

LEISURE BOOKS   NEW YORK CITY

With special thanks to Barbara Cummings, Sandra Loeb, and Patricia Griffith, who read this manuscript in its early stages and made invaluable suggestions.

A LEISURE BOOK

October 1990

Published by

Dorchester Publishing Co., Inc.
276 Fifth Avenue
New York, NY 10001

**TO EMILY,
MY SHINING STAR
AND INSPIRATION.**

Prologue

The burly, dark-skinned Italian entrepreneur positioned himself right where the runway split the seating. There, everyone of importance—especially those Americans to whom he had sent the best reserved seats—would see him, would recognize that G. B. Giorgini was the genius behind this glorious event. At last, this morning, the world would become aware of Italy's talented fashion designers. And Giorgini, who had put it all together, would show a tidy profit.

"This ballroom is magnificent! Imagine, this hotel was once the home of a duke! Such splendor!" exclaimed Carmel Snow of *Harper's Bazaar* to the Bergdorf's buyer as she swept past Giorgini with a perfunctory nod and claimed her front row seat.

Thirty musicians, dressed in black tie even though it was only ten in the morning, serenaded the burgeoning crowd of buyers, international fashion reporters, photographers and textile salesmen there to preview the fall collections of Italy's eleven finest designers.

More and more American buyers filed into the front rows, most of them old acquaintances of the others from years of buying trips to Paris and New York.

"Don't you just love Italy?" said Celia Gleason, the handsome, highly respected fashion writer for *The New York Times*. She hadn't been formally introduced to the gentleman seated on her left yet, but she did know that he was buying for Saks Fifth Avenue.

"One of the most beautiful countries in the world for my money, but couldn't you just weep over the terrible damage from the War? By the way, I'm Jim Clark. I know you are Celia Gleason." He shook her hand, then asked, "Have you been to Venice?"

"Not yet, but I'm planning to go right after this week in Florence."

"You'll love it, I promise you. And don't miss the beach at the Lido. It's right out of a Scott Fitzgerald novel."

The house lights flickered, encouraging everyone to be seated. Waiters passed out French champagne while buyers and press alike opened notebooks and pulled out pens. Carmel Snow turned to her right and acknowledged her old friend, Celia Gleason, and newcomer Jim Clark. "Exciting, isn't it? This is the first time Italy's tried to play in the big leagues, to compete with France. And I understand the prices will be about half those of Paris couture."

"Yes," Jim agreed, "and isn't it great fun to add another country to our itinerary?"

The lights went out, the orchestra sounded a fanfare, and G.B. Giorgini took the microphone to welcome his guests—especially the Americans.

The first model, a tall Italian, skipped down the runway in a pale taupe wool coat-and-dress ensemble by Simonetta. A mild smattering of applause followed her off the stage. Buyers wrote down the number 1 and, in some cases, the name and size of the client they had in mind.

The second model, a Scandinavian type, pivoted directly in front of Carmel Snow. The chocolate-brown wool suit trimmed in mink by Fabiani brought enthusiastic applause, a couple of whistles, and much scribbling.

South-Dakota-born Lorna Brown appeared at the top of the runway. She stopped dead still, waiting for the spotlight to find her, waiting for the flute soloist to complete the haunting, almost eerie opening bars of "Claire d'Lune." Only when the violins began to swell behind her did she begin to glide down the runway, a calm, disinterested look on her unsmiling face. Slowly, ever so slowly and gracefully, without even a flicker of recognition to her acquaintances in the front row, she floated to the end of the runway. Her hair, looking like sun-washed corn-silk, cascaded around her face and touched her shoulders. Her flawless complexion was like fresh, warm cream. Slowly, letting the audience drink in her cool beauty, she unbuttoned the black silk velvet evening coat to reveal a blue satin cocktail dress the exact shade of a robin's egg, the exact color of her eyes. Effortlessly, in no rush, she slipped the coat off and held it in one arm. Still at the end of the runway, she pirouetted once for the audience on the left, then once for the audience on the right.

Then, without ever seeming to have made eye contact with anyone in the audience, she floated regally back to the beginning of the runway. Halfway back, the audience exploded in wild applause and whistles.

"Like royalty."

"Breathtaking!"

"Such cool beauty . . . she's a sensation."

"We must put her on our cover," Carmel Snow whispered to her assistant, then turned to Celia. "She's everything you said, Celia! Absolutely smashing!"

Jim Clark looked questioningly at Celia.

A bit flustered by the attention, she explained. "Lorna, that model, is my niece."

"Incredible! It will be every man's fantasy, to melt that ice. But does she ever smile?"

Count Antonio Dandolo, who had been leaning nonchalantly against an ancient marble pillar in the back of the room, perked up, joined in the applause, then summoned an aide with a glance. After a whispered conversation, the aide hurried backstage.

Ninety minutes later, Lorna Brown sat down in front of a mirror and began to slather her face with cleansing cream. Now, at last, she could let her insides tremble, she could let loose the awful fear she had bottled up all morning. As she massaged her aching eyes and throbbing temples, she felt her icy hands begin to warm. She wiped her hands and searched in her purse for aspirin, then swallowed four with a glass of water.

"Hey, kid, you were great." Designer Roberto Calvani clapped her shoulder, then congratulated the other American model, Kathy Schaeffer. "You two brought the house down every time. It was a stroke of genius to bring American girls over here."

For the hundredth time, Lorna swore under her

breath at the lack of privacy in the dressing rooms. Men were always walking in and out with no concern for anyone's modesty or state of undress. She would never get used to it.

She nodded her thanks to Calvani and continued cleansing her face.

After he was out of earshot, Kathy asked "How ya' doin', Lorna? I told you it wouldn't be bad— just like back home, only the men are more expressive."

"Give me a photo session any day over a runway show. I hate this part of it."

"Strange . . . it's my favorite part of being a model. That, and the travel. I must admit, I love the applause. Most of the photographers I know don't applaud; they just try to screw you."

"It'll be another hour before I get over the shakes. I've never been so scared in all my life."

"You'd never know it. You look so totally relaxed, so above it all . . . ."

Calvani's assistant, Rosa Machelli, cautiously approached Lorna. "Miss Brown, you have been invited to lunch by the most exciting man in all of Italy! May I assure him of your acceptance?"

"No, Rosa, really. I must go back to my room—"

"Who is it, Rosa?" Kathy interrupted.

"Ah, he is charming, a rascal but so handsome. You surely must come, Miss Brown!"

"For God's sake, who is he?" Kathy demanded.

Rosa looked sadly at Kathy. "It is Miss Brown he wishes to know. He is Count Antonio Dandolo of the great Dandolo family. You really must go, my dear." Rosa patted Lorna's shoulders, then, inspired, began to massage the back of her neck. "There, you feel better soon, you'll see . . . some wine, some pasta, a nice lunch. . . ."

"I will accept only if Kathy is included," Lorna declared with a sigh. "It might be an interesting story to tell Aunt Celia."

"I speak with Count Dandolo," Rosa said, clearly annoyed with both girls.

Count Antonio Dandolo and his three guests—Roberto Calvani, Kathy Schaeffer, and Lorna Brown—were seated immediately in spite of a waiting line at Buca Lopi, a restaurant converted from the ancient wine cellar of the Antinori Palace. He brushed his wavy black hair off his sun-browned forehead, removed his sun glasses, and instructed the waiter to bring a bottle of Vernaccia. Then he turned his attention and his piercing, slightly mocking, velvet-brown eyes on Lorna. He switched to English effortlessly. It was one of five languages he spoke fluently.

"If I were a buyer, I would've bought everything you wore this morning—which makes me suspicious of the whole business."

Lorna lowered her eyes, feeling a deep flush spread across her face. She knew only that Dandolo was "in textiles"—and terribly important to Calvani. Before she could think of a response to the count's flattery, Calvani chimed in, "Why do you think we brought Lorna and Kathy here? For exactly that reason. American buyers want to see the clothes on beautiful, leggy, corn-fed American girls!"

Then, before she could say anything, they reverted to Italian. Lorna didn't mind, for she had been squirming under the count's scrutiny. His arrogance shocked her and at the same time attracted her. The men laughed, and she knew it was at her expense, set off by some sort of affectionate remark from Calvani. In spite of the count's relative youth—she guessed he could not be more than thirty—he dominated the table. She gradually realized that he was, in some business way, Calvani's superior even though Calvani had to be twice his age.

Lorna glanced directly at the count, as if compelled by an unspoken command. His eyes bewitched her with a piercing magnetism and held her in thrall; they demanded that she recognize his intense attraction, his vow to possess her. A shudder overwhelmed her body; she felt her arms break out in goosebumps, her throat go dry. She recoiled in fear. Lowering her gaze, she studied the cuticles on her nails and gripped her water glass for dear life. How could he so flagrantly announce his baseness? Then she wondered if it was his directness that she found so compelling.

They launched into a discussion of the show that morning, leaving Lorna out of the conversation except when one of the three would translate some remark thought to be of particular interest to her. They discussed Simonetta and Fabiani, then the Fontana sisters, who were the favorites of both the buyers and the press, exactly as Calvani had anticipated.

The count ordered a chestnut cake for dessert, then turned to Lorna and declared, "Emilio Pucci has invited a small group of us to his villa tonight. I would be pleased if America's most beautiful model would accompany me."

"But I . . . I had promised Kathy that we . . ."

Roberto frowned at Lorna, but the count instantly understood the situation. "But of course. Both you and Kathy will accompany me. Emilio will be delighted."

* * *

That first evening was a prelude to the next three.
The Count—"you must call me Tony, and I will
call you Lorna. After all we will soon be intimate
friends!"—insisted on occupying Lorna's evenings
and Lorna insisted on including Kathy. Not because she was concerned for Kathy's feelings, but
because she was nervous about being alone with
Tony. He would not hesitate to press his attentions
on her and she doubted her ability—and will—to
resist him.

After three hectic days and glorious evenings in
Florence, Lorna and Kathy were whisked into
Paris, into the world of Dior, Balmain, Patou,
Balenciaga, and Schiaparelli. The great fashion
houses of the world and Paris, wonderful Paris, all
in one week! Between shows and tedious photo-
graphic sessions for the American magazines,
Kathy and Lorna, always in tandem, visited the
Louvre and the Eiffel Tower, and saw Jean Babilee
dance in "Till Eulenspiegel" with the Ballets des
Champs-Elysees.

On their third evening at the newly reopened
Crillion Hotel, Lorna had an urgent message to call
the Countess Catarina Dandolo in Florence. Mystified, and not entirely certain whom she was calling,
Lorna returned the call. Catarina was Tony's mother, she learned, and she was inviting—insisting
that Lorna and Kathy attend a ball at her home in
honor of the director of the Teatro alla Scala that
coming Saturday. Lorna began to make excuses,
thinking of her limited money, but Countess
Dandolo said: "I'm wiring two tickets, and you
shall be my house guests. Tony will arrange for your
return to America on Monday. Now, it's all settled."

Lorna could think of little else in Paris, so eager

was she to see Tony again and meet his vivacious and youthful-sounding mother. She convinced the manager of Dior to sell her a sample gown for the ball and made a Friday appointment with the famous hairdresser, Carita. Lorna was determined to return to Florence in style.

And so she did, though to her disappointment, Tony did not personally greet them. A chauffeured Rolls Royce emblazoned with the crest of the Dandolo family drove them directly to the Villa Dandolo high on a hill overlooking the city of Florence. The stately car entered the grounds through a tall, wrought-iron gate and drove down a long, cypress-lined drive before the house—in truth, a palace—came into view. The young ladies were ushered into the huge marble entrance hall, then into the library where the butler offered them sherry. Moments later, a striking brunette in riding jodhpurs strode in and gleefully extended her hand to Lorna. "*Buon giorno!* I am Catarina Dandolo. I'm so pleased you could come!"

Lorna was stunned by Catarina's youth and her informality in this very imposing setting.

"And you are Kathy, the beautiful blonde," Catarina continued, shaking Kathy's hand. "Both of you are every bit as lovely as Tony told me you were."

She can't be more than forty, thought Lorna, yet she must be older if she's Tony's mother. This slim, fair-skinned beauty was the opposite of the matronly, heavy-set, dark-skinned Italian mothers Lorna had glimpsed on the Ponte Vecchio the previous week. Yet, there was a decided facial resemblance and an engaging directness in Catarina's personality that reminded her of Tony.

"You must forgive Tony for not meeting you. We

had an emergency at one of our factories in Milan. I promise you he will be here by dinner. Meanwhile, let me show you around. Tony told me you love art and horses," she said to Lorna. "We have plenty of both."

Catarina then began a tour of the villa. Lorna could scarcely believe what she was seeing—that such masterpieces were privately owned! Rubens, Titian, Tiepelo, Rembrandt—the paintings had been acquired generations ago and passed down, Catarina explained. Lorna especially loved the more recently acquired Renoirs, Monets, Manets, and—in Catarina's bedroom—three romantic Fragonards. The paintings and sculptures were priceless—and in the back of Lorna's mind was the knowledge that Tony was an only child, the sole heir to this vast collection. She barely noticed the porcelains, tapestries, and antiques. Her eyes were riveted to the paintings.

Catarina then led them out through the formal gardens down the long path to the stables, where they met fourteen fine thoroughbreds, each in its own large stall with one groom for every three horses. No wonder the stable was so immaculate! In the tack room, Lorna viewed, awestruck, the cases full of ribbons and trophies.

"My husband's family has been breeding and training horses for generations. Unfortunately, during the War we had to farm them out all over Italy to protect them. Tony has been slowly bringing them home these past two years. But he's so busy, and he has so much on his mind these days . . . ."

As she listened to Catarina catalogue their breeding and accomplishments, Lorna understood that Catarina cared much more about the horses than the priceless art collection.

"Now that I've exhausted you, let me show you to your rooms. Do nap for a while. Our parties last into the wee hours. Dinner will be served at nine, but we'll begin to gather in the library for cocktails at eight."

As they made their way to separate suites on the third floor of the west wing, Catarina explained that the villa was still being renovated following the German, and then the American, occupations at the end of the War. "Luckily, with Emilio's connections, the Vatican stored our art, so nothing was lost. But the furniture, that's another story . . . ."

The bedroom door closed behind her. Lorna collapsed into a coral velvet-covered chair, relieved to be alone to collect herself, to understand her myriad feelings. She scrutinized the bowerlike confection she found herself in. The huge room was dominated by a massive four-poster bed. The headboard, the pagoda-like top, and the four posts were draped in pale blue chintz enlivened with small coral roses. The same fabric had been used for ceiling-to-floor draperies and to upholster the walls. Circular tables covered in floor-length cloths of the same chintz were stationed on each side of the bed. Fragrant roses in crystal vases and crystal lamps with coral silk shades provided the only relief from the floral chintz exuberance. The floor was carpeted in an even paler shade of blue, and through the open door to the mirrored bathroom, Lorna could see gold and crystal fixtures glistening in the sunlight pouring in from the open windows.

Never in her most glamorous fantasies back in South Dakota—or even in New York City, for that matter—had she imagined a bedroom as splendid as this one. It was larger than her mother's living room, dining room, and kitchen combined!

Lorna walked into the bathroom and stood spellbound at the window, watching the spectacle beneath her. Bustling waiters were setting up circular
tables with gilt chairs on the terrace. The intricate
mosaic terrace had been created centuries ago,
Catarina had explained, by skilled artisans using
different kinds of local stones. From her vantage
point, Lorna could see that the mosaic's triangles,
diamonds, and stars led one's eye inexorably toward the center, where the spray from a glorious
fountain cooled the hot July air. The terrace was
partially enclosed by manicured, ancient boxwood.

Off to the left, Lorna spied four graceful swans
floating serenely in a small lake surrounded by
lemon trees, groupings of topiary animals, and
welcoming benches. Groves of tall, deep-green cypress provided a distant backdrop for the shimmering lake, creating the illusion of a large outdoor
reception room.

I would love to paint this scene, thought Lorna as
she watched the swans dunk their heads to cool off.
She glanced to the far right and remembered the
immaculate stables, hidden from her view now, but
accessible by a gravel pathway through gardens of
roses, lilies, herbs, and thousands of blossoming
flowers.

"I love fresh flowers in every room of the house,"
Catarina had confided as they walked through the
narrow passageway toward the stables. Everywhere
Lorna had seen servants, gardeners, stableboys—
and Catarina, reading her mind, had gaily commented, "As you can see, we do a lot to boost the
employment rate here in Firenze!"

Lorna thought of Tony and Catarina's horses and
remembered with a pang her own beloved Nicky
and the bitter tears she had shed when her mother

had sold her pony. She had been happy galloping over the meadows on Nicky. A few hours of happiness in an otherwise miserable daily life.

The fundamental agony of her childhood was that her father had deserted her—rather, had deserted *them*, her mother and herself.

PART ONE
Corinna

Chapter One

BARNESVILLE, SOUTH DAKOTA, 1929

Barnesville, South Dakota, was a dreary, two-block-long farming community in the southeastern corner of the state, thirty-seven miles north of Nebraska. Originally populated by God-fearing descendants of the English colonists and French fur trappers, Barnesville had come into its own after passage of the Homestead Act in 1862. Thousands of German sodbusters had flooded Wisconsin, Nebraska, Iowa, and South Dakota, followed shortly thereafter by the Irish who came to lay the transcontinental railroad. There were a few Polish and Scandanavian families scattered throughout the countryside, but the town merchants were principally of English, French, and Irish background.

When Agnes and John Gleason married, they united English and French genes that dated back to the *Mayflower*'s arrival at Plymouth with the more recently arrived German and Irish. Somewhere in

John's genealogical past there appeared to be Sioux blood, though no one in the family would admit to it or even discuss the subject.

On the tranquil surface, Barnesville families seemed to live simple, peaceful lives filled with small joys, unceasing hard work, and a deep concern for the next day's weather. The older folks who passed the time of day on the bench outside Snyder's Drugs could tell the history of family feuds fought out through three generations. As in all small towns, the greatest desire was for respectability, the greatest fear was scandal and gossip. Children were taught to worry about "what people will say" while they digested their pabulum. Social life revolved around church events, school events, revivals, the annual county fair, funerals and weddings, and, with the coming of a movie house (which had been fought by the Methodists), the Wednesday and Saturday night movie.

The reality was that everyone knew everyone else's business and with the advent of telephones and party lines, the housewife found herself distracted from her daily chores by the need to listen to everyone else's calls. Nothing, absolutely nothing, was a secret for long in Barnesville.

"I made lunch for us," Celia called to her older sister Corinna as she carried a tray out onto the back porch, letting the screen door slam behind her.

"Well, I'll be . . ." Corinna muttered with a shrug of her shoulders. Then, thinking better of it, she called back, "I'll just finish this basket first." She continued hanging the sheets and pillowcases on the clothesline. "When's yer next one comin'?"

"Alyce Peterson comes in half an hour."

"Ugh! She's been playin' the same three pieces

for the last month. I 'speck her parents don't think much of yer teachin'."

"It's her mother's fault. She doesn't make Alyce practice."

Corinna hung the last sheets, dropped a few clothespins into the empty basket, then carried it to the porch and sat down beside Celia on the steps. She picked up the egg salad sandwich, but before she took a bite she asked, "Did you see to mother?"

"Yes, she's eating now. She's complaining of a headache. I think we need to rig up better lighting for her if she insists on working with such dark thread."

"Maybe she'd like to eat with us. It's not too hot, and her roses and hollyhocks look right good today."

"No. I asked her. She's listening to that choir from Salt Lake City on the radio. You know how she is."

"Yeah." Corinna brushed some crumbs off her blue cotton skirt. "Maybe the headache's from listening to all that racket yer pupils make."

"She says that doesn't bother her at all. She loves to listen to music, you know that."

"Maybe so. But that ain't music. If you weren't learning the kids today, she'd be listenin' to that preacher from Sioux Falls. I'spose it don't make no difference."

"*Doesn't* make *any* difference," corrected Celia.

"You know I hate that. Why do you keep trying to shame me? Mama says it's wrong to correct yer elders, an' I'm yer elder!"

" 'By your language you shall be known.' Honestly, Corinna, I wish you'd try to sound a bit more educated. I know you didn't finish high school and you always hated studies, but that isn't any excuse."

"I talk like everyone else in Barnesville. I ain't stuck-up like you." She watched a bumble-bee sample the pollen of a red dahlia, then added, "Celia, people talk about you down at the store. Yer 'big head', yer 'big ideas.' Puts me in mind of the Clark girl, left for New York six years ago and her parents ain't heard hide nor hair of her since."

"Which people, exactly?"

"Reverend Miller's wife was in the store yesterday. She asked me if my 'smart sister' was still planning on leaving for New York the day after graduation."

"What did you tell her?"

"I said I didn't rightly know. But I'm 'fraid Reverend Miller is gonna come see mama and tell her to put a stop to your wicked ideas. Also, Sarah Fields saw you at the movies last week. Mama knows you sneak to the movies even though you're forbidden to go. She says that's where you get all your high-falutin' ideas, from the movies."

Celia slammed down her plate on the gray porch floor. "All I've ever wanted to do is get out of this boring town where nothing ever happens and go to New York and make something of myself. But in this miserable town it's a scandal to even think out loud about leaving. Makes me so gosh-darn mad!"

"How much money you got saved?"

"None of your business."

"Are you giving me half of everything?"

"You know I am Corinna, that's our deal and I don't cheat."

Celia and Corinna Gleason had made a deal between themselves three years previously. Corinna, who didn't mind housework and cooking, would take care of the house and their mother, who had been in a wheelchair since being struck by lightning seven years previously. Celia, recognized by everyone as the bright and talented sister, would teach piano lessons. Celia would give Corinna half of all the money she made to compensate for not helping with the housework. Corinna, meanwhile, had dropped out of school after her sophomore year when she'd been offered a clerk's job in the grocery store. Her one strength, in addition to being considered pretty, was that she was good with figures.

Meanwhile, their three older brothers hired themselves out to farmers in Nebraska. Their father, hardly ever home, was an electrical engineer who traveled from town to town designing and creating electrical plants. Though the Depression was beginning to make itself felt in South Dakota, so far the Gleason family had not seen any measurable changes in their quiet lives.

"How much you got saved for New York?" Corinna persisted.

"I told you, it's none of your business. If you didn't spend every penny you made on the latest gewgaws, you'd have some money saved too."

"You should see what I bought yesterday. Nail polish and lipstick!"

"And you think Reverend Miller is going to talk to mother about *me!* My gosh, Corinna, you'd better not let Mama see you with any lipstick or polish. She'll have a stroke!"

"I got polish remover, stupid; I can take it off anytime I want. She'll never see it."

At that moment, Alyce Peterson arrived for her piano lesson, so Celia quickly gathered up the remnants of their lunch. Corinna went back into the house to get more laundry.

As she hung out her brother's overalls, she

thought about herself and her sister. *Mostly, we love one another. But we're so different. We've always been the 'pretty Gleason girls' and there's no doubt about it—we're the prettiest girls for miles around, maybe in all of South Dakota. People say Celia's the brightest, but whatta they know? She 'will go places,' but I 'have a way with the boys.' And that's more important. And it's true, I do, and I am the prettiest. (Mama, forgive me, I know vanity's a sin.) I'm going to marry Ed Brown, the best catch here 'bouts. He makes nearly a thousand dollars a year and he's so good-lookin, like a movie star. Someday he'll own his father's gas station, it'll be all ours. Poor Celia, can't attract boys, no boys interested in her at all. She don't care none. T'wouldn't surprise me if she ends up an old maid. No boy in this part of the country would have such a stuck-up girl. "Too smart for her own good," our dad says and it don't please him none that she'll be valedictorian. I s'pect Mama is secretly happy, but daren't say so in front of dad.*

Funny about Mama. . . . Some days she acts as if it's okay for Celia to leave and go east, even to be an actress. Everyone knows that's the wickedest profession of all. Celia imagines she can be an actress just 'cause she recites better than anyone here'bouts. Other days, Mama calls down Celia 'bout wickedness, and God's will, and vanity and 'the ways of the world.' Seems Mama can't make up her mind whether to force Celia to stay home or let her go. At least I won't be no cause of trouble. I'll do exactly what Mama wants me to do, marry Ed and settle down.

After Celia's piano lessons were finished and Corinna had seen to their mother's dinner, the two girls found themselves together again in their bedroom. Corinna was dressing for a date with Ed.

They were going to a church supper where all the Barnesville Methodists could see what a fine match Corinna was about to make.

"When's the big day? When are you and Ed going to get married?"

"Pshaw! I don't know. He ain't even asked me yet."

"But you know he's going to. He's just got to save up money like our dad said."

"He'd better not come round here asking for your hand unless he's got five hundred dollars saved up," Jason Gleason had said several times during the past year. Corinna had promptly repeated it to Ed.

"You're going to marry him and have ten children. I know your whole future. I only wish I knew as much about mine," Celia said as she picked up the poetry book and began again to memorize "How do I love thee?"

Corinna stopped brushing her hair for a moment. "No, not ten children. Maybe five."

"Yeah, we'll see! But you'd better hurry up and set the date 'cause I'm not waiting around this hick town forever just to be your bridesmaid."

Corinna looked hard at Celia. "Are you really fixin' to leave the day after graduation? Do you really have that much money put by?"

"My plans are my own business. But once I leave, I won't be able to afford to come back for your wedding. So if you're really going to marry Ed I wish you'd hurry up and set the date so I can make my own plans."

"Ed is gonna surprise me with something tonight. I can't wait to see what it is . . . maybe a ring?"

"You'd be better off if he bought a car of his own. That's what you'll need." Celia took her book and fled to the kitchen where there would be no distractions.

Corinna was slightly miffed to realize Ed had her sister's practical turn of mind when he arrived in a used '27 Ford he'd proudly purchased for fifty-seven dollars. Even so, she tried to cover her disappointment and act thrilled for him. Owning his own car was one more step on the way to marriage, that much was sure.

The Methodist men looked over his car and the women clucked over her new store-bought blue and white linen dress in the latest middy style. Corinna, probably the most fashion-conscious person in Barnesville, wore white calf shoes, silk stockings, and a white cloche hat. She was pleased that she stood out as the fashion plate of the Saturday night box supper.

"I was hopin' you'd bring your dear mother, Corinna," Mrs. Miller, the minister's wife, scolded. "T'would do her a world of good to get out more."

"She's been poorly all day—her eyes, you know."

"And Celia? Didn't she want to socialize with our young people?" Eleanor Peterson asked in a mildly sarcastic tone.

"No, she's memorizing poems by that English woman—for the graduation exercises."

Ed and Corinna ate their chicken supper, gossiped with the other young people, and while it was yet light they escaped for a ride in the country. It really was quite daring, Corinna thought, as they drove away, to go riding in his car, just the two of them alone. People would definitely talk. They talked about everything in this town.

They drove four miles into the country, then without warning Ed drove down the long drive leading to his cousin Burt's farm. "Oh, you're gonna show Burt your new car!" They came to an abrupt stop in front of the large white farmhouse.

"Nope," Ed answered as he climbed out of the driver's seat and slammed the door. He opened the door on her side. "Careful, don't slip with those fancy shoes of yours." She stepped gingerly onto the running board, then into his arms. He kissed her soundly as he lifted her down. "You like it then, my roadster?"

"Oh, yes, it's grand!"

As they walked toward the kitchen door, Ed fumbled in his black Sunday suit coat for a key. "Burt's gone to Sioux City with a load of hogs. Asked me to do the chores and look after the place for him. Thought you'd like to see his fancy house."

"I'd hardly 'spect a bachelor's house to be fancy," she said as she followed him into the kitchen. "Oh my! Look at that sink!"

"Turn the faucet on."

Corinna turned the handle on the left. Then put her hand under the spigot. "It's hot!"

"Yes, indeedy. Some house, this her'in. Wait till you see what's upstairs."

They prowled around the main floor opening closet doors and feeling like two guilty spies. Then Ed led Corinna by the hand up the pine staircase.

"My, he really took time with this finishing. It's like glass."

"Yeah. He likes to mess with wood. He did all the sanding and finishing himself. Maybe he'll build a house for us someday."

"D'ya think?"

Ed smiled secretively and leaned down to kiss her again. "If I ask him to, he will. Now, close your eyes and don't open until I tell you." Corinna obeyed, heard him open a door and lead her in, then he told her to open her eyes. She stared at a gleaming white porcelain bathtub on claw feet and then at a white toilet with a pine cover.

"Watch," he said as he pulled the chain.

"An indoor bathroom! I'll be, how wonderful! I didn't know Burt was so rich." She turned the faucet in the sink and tested the water with her hand. "How do you keep it warm like this? Land-a-goshen, I do wish we had hot water in our house. T'would make doing laundry so much easier, no more haulin' . . ."

"With a water heater in the basement, silly."

"Oh, I can't wait to tell Mama and Celia."

He frowned and became thoughtful. "I don't think you'd best tell your folks you was out here like this with me. It might not set too well with them."

"Oh . . . well, okay. Now show me the rest of the house."

"Well . . . it's just two bedrooms up here."

Corinna began to finish the tour by herself. She went into Burt's bedroom, examined the odds and ends on his dresser, looked in his closet, and saw a wall of girlie pictures. "Ah, ha! What a bad man!" she grinned back at Ed. "Do you have pictures like this?"

"Maybe I do and maybe I don't," he teased as he walked over to her. He kissed her solidly, then let his hands wander down her back. She reached up and teased him with her tongue on his lips.

"You'd better be careful, young lady, you're going to get yourself in trouble."

"Maybe I want to and maybe I don't."

He let himself go then and pressed her body back against the wall with his own. Somehow, without consciously planning it, his hand was on her naked breast and then her new linen dress lay on the floor beside them. He picked her up and carried her to Burt's bed.

Afterwards, their passion spent, they lay quite still contemplating what they'd done.

"I'm sorry. Corinna? I . . . I didn't mean to . . ."

"Hush. It's okay. I love you, Ed. Now you know how much I love you."

"I love you too, Corinna."

"When did you first?"

"I don't remember. For a long time now."

"I loved you my first day in high school. I saw you at the pep rally. You were captain of the football team, the best lookin' guy in the senior class. I knew I loved you that moment and I've loved you ever since."

Ed was very quiet. Then he said, "We shouldn't have done it today. It's wrong, Corinna."

"No, no, it's not, because I love you. We love one another."

"Yes."

"But we should get married soon."

"If you think so. But I've only saved three hundred dollars. Your dad—"

"I'll take care of my dad."

Ed reached over cautiously and took Corinna's hand. "Would you like to take a hot bath? In a real bathtub, like rich folks do?"

"Oh yes, that's a great idea. Will you take one with me?" She looked at his large, lean body and her pleasure glowed in her eyes. He reached over and caressed her creamy breast, then kissed it.

"Maybe we'll wait a few minutes before that bath . . . ."

Twelve weeks later, in early August, Edward Brown and Corinna Gleason were married in the Methodist Church before the townspeople of

Barnesville. Jason Gleason managed to be home for the wedding, having traveled from Long Pine, Nebraska, where he was working on a major electrical job. The bride wore a slipper satin gown made by herself and her mother. She had decorated the shoulder-length veil exactly like one she had seen in *Woman's Home Companion*, with white roses and lily of the valley. Her sister Celia doubled as bridesmaid and soloist. Burton Brown served as his cousin's best man.

After the punch-and-wedding-cake reception in the church hall, the happy couple left for a wedding trip to Lincoln.

Unbeknownst to her family and the townspeople, Celia slipped away the next day. She took the bus to Sioux City, then the train to New York City.

Seven months later the focus of town gossip shifted away from Celia's escape and back to Corinna. She gave birth two months prematurely to an eight-pound baby girl whom they named Lorna. The baby was born with glowing pink skin, a robust cry, chestnut hair, and intensely blue eyes.

Years later, Corinna would look back on her first two years of marriage as the only happy time in her life. Perhaps it was her imagination, as her mother said, but after Lorna's birth she felt herself being repeatedly snubbed by the people of Barnesville, especially the members of the Methodist Church. She could feel them whispering about her every time she walked into the church or social hall. She knew they were constantly judging her to see if she could overcome the stigma of Lorna's "premature birth." Would she humble herself enough to regain full membership in their tight Christian society? Churchwork was the only social world open to a young woman in Barnesville, so Corinna, in her hunger for respectability and acceptance, redoubled her efforts. She baked and put by preserves for church sales, she visited the sick every day, she did housework for the bedridden, and, because she had no money, she began to dress in homemade clothes like everyone else. Reluctantly, she surrendered her image as the town's fashion plate.

As she slowly worked herself back into the good graces of the Methodist ladies, they confided to her their concerns about her husband's family and future. It was well known that the Browns had once been Roman Catholics but had fallen away when Ed's father had a violent disagreement with Father Henley. They had raised no objection to Ed's marriage in the Methodist Church, nor did they seem to mind his weekly attendance with Corinna. She knew Ed's father, Bill, broke the rules of the Methodists, as most Catholics did. He smoked cigars, always had a stash of beer and whiskey in his barn, and regularly played cards. Bill and Clara Brown even liked to travel down to Hardington, Nebraska, where big dance bands played on Saturday nights. Their favorite was a local boy, Lawrence Welk. They never missed him if they had the money to spare. Once, shortly after their marriage and before Corinna was visibly pregnant, they had invited her and Ed to come along. "But I can't," Corinna had protested. "I couldn't possibly. Dancing is against my religion!"

In the deepest, most hidden part of her heart, she wondered how she could have thought so little about the Brown family before she'd married Ed. It seemed to her now that she had to overcome not only the stigma of her daughter's untimely birth, but also the Brown family's disrepute in Methodist circles.

She was not prepared, however, for what Ellen

McClintock confided to her one morning when she was making a round of sick visits. Ellen, a portly woman in her late fifties, was recovering from a bad bout with pneumonia and Corinna had visited her several times a week for over a month. Mrs. McClintock had thought long and hard and prayed over what she was about to say.

"My dear, please stop fussing with my bedclothes and come and sit by me. We must talk."

Corinna sat down, smoothed her long, burgundy wool skirt and unrolled her sleeves and buttoned the cuffs. She sipped the tea she had poured for herself a few moments earlier.

"I must talk to you about Ed, my dear. Strictly confidential."

Those words, uttered in such an ominous tone, caused a sinking feeling in Corinna's chest. "Yes?"

"His father is about to lose the gas station. Gambling debts, you know. The bank is going to forclose next week."

"But—that's impossible! Ed would know."

"He may be trying to spare you, my dear, or he may not know."

"Are you sure?"

"I'm positive, my dear. I'm so sorry."

My foot, you are, Corinna thought meanly. *You and the rest of the Methodists are just waiting to see bad things happen to us.*

Corinna thought hard. Ellen McClintock's best friend was married to the owner of the bank, so her information was probably reliable and lots of other people probably knew too. She quickly calculated what she would do. She would wheel Lorna's buggy down to the gas station—quite a bit farther than their normal outing—and she would confront Ed with this information.

"I've only told you, my dear, because I know Ed works for his father, and what with jobs being so hard to come by these days . . ."

"I understand, Mrs. McClintock. Thank you. And now, if you'll excuse me, I think I'll take Lorna home. It's time for her lunch."

"Yes, of course. My dear child, we will all be praying for your well-being."

What joy she got out of telling me that, Corinna thought bitterly as she pushed the baby carriage toward the gas station. She was prepared to surprise Ed and his father, but she was not prepared for what she saw when she walked into the back room. There had been no cars demanding service, as it was February and business was slow. When she entered the back room unannounced, she was stunned to see her husband playing cards with his father, his cousin Burt, and a local farmer. All four of them had open beer cans beside them, and Ed was dragging on a cigarette as she walked into the room. After the initial shock, Corinna walked directly to the rusty metal table.

"Corinna, what a surprise . . . ."

"Hell's bells!"

"Well I'll be God-damned . . . ."

She looked directly at the pile of bills and coins in the middle of the table.

"So, Father Brown, is this how you're going to keep the bank from foreclosing on you next week? Is this how you're going to protect your family's future?"

"Ed, I think you'd better get your wife outta here." Bill Brown looked as if he might strike her if she didn't disappear instantly.

Ed had already stood up. He crushed his cigarette with deliberation, looked angrily at her, and said,

"I've told you to stay out of men's business. I've told you not to come here."

"Yes, and now I understand why!"

The bank did foreclose, not only on Bill Brown's gas station, but on his farm too. The Brown family, in a useless attempt to save face, announced they were moving to Detroit, where Bill would go into "automotive manufacturing."

A dispirited Ed Brown visited every town within a forty-mile radius during the next six months looking for work. The following October, he accepted a job as a shoe salesman in Vermillion, deciding to drive back and forth each day rather than uproot Corinna and Lorna. Besides, Corinna could not leave her mother.

Money had become increasingly scarce for the Browns, but that only endeared Corinna to her church friends. The Depression had begun to take its toll on small-town America; why should Corinna and Ed be exempt?

It was Celia's former student, Alyce Peterson, who delivered the next blow to Corinna's sense of family honor. They bumped into each other pushing grocery carts, each with a toddler inside the cart, at the same store where Corinna had once worked.

After exchanging pleasantries, Alyce, whom Corinna had never considered very bright, blurted out in a hushed voice, "I'm so sorry . . . about your father . . . ."

"What about my father?" Corinna demanded.

Alyce's face turned bright red as she hastily grabbed two cans of tomato soup from the shelf. "I thought you knew . . ."

"Knew what?" Corinna took hold of Alyce by the

shoulders. "Tell me what you are stammering about. Is he ill? Now talk!"

"His—his woman . . . . You know."

"I don't know . . . ." Corinna felt a stab at her heart. She should have known, but who would suspect that kind of thing about her own father?

Corinna let go of Alyce's shoulders. "Yes," she said calmly. "Does everyone in town know? Is everyone talking?"

Alyce nodded her head, now totally abashed.

"Tell me. I won't be mad at you, Alyce. What is the gossip? Tell me." Corinna begged her, in a soft pleading voice.

"He has a woman, young and red-headed, with a baby boy. The baby has black hair like his. She moved into his place down in Long Pine maybe six months ago. Reverend Miller went to see him on account of your mother. He's drinkin' lots now. He cursed the Reverend out, told him he'd never come back to your mother, never step foot in Barnesville again. Said Celia's gone, the boys are growed, you're taking care of your mom. Now he's gonna live his real life, he told Reverend Miller."

So the whole world knew, Corinna thought with a weary sigh. Why was she always the last to hear about her own family? "Thank you, Alyce. Thanks for telling me."

Later that afternoon, after Lorna's nap, after Corinna had wept bitter tears and cursed her father herself, she put on her hat and gloves and walked with Lorna, who was now three, the two blocks to her mother's house.

Slowly, gravely, with tears in her eyes, she told her mother what she'd been told that morning.

"Yes, yes, I know." her mother responded as she attempted to console her daughter. "I've known—

somehow a wife just knows—for years now. But I needed to be sure before I talked to lawyer Nelson."

"You've spoken to a lawyer! Why?"

"To get a divorce. Under the circumstances— desertion by my husband after all these years—I think that's the right thing to do."

"No, mother, you musn't even think of it! A divorce is such a disgrace. I won't be able to hold my head up . . . ."

"Nonsense, my girl. He left us. For that red-headed hussy. They've been together for years. Since before you were married, before Celia left. I've always known."

"Why didn't you do something? Something to keep him?"

"Because I wanted to be free of him. It is God's will."

Corinna felt, as she looked at the wheelchair her mother sat in, that she herself had just been struck by lightning. Her father had deserted them and her mother was glad! It was beyond belief.

That Sunday, for the first time since her marriage, Corinna did not go to church. She took to her bed and felt herself sink into despair. She simply couldn't face the busybodies who would by now know that she had not known what everyone else knew about her father.

He had cursed out the minister. She could never face Reverend Miller—or his busybody wife— again.

She justified staying in bed by the fact that she was seven months pregnant. Hopefully, she would now give Ed the son he so badly wanted.

She wondered how much Celia knew, Celia who had escaped all this misery by fleeing to New York so long ago.

That first letter, arriving eight months after Celia

left, had been personally delivered to her mother by the postmistress, Helen Adams. So anxiously was the town awaiting news of its errant daughter that Helen had simply tucked the letter postmarked "New York" into her apron pocket and had personally driven it over to Agnes Gleason on her lunch break. She had then waited quietly while Agnes read it with tears of relief running down her cheeks.

Celia was well. She was working as a waitress and taking university courses at night and "trying out" for plays almost every week. She'd had one small walk-on part in a crowd scene, so her acting career wasn't blooming, but she loved the city. It was everything she wanted and she had new friends and had joined the Epworth League and lived in a decent rooming house.

"She sounds so happy, don't you think?" Agnes asked brightly as she took the letter back from Helen.

After that first letter Celia wrote every three or four weeks. Corinna grew accustomed to being asked "What do you hear from Celia?" exactly one day after each letter arrived.

Now, nearly four years later, Celia's success was commonly applauded. She had given up acting for journalism. She had put herself through City College of New York, then taken a job with *The New York Mirror* as a cub reporter. One day, when covering a labor dispute in the garment district, she'd met Larry Rosenblum, the business manager for Adele Simpson, who subsequently introduced her to the editor of an industry newspaper. She was now making more than four thousand dollars a year as editor of this garment industry newspaper. And she was buying wholesale all the latest fashions.

Each letter from Celia seemed to be an additional blow to Corinna's pride. As Celia's good fortune multiplied, Corinna's sense of herself and her family diminished. She had half a notion, as she thought of her now total responsibility for her mother, to write Celia and demand that she come home and share the burden, or at the very least, send money regularly.

As a morbidly gray winter finally turned into a golden-green spring, Corinna alternated between hopeful good feelings about the birth of the baby she was certain would be a son, and a sudden, overwhelming conviction that her son would not live. She couldn't explain or rationalize away these visions of a tiny baby, dead, in a white, satin-lined casket. She confided to no one but her doctor, and he assured her that her fears were groundless.

On the tenth of May, Corinna and Ed became the proud parents of nine-pound baby Edward Brown, Jr., in the Vermillion Lying-In Hospital. Nothing about baby Ed's arrival had been unusual. Ten days later, mother and son went home. Three days after that, the baby lay dead from pneumonia in the white casket Corinna had seen in her vivid premonitions.

Not Ed, nor little Lorna, nor any of the church people could raise Corinna from the deep depression and grief she succumbed to after her baby son's death. She languished, caring not what anyone thought, unconcerned for the first time since her mother's accident whether anyone was caring for her mother. She retreated into complete self-pity and tallied up all the wrongs done to her during her twenty-three hard years. Ed, distraught himself, took Lorna with him each day to Vermillion, where an elderly woman cared for her while he sold shoes to the few folks who could afford to buy them.

As Corinna sunk deeper into despair, her mother came to life. Each afternoon she tidied her little home, put on a fresh dress, rearranged her gray hair into a neat bun—and received a gentleman caller, a Mr. Robert Appleby who had recently been widowed. His late wife, Eileen, had been one of Agnes's closest friends. Eileen had succumbed to the heart disease which had plagued her since her last child was born—a lifetime ago, Bob Appleby said. "It was God's will," he said. "I cannot question God."

They were looking forward to the early summer Revival to be conducted by the Reverend James Bantry in Sioux Falls. Eileen Appleby had gone the previous summer and had felt much better afterwards even though the famous preacher who had performed many miracles had not cured her heart disease.

Bob Appleby had suggested to Agnes that he drive her over to the Revival. "If you really believe in Jesus, and your heart is pure, you might be cured of your paralysis." Agnes had no trouble with purity or belief; she had trouble with her daughter.

"Mama, if you must go, I'll take you." Corinna pleaded. "Can't you imagine what people would say if old Mr. Appleby took you over there? Why, you have to stay overnight. It's just not right!"

The compromise they agreed to was that Mr. Appleby would drive both women to the Revival. "Reverend Bantry might help you get over your grief," Agnes had told Corinna.

The Miracle took place. As if she had rehearsed it, when the Reverend James Bantry placed his hands on top of Agnes's head and prayed over her, "Oh God Almighty, I ask you in the name of your Son, Jesus, please heal this God-fearin' woman, Agnes Gleason. Please make her legs work again as always You intended them to work. I ask this in the name of your Son, Jesus," Agnes cautiously placed each foot on the ground in front of the wheelchair. With Corinna on the left side and Mr. Appleby on the right side, ready to catch her if she faltered, she took one small shuffling step, then another. And another.

The Reverend Bantry proclaimed it A Miracle. Reverend Miller said it was God's will and invited Agnes at least once a month for the rest of her life to recite it at their Wednesday night Prayer Meeting. All of Barnesville applauded Agnes and her Great Faith. (Only Lorna's doctor, George Murphy, told Corinna that he had his doubts.)

And no one dared criticize Agnes when, one month later, the court quietly signed a divorce decree. Nor did anyone comment adversely six months later when Agnes Gleason of Great Faith, and Robert Appleby, widowed just one year previously, were married in front of the altar of the Barnesville First Methodist Church.

All the talk about The Miracle shamed Corinna into going back to church herself. But she couldn't bring herself to go back to Reverend Miller and the Methodists. Ed, who didn't believe her mother had been paralyzed to begin with, declared he was fed up with all this religious nonsense. Corinna felt a deep need to choose something new, to start over; so she visited several Protestant churches and found herself especially drawn to the Reverend Leonore Addison, one of the new breed of female ministers.

On the Monday after her Sunday visit to the First Presbyterian Church of Barnesville, Corinna called Reverend Addison and asked for an appointment.

"Why don't you just bring precious Lorna over here to my kitchen right now. I've got a pot of coffee brewing and some crayons to keep Lorna busy while we visit."

That Monday morning chat had unaccountably cheered Corinna. Reverend Addison had said right off, "Oh, please call me Leonore. After all we're just two women friends together trying to figure out how best to cope with life. I don't stand on titles."

Leonore had heard for months about Corinna's dedication to her mother and about her multitude of family problems. She wanted to help the woman, but she also relished capturing one of the Methodists into her grasp. She challenged Corinna to "be her best person."

"You seem to have such a wonderful way with children," she said. "Would you consider teaching a Sunday School class?"

Stunned and flattered to have been asked, Corinna began to say yes, but was interrupted by Leonore. "One thing we'll have to do first is work on your grammar. Children learn by what they hear, but it's not a major problem. I'll give you a book and if you'll just stop by, oh, say three mornings a week, we'll break those bad habits in no time."

Six months later Corinna seemed a different woman. Leonore was her best friend. Corinna spoke with perfect grammar—"Celia would be proud of me," she had confessed to Leonore—and taught twelve fifth and sixth grade children each Sunday. She visited her mother only once a week instead of several times a day. And at Leonore's suggestion, she began to check books out of the public library for herself and Lorna.

Lorna, meanwhile, began school and spent her

after-school hours drawing pictures to show to Leonore, who always rewarded her with praise and cookies.

"Corinna," her mother's excited voice chimed into the telephone, "you must bring Lorna and come immediately. I've such a surprise, you'd never guess. Oh, and have Lorna wear that blue smocked jumper I made last Christmas. Come as soon as you're cleaned up. We'll be waiting . . . ."

"What in the world . . . ? Corinna muttered as she deposited her gardening gloves and trowel in the kitchen sink.

It was a Monday afternoon in June of 1937. Corinna spent every Monday in her garden weeding and watering, trying to produce as much food as possible for herself and Lorna. During the rest of the week, she clerked at Alban's Hardware while Lorna attended public school or church school in the summer.

Ed had gone off to Detroit in search of employment right after the first of the year. "He must not have found work," she told her stepfather, Bob Appleby, "or he'd have sent us money by now." Each day she went to the post office with hope in her heart; each day the disappointment and fear grew like a cancer in her heart.

She washed and dressed in last year's green bombazine Sunday dress, but left her legs bare because it *was* summer and she couldn't afford stockings anyhow. She put a small beige straw hat on her head and then called to Lorna. "Are you ready, dear? Come, let me see your hair." Lorna was adept at dressing herself but hadn't yet mastered brushing her hair.

"Oh, darling, you didn't get all the paint off yourself." Corinna took Lorna back to the kitchen sink and scrubbed the water colors off her elbows.

"I love Leonore dearly, but I'm not sure you're old enough for finger painting." Reverend Addison had given Lorna paints for her seventh birthday.

"But I love it, Mommy."

"Well, never mind. Now, hold still while I brush your curls. Grandma wants you to look especially nice for some guest she's got. I can't imagine who . . . ."

As they approached her mother's home, Corinna recognized the three cars out front, all local townspeople and no one special to get so excited about. But why did her mother have so many guests on a Monday afternoon? Instead of walking unannounced into the kitchen as she usually did, Lorna and Corinna went up the front steps onto the porch, and Corinna gingerly pushed open the front door and they walked in.

A strange woman sat on the parlor sofa next to her mother. On her lap she held a large photo album. For a moment she stared at Corinna and Lorna, and Corinna stared back, unable to speak. It was Lorna who broke the strained silence.

"Aunt Celia New York, Mommy! It's Aunt Celia New York." Everyone laughed nervously at the child's apparent misunderstanding of her aunt's name.

Celia grinned at the child, stood up and offered her open arms. "That's right, Lorna baby, it's your Aunt Celia from New York. Come give me a big hug and kiss!"

Corinna followed her daughter and waited her turn for a hug. After all, the whole town seemed to be watching. "You look . . . stunning."

"And you look like a mother, exactly like I expected."

What was that supposed to mean? Corinna groaned inwardly as she surveyed Celia's costume.

"Like a moviestar" was the phrase that swept across her mind, but Corinna never went to the movies so she couldn't really know.

Celia wore a crisp, black linen, short-sleeved suit which emphasized her trim but voluptuous figure, silk stockings, very high black patent sling pumps with jaunty red clips on the instep, and a sleek black straw hat with a mini-bouquet of red roses just as it dipped over her face. Her bright, glossy lipstick matched the flowers. Her dark brown hair was fashionably bobbed and waved. On her ears and around her neck were pearls. Her eyes were vibrantly alive, outlined sharply in black pencil and mascara. All in all, Corinna recognized, Celia was breathtakingly glamorous and sophisticated.

"You should have let us known you were coming," was all she managed to say.

"But I thought a surprise would be such fun!" Celia countered. "Don't you think so, Mother? Bob?"

How dare she call him Bob? Such nerve!

With her mother's friends watching the little drama being played out, Corinna suddenly became acutely aware of how she must look to her sister. Dumpy, frumpy, "gone-to-fat," almost middle-aged. And faded. Faded hair, faded clothes, faded skin. A faded beauty.

"What a beautiful child you are, Lorna darling! You must come back to New York with me. You'll put all those insipid imitations of Shirley Temple to shame!" Then to Corinna she said, "How does it feel to have such a gloriously beautiful child? You must be so thrilled!"

"We try not to emphasize it, if you know what I mean . . . ."

"Well, here, you two come sit beside me and we'll look at these pictures together." Corinna and Lorna sat next to Celia then and heard, and saw, her life in New York. She was assistant fashion editor of *The New York Times*. She traveled with the "best people," wore the "best clothes," went to the "best shows," and visited and dined with "the 400."

For the next six days, Corinna listened patiently as Celia told tales about Barbara Hutton and her Danish count, about Brenda Frazier ("she spends six thousand a year on clothes"), about the Whitneys' home in Kentucky where she had been a houseguest during the recent Kentucky Derby and the Vanderbilt mansion in Asheville, North Carolina, where she had covered their ball.

"Mrs. Roosevelt has no style, none whatever," she announced while defending the President's New Deal policies, "but I like her son James." She traveled to Washington several times a year to cover White House dinners, Celia confided.

Each night Corinna went to bed exhausted from Celia's non-stop chattering and from her own conflicting feelings of envy. She tried to tell herself that she was happy for Celia's success, and she loved her younger sister. But it was a bitter pill which stuck in her throat.

Celia's life was filled with sin and evil. Corinna was convinced of that, even though her mother didn't seem to see it. Celia wore strapless dresses. She danced and drank cocktails. She probably even smoked cigarettes, though there were no pictures of her smoking. She was too smart to let Mama see pictures like that.

Whenever the opportunity presented itself, Corinna tried to tell Celia that she was missing a lot by not being married and having a child, but Celia pooh-poohed that idea. She felt her life was perfect, and there was nothing she would do to change it. Celia seemed interested in Corinna's life, sometimes prying too deeply into her relationship with Ed. When she pressed her about Ed's absence, Corinna snapped, "Oh Celia, you can't possibly understand, you've never been married."

"Just because I'm not married, my dear sister, doesn't mean I've never slept with a man. As you know very well, lots of women don't wait for marriage. I just make it my business not to get caught."

"And what's that supposed to mean?"

"Figure it out for yourself!"

The last morning of Celia's visit, Sunday, she came to Corinna's house early to say good-bye. "I've been thinking about you and Lorna, honey, and I think you should come live in New York. I'll help you get a job. Lorna's opportunities will be so much greater."

Corinna was aghast. "I wouldn't even consider it. Ed will be coming back soon and we've got to be here."

"Corinna, honey, you're only fooling yourself, not anyone else. He's not coming back. It's been more than six months. The whole town knows you haven't heard a word. It's time you faced—"

"That's not true!" Corinna slammed her hand down hard on the table to keep from hitting her sister. "It's not true, do you hear me, it's not true! Get out of my house. Don't you dare come into my home and say something like that about my husband—about Lorna's father!"

Celia stood up and backed out of the kitchen door. As she left, she saw the tears begin to flow down Corinna's cheeks.

PART TWO
Lorna

Chapter Two

FLORENCE, ITALY, JULY, 1951

Lorna turned the double handles above the blue marble tub, testing the rush of water from the burnished gold faucet with her fingers. Then, while the tub was filling, she unpacked her clothes, taking special care with her Dior gown, a marvelous creation of white tulle ruffles with a snug, sheared bodice and off-the-shoulder neckline.

Not many years ago, she reflected, she had worn dresses made from chicken-feed bags, and had been forced to wear those horrid Buster Brown shoes with the toes cut out. Her feet had grown faster than her mother had planned, so rather than let Lorna get callouses when she was only eleven, her mother had taken a butcher knife and cut huge holes in front, "for your toes to spread out." How the kids had laughed at her! Even though most of them came from families as poor as hers, most of them had two parents, and most of them could afford shoes that fit.

Corinna Brown could not. "It is all I can do to feed the two of us, and if my sister Celia hadn't begun sending her old clothes to Lorna, heaven only knows what the child would have worn to high school!"

So many times Lorna had heard her mother's litany of woe, her excoriation of Ed for having left her with a daughter to raise, her boast of her own efforts to keep a roof over their heads.

It's a long way from Barnesville to Florence. And there's no going back. I'll never go back home. That much I've learned from Aunt Celia!

Celia Gleason was her fairy godmother, the person who had made it possible for her to leave Barnesville. Her mother's younger sister had left home immediately after high school graduation. Lorna could hear her grandmother's voice explaining, "Celia originally planned on being an actress on Broadway, but she makes the most of every opportunity. She is a fashion writer for *The New York Times*, an assistant to Virginia Pope."

Though Celia rarely returned to Barnesville, she kept in touch by mail and her mother regularly sent pictures of Lorna. During Lorna's sophomore year, Celia wrote Corinna suggesting that Lorna come to New York as soon as she finished high school; she would find her a job, surely a better job than anything South Dakota had to offer. Lorna's fantasies fed on dreams of studying art in all the great museums in New York, but Celia, having studied her photographs carefully, had other plans.

Using her connections, she secured an appointment with Eileen Ford of the Ford Agency, and sure enough, her hunch that Lorna had exactly the looks and carriage that designers and magazine editors required, paid off. Lorna was snapped up and began a career that brought her, two short years later, to Europe and into the home of one of the wealthiest and most famous Italian families.

After her luxurious bath, Lorna wrapped her slightly damp hair in rag curlers. Next to her eyes, her hair was her best feature—thick, brown, and worn shoulder-length, in the popular page-boy style. Long hair was every man's favorite.

Gingerly she turned down the heavy, quilted-chintz bedspread, discovering beautifully embroidered sheets made of soft cotton that felt like silk. She climbed into the bed and lay there, too excited to even consider sleeping. She looked at the marble fireplace across from the bed, imagined a big log fire burning in the middle of winter, and Tony in bed beside her. . . .

No, I mustn't think that! . . . She shut the thought out of her mind. *I don't belong in this bed, in this house! Nothing has prepared me for such luxury, such wealth. Mother would say I am "out of my element." Even Aunt Celia would be astounded if she knew where I am and what I am doing. But Kathy is here with me. And the Countess Dandolo. We are well chaperoned. There is nothing scandalous about being a house guest . . . .*

Her thoughts trailed off. She was excited, yet felt guilty for reasons she couldn't trace. The kernel of a thought again slipped across the back of her mind: *Someday I will live like this. Someday I will become . . .*

Before the thought could be realized, she forced it out of her consciousness.

Several hours later, as she was putting the finishing touches on her makeup, the phone beside her bed rang. It was Tony and he sounded breathless.

"Lorna, welcome! I'm just in from Milan. I'm almost finished dressing. I'll knock on your door in fifteen minutes. Are you ready?"

She assured him she was, even though her stomach was doing flip-flops. Anxiety flooded through her. This was as bad as walking down a runway. Worse! She had to make conversation! What had she gotten herself into? How would she know what to say to the "leading citizens of Italy," as Tony had described the guests at his mother's parties? Never had she dined in such a fantastic home . . . how would she know which piece of silver to use?

Over and over again, she assured herself that she would do fine. She would listen and observe, she would ask intelligent questions to keep the attention off herself. She would be a "quiet, introverted beauty"—she had heard Calvani describe her that way—and she would carry herself with the cool, regal dignity she had learned during countless modeling sessions. The truth was, she was a consummate actress, and modeling was nothing more than acting. Never would she let these people imagine her true background. Tony especially would never know how different his life was from hers.

He tapped lightly, then abruptly opened the bedroom door. He gathered her in his arms in a massive bear hug, followed by a kiss on both cheeks, then a soft, warm kiss directly on her lips.

"Tony, you mustn't. You'll mess me up!"

He released his tight grip on her. "*Ah, si, mia carissima*. Later, *then*. You *do* look scrumptious, absolutely delicious!"

His eyes traveled from her face down to her breasts, snuggly outlined in the sheared white tulle. "What a lovely gown! You are more beautiful—much more beautiful—than I remembered." He looked her up and down again, undressing her with his eyes. Lorna felt her face burn and turned from his wicked eyes to look for her evening bag. Why did he always make her feel like a fallen woman? How could he be so elegant and so—so crude at the same time?

They stopped for Kathy at her room and then proceded down the grand staircase toward the library. Kathy was dressed in gold lamé and white organdy, with each tier of the organdy skirt edged in the gold threads of the sweater-like top. The gold in the sweater made her blonde hair gleam even more, Lorna thought as she noticed Kathy's green and gold gilt eyeshadow. It made her eyes an even more intense shade of green, almost the color of emeralds. Kathy wore the diamond earrings her parents had given her on her twenty-first birthday. *It must be nice to be born rich*, Lorna thought meanly, as she descended the staircase on Tony's arm. Somehow, Kathy seemed to know precisely what was expected, what this evening would be like. *She is an American aristocrat, just as Tony is an Italian aristocrat.* The thought struck Lorna with sudden enlightening power. *How I would love to trade places with her! Why couldn't I have been born into her family?*

When they entered the large, mahogany-paneled library, Lorna's eyes were riveted to Catarina. She stood in front of the fireplace, flanked by a tall, distinguished, older man—Tony's father, most likely—on one side and by Victor de Sabata, the Director of the Teatro alla Scala, on the other. Catarina was wearing a pale blue and violet silk taffeta and moire strapless gown. Monet might have painted the fabric. Her only jewelry was a diamond bracelet composed of large, emerald-cut stones and the largest diamond earrings Lorna had ever seen.

Though she had always stopped to gaze wistfully into the windows of Van Cleef & Arpels, Tiffany, and Cartier, she had never seen diamonds so large. The huge, pear-shaped drops had to be at least thirty carats each!

Oh, why can't Catarina be my mother? She is elegant, refined, so warm and understanding. If only I had been born into a family like this . . . my God, how can I be so disloyal to my mother, to have these feelings? God should strike me down!

Tony propelled the two young women across the room, past a dozen people, directly to his parents.

"Ah, here are the American beauties I've been hearing about!" exclaimed Count Emilio Dandolo with a twinkle in his eyes and a big wink to his son.

"Yes, Father, I'd like to present Miss Lorna Brown and Miss Kathy Schaeffer."

"What a great pleasure this is. We are delighted to welcome you to our home!" He bent and kissed Lorna's hand first, and then Kathy's.

"You look lovely, Lorna!" Catarina added. "Absolutely regal! I saw that Dior and almost bought it myself!" Lorna blessed herself for having chosen a dress from the finest French couturier. "And Kathy, that is a most exquisite, a most unusual dress. It must be American?"

"Yes, Adele Simpson. I brought it along, just in case."

"That was very clever of you. Has Tony told you about Rugierro yet? He is one of Tony's cousins, an architect. I hope you will enjoy his company . . . ."

After introductions to the guest of honor, as well as to Maestro Arturo Toscanini and composer Giancarlo Menotti, Tony guided the women to the opposite side of the room, where a waiter immediately offered them champagne. Kathy casually picked up one of the tall crystal glasses. Then it was Lorna's turn.

Slowly, hesitantly, she took the glass, then tentatively sipped its contents. She had never tasted an alcoholic drink before, not even a beer. It was one of the evils her mother had warned her against. "Don't ever take your first drink and you won't be sorry," Corinna had told her. "Drink is evil, it will destroy your life. Mark my words, it will lead to your downfall if you take your first drink."

The words rang in Lorna's head as she sipped a second time. *Darn it*, she thought, *why can't I escape from her*? And then she made a resolution that this would be one evening in her life when she would simply not listen, not hear, not remember all the taboos she had been taught.

Tony guided them through the library, introducing them to guests, insisting they try the fresh duck *foie gras* on melba toast and the Beluga caviar which was being passed by waiters. Rugierro arrived, and much to Kathy's delight he turned out to be powerfully built and ruggedly handsome. Best of all, he towered over her at six feet, three inches. Kathy's five-foot-eleven made it especially difficult for her to meet attractive, eligible, tall-enough men. Rugierro was perfect! And at thirty, he was sufficiently older than her twenty-one to seem very sophisticated. Lorna, happy that Kathy had been well provided for, began to relax and enjoy the evening.

After an hour-and-a-half, when Lorna was beginning to feel light-headed and very hungry, the butler passed through the rooms announcing that dinner was served, and the two hundred guests drifted to the terrace where a dream-like scene greeted them. Twenty tables were dressed in white hand-embroidered organdy cloths with yellow underskirts. In the center of each table sat a yellow-rose topiary tree. A dozen small vigil lights surrounded the rose tree, and the table gleamed with crystal, Buccellati silver, and Royal Crown Derby china embossed in gold with the Dandolo crest. Thousands of candles sparkled like small stars flung across the terrace and gardens. The full moon illuminated the lake, and the swans seemed to crane their necks to see what all the chattering was about.

Tony held her chair and she slipped into it. She was again struck with the eerie feeling *that she didn't belong there. What was she doing there?*

The mingled fragrance of jasmine, honeysuckle, orange blossoms, and roses floated through the soft night air, captured and held aloft by the violins. Lorna breathed deeply, resolved to relax and let the glowing atmosphere work its magic.

It's easy to be Tony's date, Lorna decided halfway through the five-course meal. He does all the talking. The heir apparent to all this opulence was living up to the role. He brashly forced the conversation into subjects he introduced, all the while being charming and gallant and only a bit argumentative. Lorna observed him, fascinated by her own conflicting judgments. *He takes for granted his primacy at the table, or is that a cover for the insecurity he feels being the youngest? But he's so certain of his superior knowledge, his facts.* She had only to follow his lead, eat with the same fork, taste each different wine as it was served, and nod her head in occasional agreement with something he was saying.

Kathy, on the other hand, was much more courageous, much more outspoken, for example, about American architecture when it was rigorously attacked by Rugierro. He listened to Kathy's comments and cautiously responded, always coming back to defend his favored Italian designs.

Catarina had taken great care to seat an interesting table for Tony and Lorna. In addition to Rugierro and Kathy, they had Salvatore Ferragamo, one of Italy's most talented designers of leather goods, and his wife; Ettore Sottsass, Jr., a young designer-engineer who was creating new ideas for Olivetti; and Enrico Mattei, soon to be named the head of Ente Nazionale Idrocarburi, Italy's state-owned industrial combine, and his Viennese wife.

Mattei, Tony had explained during their first dance, was the most important person at the table, a real "comer" in the world of industry and finance. "He is one of my heroes, he has incredible willpower—and his influence will grow!" Mattei was seated on the other side of Kathy, and Lorna wondered how Catarina had known that Kathy would be a much better conversationalist than Lorna. Yet Lorna had to admit to herself that it was true.

"Enrico is all work and no play," Tony explained as they danced. "I think we are lucky to have lured him to this party. Even my mother and father were surprised when he accepted. He has a reputation for never going out socially, except with people like the Shah of Iran or the King of Morocco!"

Knowing that she was at a party with "the superstars of the new Italy," as Tony had put it, intimidated her. She watched Kathy out of the corner of her eye. Her friend was chattering away as if she attended dinners like this every day. Kathy was "to-the-manner-born" and it was as natural for her as riding a horse had been for Lorna—a matter of breeding.

After fresh raspberry meringue cake was served, Emilio Dandolo began the toasts, telling of the great feats of the guest of honor. Sabata responded, and then several guests stood to thank their hosts for providing such a splendid occasion for the supporters of Teatro alla Scala to become better acquainted. "Dancing will continue until the last dancer is exhausted," Emilio told his guests, amid much applause and laughter. Then he came to claim Lorna's hand. Momentarily stunned, she stammered a yes, then rose to precede him to the dance floor.

The tall, somewhat stocky count held Lorna very properly at arm's length—unlike his son who had crushed her to him and kissed her forehead and the side of her face until she had squirmed in embarrassment.

"I do hope my son is showing you a good time while you're here," began Emilio in perfect English. "Catarina and I worry about him. He never relaxes enough. He is always thinking, scheming, planning his next coup."

Lorna began to relax, content to let Emilio carry the conversation. He seemed very old to her, weary and sad.

"When the war was over, we returned home from Switzerland—Tony told you about our exile in Switzerland, no? Those of us who survived and had been part of the resistance felt it was our obligation to form a new government. My family never before held government office—we had been bankers and land owners and industrialists, but never actually participated in the government." He paused to cough.

"My father was too old to begin anything new, but he had done his part already. All during the exile he taught Tony about business, about banking, textiles, and minerals. Of all the tutors Tony had, my father was the best. He taught him everything about the family businesses."

Emilio stopped dancing, coughed again, then led Lorna off the dance floor toward a bench on the edge of the terrace. "I'm too exhausted to dance to this fast music. It's awful, growing old! But I want to talk to you." He mopped his forehead with a linen handkerchief. "As I was explaining, I feel it is my duty now to participate in the government as a member of the Chamber of Deputies."

Lorna nodded her head. She wondered why Tony's father was so determined that she understand their relationship. *How wonderful it must be for Tony to have a father who is really there for him, who cares, who worries about how hard he is working.*

"But it means Tony has to manage all the businesses—our conglomorate is the second largest industrial operation in Italy," he added with pride. Then, as if he could scarcely believe it himself, he said, "Imagine—he's only twenty-five!"

Lorna gasped.

"What's the matter?"

"I—I thought he was older."

"No. He thinks older and he acts older, and when he's tired he looks older. We called him home from the London School of Economics after only one year. And let me tell you, he's taken chances I never would have taken. Did you know that he's brought an American designer, Ken Scott, over here to design fabrics for him? A new synthetic fabric, I think it is called 'banlon.' Well, that's all Tony's doing. He has a knack for management, and he is also a genius at banking and international finance." Emilio stopped to cough again, then continued. "It bothers me to see him so tired-looking and thin. I don't think he eats well. He needs someone to take care of him. He needs a wife."

Lorna blushed at Emilio's pointed statement. It was ridiculous for him to imagine his handsome, aggressive son lacked the company of women! Surely Emilio knew . . .

"Well, I've been watching the two of you out of the corner of my eye this evening, and it's clear to me that Tony adores you. I only hope he's remembered how to court a real lady."

"Oh, but he's been wonderful to me," she protested quickly. "He has shown us Florence, he has taken us to the best restaurants. We've had a perfectly marvelous time."

"*Bene*! I've been worried about him. We put too much responsibility on him early in life." Emilio hesitated for a moment, then added, "He should be settling down by now. After all, I want to live to see my first grandson!"

Count Dandolo had delivered his message to Lorna. Now he escorted her back to Tony, who was deep in conversation with Enrico Mattei.

That was the strangest exchange, Lorna mused as she half listened to the conversation between Mattei and Tony—something about building fertilizer plants and synthetic rubber plants. Why did the Count feel he had to give her a sales pitch on Tony? Tony didn't need his father's help to find a wife. But then, the Count was old—so much older than his wife—and he wanted grandchildren . . . .

Tony smacked his hand on the table to dramatize

a point, then turned to Lorna. "Time for another dance, *carissima*. You must be bored to tears with all this talk."

Mattei stood to join the throng of those guests who had decided it was time to depart. *"Buona notte, arrivederci."* He kissed her hand, his eyes never leaving her face. "Be good to my friend Tony!" Then the two men lapsed into Italian again and Lorna was left out of their fond farewells.

Later, on the dance floor, Tony announced to Lorna, "Kathy and I had a wonderful dance. It was the first time I've had her to myself, and I learned she is a very sharp, very astute lady. Tell me about your gorgeous friend."

Lorna felt as if he had stabbed her. Then she wondered at those feelings. She picked her words carefully. "Kathy belongs in this kind of social setting, it's exactly like her parent's life back home. She is, you might say, an American aristocrat."

As she said the words her anger grew. *Why tell him anything about Kathy? Let him find out for himself! Kathy will steal Tony from me. She is a friend, but friendship only counts for so much. If she can steal him, she will.* Then her inner voices contradicted one another. *What am I thinking? Steal him from me? He isn't mine yet, not by a long shot!*

With teasing eyes, Tony needled her, "What about you? Aren't you an aristocrat?"

Lorna hesitated, then responded icily. "Where I come from, there is no aristocracy. Everyone is of the same class in South Dakota." She let that sink in a moment, then added in a softer voice, "You must have places like that here in Italy. Rural, farming areas?"

"Yes, we do," Tony said thoughtfully, "but even

there we have class stratification. Most of the land is still owned by absentee landlords. It's not quite the feudal system of the Middle Ages, but it's not far removed."

Tony pulled her closer, bored with the direction their conversation was taking. He whispered in her ear, "You are by far the most beautiful woman here this evening, and I've neglected to tell you that for much too long." He kissed her forehead, then added, "Your eyes are like magnets, the most beautiful pools of blue . . . . Why do you squirm so when I kiss you? Don't you like my kisses?"

Embarrassed, Lorna pulled away from Tony far enough to look into his eyes. "Your mother is the most beautiful woman here. She is truly splendid."

"She comes in . . . well, I guess a close second to you. Pretty good for a fifty-one-year-old woman, wouldn't you say? And it isn't just her looks; she's young at heart. She is one of my favorite people in the world to talk with. We have long conversations on everything imaginable—even sex!"

It was nearly two-thirty in the morning when the last guest left and Tony's parents retired. He was still wound up, not at all ready to go to bed. He led Lorna outside, through the dance floor where the musicians were packing up, down into the garden, around the lake, to a bench on the other side. They looked back at the villa and watched the waiters pack up the tables and chairs and tidy up the terrace. The full moon shone brightly on the swans huddled in one corner of the lawn. For a long time Tony and Lorna watched the activity, holding hands, letting the emotions of the evening wash over them again.

Tony squeezed Lorna's hand and asked: "What do you think? Did it meet your expectations?"

"It was spectacular, Tony! I've never imagined anything so lovely. Your mother has wonderful taste. Everything—the food, the flowers, the wine, even the guests—everything was perfection."

"I thought so too," he murmured so quietly she could barely hear him. "Do you suppose you could give a party like this?"

"Goodness no! I mean—I wouldn't know where to begin."

"It's easy to learn—just a matter of taste and attention to details. Then of course, one has to be able to afford it, but that will never be a problem, at least not here . . . ."

He seemed caught up in a deep reverie, struggling with some sort of decision. Then he seized her hand and said, "Come. Let's walk."

They walked away from the house toward the swaying cypress trees. When they reached a small arbor, like a tiny room with walls made of shrubs, he stopped and placed his hands on her hips, forcing her to face him directly. He stood very close, so close she could feel the heat of his body radiate toward her, even though the evening had become chilly.

"I wanted you to come to this party because I wanted you to see how I live, to see the tradition I must uphold. My father is old and not well; my grandfather is on his deathbed. I am the only one left. I must carry on . . ."

Momentarily embarrassed, he stammered, "Well, I don't know . . . I just wanted you to understand. You can't really know me unless you understand their expectations for me."

Did he feel he had said too much? Had he revealed more of himself than he intended? Lorna searched for a way to put him at ease again. "I'll bet when you are in Rome and Milan at your bachelor apartments, you manage to forget what's expected of you!" She had meant to lighten his mood but instead incurred his anger.

"And what is that supposed to mean?"

She removed his hands from her hips and walked a few steps toward a statue of a small boy. She reached out to feel the smooth, cool carved stone, taking time to gather her thoughts. "It is true, Tony. You were right to bring me here, because if I had only known the you I met last week I would have thought of you as a rich Italian playboy. Meeting your parents, hearing your father talk about you, has given me a new appreciation for the responsibility you have."

Slowly his angry face softened. "Ah, my father has been talking again. No doubt bragging."

"I love your father. He is one of the kindest men I've ever met. And he loves you so."

He could discipline himself no longer. He took her upturned face in his hands, caressing it softly as one would a child. He moved one step closer, leaving her no escape. His arms were around her, pressing her so tightly she could barely breathe. His lips sought her lips. For a split second she resisted, hearing her mother's words in her ears: "Don't give in to that first kiss and you'll never have anything to regret!"

Go to hell, Mother, she thought, as she opened her mouth to let his probing tongue find hers. He kissed her unrelentingly until they both had to stop for air.

"You are so beautiful! I want you so!" And then once again he was kissing her, her mouth, her neck, the top of her breasts. His hand found her breast and she pulled away with a slight sigh. But he pulled her back and stilled her objections by kissing her mouth again, his hands meanwhile caressing her back and shoulders.

"I must have you," he muttered again as she pulled away. Again and again he kissed her and she responded fully, but when his lips made their way down to her breasts she stopped him, pulled away, and finally turned her back to him, looking toward the villa.

"Don't you think we should be going in?" she asked in a quavering voice, afraid of him, afraid of the passion he had stirred in her.

"Yes, I do," he agreed. He reached for her hand. "You turn me on, you know that, Miss South Dakota? When are you going to invite me to visit you? It's traditional, you know. One invitation deserves another."

Her heart thundered in her temples at the thought that he might actually visit her family in South Dakota. *That will never happen*, she silently vowed. "I'd be delighted to show you New York City, but there's nothing to see in South Dakota."

"I accept. When?"

"What do you mean—I mean, when can you come? New York is dreadful in August. Wait till September at least."

"Sounds good. I've been wanting to go to New York for some time now; now I have two reasons— no, make that three—business, you and Kathy."

"In that order of importance?"

"Of course. Business must always come first in my life." He hesitated, then his mischievous eyes twinkled and he added, "Oh, I get what you mean. Actually, I'll rearrange it—business, Kathy, and then you!"

You should be dating Kathy, Lorna thought sourly, *she's more your speed. She'll hop into bed with*

*any man who has money, even some who don't.
Besides, she's from your world.*

"Hey." He stopped her and made her face him.
"Are you jealous? Really? *Dio mio*! I was only
teasing you, you silly little duck! Haven't you
figured out yet that you are the one I want? Do I
have to draw pictures? Or put a diamond on your
finger?" He held her close once again, not a passionate embrace but one full of understanding, an
embrace that seemed to promise he would take care
of her, would let nothing hurt her.

She was overwhelmed with emotion, so willing to
surrender that she could only blurt out, "It really is
getting late, and I'm cold!"

"I guess I deserved that. You know how to insult
a guy. He wraps his arms around you and you tell
him you're cold!"

They crossed the deserted terrace, now in need of
a good sweeping, and entered the quiet house. The
grandfather clock chimed three-thirty as they
walked slowly up the grand staircase. At the top of
the third floor they parted, after he had kissed her
one last time on the forehead.

"See you soon."

Lorna dressed in her father's old yellow pajamas
that she had managed to sneak out of her mother's
house. Corinna had never thrown out Ed's clothes,
perhaps still imagining he would return. She
washed her face, brushed her hair thoroughly, and
climbed into the big canopied bed. She felt encap-
sulated in decadent luxury. *What a magnificent
feeling! This whole evening has been a dream . . .
I'll never get to sleep . . . .*

Then she remembered a book she had glanced at
earlier in the afternoon, a life of Michaelangelo

with color plates. She retrieved it from the book-case. *No point in wasting valuable time. I may never get another chance like this. I can always sleep back in New York.*

She was reading the second page when she heard a sharp *tap-tap* on the door, then watched it open. Her stomach lurched as she saw Tony, dressed in a wine silk robe.

"Tony! What . . . ?"

"Sshhh. Don't wake the whole household!" he commanded as he came to her bed and reached for her.

Before she could protest, he had gathered her in his arms and was kissing her profusely, all over her face and neck, then beginning to fumble with the top button on her father's pajamas.

"Tony, don't . . . you mustn't . . ."

She was stunned, so breathless she could barely hear the voices in her head saying, *Okay, this is your big chance, don't blow it! No man will marry a woman who isn't a virgin! If you go to bed with a man before you marry him, he'll spend the rest of your life together calling you a tramp!*

"Tony . . . we mustn't . . ."

"Don't be silly Lorna. I love you! Don't you understand that?" He tongued her nipple, causing the most delicious ripple of pain in her groin. She was swimming, trying to save herself from drown-ing.

My God! He said it! He loves me! It's all right!

Don't ever let a man trick you into bed by telling you he loves you, the voices countered. *Every man tries that ploy, but once they've had their fun and left you pregnant, you'll find out how much they love you!*

But it feels so wonderful . . . don't stop, Tony,

please don't ever stop . . . whatever you are doing to me, may it go on forever . . . .

Her disciplined self took over at last, and she struggled away from him. "Tony, I'm really sorry," she began, with tears streaming down her face. "But you must leave. Really, you must. I've . . . I've never . . ."

"You can't be serious! I love you, Lorna. My God, I've waited all night. All last week, the week before—I could barely control myself out on that dance floor. What's wrong with you? Don't you see . . ."

What had been trickling tears became hysterical sobbing. Tony's passion disintegrated, and anger took over. He stood up and rearranged his robe. "If this is the way you want it, Lorna, then this is how it will be. No one has ever accused me of rape. But you're making a mistake. You will regret this tomorrow."

He walked out of the room, shutting the door very quietly in spite of his controlled fury.

How dare he imagine he can barge in on me like that and demand sex—as if he could buy me like some possession! As if I'll capitulate if he asks—or threatens—me! My God, he's the most arrogant . . . !

She climbed out of the bed and hurried to the sink to wash her hands and face, to wash all traces of his ardor and her shame away.

He will never buy me. He'll have to earn the right to possess me. I'll teach that spoiled Count a thing or two!

Tony did not appear the next day until midafternoon when the six of them—his parents, Lorna and Kathy, and Ruggiero—were scheduled to take a long horseback ride through the fabled countryside of Fiesole, then end the evening with a picnic in the Roman theater of the ancient monastery of San Francisco.

When he joined them, Tony greeted her noncommittally, presuming his mother had apologized for his absence earlier in the day. After a long, peaceful ride on the "gentle" thoroughbreds, the group dismounted and admired the magnificent view of Florence laid out in the distance before them. Emilio, too, stared at the red tiled roofs, shimmering in the late afternoon heat, then turned toward the others seated on the large blanket.

"If I could live my life over again, I would live it exactly as I have. There is no place as wonderful, as cultured, as civilized, and as beautiful as Florence."

"We'll all drink to that!" agreed Tony as he popped the cork on a bottle of champagne.

"What a shame we have to go back to New York tomorrow. I could stay here forever!" Kathy exclaimed.

"And I'll drink to that!" said the obviously smitten Ruggiero.

"Tony is going to be glad to be rid of us so he can get back to Milan," Lorna said with a wry smile in his direction.

"I do have a lot to do, but I'd like to offer a toast to our beautiful Americans. May your pictures sell lots of Italian clothes—made with our fabrics, of course."

That's finally what it all comes down to, Lorna mused sadly. *Business will come first . . . then Kathy . . . .*

"Well, Lorna, that was quite a trip to Europe, wouldn't you say? We sure did it up right!"

They had gone through all the formalities at the gate in Rome, climbed aboard the TWA Constellation, and were awaiting takeoff.

"Like a dream. It will be a wonderful memory to cherish the rest of our lives." Lorna had already resigned herself to the dream's end.

"You don't think that's the last you'll see of Tony, do you?"

"Yes," she responded quietly but without hesitation. *He understands we don't belong together, that we have no future together.*

"Lorna, I don't believe you! That guy is nuts about you! What kind of an idiot are you? You're so damn cerebral, Lorna, sometimes I don't think you have a heart."

"Actually, he's much more suited to you. He—"

"Nonsense. When I was dancing with him, all he could do was ask questions about you. He wanted to know about your mom and dad."

Alarmed, Lorna glared at Kathy.

"What did you tell him?"

"I told him the truth—that your father had abandoned your mother when you were young, that your mother supported the family by working in a store . . ."

"You told him that?" Lorna angrily retorted.

"Yes, damn it, what did you want me to do? Lie?"

"What time—I mean, when during the evening . . ."

"I don't know what time. When we were dancing, early. Right after dessert was served."

He already knew that when he told me he loved me. It was after that and still he wanted to make love to me . . . but no, I must put that out of my mind. . . .

"Well, it is all over with now. We've had our little

Italian fling, and I really don't ever expect to see Tony again." Lorna said it angrily, but then after a while she quietly added, "I did enjoy it, though. I liked his parents very much."

"Yeah, right. I swear! You *are* crazy, Lorna!" Kathy opened the copy of *Vanity Fair* she was holding in her lap and began to read.

Chapter Three

Doesn't do her justice, she's much more beautiful than this, Tony mused as he put down his advance copy of *Vogue*'s Italian fashions issue. The picture of Lorna had caught him off guard; he had been struggling for weeks to put her out of his mind, to forget he had ever met her. He walked over to the window of his chrome-and-glass office. From his sixth-floor vantage point, he looked down on the parking lot where his chocolate-brown Ferrari was parked. It was his favorite toy, and he was happiest when he was in it barreling down the autostrada from Reggio Calabria to Milan.

He turned from the window. His great-grandfather Emiliano Dandolo glared down at him from the dark oil portrait above the credenza. Emiliano's son, Paolo, was now ill and the future of the dynasty rested on Tony's shoulders. For as far back as the history of Italy was known, his father's ancestors had been among the leading families. Descended from the sister of the medieval pope Gregory II, the Dandolo family first gained prominence as financial backers of artists and thinkers during the Renaissance.

Initially, their money came from farming vast tracts of land in southern Italy. Tony's great-grandfather had recognized that the future of the land lay in making its workers as happy and prosperous as possible, so he had instituted a system of crop sharing, profit sharing, and fair wages among the people who worked his land, selling plots to those peasants who demonstrated an ability to make a success of a farm of their own.

Using the income from agriculture and the sale of land, Emiliano had invested in the fledgling steel and rubber manufacturing industries. His son Paolo, a graduate of the University of Piedmont, had diversified the family businesses even further into chemicals and textiles, and had begun to export agricultural products. The Dandolos had inevitably become involved with the government of Italy. Their home in Florence had become the scene of frequent dinners and meetings where men of industry, finance, and government met to plan the nation's future. Grandfather Paolo was already a power behind the throne when Emilio was born in 1891.

His father, Tony reflected, was more suited for thinking, for creating the future, than for managing. He had always been an intellectual, a voracious reader, an idealist. He had been ardent in his opposition to Mussolini, though he had been smitten in his youth by Marxian economic theory, only to become bitterly disillusioned with Marxism during the twenties and thirties. Ultimately, his soul had found its home in the Social Christian Party, and it was as a leader of that party that he helped organize the postwar government of Italy.

Throughout the twenties and the reign of Mussolini, more and more industry was nationalized, and the militant and fanatic structure of the regime became apparent. Paolo began to make investments overseas with relatives who had emigrated to the United States after World War I, and Emilio followed his example. The Dandolos also began to deposit large sums of money in Swiss banks.

After Mussolini invaded Ethiopia, Emilio had sent Catarina and nine-year-old Tony to live in Geneva, ostensibly for a "vacation." That vacation lasted ten years, until 1945, and Paolo and Emilio joined them in Geneva in 1936.

Tony enjoyed life in Switzerland because he could command the total attention of both his father and grandfather, a feat which would have been impossible back in Italy. Since they had been forced into an early "retirement" by Mussolini's nationalization policies, they had all day to tell Tony over and over again the history of his family and the grand history of Italy, with heavy emphasis on the glories of Firenze. Tony had absorbed their love for Italy, as well as their love for history and the intrigues of the world of high finance.

From his grandfather he had learned everything the man knew about business and politics; from his father he learned about the world of ideas, about the great Renaissance thinkers such as Leonardo da Vinci, Dante, and Machiavelli. Their conversations, together with the daily ministrations of his tutors, provided Tony with a finer education than he could have received in the finest boys' schools in England. Nevertheless, as he approached the age of fourteen, his parents arranged for him to attend The International School of Geneva, the best private school Switzerland had to offer.

During the war years, the family spent much of its time huddled around a wireless radio set which Emilio had erected in the basement of their rented villa. Though it was highly illegal and dangerous, they could overhear Swiss, and occasionally German, military communications. Three hundred thousand German troops massed on the Swiss border and the Swiss military made plans to dynamite the Simplon and St. Gotthard Tunnels in order to prevent an invasion by the Germans. Fortunately, that invasion never took place.

When the war was over, the Dandolos returned to Italy, found much of their diversified empire still intact, and set about restoring the family home and recouping their losses.

Emilio, because he had been an active member of the anti-fascist exiles, was called upon to help form the new government. After some hesitation, he did what no Dandolo had done before—he announced his candidacy for Parliament as a member of the Social Christian Party. He was elected by a wide margin.

Catarina and Emilio then faced a difficult decision. Paolo was too old and ill to run the restored family businesses, so they asked their son Tony to leave the London School of Economics, where he had begun his second year, and return to Firenze. There, at the age of twenty, he took over as executive vice president of Dandolo Enterprises, with Paolo serving as the nominal president.

Tony's thoughts turned to the call he had received that morning from Mattei, wanting him to invest in a fleet of oil tankers. Mattei's judgments were usually flawless, and yet . . .

It's all on my head, he thought. *It's up to me to*

*continue the family fortune or destroy it. To continue
the empire, the dynasty . . . what the hell . . . Why
couldn't Mom have had more children?*

He walked back to his desk. There, smiling
blithely up from the page was beautiful Lorna
Brown, the first woman to shun his embraces in
years. Damn. Why couldn't he get her out of his
system? What was it about her?

*She's a challenge, that's it. She's the first woman
who has turned me down since I was a kid in
Switzerland and those girls at that fancy Swiss
boarding school . . .*

"I've got to get back to work," he muttered to no
one and buzzed for his secretary.

Two weeks later, Tony Dandolo impulsively accepted the government's offer to be part of the
official delegation going to New York for the Italian
promotion at Macy's. The "Italy-In-Macy's,
U.S.A." event would officially premiere the afternoon of September 10 on the fifth floor of the New
York City store. After a month in New York, the
exhibit and the craftsmen would visit various department stores throughout the states, hoping to
create a market for Italian clothing, ceramics, glass,
leather goods, and decorative wood carvings. Tony
was a natural choice because of his family's in-
volvement in the textile industry, and more recently their aggressive move into synthetic fabrics. But
Tony also suspected that his father had recommended him for the trip. On more than one occasion, Emilio had commented to his son that "some
American blood might be just what our family
needs." There was no doubt his parents had liked
Lorna—and would be very pleased if she became
their daughter-in-law.

The trip to New York City, Tony rationalized,

would also give him an opportunity to visit the American designers and entice them into using his silks and synthetics. If the top designers began using synthetics, the rest of America's fashion industry would follow suit. Normally, these negotiations would have been handled by his vice-president for marketing, but Tony had only been to America once before, three years earlier, and he looked forward to another opportunity to explore the wonders of New York City.

He booked a suite at the Hampshire House on Central Park and ordered a limousine to meet him at Idlewild. He arrived the Friday afternoon before the Monday opening at Macy's.

After checking into his room, he placed a call to Lorna. It was late afternoon, he had not notified her of his visit, and he felt his stomach tighten as the voice on the other end answered with a sultry "hello."

Instantly he remembered Kathy, and Lorna's apparent jealousy of his feigned interest in Kathy. "This must be Kathy."

"Yes, it is," the voice purred.

"And this is a voice out of your past—your past in Florence, Italy, to be exact."

"Tony! Tony Dandolo!" shouted Kathy.

After a few minutes of flirtatious pleasantries, Tony asked for Lorna.

"Oh, she's not here. She is back in South Dakota . . . phoo! I was hoping you were calling me."

"Is she coming back to New York?" Tony asked impatiently, stunned that Lorna was not there waiting for his arrival even though he hadn't notified her he was coming. At the same time, he was becoming vaguely annoyed with Kathy's flirting.

"Yes, too bad for me, she's arriving Sunday

afternoon. She had to go home to put her mother, who had another stroke, in a nursing home, poor thing."

"That's terrible! Why doesn't she bring her to New York City?"

"Oh, heavens no, Lorna wouldn't even consider something like that. Besides, nursing homes in New York would be too expensive. Mrs. Brown has some family, her brothers, near her. It's much better for her to stay in South Dakota."

"I see," Tony responded, thinking he could never do anything like that with his parents or even his grandfather, who was deteriorating rapidly.

"Look, Tony, I know you came to see Lorna, but since you've probably nothing better to do, why don't you come with me this evening? My parents are having a small dinner in honor of the president's foreign affairs advisor, Averell Harriman. It will be a lovely evening and I'd simply adore it if you'd be my escort."

"Well . . ."

"C'mon, I'll be insulted if you turn me down. It's the least I can do to repay the wonderful time you showed us this summer."

Against his better judgment, Tony accepted her invitation, hung up the phone, and began to unpack his clothes. He was devastated that Lorna was not in New York. Yet, she would be returning Sunday . . . and he had not made return reservations to Rome. He would stay in New York as long as necessary.

Later that evening, Tony regretted his decision to escort Kathy to her parents' dinner party. Sure, it had been a lovely evening, full of Wall Street's wisest men and some of New York's most glamorous women. Excellent food and wine were served in a setting only a little less magnificent than his family home in Firenze. But Kathy had become quite tipsy, and then embarrassingly giddy, and when they took their leave for the drive back to New York she had managed to convey the impression to her parents that they were sleeping with each other, something Tony was determined to avoid.

As he drove her Cadillac convertible down the Merritt Parkway, Tony surveyed the sleeping, but nevertheless gorgeous blonde cuddling next to him. No doubt about it, she was a beauty. From her perfectly shaped long legs to her ample bosom to her tiger-like green eyes, she was as nearly perfect a specimen as a man could want. And as Lorna had pointed out, she was an American aristocrat. Yet she interested him not at all. He knew he would walk away from her apartment, having turned down her overtures as gracefully as possible.

Christ, this must be love! he said to himself as he wondered at his self-discipline. It simply was not like him to walk away from a night in bed with a gorgeous woman like Kathy, to walk away from a non-entangling, one-night stand. Yet he also understood that if he so much as kissed Kathy, she would find some way to let Lorna know, and that would kill his chances with Lorna. And it was his obsession with Lorna, after all, and not a need to sell his fabrics, that had brought him on a twenty-one-hour flight across the ocean.

After successfully depositing Kathy in her apartment, Tony grabbed a cab back to his hotel and dropped into bed, finally feeling the effects of the long plane trip. He slept the clock around, awakening late Saturday afternoon. Then he began to plan his not-so-subtle strategy to win Lorna's heart. He contacted the hotel concierge and ordered theater, opera and ballet tickets for the next two weeks. He questioned the concierge about the best night clubs, restaurants, and supper clubs. Tony ordered an orchid plant to be delivered Sunday afternoon to Lorna's apartment. He ordered *The New Yorker* and *The New York Times* to be sent to his room so he could have a complete picture of which evening spots were the most romantic.

When he opened *The New Yorker*, there, smiling at him from the third page, he saw Lorna in a full-page ad for Saks Fifth Avenue. It was a wonderfully carefree and happy picture of Lorna. The camera had caught a glimpse of her he had never seen, but it was the way he wanted her to feel for the rest of her life—cherished, loved beyond measure, without a worry in the world. That was what he would promise her.

Lorna was met by the Reverend Leonore Addison when she stepped off the plane in Sioux Falls. During the long drive back to Vermillion, her mother's best friend began to prepare her for what she would find at the hospital.

"Your mother's stroke was a major one, and her ability to speak so a person can understand her hasn't returned yet. But it's good you've come because she surely will recognize you and feel your love and concern."

"What do the doctors think about her chance of recovering?"

"They don't seem too hopeful. I'm sorry, dear." Reverend Addison patted her hand as she saw a tear run down Lorna's face. "She can't walk or use her hands right. Someone has to feed her, dress her, nearly everything."

"I see. Have you checked out the nursing home?" Lorna folded and refolded her handkerchief.

"Yes. I've been visiting my people there for years. You'll see it. It's quite nice, very bright and spacious, not too large or crowded. And they welcome visitors at any time, which is always a good sign. They have a lovely chapel."

"Couldn't this have been prevented? Was Mom sick first? Did she complain?"

"Well, that's hard to say. Yes, she did have headaches a lot and complained of light-headedness now and then. But, land sakes, we couldn't get her near a doctor! She hadn't been to a doctor since you were small. Wouldn't go because some doctor back then had doubted your grandmother's miraculous cure. Corinna hated all doctors after that. Could be, though, that she's had dangerously high blood pressure for years and no one knew it."

"Mom was always so angry and so tense."

"Yes, your dear mother had lots of heartaches."

"I suppose my going to New York added to it."

"Now don't you go blaming yourself, Lorna. Corinna knew it was best. She knew your grandma was right about taking advantage of your Aunt Celia's offer. Corinna would never have sent you herself, but I think she was relieved—she knew deep in her heart it was the right thing—when your grandma sent you off to Celia."

Nothing Reverend Addison said adequately prepared Lorna to see her sick mother. Corinna had gained a great deal of weight in the nearly three years Lorna had been in New York, and her brown hair had turned almost completely white. Her dull eyes seemed to smile recognition, nonetheless, when Lorna stood beside her bed and spoke to her, steeling herself against tears, as Reverend Addison and the nurse had advised.

She talked soothingly to her mother, first about the illness, then about the happy parts of her career in New York. Corinna's only response was a tightening pressure on her hand.

After about twenty minutes, she left at the nurse's insistence, promising to return the next day.

"You'll stay with me at the parsonage," Reverend Addison said as they left the hospital. "It would be too dreary for you to stay alone in your mom's house."

For three days, Lorna traveled back and forth to the hospital and visited the nursing home to sign the necessary papers. On the drive back from the nursing home, Lorna cautiously broached a subject which had been much on her mind.

"Do you know, Reverend Addison, if my mother ever heard from my dad or his family? Did she ever try to find him?"

"No, she never heard from him, and yes, she did try to find him. About two years after he left, she traveled to Detroit and tried to find anyone by his name. She found six different Edward Browns, but none of them was your dad. And she couldn't trace his family either."

"Why do you think he left?"

"I think . . . you know I love your mother dearly, Lorna. . . ."

"Yes, please tell me."

"Well, I think it may have been at least partly your mother's fault. She was a bit of a nag. She was obsessed with what she considered Ed's evil habits. She wanted him to be a perfect Christian according to her definition."

"I see." Lorna's eyes followed the dust cloud stirred up by a flock of wild geese in the field next to the highway. "I have only happy memories of my father."

"As well you should, dear. Your father was a good man, a kind, decent man who struggled against hard times. And he worried about your mother's harshness toward you."

"Sometimes I wonder about religion and what it does to people."

"I understand what you're saying. Especially in small towns like Barnesville, people like your mother sometimes take religion too much to heart. They lose perspective. I tried hard—God knows, I tried with Corinna—but she got worse and worse in judging folks. Everyone was guilty, wicked . . . it's sad, it really is sad."

Lorna suggested, only half-heartedly, that perhaps she should stay in Barnesville and care for her mother.

"I won't even discuss it. It would be wrong for you to give up your chances when life is just beginning for you. Your mother—yes, even your mother—would be horrified. We'll take care of her; we church people will see to it that everything goes well for her. She helped us all, visited our sick. Now it's her turn. Remember all those Sundays she spent teaching those children? Now we'll take care of her. You just write happy letters, send money when you can, and come visit every couple of years."

On the fifth day, they took Corinna from the hospital to the nursing home in an ambulance, and two days later Reverend Addison drove Lorna back to the Sioux Falls airport. She had to be in New York Monday for a special show at Macy's department store.

She disembarked from the American Airlines flight from Chicago and walked into the airport waiting area carrying *From Here to Eternity* in one hand, her make-up case in the other, and a heavy shoulder-bag over her right arm. She was deep in thought, attempting to decide whether or not to tell Eileen Ford that she would, after all, make herself available for Saturday jobs. Previously she had kept Saturdays free for all-day art classes at the Art Students League, her one big self-indulgence. But if she agreed to work on Saturdays, she would not only make the extra income which she now desperately needed to keep her mother in the nursing home, but she would also save the eighteen dollars a month it cost to take the classes. Yet, it was a difficult decision, giving up the one thing in her life that meant the most to her. And if she gave up the classes, she would also be giving up the dream—which had nourished her since childhood—of becoming an artist.

Suddenly her senses told her someone was deliberately walking behind her, then next to her.

"Can I help you with that bag? You seem to have your hands full."

The deep male voice brought shivers to her spine. She was afraid to look at the tall, dark-haired man who had materialized beside her and was walking step-in-step with her. She was afraid it might not be the man she hoped it was, that her imagination was playing tricks on her.

"Tony! My God! Tony . . ."

She dropped her bag to the floor and wrapped her arms around the man she had given up hoping she would ever see again. "Oh Tony, you look so good to me!" But his greedy kisses, first on her forehead, then directly on her mouth, silenced her. She hugged him thoroughly, then hugged him again, as tears formed in her eyes.

"Lorna, you're as beautiful as I remember."

"Sshh . . . just let me look at you! What a surprise! What are you doing here? How did you know

I was arriving? How long have you been in New York?"

"The answer to all your questions is Kathy. Come, now, let's get your bags." He took command of her, moving her light-headed, floating body toward the front of the terminal. "I have a car and driver waiting."

As he propelled her toward the baggage claim he told her about his official reason for coming to New York, the Macy's show.

"You won't believe this, but I'm modeling in that show tomorrow. In fact, that's why I had to hurry with the arrangements for mother. I'm modeling lingerie—it's the first time I've ever accepted a lingerie assignment, but Macy's isn't carrying the Italian couturier designs, only the gorgeous hand-made lingerie." She was breathless at the wonder of seeing him and at trying to keep up with his stride. "My memories of Italy are so wonderful, I couldn't resist the offer to be in this show . . . are you shocked?"

"Shocked? That you're modeling lingerie? Hell, no! I only want to be in the front row seat!" He paused, then with a rakish grin continued, "You might even want to buy some. The last time I saw you, you had on some man's old pajamas!"

Lorna looked sharply at Tony to see if he was teasing or serious. Surely he couldn't believe her father's pajamas were a lover's . . . ?

"I'm only teasing you. Don't take everything I say so seriously. By the way, I love the picture of you in *The New Yorker*. It is the best one of you I've seen so far. Seems like every time I pick up a magazine, I find a picture of you in it. But that's the best one."

Lorna glowed in his praise, then realized it was showing all over her face and shyly looked away.

"I'm so surprised . . . I just can't believe you are here!"

"You mean you didn't realize that I always go after what I want? You thought the Atlantic Ocean would stop me? You silly little duck, don't you know I love you?"

When they were finally ensconced in the velvety softness of the Lincoln limousine, Tony turned his full attention to an appraisal of her. With a roguish sparkle in his eyes, he looked her up and down, undressing her and caressing her body with his eyes. Lorna was overcome by his staggering good looks and his powerful masculinity. Her heart lurched unexpectedly as she thought in a rush of clarity of how she had been transported from the poverty and dreary bleakness of South Dakota to the luxury of great wealth by this amazing man, walking back into her life brashly, unexpectedly, with such self-assurance, such overpowering arrogance. But the question remained—this time . . . this time, would she be smart enough to hold him?

"I figured you'd be tired, so I've made reservations for us at the Pierre Grille tonight," Tony announced as he dropped Lorna off at her apartment. "But tomorrow night I have a special treat for us—dinner and dancing at the Starlight Roof to the music of Vaughn Monroe—if you're not too tired from modeling nightgowns."

"Oh, that sounds glorious," Lorna responded even as she wondered at his assumption that she would be available to go out with him every night. Yet it wasn't very often that she was invited to places like the Starlight Roof.

"And we have theater tickets, sixth row center, for "Call Me Madam" with Ethel Merman on Tuesday, to be followed by dinner at Frankie and Johnny's."

"Hey, I thought I was going to show you New York! Sounds like you are giving me the grand tour!" she said as the doorman opened the door to her building.

"Only the best places—only the best for you, my darling." Then he kissed her lightly on the forehead and strode back toward the waiting limousine.

It was a week she would remember for the rest of her life, an imperishable, vivid fantasy—yet it really was something she had lived. Every moment she was not working, she was with Tony. They not only saw "Call Me Madam", but such was Tony's enthusiasm for America's own special musical art form, they saw "South Pacific," "Gentlemen Prefer Blondes" with Carol Channing, and Gertrude Lawrence in "The King and I." They held hands through two movies: "Jim Thorpe: All American" and "People Will Talk." They watched Patricia Wilde and Frank Hobl in a new ballet produced by The New York City Ballet, "The Cakewalk." And they visited every major museum, returning a second time for the Toulouse-Lautrec drawings at the Metropolitan Museum.

They walked in Central Park, and every night after dinner or the theater Tony insisted on one last hansom carriage ride. They even had a favorite horse, a dalmatian-spotted old nag with a driver in top hat and tails who dropped them off every night at Lorna's apartment.

The following Saturday morning Tony announced that they were returning to the Starlight Roof. "Wear your most gorgeous gown and put your hair up on top of your head. I like it like that."

Lorna dressed in an ice-blue, silk peau-de-peche, off-the-shoulder gown by Jacques Fath that she had been saving for a very special occasion. She added

pearl-studded combs to her dark hair and wore a
simple strand of pearls around her neck. Then,
after a final spray of Arpege, she was off for one
more dream-like evening with Tony.

Dominique, the maitre d' at the Starlight Roof,
led them to a table with a banquet for two in the far
corner of the dining room, secluded by two tall
palms. Next to the table, already cooling in the
silver bucket, was a bottle of Mumms champagne,
and on the table awaiting her arrival was a small
bouquet of red sweetheart roses.

Strolling string players serenaded them while
they sipped their first glass of champagne. Then,
with much bowing, the maitre d' placed a magnificent gold-embossed plate in front of Lorna. The
center of the plate was filled with a deep blue
crushed velvet nest in which lay a bristol-blue
Fabergé egg. Lorna looked at Tony, totally mystified.

"Open it up," he quietly ordered.

She picked up the precious gold-encrusted egg
with trembling hands. A roaring filled her ears even
though the violins had ceased and the room had
become quite silent. Finally, the clasp gave way and
the egg opened to reveal a huge diamond solitaire
nestling inside.

"Oh my . . ."

"I love you, Lorna," Tony softly intoned as he
reached for her hand. "May I put it on?"

Tears formed in her eyes as she looked from him
to the ring and then back at his soft brown eyes. In
that moment her entire life passed in front of
her—all her mother's stern admonitions, her
grandmother's strict love. They had been right,
right to counsel her to remain a virgin, to make a
man declare his intentions. She had followed their
admonitions and she had won the prize, a greater

prize than they could ever have imagined for her. She looked at Tony and saw all the love and devotion in the world pouring out of his eyes—all the love she could ever absorb.

"Oh, Tony, I love you too!"

He slipped the ring on her trembling, icy hands and then held them for a long moment. "You are a dream come true for me, Lorna, the woman I have been searching for all my life." Then he stood and gathered her into his arms for a dance.

The rest of the dinner was a blur in her memory—oysters on the half shell, rack of lamb with rosemary sauce, asparagus in mustard dill sauce, and more and more champagne. Vaughn Monroe dedicated several ballads to the "newly engaged couple," mentioning Lorna as a "famous New York model and cover girl." Finally there came a time on the dance floor when Tony could no longer contain his raging passion. "Let's go!" he commanded, and even though it was early in the evening he instructed his driver to take them to the Hampshire House.

Suddenly Lorna understood where they were going—back to his suite at the Hampshire House—and she knew she would not resist this time. Nor did she want to.

As he inserted the key into the door of his suite, Lorna remembered Emilio Dandolo's concern: "I only hope he's remembered how to court a real lady." And she was so happy she had fended off his advances that night in Florence. For everything there is a time.

The suite was champagne colored—silk damask-covered chairs and sofas, plush champagne carpeting, moire walls. Crystal vases filled with glorious spring bulbs sat on every surface. Tony had arranged everything perfectly, from the softly piped strings of Montovani to the flowers to the silver bucket with more champagne. Indeed, he had remembered how to court a lady!

After pouring two glasses of the bubbly, he broke the tense silence with a toast: "To the woman I love, to you Lorna, the person who has taught me that there are some things in life more important than work—to you, my dearest."

"Am I allowed to drink to that?" she shyly asked, her face flushed with happiness.

In answer he put his glass on the coffee table and took her in his arms. "Hurry up and drink to it, so I can kiss you." She took one tiny sip, then he removed the glass from her hand and said with a mischievous grin, "You don't really want any more champagne now, do you? I've other things in mind."

He picked up her hand, now bejeweled with the twenty-two carat marquise. He kissed each finger, then the back of her hand. "You taste lovely, as good as candy!" As his kisses traveled up her arm, she felt a tingling that flooded through her arms and legs, then traveled at lightning speed down her spinal cord. He nibbled a moment on her bare shoulders, then began to kiss her neck under her left ear. "I love you, I'll always love you my darling." Then he roughly crushed her to him and kissed her mouth hard, probing to find the delicious sweetness her mouth would yield, as his strong hands massaged her back and shoulders. Abruptly, he stopped the kiss, lifted her in his arms and carried her to his bedroom.

As he placed her on his bed, she glimpsed boxes, large and small, wrapped in beautiful silver and blue papers and ribbons, piled on the chaise. But she had no time to think about them as he began undressing her.

"You'd better help me so I don't tear this creation," he muttered impatiently as he tried to unzip the silk gown.

Then, as she struggled to undo the dress, his mouth once again found hers and made the singing inside her head start all over again. His kissing somehow calmed her nervousness, her trembling hands. It was so strange to be doing this, undressing before the eyes of a man.

When she had the dress off, she still had her strapless bra and garter belt to contend with, but Tony stopped her. "No, no, let me do that," he offered with a wicked grin. "That will be my greatest joy."

Slowly, savoring his anticipation, he unfastened each garter and drew the sheer stockings off her legs. When the first leg was bare he took her foot in his hands as if it were the most cherished of objects, then began to kiss each polished toe. Her entire body shuddered and broke out in goosebumps. Finally, when Tony had removed every article of clothing, he stood and looked down at his prize. His eyes traveled from her face to her breasts and down her legs to her toes. Then back up again. Slowly. She couldn't believe the feelings she experienced as his eyes traveled over her, feasting on her body. Then she wanted him fiercely; she wanted him in a way she had never felt before. She wanted him to smother her own body with his, to enter her, to pierce the very center of her being.

"Tony . . ." she gasped, "you must get undressed too. . . ."

"I will . . . in a minute." He sat down beside her naked body and began to gently explore it with his hands. He pressed her breasts, cupped them in his hands, teased the nipples until they stood rigidly at attention. Then he bent down to tenderly tease each swelling bud with his tongue, then began to suck fiercely while he continued to prod the other with his fingers.

A liquid heat began to take over Lorna's abdomen, began to seep through her loins; she heard herself moan. It came from the very depths of her, a sound she had never heard before, and she couldn't stop it. The more he nibbled on her breast, the more her moaning grew. She felt as if she would soon lose consciousness, as lightheadness took control of her body, a delicious drowsy otherness catapulted her away.

His free hand left her other breast and began to travel lightly down her belly to her thigh, between her legs. First gently, then with more pressure he began to probe her. Unexpectedly, involuntarily, she felt her hips arch up in rhythm with his hands. She felt a gush of warmth and waves of spasms. He seemed to know what she was feeling, and after looking at her face to gauge her response, he quietly reassured her, "Relax darling, I'm going to give you the most marvelous experience you've ever had." He spread her legs then and began to explore with his mouth and tongue.

Fiery sparks sped through her body, the most amazing, most incredible feeling in the world. The spasms spun off and increased in intensity. Suddenly she felt it take her over, and her entire body lurched, straining uncontrollably, begging him to continue his glorious torture. Her body flushed, her pulse exploded, pounding in her temples. She was beyond consciousness in a world she had never traveled to before. Then, slowly, he brought her down. Slowly, slowly, he calmed her raging fever, the pounding in her head. His lips traveled up to her breasts again, then to her lips, and she could taste her own juices on his tongue when he kissed her mouth.

"Now it's my turn," he said as he stood and began to remove his shirt.

Lorna sighed a huge sigh, thinking, *what have I been missing all these years?* Meanwhile, she stared at his strong chest, his muscular biceps. He removed his pants and she averted her eyes from the huge bulge in his shorts. Then she looked back, unable to resist. Slowly he removed his shoes, his socks, then at last his shorts. It was amazing, she thought, the size of it. It could never fit inside her!

As if he could read her mind, he said, "Now you know why I had to get you ready first. I'll try not to hurt you."

He lay down beside her, resting his hand calmingly on her thigh, letting her get used to the whole idea. He turned his head toward hers and commanded, "Kiss me, touch me, Lorna."

At first, not understanding, she kissed his mouth. After a moment he chuckled at her innocence and said, "You are permitted to touch."

Hesitantly at first, then with real appetite, she began to explore his body with her hand: his hairy chest, then his tight abdomen, his thigh. Finally, after much resistance, she lightly touched his golden-pink shaft. He grabbed her hand and pressed it to him, and she felt the hot throbbing inside him, and for a moment was terrified.

"Darling, I'm not going to hurt you, I promise. Just relax." And he moved over on top of her.

She wanted him deep inside her. She arched her hips upwards to receive him, and felt a searing pain as he thrust deep inside her. The magical rhythm began, first small spasms of delight, then huge muscular contractions. She had no control over her moaning body. Blood rushed from her head and she lost control of her mind. That delicious flowing and pulsing, that wonderful earthquake that was happening inside her, took over and she climbed with him to the heights, to marvelous peaks of emotion she had never dreamt of. She felt his first tremendous shudder, then more, smaller ones. He collapsed on top of her. For a long time they lay entwined, silent.

He moved his chest weight from her, keeping their lower bodies interlocked. It is heaven, sheer heaven, she thought. I could die now.

"Chiave d'oro apre la porta di ferro."

"What?"

He smiled broadly, then translated for her. "A golden key opens the iron door."

"Tony!"

"Did I hurt you?" he asked tenderly.

"Only for a moment. But it was glorious . . . so wonderful."

He looked at her radiant eyes, her glowing skin, her long beautiful body. For a long time they lay there, each replaying their wonderful lovemaking in their minds, their hands and bodies intertwined.

"I have an idea. Let's take a bath."

"Together?"

"Of course. I even bought bubble bath. Come see."

She followed him into the champagne-colored marble bathroom where she saw the biggest tub she had ever seen, mirrored on two sides. She watched the two of them, naked, holding hands, her hair thoroughly love-messed. She felt no embarrassment and was surprised. She realized she was no longer the same person she had been before . . . before love. Tony had transformed her, turned her into a real woman. She loved what she saw in the mirror.

For two more weeks he stayed in New York, wining and dining her every evening, teaching her everything he knew about the pleasures their bodies could bring them. She felt addicted. She could barely bring herself to get up out of bed to dress and leave him when she had a modeling assignment.

All during the day while she pranced down runways and pirouetted before the cameras, she thought of Tony, of his splendid body, of his marvelous plans and dreams.

They would be married in Florence early in January and spend the month honeymooning at the Dandolo ski chalet at Cortina D'Ampezzo.

"You will love skiing," Tony had promised her, "and you will love what we do *après-ski* even more."

Chapter Four

At precisely five minutes before eight o'clock, His Excellency, The Ambassador of Italy and Mrs. Dandolo, followed by their daughter Tanya and her nursemaid Rosina, descended the majestic marble staircase. The ambassadorial couple were in evening clothes. He had accented his black Italian-cut silk-and-linen tuxedo with a white ruffled shirt; she wore a yellow silk-organdy Valentino creation. Five-year-old Tanya had been told she could "spy on the party" from the top of the staircase "but for thirty minutes only—then off to bed!"

Bruno, the major domo they had brought from Florence, greeted the family and offered them sherry and ginger-ale. "Would you like to see the solarium, Excellency?"

"Yes, indeed," Tony responded, knowing how excited Lorna was with the results of her creation. Tonight, at their first major dinner party since arriving in Washington, they would begin the evening with cocktails in the intimate setting Lorna had designed.

They followed the butler through the fifty-five-foot living room. "An abomination!" Lorna had said when she first glimpsed it. "It would take at least one hundred guests to begin to fill this room up! And I hate large parties." She had immediately turned her imagination toward creating a warmer atmosphere, much as she had at their renovated palazzo in the heart of Florence, for the much smaller gatherings she preferred.

At the end of the long living room, they came to French doors leading to a solarium. Only yesterday had the tile floor been finished; today, florists had worked their magic. Her decorator had delivered a few pieces of furniture and Lorna's vision had materialized. Seventeen varieties of orchids hung from the ceiling and sat on the deep window ledges; numerous green plants transformed the modern, glass-walled addition to the century-old embassy into something the ambassador had not seen before. It was not a sidewalk cafe or a moonlit garden but something special—both European and tropical in atmosphere.

On the one real wall, the brick wall which had been the outside of the building until the solarium was added. Lorna had hung her most prized possession, the one item she had insisted on carrying onto the airplane herself—an original Monet canvas, one of many Monet had painted of the bridge at Vetheuil. She had wanted it instead of a multi-carat diamond wedding band from Bulgari, but Tony had bought the Monet for her, and then surprised her with a diamond wedding band cut to fit her solitaire. It was typical of his generosity, she later understood.

Bruno began to light the dozens of candles tucked in with the orchids on the deep window ledges.

"Oh, Mommy, it's like a fairy tale!" Tanya exclaimed as she very tentatively touched one of the orchids.

"Yes," Lorna answered, calmly taking Tanya's offending hand in hers and thinking, *it is exactly as I dreamed it would be. . . .*

They had been asked to come to Washington by Italy's newly elected prime minister, Amitore Fanfani, the day after his election. That was in July. Now, only seven weeks later, they were hosting their first dinner, in honor of the American secretary of state, John Foster Dulles. With his usual managerial efficiency, Tony had arranged for several cousins who had been working for him to take charge of the various components of the Dandolo family conglomorate. He would receive monthly reports from each of them, uncensored by any one overall manager. It was a big order—manage the conglomorate from across the ocean and run the American embassy, Italy's most important diplomatic post.

Lorna had stored their priceless furniture and art collection and rented their palazzo to a nephew of Bernard Berenson, assuring Tony that it would be better to rent it out than leave it empty, a temptation to vandals. After all, when they did make short trips home, they could stay with Catarina and Emilio at the Villa.

Lorna had also garnered a fresh wardrobe from the Italian designers, knowing she would be their premier showcase in the United States. She had gone to Oltrarno and ordered hand-embroidered organdy and linen table cloths, as well as bed and bath linens. She had become spoiled during her seven years of marriage to Tony—nothing but the finest, preferably Italian and handmade, satisfied her now.

"Bruno, let's take one last look at the dining room and the seating arrangements," Tony ordered as he swept Lorna before him, heading back toward the marble foyer and across it into the massive dining room. Eight circular tables now covered with the embroidered organdy cloths, creamy Limoges china, and amethyst and gold Venetian crystal, were each set for ten guests. Small vigil candles and gracefully arranged exotic orchids were the final dramatic touch in the center of each table. Lorna's secret was that the orchids were not cut flowers, but plants, their pots carefully concealed in Italian porcelain. The next morning they would be moved to the solarium where they would reside until the next big occasion.

"This is incredible, simply amazing!" Tony said as he again checked the seating chart, amazed at how quickly they had been able to attract such a stellar group—the movers and shakers of the Senate, the Washington press corps, and the Eisenhower administration. "I'd like to bet we have at least one future president here tonight!"

"And you gave me the best-looking prospect," Lorna reminded him mischievously.

"Oh, you mean Kennedy. But I put him across the table from you, so you would have no opportunity for an intimate conversation. Don't worry, I'll be keeping an eye on you, my darling."

"Is everything going well in the kitchen, Bruno?"

"Yes, madam. Cecilia hasn't blown up since early this morning when she fought with the fish market. She claims the red snapper was frozen, that she can tell by touching the fish. She made them take back their delivery and send over another batch. That lady has some temper, madam. She terrorizes everyone."

"Yes," Lorna agreed, "but she gets results."

"Can't deny that, can't deny that . . ."

The doorbell rang and Rosina quickly led Tanya to the top of the staircase. Lorna and Tony prepared to greet their first arriving guests with a conscious attempt at ambassadorial dignity. Louvie and Drew Pearson walked through the door first, and immediately following them, Dr. and Mrs. Henry Monat.

As Tony took over, the way he always did with such instantaneous and genuine warmth, Lorna thought again that he was a natural politician. How much he loved people, how easy it was for him to be a gracious host! But how hard it was for her . . .

Hours later, after the last guest had gone home, Lorna and Tony collapsed in the rosewood-paneled library. Bruno brought them both a brandy. "Will there be anything else, Excellency?"

"No, Bruno. But tell the staff everything was just fine this evening. Mrs. Dandolo and I are both very pleased."

"Thank you, sir. I'll just check one more time and be certain everything is locked up."

Lorna moved closer to Tony on the brown leather sofa. "Well?"

"It really was something. It was very gay. I was amazed at how everyone danced so late. I'd heard Washington wasn't much for late nights."

"They loved the food, especially the dessert. Several ladies asked me for the recipe, but I know Cecilia won't part with it."

"Lyndon Johnson is a fascinating man. I am

surprised at how much I liked him after everything I had heard. What did you think of Kennedy?"

"He's gorgeous! And brilliant, and charming, and everything. He'll be my candidate for president any day."

"Sorry, kiddo, you can't have a candidate. Diplomats are not allowed favorites, not even diplomats who were once American citizens."

"But you must admit he's sexy."

"Hey, I'm not sure I like this!" Tony responded as he pulled Lorna closer. "Don't think I like it at all . . ."

After he had kissed her resoundingly, Lorna asked, "Do you want to hear something funny? I don't know who the woman was, but at the table next to me I caught a glimpse of a middle-aged woman, sort of brownish-grey hair, stuffing a roll in her evening bag! Can you imagine? I must look at the dinner chart and figure out who that was. I couldn't believe my eyes."

"Yes, tomorrow morning we must both make notes on everything we remember about each guest. And Lorna, you really must begin to interview for a social secretary. That is absolutely urgent." Tony stood and began to pace as he reeled off the qualities he wanted in a social secretary. "She should be an American, she should come from one of the best families, young and energetic, and very attractive. We'll include her in the parties. And I don't think we'll have to pay her much, as it's a prestigious job. Preferably, she should be single, and if she's well connected with the White House, it would be a plus. Yes, let's get a Republican, Lorna."

"I mentioned it to Louvie Pearson, and she said she would think about possibilities overnight. I'll call her in a day or two."

"Yes, and you really ought to cultivate that friendship. She can give you lots of good advice."

"And they have a big farm out in Potomac and horses to ride. . . ."

"But you must be very careful what you tell her, Lorna. Always remember that she is married to a member of the press, and they—all of them—will use us to their advantage when they can. You can't trust any of them. So please, for God's sake, be careful when you make friends, what you confide in them."

Lorna sighed. It was the twentieth time he had given her this lecture. Why, oh why did he have to get into politics too? Wasn't one member of the family in the public eye enough? Now she had to guard everything she said, everything she did, and he had told her the embassy itself was wired for sound by the U.S. State Department. The only place they could hold a private conversation was in the shower, together, with the water running! What had he gotten her into?

As they walked up the stairs toward their private suite of rooms, Lorna hugged Tony. "I do love you, darling, but I hate this life, I really do."

He hugged her in response, then kissed her forehead. "Try, darling, try."

"I will. I promised you I would, and I will try to like it. But I don't know . . . I truly don't like being such a public person."

They continued discussing the party while they prepared for bed. Tony was already in his pajamas, seated on the mauve chaise with a book in his hand when Lorna emerged from her dressing room wearing a thin blue-silk, floor-length negligee. "That Jennifer O'Neal is one woman I don't think we'll invite again. She acted like a slut on the dance floor. It was bad enough, the way she carried on with

Senator Page and Senator Henson, but when I saw her take up with you and watched you respond, I decided it was the last time she'd dine under my roof."

"I love to see you jealous!"

"It's not jealousy. I think she is common!"

"What could you possibly be jealous of Jennifer for? I was actually quite taken with her. She is so full of the devil and a terror on the dance floor, and she's easily one of the wittiest women I've ever met. A blonde bombshell."

Lorna was aghast at Tony. Without thinking, she threw her hairbrush at him. Tony ducked, then stood and walked toward her with a menacing look in his eyes. He held her firmly by the shoulders and forced her to look in his eyes. "Don't you believe that I prefer you? You, Lorna, to any other woman in the world? You are my woman. You belong to me. I love you. My life couldn't go on without you. But damn it, I love to see you jealous. You're a holy terror when your eyes blaze like that. I like to tease you, *mia cara*, because it proves you still love me when I see you that angry. I saw you watching Jennifer and me tonight. I watched you begin to burn."

"You bastard! That's what you are, Tony, a real son-of-a-bitch!"

"My, the lady's grammar has changed in the seven years I've known her. For shame!" And then he grinned at her and smacked her bottom.

Lorna had been watching Tony's eyes all the while he made his little speech—the one she had heard so many times she could recite it herself. It was hard to know, she reflected, how much of it he genuinely believed and how much was part of his line, that he was only saying for her benefit. She remembered with sadness that afternoon last June when she had accidently stumbled upon Tony making love to blonde, seventeen-year-old Colette—Colette, her houseguest, one of her art students. She had backed out of the bedroom quickly, unobserved. She had fled to her studio and wept in humiliation. It was bad enough to realize that Tony needed other women, but she had guessed at that and unconsciously accepted it. But how could he defile her bed, her bedroom? How could he take another woman there? Several hours later, she had returned to the palazzo with no trace of tears on her face. With the dignity of the "contessa" she rightfully was, she quietly asked her maid to change the bed and bathroom linens. Tony never suspected what Lorna had seen. And Colette decided—quite on her own—to return to France.

These images were reverberating in Lorna's brain when Tony turned her around to face him again. "You're not really jealous of Jennifer, are you darling?"

"Not tonight. Not this moment. You're here with me now. I don't have to be jealous of anyone."

Later, after they had finished making love and Tony's heavy body was dead weight on top of hers, a thought which shamed and titilated her flashed, unbidden, through her imagination—*would Senator Kennedy feel this heavy if he were lying on top of me*? She felt a tremor of heat and excitement flush through her veins. *Could it be? Will I change? Will coming back here change me? Could I have a love affair? Of course not! I love Tony. I could never love another man. I could never stoop so low. Never!*

"Good morning, Tamara. My, you look lovely. That's a beautiful suit!" Lorna looked up from the stack of invitations to greet her new social secretary, Tamara Thompkins.

"Today's a big day and I wanted to look my best."

Lorna loved her enthusiasm. At a time—ten o'clock on a Monday morning—when most secretaries were still trying to get over a full weekend, Tamara exuded pep and energy. She was dressed in a bronze-colored tweed suit only a shade darker than her hair. Her dappled-green eyes glistened with happy anticipation.

"The Ambassador is excited about his debut too," Lorna said. "He showed me the outline and text last night. Tell me, are the questions usually tough at the Press Club?"

"Depends. On what the big issues back in Italy are, on whether they want to pin him or let him slide. So far, you and the Ambassador haven't made any mistakes, and you have no enemies in the press corps so far as I can tell. So I don't think they'll be too rough."

"Would you find out for me who will be at the head table? I know it probably sounds silly, but I feel so much better when I know in advance who I'll have to make small talk with."

"Sure. I'll call right now." Tamara began to dial the phone, then stopped. "Do we have advance copies of the speech to send over now?"

"The problem with that is that Tony never sticks to his text. He mostly ad-libs—I think you'll be surprised at how good he is."

"I expect him to be terrific. But he'll have to be prepared to comment on his opinion on shutting down Italy's 'houses of tolerance,'" Tamara added mischievously. "Those men are going to resent having the last legal brothels in the western world closed! Takes all the fun out of a visit to Italy."

Lorna laughed, thinking at the same time that Tamara had done a remarkable job of becoming familiar with issues back in Italy. "Tony's opinion is that the government is acting very foolishly because they are giving up twenty million dollars a year in taxes and license fees."

"Seriously, Lorna, is it really true that thirty percent of the women in Italy are prostitutes? I read that in *Newsweek*."

"Not in the sense of being street walkers or call girls, I don't think, but rather—oh, I don't know Tamara—it seems the women of Italy have a strange set of rules they live by. I don't understand it even after living there seven years. The upper class has its set of morals, a ridiculous double standard—but then it is also true that many of the poorer girls end up as prostitutes or mistresses. Believe me, it's refreshing to be back in the United States."

"Aren't Italian men fabulously sexy?" Tamara paused, then continued, "I mean, when I was there I was certainly pursued down every street, and by some of the best-looking men I've ever seen."

Lorna responded with a terse, "Italian men take great pride in their sexual prowess," leaving Tamara with no doubt that that conversation was not her cup of tea.

She stood up from her desk. "I've got to shower and dress. Later this afternoon I want to work with you on the dinner for Mrs. Longworth. I think we'll plan it for October 30th if she's available on that date."

Tamara Thompkins had been recommended to Lorna by Luvie Pearson. She had called the Monday after the Dulles dinner to tell Lorna that Tamara was available and would be splendid in the job. She had been raised in Main Line Philadelphia, the daughter of a wealthy industrialist who was a large contributor to the Republican party.

Tamara had graduated from Sarah Lawrence with a degree in politics, had married immediately and divorced her husband three years later. Since then, she had worked as a case worker in the Senate, as a press relations officer in the State Department's office of protocol, and as a press assistant to Senator James O'Neill. Her most important qualification, Luvie had pointed out, was her knowledge of how political Washington worked. Largely because of her father's contacts, she could get through to anyone, and now her own contacts were numerous and at the highest levels of government.

Lorna had agreed to interview her, thinking that she was probably sleeping with the Senator and wanted, for whatever reason, to break up the relationship. Why else would she be interested in changing jobs? Lorna thought, without even meeting her, that she wouldn't like her and Tamara probably wasn't competent anyhow.

Luvie had not prepared Lorna for the vision of red-haired loveliness dressed in a Mainbocher suit who arrived the following morning. Not only was Tamara gorgeous, but she was gracious, tremendously intelligent, and well educated. Her most overpowering asset was her bubbling enthusiasm and energy. Lorna was overwhelmed and immediately decided that Tamara was clearly overqualified for the job of social secretary.

On the other hand, she was exactly what Lorna and Tony needed to make this city notice them.

After chatting for a half hour over tea, Lorna led Tamara through the solarium to the ambassador's office. The three of them discussed the position and Tamara's obvious qualifications for it for about an hour. It was clear to Lorna that Tony had taken an instant liking to Tamara. The only hitch was that Lorna felt she needed a secretary on a part-time

basis, and Tamara wanted a full-time job with a
large salary. Tony hired her on the spot, saying that
her first priority would be to serve as social secretary. When she had time left over, she would work
at the embassy as special assistant to the ambassador, concentrating on press relations and cultural
affairs.

That evening Tony talked non-stop about their
wondrous good luck in having found Tamara.
Lorna couldn't repress the nagging thought that
Tamara reminded her of the friend of her modeling
years, Kathy. Like Kathy, Tamara had been born
with everything Lorna didn't have—wealth, a position in society, a fine education. Those assets,
coupled with her professional experience, gave her
a sophisticated elan that Lorna could never hope to
achieve. In truth, Lorna admitted to herself, she
was intimidated by Tamara.

Her early doubts quickly disappeared. Within
two weeks, Lorna felt more relaxed in Tamara's
presence, knowing they had found a true gem.
Tamara was organized, efficient, and totally reliable. She was witty and had a wonderful sense of
perspective. The two women became fast friends.

"I positively never will go to another charity
luncheon!" Lorna announced angrily as she flung
open the door to her office, threw down her bag,
and plopped down at her desk.

Tamara laughed, then asked, "But you enjoy
women—at least some of them—don't you?"

"Yes, but I prefer them one at a time. I hate hen
parties. I hate luncheons and teas! I tell you,
Tamara, I was never meant for this job."

Tamara realized how serious Lorna was, but
there was no help for it.

"Honestly, I'm so sick of parties that I'd like to

go into seclusion for a month. And I've only been here a little over two months. But you know Tony. He's indefatigable. He loved every one of them. From now on, I'm instituting a new rule. I've asked the mail clerk to bring all invitations—every one of them—directly to this office. I'll go over them first and write "No"—you can make up the excuses, Tamara—on the ones I can't face. That will take care of seventy-five percent of them. Then I'll discuss the rest with Tony."

She took a small hairbrush out of her bag and began to tidy her long, bouffant hairdo.

"As for invitations to me personally, there have to be rules too. I simply must discipline myself or I won't have time left to think. You know, a person can't go to parties day after day without becoming terribly dull. Sometimes I have nightmares about my face freezing into a smile—like this!" Lorna grimaced dramatically and both women burst into laughter.

Then Lorna added, "Besides I need more time with Tanya."

"Okay. Let's try it. What are your rules?"

"No more diplomatic calls—to hell with the rest of those wives! I've made forty calls in two months. The other countries aren't important to Italy anyhow."

"I love that! Do you realize how many hours I've spent on the phone arranging those stupid calls—trying to get a day and an hour that is mutually agreeable? That's fine with me!"

"And don't accept any luncheon invitations for me. I mean, private luncheons and charity luncheons. Not unless the Ambassador is speaking or the whole theme of the luncheon has something to do with Italy. It's foolish for me to waste my time—and they all last three hours—unless it will really do Italy some good. And no more charity balls at night. Those balls have wall-to-wall ambassadors and cabinet officers. Tony and I get lost in the crowd. There's no point in it."

"But how can you say no to people like Mrs. Merriweather Post?" Tamara asked, holding up the beautifully addressed, heavy cream invitation which had been sitting on her desk for two days.

"Plead a previous engagement or say the Ambassador is expecting to be out of the country that week—he has a crisis at home—God knows Italy has enough of those! I don't know, Tamara, you think of something. Make yourself a long list of reasons why we can't accept an invitation, post it on the bulletin board and close your eyes, throw a dart, and wherever it lands, use that excuse!"

Again both women laughed.

"Now, about the dinner for Mrs. Longworth. Please make up a guest list. I want a good mix— press, columnists, three or four senators, two or three outstanding congressmen, preferably some with beautiful wives. You know, Tamara, I never knew how much that mattered, how many people get invited back again and again because of physical beauty. It astounds me. But Tony always insists that we have several really gorgeous women—besides you and me, of course!

"Anyhow, try to get either the Kennedys or the Coopers, then get some people from other worlds —the arts, the theater. If you'll make up a list and leave it on my desk, I'll go over it with Tony tonight. Oh! Be sure to call Mrs. Longworth and ask if there is anyone she would like invited." Lorna stopped for a moment, looked in her purse to be sure she had her wallet, then stood. "Now, do you have any questions?"

"If you are getting an opera star from La Scala,

what arrangements should I make for accompaniment?"

"Call the National Symphony and see if they can recommend a pianist and a couple of violins—but wait till I've made arrangements with the soloist. And call Devron and make arrangements for dance music—a small combo from ten to one o'clock. I'm going down to the kitchen now and talk to Cecilia about a special menu."

Lorna walked briskly away from her desk, but at the door she smiled back at Tamara. "You'd better start compiling that list of excuses for me. I've been seriously contemplating pneumonia!"

Chapter Five

A week before the dinner for Mrs. Longworth, as the three of them were returning to the embassy after the ambassador's speech to the Woman's National Democratic Club, Tamara informed them that *Town and Country* magazine had asked if they could send photographers to cover the dinner.

"Would it be one extra cameraman or several?" asked Lorna.

"They mentioned a reporter and a photographer. They want to come an hour early to take portraits of you and the Ambassador and the dining room. They hinted that they want to put you on the cover, Lorna."

"What do you think, Tony?"

"Why not? Two more press people won't add that much to the crowd."

"Sometimes I wonder, Tamara, if it's a blessing to have a social secretary with such connections!" But even as she teased Tamara, Lorna knew it was her Washington connections that made her invaluable to the embassy.

"Have the two of you made a decision about a spring fashion show?"

"Ugh!" Lorna grimaced.

"You've got to do it, Lorna, you've really got to," Tony admonished.

"Damn it, Tony! You make the arrangements. Let your commercial office make the decisions with the designers, stores, models—all that nonsense. Tamara and I will arrange for a lovely cocktail-buffet reception. We'll take care of that, but I will not personally deal with those designers. And only two a year, spring and fall. I will not give a show for each individual designer the way the French do. Italy has better things to show America. That's why I want to bring some of our artists and musicians over here. If the foreign office can budget to send hundreds of people over here for fashion shows, they can budget some money to send over art and artists and musicians and writers."

"For Christ's sake, be realistic. Fashion is one of the main things Italy sells to America."

Tony continued his sermon, but Lorna tuned him out. When the car was finally silent, she turned to him and in an intimate voice said, "Let's cancel out of those two parties tonight and you and I sneak out to see that new Antonioni movie—could we?"

"I don't know. What parties are we scheduled for tonight, Tamara?"

"The Kreegers are having a cocktail party from six to eight and the Embassy of Kuwait is having a big blast."

"I think not Lorna, though I'd like to. The Kreegers would be hurt. I know they are expecting us, and he's got good connections."

"Then you go alone, Tony. I mean it. I haven't spent an evening with Tanya in a long time, and I'm really tired."

"If you wish. But you know I hate going without you."

"Please do, Tony. I need the rest."

"Will you need me for anything this afternoon, Ambassador?" Tamara asked as they were getting out of the car.

"The only thing would be calls about the speech. If anyone calls the press office, I'll have Petrini refer them to you. But tomorrow I'll need you in the morning. Can you do without Tamara tomorrow morning, Lorna?"

"Yes. I'm going to sleep late and read. In the afternoon I have an appointment with J. Carter Brown at the Gallery. He's going to give me a private tour. Tomorrow is a day I have set aside for myself."

"Good. You should do more of that."

"And what about more time for us?"

"Ah—that's another story!" Tony pecked Lorna lightly on the cheek before they parted, she for the house and he for his office next door.

Later that afternoon, after Tanya had left with friends to go ice skating and Lorna had at last settled down on her chaise to read *Dr. Zhivago*, the telephone rang. It was Bruno.

"Bruno, I asked you not to disturb me!"

"Yes, I'm sorry, madam, but there are two officers from the metropolitan police here asking for you."

"It must be a mistake, Bruno. I'm sure they want the ambassador."

"No, Madam, they insist on talking with you."

"Bruno, I will not come down there and speak to the police. Please call the ambassador immediately and ask him to come to the library. Meanwhile, ask the officers to be seated in the library."

Lorna slammed down the phone, unusually angry and impatient with Bruno for not obeying her wish for a quiet hour alone. But after she turned back to her book, she could not concentrate. She wondered why the police were asking for her. Moreover, she was ashamed of her display of temper to Bruno.

Her mind slipped back to the previous visit they had had from the police. Two weeks previously, she had been suffering from insomnia and had gotten out of bed and gone downstairs to pace. She decided to sit in the solarium and look at her Monet. She unbolted the French doors, walked out and sat down. Minutes later the yard outside the glass walls was ablaze with search lights and she found herself surrounded by a dozen police. No one had told her that when the French doors were opened after Bruno had locked them for the night, a burglar alarm went off at the police station.

"In that case, let's take the burglar alarm off the French doors and put it on the door leading into the solarium."

"That door is already wired," Tony had explained, as he rubbed his puffy eyes and tried desperately to look like an ambassador in front of the police force at three-thirty in the morning.

"Then take the alarm off the French doors!" Lorna demanded.

"We couldn't do that," explained the police officer. "It would be too easy for a burglar to get inside the solarium undetected, then open the French doors and get inside the embassy. After all, Mrs. Dandolo, it's your lives we're protecting. And if that painting is valuable, please move it inside the embassy proper. This glass room is no place for anything valuable."

As she sat remembering that encounter with the police, the phone again shattered the silence of her bedroom.

"Darling, you really must come down here. These officers want to speak to you and I completely agree you must hear what they have to say."

Lorna sighed audibly into the phone and then obediently answered Tony, "Okay, I'll be down in a minute."

When Lorna arrived at the entrance to the library, the two officers sprang to their feet. "Lorna, this is Captain O'Connor from the police department, and this is Sergeant Jones."

As Lorna graciously shook hands, she detected an embarrassed attitude on the part of the young sergeant. Whatever they had to tell her, she thought, they didn't relish the job.

"Mrs. Dandolo," began Captain O'Connor, "we have come to ask you not to go walking alone in Dumbarton Oaks Gardens. Our vice squad has been searching for several known sexual perverts for the past two months. We have good reason to think one of them has been hanging around Dumbarton Gardens recently. Please don't go there unless you are escorted by a man."

"But it's the most beautiful garden in Washington—where else can I go for a long walk alone?"

"Unfortunately, you really shouldn't go walking anyplace alone."

"But my daughter and I love to go there in the late afternoon. It's peaceful, the flowers are lovely . . . I thought I had discovered a wonderful oasis."

"It's not safe to go with your little girl either."

"But how did you know I go there? Have you been watching me?"

"Yes." The graying officer blushed. "One of our men saw you there several afternoons in a row, walking and reading. He was concerned, so he followed you back to the embassy. Later we contacted the protocol office and he identified your picture. Mrs. Dandolo, I'm sure you understand how embarrassed the police would be if the wife of a foreign diplomat was accosted. We simply cannot take that chance. We're hoping you'll cooperate with us. Please."

"Darling, you must promise me and these officers that you won't go back there alone, or with Tanya. If you must go back there without me, then have your chauffeur sit on a bench not far away and act as a bodyguard."

"But the whole point is that I want to get away from people, from servants . . . from everything."

"We'll have to find some other way, Lorna. Now, Captain O'Connor, I give you my word we'll cooperate fully." The ambassador stood up, indicating that the interview was finished.

"Yes, good-bye." Lorna, reeling with anger, abruptly took leave of the three men and escaped back upstairs to her bedroom. As she fled up the steps, she thought, *And now I can't go walking in the daytime! Two weeks ago I was told I couldn't walk in my own house in the middle of the night. I'm a god-damn prisoner here! Upstairs here, in these rooms, and those damn phones with all those flashing lights are my tormentors!*

After that, Lorna stayed away from the Dumbarton Oaks Gardens for ten days. Then, one afternoon, feeling desperate to get out—anywhere —she took Tanya and her nursemaid Rosina, as well as the chauffeur to the Garden. Rosina watched Tanya chase a ball through the flowers while the chauffeur sat on a nearby bench. Lorna, feeling very put out, sat on another bench nearby and tried to read her book in the late afternoon sunlight. The leaves had turned and were beginning to splash their vivid colors over the grass; the air was brisk. It was a wonderful time of year in Washington, one of the most beautiful cities in the world, Lorna thought, as she took a huge breath, closed her book and allowed her mind to float with the leaves.

She thought of her mother, a woman whose greatest enjoyment had been working in her flower garden. That had ended with her first stroke, which was followed mercifully soon thereafter by her death. Corinna had never met Tony—by Lorna's design of course—and she had died from her third stroke two weeks before Tanya's birth. It was a continuing source of sorrow, mixed with guilt, that Lorna had not been permitted to fly back to South Dakota for her mother's funeral. At the time, the doctors had suggested that she might make a pilgrimage back after she recovered from childbirth. But her delivery had been extremely complicated, both she and Tanya had come close to death during an emergency Caesarian, and when Lorna began severe hemorrhaging two days later, Dr. Zoli had performed an emergency hysterectomy. Lorna's life had been spared, and Tanya was a robust, healthy, six-pound miniature of her father. But along with their joy at Tanya's birth, they had the deep sorrow of knowing that they would never have the son Tony and his parents had wanted so badly.

Lorna never did make that trip home to South Dakota.

Her mother had not shared the happiness she had felt during the early years of her marriage, had never seen the splendid home she and Tony had recreated out of an old palazzo, damaged during the war. Corinna had never seen the fine paintings Lorna had turned out under the watchful eye of her dear friend, Bernard Berenson. Of course, she was still an amateur—but she was growing closer to being a professional painter every day.

Then their lives had been rudely interrupted when Tony was named ambassador. Damn. Why did he have to go from one challenge to another? Why was he never satisfied? He needed to prove himself, then prove himself again. And yet, a part of her understood his need. She needed to prove herself too, but in a different way. She had long since given up trying to emulate her mother-in-law, truly one of the finest women in all of Italy. Not only was she beautiful, gracious, and thoughtful, but she possessed that innate sense of style only the very rich are born with. Lorna would never measure up when it came to being a hostess. She just didn't care that much. She really didn't like people that much, if the truth were told. What she loved was solitude, being all alone in her study, painting her heart out—that and being with Tanya, her precious little girl, who at that moment was running toward her.

"Mommy, Mommy, come quick, we found a bunny rabbit. Come quick!"

Tanya grabbed her mother's hand and they ran to the flower patch where the bunny had been sighted. It was a wonderful feeling, following that dark-haired bundle of joy, knowing she would grow up with everything Lorna had missed, knowing how cherished and protected her life would be.

Chapter Six

The waiter served the chocolate and raspberry souffle and refilled their glasses of champagne with great flourish. Then he backed away to let them enjoy their dessert.

"Beautiful!" Lorna crooned, "absolutely the most beautiful restaurant I've ever been in. I can see why the magazines and newspapers are touting it so!"

Tony tasted his chocolate souffle, then sipped the champagne. "I have to give you credit, Lorna, this Valentine present you dreamed up—a weekend together in New York City—was a stroke of genius. I needed it—*we* needed to get away together. How is your raspberry souffle?"

"Here, taste it." She held a spoonful toward him.

"Don't we have awful manners?" he chided. "We must look like a bride and groom."

"That's what I feel like this weekend. I haven't had such a good time since we came to America!"

Tony glanced around the room again, wondering if anyone had recognized him. Surely some member of the international press corps must be at Manhattan's newest gourmet extravaganza. The room was filled with massive arrangements of multicolored spring flowers in huge crystal vases, and mirrored walls multiplied the effect endlessly. He wished he could share Lorna's enthusiasm for things visual. He had spent most of the last two days following her through the art galleries of New York, and though he tried to appear interested, he tired quickly and found his mind wandering to political matters, the morning's headlines, and a labor problem at his Milan optical plant. Lorna had the kind of mind—a painter's mind he supposed— that reveled in physical beauty of any kind. Tonight she seemed to take on the glow of the scene she was enjoying so thoroughly.

"I wish you could always be as happy as you seem tonight," he told her as he reached for her hand and squeezed it. "Nothing makes me happier than to see you so content."

He finished his dessert and pushed the crystal bowl slightly away from himself. "And now I have a surprise—I know you thought this nostalgic trip was your Valentine present from me, but I have something else." As he spoke, he reached into his suit pocket and pulled out a small brown envelope and handed it to Lorna.

Mystified, she opened it and found a door key with a paper tag on it.

"I have rented a studio for you."

Lorna's face broke into a broad, surprised smile.

"In Georgetown. It's a huge room on the top of

an old warehouse on the waterfront, with lots of
light. It's really not the best neighborhood, but safe
enough, the real estate lady told me, if you only go
there in the daytime and lock yourself in."

Lorna was overwhelmed. How had he so clearly
read her mind, figured out what she wanted most in
life if he wouldn't give up being an ambassador?

"I'm acutely aware," Tony continued before she
had a chance to say anything, "of how much you
hate being an ambassador's wife and of how much
you wish we were back in Florence. Tamara and I
talked about it, and she suggested that we find you a
studio here where you could go, no telephones or
servants to distract you, and paint to your heart's
content."

Lorna could contain her enthusiasm, her gratitude no longer. Ignoring the quiet decorum, the
terribly proper and elegant atmosphere of the restaurant, she reached for Tony's face and kissed him
soundly on the cheek, then quickly reached for her
napkin to wipe away the offending lipstick. Her
eyes were brimming with tears of happiness.

"You should mark off three days a week on your
calendar, leave Tamara in charge of the office, and
simply hide away in your studio until it's time for
Tanya to come home from school. That would give
you about eighteen hours a week of solitude, time
to regain your 'center,' whatever the hell that is."

"Tony, I'm so grateful, I can't tell you—"

"One of the things I've learned about you, my
darling—actually Tamara pointed it out to me—is
that I can't expect someone as creative as you to
spend the rest of your life basking in my 'reflected
glory'—Tamara's words! You need your own sense
of accomplishment, of success, you need your own
identity. And because I love you more than anyone

in the world, I want you to have what will make you a satisfied, complete human being. Even if I don't always understand it."

"My, that was quite a speech, Mr. Ambassador!"

"I haven't finished. You might even want to consider coming to New York two or three times a month to take a master class. Tamara says you'd give your right arm to study with Hans Hofmann."

"Oh, yes!"

"Here, let's drink to our budding artist, to your new studio, to your success."

They clinked their fluted glasses and sipped the last of the champagne. Tony reached again for Lorna's hand. "And now I want nothing more than to take you back to the hotel—urgently!"

Tony climbed into the back of the limousine, breathed deeply, and began to savor the exhilaration he always felt after a successful speech. Of all the responsibilities of an ambassador, he loved most making public appearances, especially when he was called upon to debate, as he had been at the Naval Academy in Annapolis that afternoon.

"You were wonderful, simply marvelous!" Tamara said as she adjusted her skirt and placed her briefcase at her feet.

"It was a super audience. I love it when they have some knowledge of Italy's political history. Those midshipmen did their homework."

"Yes, it was one of the best groups ever. Their questions were right on target—and you, my darling ambassador, rose to the occasion. By the way, isn't this a wonderful little town? Sometimes I come over here on Sunday afternoons and browse in the little shops. There are several good restaurants here, too. You should bring Lorna . . ."

"That sounds so idyllic. When would we ever find time to do something like that? Though I must admit, Lorna would love it if we could."

"Yes, she would. There are lots of wonderful places a short distance from Washington— Middleburg, Alexandria, St. Mary's on the eastern shore of Maryland, Annapolis. . . . You should try to see some of the countryside before . . ."

"Before I am recalled you mean."

"Well . . ."

"Let's be honest about it, Tamara. With politics the way they are in Italy, I could be recalled at any moment. I am delighted that Prime Minister Segni asked me to stay on. But who knows when the next change of government will take place. Lorna would welcome it—our return to Italy. She hates playing the role."

"I know. What a pity! Most women would give their right arm for such a chance."

"I want you to know, Tamara," he said in an intimate voice as he reached for her hand, "how much I appreciate everything you are doing for Lorna to ease the job. We both consider ourselves extremely fortunate to have you to guide us. You've become Lorna's best friend, perhaps her only real friend here."

"I guess that's true. She really is quite a loner, isn't she?"

"Yes, she always has been, although back in Italy she had made a few friends among the artists. When she wasn't at art school she was in her studio painting, or wandering around the museums. Art is her one great love."

As Tony looked deeply at Tamara, her copper hair glinting in the afternoon sun, he felt again the conflicting emotions that had become more acute in recent months. At first he had tried to deny, even to himself, the great attraction he felt toward Tamara. Then, finally, one evening when they had been working late on a speech he was to give the next day to the Cosmos Club, looking over her shoulder as she typed to his dictation, he had impulsively bent down and kissed the back of her neck. She had shuddered, and murmured, "No, please . . . we mustn't, Tony." And in that split second, he had realized that she felt the attraction too, and that she had made up her mind that nothing would ever happen between them.

He had moved away from her, silently berating himself for having displayed his vulnerability. He too had made a vow to himself that they would not betray the love they both had for Lorna for what was simply a sexual attraction.

A few minutes later, unable to bear her presence any longer, he had sent Tamara home with the assurance that he would study the speech before retiring and again in the morning. Then, as was his habit, he would stand up at the Cosmos Club without a note, having committed the speech firmly to his computer-like memory. Tamara would give out prepared texts to the press afterward.

They had become quite a team, Tony and Tamara. She proved adept at speech writing, including names of people he needed to recognize, adding a few good jokes, always keeping the speech short and pungent. They both enjoyed the collaboration, and finally they both began to realize why they looked forward to speech-writing sessions. They were falling in love.

Inevitably, Tony began to make mental comparisons between Lorna and Tamara. They were each majestically beautiful, poised and fashionable. But Lorna's poise was purely cosmetic; underneath a surface polish, she was horribly insecure. No one was more aware of her lack of educational background, her lack of aristocratic breeding than Lorna herself. Tamara's blue-blood background and fine education, added to her political experience, made her a much more interesting person to spend an afternoon with. Or an evening, Tony thought ruefully as he continued to hold her hand.

"Perhaps some evening you'll come back to Annapolis with me and we'll have dinner at your favorite restaurant."

"Tony, I don't think . . ."

"I don't think we should either, but I'm beginning to believe it is going to happen, Tamara darling. We are going to become lovers. I know it. I feel it. And I hope it will be sooner rather than later. As you said a minute ago, who knows when I'll be recalled? We are wasting precious time."

"But Lorna—"

"Lorna will never know. And what she doesn't know can't possibly hurt her. What are your plans for this evening? No, don't answer that—whatever they are, cancel them. I'm coming to visit you."

As he squeezed her hand, he saw her eyes mist over with the beginning of tears. And through the tears, he saw her acquiescence and happiness.

The smell of orange blossoms permeated the embassy. It had always been a favorite fragrance of Lorna's and now three huge, mock orange bushes were blooming in the back of the embassy. Lorna had directed Bruno to ask the gardener to bring in huge bunches with long stems for the large vase on the Steinway in the living room.

Nevertheless, in spite of the glorious fragrance, it looked as if it had snowed on the rug under the piano. She went into the library and picked up the telephone, dialing Bruno in the pantry. "Bruno,

I'm dreadfully sorry to bother you with this, but those blossoms on the piano are shedding awfully. Would you come in and clean them up? It would be dreadful if the ambassador were to bring someone in from his office—yes, thank you."

Bruno had already cleaned up the mess from the blossoms once that morning, so she didn't blame him for being a bit angry with her request. As she saw him pass the library, she softly called to him and walked with him to the grand piano. "Here, I'll clean off the top of the piano if you'll just take care of the carpet. Besides, I need to talk to you about tomorrow evening. There will be twelve of us and we'll eat in the solarium—it should be lovely in there if it's not too . . . hot . . ."

As she was speaking, Lorna had glanced through the French doors, through the sheer silk curtains, and then stopped in mid-sentence. Bruno was still concentrating on the floor. No, she thought, he couldn't see what she was seeing—but how could they? How could they carry on like that right in her own home? Where everyone could see them—the servants, his secretary—didn't he care? Didn't he care, for her sake?

Lorna watched spellbound as Tony and Tamara kissed. No one else, she thought, could belong to that long red hair. This was what had happened to her Garden of Eden, she thought, and then said to Bruno, "On second thought, I don't think I want dinner in the solarium tomorrow." He was on the other side of the piano and couldn't possibly see what was going on. "I think it will be too hot. We'd better plan to serve dinner in the dining room. Take two leaves out of the table and set it for twelve."

"Yes, ma'am."

"I've forgotten something—excuse me, Bruno—I must go upstairs."

She turned abruptly and rushed the length of the living room toward the marble staircase.

Perhaps they already know, the servants, the employees in the office. How long? Maybe for months, I don't have any idea. But how could he do it? How could he make love to her here in my house?

She raced up the stairs to her bedroom, then out onto the sun deck—there the air would be refreshing, and she could breathe again. She slumped down into a wicker rocking chair, thinking, *I've got to catch my breath . . . my heart is exploding . . . how could they?*

She began to rock slowly, meditatively.

But I've always known it, since that day they first met in Tony's office. I could see it then, like threads of electricity stretched between them. It was only a matter of time. . . .

And then her breath was taken away again by what she saw from her vantage point on the upper balcony. She saw them walking—casually strolling in fact, for all the world to see—toward Tamara's blue Mercedes coupe. She watched as Tony held the door for Tamara, then let himself in on the driver's side.

Where will they go? She wondered. *Oh, that's easy! They'll go to her apartment. Their lover's nest! The very same apartment where she has Sunday parties that Tony and I go to "to be nice to her," he says. Ha! He's been in love with her all along. They've been having an affair right here under my nose for—God knows how long!—and I've been too stupid to see it!*

Thirty minutes later, Lorna was in her own car, driving furiously toward the town of Potomac, toward her recently discovered favorite escape at Great Falls. She would walk, walk and think, walk and think, until she had worn herself out, until she had dissolved the core of hatred and jealousy and desire for revenge that she could feel even in her fingernails! And then she would go back to the Embassy and never, never—no never, for that would be defeat—never let Tony know that she knew. As for Tamara, she would kill her with kindness. Just as she had never told Tony about seeing him in bed with that French girl, she would never admit to either of them what she knew.

She parked her car in the nearly deserted parking lot and walked to her favorite isolated spot. She sat down on her rock and looked at the tumultuous waters of the Potomac. For several minutes, she simply looked and deliberately avoided thinking. She would let the scene calm and heal her, she would let that double Scotch she had swallowed before leaving the Embassy—*at mid-morning! What's happening to me?*—take its effect.

Why do I even care? It's not because I love him, that's for sure! Something died in me a long time ago, I guess that time I saw him with that French girl in my bed. I've never really enjoyed him since. . . .

She picked up a twig and began breaking it into small pieces.

Are all marriages alike? When the passion wears off, do we secretly wish for our husbands to take a lover? Perhaps. But not my secretary! Not someone I have to deal with every day! Not someone I'm envious of already!

Yes, she thought, she had always been envious of Tamara. She had the vitality, the youth Lorna once had—the radiance, that zest for life. And she was beautiful. Bright. An idiot would have seen that Tony would fall in love with her.

And I care . . . because I'm afraid the servants or the office staff will find out. I don't care that he is right this minute lying in her bed.

She paused in her thoughts to deliberately conjure up the image of them in bed together to test her reactions. But the vision didn't bother her half as much as worrying about whether someone else knew. And in her house! They had so little respect —in fact, so much contempt—for her that they were kissing in her solarium, in her special room!

Yet, a part of me is relieved, grateful to have discovered this.

"Do you really think we can get away with it? It seems risky to me, though of course I'd love nothing better than a trip to Italy with you, Tony." Tamara was coming back from her bathroom where she had gone to get some massage lotion.

"As long as we don't fly together, there's no reason in the world to worry about getting caught. We'll take separate flights the same day. We'll meet in Rome at the Hassler House and from there we'll travel together—a week together! Imagine, darling!"

"You don't think you'll be recognized?"

"Over there, they think nothing of seeing me with a beautiful woman!"

"I would hate to have Lorna find out. I have nightmares about that, Tony. As much as I love you and don't want to give you up, I'm terrified of her finding out. Does that sound hypocritical? How can I be so genuinely fond of Lorna and have a love affair with you at the same time? It doesn't make sense!" She warmed some of the lotion in the palms of her hands and began to gently massage his back.

"That feels so good! You're great, Tamara, really terrific! It's understandable that you love both me and Lorna. We're two lovable people! Can you help it if we're married to each other? No, I'm not being facetious! Lorna is a wonderful woman, and I know you feel guilty about this affair—you never let me forget it! Sometimes I think you are trying to make me feel guilty."

"No, I'm not, Tony! I don't want it to end either. But we must be careful. Kissing me in the solarium was dangerous. Someone might have seen us."

"You certainly don't think any of my employees would go running to her, do you? Italians are sophisticated about these things, not like Americans."

"But wouldn't she care terribly if she knew?"

"Damn right she would care! She'd ask for a divorce without batting an eyelash. Lorna is a wonderful woman, a good mother, everything I wanted in a wife—but she doesn't care that much for sex. It's simply not one of her concerns anymore. Not for years now."

"I don't believe that. I don't believe that about any woman. That's something men like to tell themselves about their wives, but it's not true."

"Oh, Tamara, you make me laugh. Can you imagine Lorna having an affair? Can you imagine her going through all the complicated plans, the secret phone calls, the little notes? She could never do it. I tell you, she hasn't liked sex all that much in years. Not since the early years of our marriage."

"You must be blind to imagine that she isn't turned on to men. Maybe not by you—after all, she's been married to you for years! Okay, turn over on your back and I'll do your legs. You know, I've always wondered why you don't have more than one child. Don't you want a son?"

"Of course I wanted a son. It seems a tragedy that when I die, the Dandolo name will disappear from Italy. Our family has been prominent in Florence for generations."

"Why don't you have more children?"

"Lorna had a difficult delivery, then she hemorrhaged and they had to do an emergency hysterectomy."

"Oh, Tony, I'm so sorry. I didn't know. . . . Then, Tanya will inherit everything. Who will run the businesses?"

"Maybe her husband if we get lucky—but you're right, it's not the same as having a son. I would have loved a son."

"Well, we can't have everything in life. I should have been a mother by now if my first marriage had worked out. I guess the grass is always greener, as they say, but sometimes I wish I were a happily married surburban wife raising babies."

"I'm glad you're not—you probably wouldn't be here, and I like having you here. I love you, Tamara."

"I love you, Tony darling, so much—too much! I can't even express it."

"Maybe we'll go to Capri. Lots of tourists go there, of course, but I have a friend who has a villa. Would you like that?"

"Anything you say. You're my tour guide. Do you give tours as well as you make love?"

"Definitely! And how did you know I'd be able to satisfy you? Huh?"

"From the look in your eyes that day you interviewed me. I could see how much you appreciated all my good qualities!"

"Well in that case it sure took you long enough to let me in on that little secret! Christ, I thought about you for months! Come up here, baby, and give me a kiss!"

"All things considered, we showed a considerable amount of restraint, don't you think?" she asked, after kissing him.

"Yes darling. What time is it? Reach my watch for me, will you?"

"It's two-thirty, Mr. Ambassador. And your next appointment is at three. Whatshisname Westerman is coming over for a little chat, remember?"

"God, he is dull! He has to be the dullest man ever to graduate from Harvard. Well, let's get dressed."

I'm getting lazier and lazier, thought Lorna as she looked at the bubbling foam of the Potomac River, which never ceased as the careening icy water smashed against the huge boulders. She knew how cold it was. One day in late June she had impulsively taken her shoes off and tiptoed over some rocks to reach that boulder. Once there she had looked backwards over the rocks she had traversed and marveled that she should do anything so ridiculously dangerous. But then, so much of what she had been doing the last few months, when she thought about it, astounded her.

She spent less and less time these days working on projects at the embassy and more and more time painting in her studio or walking aimlessly, alone, at Great Falls, or simply sitting here on this ridge as she was now, thinking about everything, past and present, trying to make some sense out of life.

She'd lost Tony to Tamara, without even putting up a fight. She'd never forgive them for being so open about their relationship. It wasn't just sex, like Tony's little flings had been before. He loved her. They had a hell of a lot of nerve going off to Italy together! That stupid Second Secretary, sending over all those newspaper accounts and pictures of Tony's trip with that innane note—"I thought you'd like to see how popular Tony is back home!"

He had clearly wanted her to recognize Tamara in that picture—but what did he stand to gain by breaking up their marriage? Perhaps Tony would be recalled. But why did Enrique want Tony back in Italy . . . ?

I should have been smart enough to realize what was happening when Tamara asked for a vacation for the same week Tony was due back in Rome . . . what a fool I am!

I should have an affair, I should find a way to get even—but damn it, I won't lower myself to their level.

Lorna stood up and broke a dead twig off a branch of the oak tree she had been sitting under. As she walked back toward the path to the parking lot, she broke the twig in tiny pieces. And dropped them.

I've got to get back to my painting, she thought. *I've got to concentrate on something that means a lot to me. Work will assuage the pain. If only we could go back to Italy. . . .*

"No, Tamara, what you don't understand is the power of the Church in Italy," Tony corrected her. "It's everywhere. There isn't a school in Italy, not a law court, without its crucifix staring down at the people. We live in a country which has always been the home of the Pope; he is there like a Great Father watching over our every action. Having the Vatican in Italy is a source of great pride—and inhibition —to us."

Tamara poured some more wine into Tony's glass. They were eating lunch on the balcony of her apartment. "But it's absurd, in the twentieth century, to let the church make governmental decisions. Why don't the people revolt?"

"Because the people like it, I tell you! And the

people have been totally brainwashed by the
Church on the subject of divorce. And it happens
that the feelings of the people and the teachings of
the Church nicely coincide. Italians are totally
family-oriented. Divorce is considered a menace to
family life. We never forget we are part of a family,
we are embedded in our families. We are each one
link in the chain of generations, in a deep and
ancient cultural tradition that is founded on Ca-
tholicism."

"You sound like a propagandist, Tony! You're
giving me a lecture! I've never noticed you were
such a devout Catholic. When was the last time you
went to mass?"

"Going to mass has nothing to do with it. Most
men don't go to Church. Only American men do
that. The point is that being a Catholic is as much a
part of my identity as being Italian or being a
Dandolo or being a man. Besides, everyone in Italy
is Catholic."

"But why do you allow the Church to decide
issues such as divorce?"

"Because the institution of the family must be
protected—that is a moral issue. The imminent,
always-there possibility of divorce is what has ruined marriage in this country. The Church has a
perfect right to speak out and guide its people on
questions of morals."

"You believe that?"

"Of course, definitely."

"Then you would never consider divorcing
Lorna?"

Tony flinched visibly as Tamara turned this abstract discussion into a personal matter. "No."

"But what if you discovered that she was unfaithful? What if you caught her in bed with another
man?"

"Then—but of course it's impossible, out of the question—I would separate from her. We would not sleep together after that. But we would probably remain together, in the same house, for Tanya."

"That's absurd! That's crazy! To ruin your lives because of a medieval religious rule! Tony, this is a side of you I never imagined! And I don't like it."

Tony shook his head, sighed, then said, after a moment, "Ah, it's so peaceful here, so quiet and lovely. You have a delightful apartment, Tamara."

Tamara sighed, then added coyly, "The only thing I lack is a permanent roommate!"

"So! So that's what all this talk of divorce is about!"

"Perhaps."

"Sorry. Don't look this direction. Out of the question."

"I think I'd better get rid of you and find a boyfriend who is eligible for marriage. There's no future in you, Tony."

"Tamara, darling, don't threaten me like that!" he protested in exaggerated fashion. "I love you too much to give you up just yet. Wait—wait until I go back to Italy."

"I hope that's not imminent."

"No, not that I know of. Oh, Tamara, it's so nice to be with you—don't make demands on me, don't spoil it. There is no way we can ever be married."

"I can't quite believe that, Tony. Somehow, I don't believe it." Tears formed in Tamara's eyes.

"Hey now, what's gotten into you?"

"Oh, Tony," she began, then used her napkin to wipe her eyes. "Don't you realize that I want a home and family, a husband and babies, like every other woman? This is miserable, sneaking around, being able to see you only in the daytime and going out with other men—or sitting here alone—at night. I love you so much. Won't you figure out a way to marry me?" Tony got up from his chair and took Tamara by the arm, lifting her gently from her chair and walking her toward the sofa with his arm around her.

"Tamara, darling, you've got to stop thinking this way. You know I love you, as much as I've ever loved anyone. But there is no way I can ever marry you. I'm one of the leaders of the Christian Democratic Party, and we've always opposed efforts to allow divorce. And if I were to get divorced here, it wouldn't be recognized in Italy. I couldn't go home. There's no way, Tamara."

"Tony, I don't believe you." She wiped her eyes again. "Even if divorce were allowed in Italy, you'd never give up Lorna. I've seen how proud you are of her, how much you love her."

He kissed her forehead in answer. It was easier than lying to her, and he would have been lying if he had denied what she realized was true. No, he thought, as he kissed Tamara, I would never give Lorna up. I love her. I love them both. And I've got them both now. There's no need to change anything. "We've got to be getting back. Be a good girl, now. Dry your eyes and get dressed. I've got an appointment at three-thirty. Please, darling, go get dressed. We'll come back here tomorrow and talk some more if it will help."

Tamara stood up reluctantly, wrapped her robe tighter, and went out to the balcony to bring in the dishes left from their lunch. Tony went into the bedroom to get dressed.

God damn it, he thought, *why do women always get like this? The minute you really get comfortable with them, begin to enjoy them totally, they want to make something permanent out of it. Poor girl, she probably really does crave a family. She's getting up*

*there in years after all. Well, there's nothing to keep
her from looking around for a husband. It's a wonder
she hasn't found one by now.*

But not me—hell no, not me!

Late the next afternoon, Tony drove to Rehoboth
Beach, Delaware, to spend the weekend with Lorna
and Tanya. Lorna had rented a lovely old home
from the Randall Hagner Shaw family, and typical
of her, he thought as he drove up Henlopen Avenue,
she had refused to let any of the other members of
the diplomatic corps who summered at Rehoboth
Beach know they were also there. Lorna's routine
consisted of riding a bicycle with Tanya on the
boardwalk every morning, sunbathing on a private
beach all afternoon, sketching and painting, then
reading in the evening. She was perfectly happy
there, he told himself, as happy as she had been
since coming back to the United States.

No sooner had his car come to a stop than little
Tanya was in his arms. "Daddy, Daddy, you should
see all the stuffed animals I've won on the boardwalk! It's such fun here, I wish we could live here all
year! Tonight I'm going to beat you at miniature
golf!"

He hugged Tanya, then picked her up in his arms
and carried her toward the front door where Lorna
was waiting. "Darling, you look marvelous, simply
wonderful with that tan." Lorna, still dressed in her
bathing suit, had just returned from the beach.

After kissing Tony, Lorna asked him if he wanted
a drink. They walked together to the kitchen, where
she made him a scotch and he greeted Rosina, the
only servant they had brought along on their vacation.

They ate hamburgers on the screened porch, and
then decided to go for a long stroll on the board-

walk with Tanya. Lorna was relaxed and gay, happy away from the responsibilities of embassy life. They played a round of miniature golf, then sat on a bench to watch the teenage volleyball game being played on the beach. "Isn't it great to be anonymous like this?" Tony asked as they munched on their candy apples.

"That's what I love about being here."

"Don't you miss me a little bit?" Tony asked with a twinkle in his eyes. "Especially late at night?"

"My bed is awfully empty, that's true."

"And so is mine."

"But I'm sketching and painting—and the sound of the ocean is so wonderful when I wake up in the morning." And, Lorna thought, I'll bet your bed isn't so empty.

Later that night, he made love to her. Carefully and silently he explored her body with his hands and lips, trying to break through her barriers. Finally, he gave up, groaned inwardly, and gave himself release. They fell asleep back to back, each of them mourning the magic they had lost.

The next morning Lorna prepared breakfast for them and served it on the screened porch. They lingered over their fresh croissants, raspberries, and coffee. Tony breathed in the scent of pine mingled with the salty air and gazed across the room at Tanya, who was patiently playing with her stuffed animals while waiting for them to take her bicycling. This beautiful woman and this precious little daughter were all he wanted of life at the moment. And this peaceful setting. But even as the thought was forming in his mind, he knew he would quickly be bored with the tempo of beach life, and the love he felt for his family at that moment would be replaced by fiery passion on Monday afternoon in Tamara's apartment.

Am I so fickle? he mused, then thought, *what the hell, I'm a Dandolo. We always get everything, everything we want. I can have Lorna and Tamara too. I'll never give up Lorna and Tanya, not for Tamara, not for any woman.*

"Tanya, if you come here this minute and give me a big kiss, we'll rent that bicycle-built-for-two you want so badly."

"Oh, Daddy, that's wonderful," Tanya shrieked as she bounded across the porch to smother her father with kisses. "And can I have some cotton candy today? Remember, it's Saturday, and you promised once a week."

Chapter Seven

"It's a good thing the Pilgrims invented Thanksgiving—good for the diplomatic corps, don't you agree, Tony?" Lorna said as she put the needlepoint she was working down in her lap and stretched her legs out in front of her chair.

"Hmm?" Tony looked up from *Dr. Zhivago*. "What did you say Lorna?"

"I said it's a good thing the Pilgrims invented Thanksgiving—a long weekend like this, empty of social obligations, is really what we needed."

"Absolutely. I've enjoyed Tanya and you immensely the last four days. It's a good feeling not to have to deal with a staff, a bunch of visitors, and to be able to go out to the movies like we did last night." He puffed on his cigar and looked at the blazing fire. "That's a beautiful fire, Lorna. You gals from South Dakota sure know how to lay a fire."

"Mother taught me that when I was very young

—but I was never allowed to strike the match. That's what I wanted to do most."

"You know, this is a terrific book. Pasternak is a great writer."

"I'm glad you like it, it's nice to see you enjoying something like that. A good book seems to be the right antidote for Washington's miserable party scene. There's something stiff and hypocritical about parties these days."

"Yeah, well, it'll change soon. The Democrats have always been more lively." He puffed again on his cigar. "Everything's sort of dead, waiting for the holidays and the inauguration."

He put his book down and rose, walking to the fireplace to stoke it with the long black tongs. "Except at the Arab Embassies. That's where the action is, and if you've got money—almost every citizen of Kuwait is a millionaire from oil—you can spend as lavishly as you want with no fear of criticism in the home press. Some of the parties they give—well, you've seen them, Lorna—they cost as much as forty or fifty thousand apiece. They'd roast me alive back home if I did anything like that."

"Which reminds me," Lorna interjected. "I've been toying with the idea of having a New Year's Eve party this year—not a fifty thousand dollar blast, but something very gay and relaxing. Would you like that?"

"Terrific!" Tony looked at Lorna with amazement. It was perhaps the first party she had suggested since they came to Washington. "My God, Lorna, I think that's a great idea! I must say, though, it's a surprise coming from you."

"I'm in the mood for something like that. And I always enjoy my own parties more than anyone else's. We'll go to work on it tomorrow."

"Fine."

Lorna stood up and laid her needlepoint on the table next to her chair. "I'll get us some tea. Would you like a pastry, dear?"

"No, only tea. I'm about ready to go upstairs. Being lazy all day is very tiring!"

"Tomorrow it's back to reality. Tamara and I have to face those three thousand Christmas cards. Ugh!"

"I'll send some extra help over from the office if you need it. Things are pretty quiet now."

"Thanks, Tony. I'll be back in a minute with the tea."

"Good morning, Tamara. Did you have a nice weekend?" Lorna felt fresh and full of energy—a euphoric mood, she realized, that was the result of having finished a painting over the weekend.

"Yes, it was okay. I read a good book." Tamara looked unusually pale, Lorna noticed.

"Would you believe that's what we did here too? We went to two movies in four days! Our record in this country. And Tony spent the better part of every day reading." Lorna paused, then asked, "Are you feeling okay, Tamara?"

"Yes, I'm fine. My stomach's been a bit queasy. It has been for several days. I might have a bug."

Could you be pregnant? Lorna thought with alarm. *But you're too smart. You'd use something. . . .*

"You shouldn't have come to work if you're not feeling well," Lorna protested. "You should have called me."

"I knew we had to get started on the Christmas cards."

"Oh, don't even think about that. Tony said last night that he'd send help from the office. Besides, we have a party to plan this morning. We've decided to give a very gay New Year's Eve party—Tamara, what is it?"

Tamara had jumped up from her desk and run out the door, headed for the bathroom. She was holding her mouth as if she were about to vomit. In a few minutes, she returned, looking somewhat better.

"Tamara, I'm so sorry you're feeling badly! Why don't you come into my room and lie down until you're a bit better? I'll call down for some tea and soda crackers."

Lorna led Tamara into her bedroom, where the maid was making up the bed. "Here, sit down on the chaise until the bed is ready. Would you like me to call your doctor?"

"No! It's only a bit of an upset stomach. I'm feeling better already."

"As soon as you feel well enough to ride in a car, I'll call Tony's chauffeur and he'll take you home. And don't bother to come in tomorrow unless you're feeling much better. Don't trouble yourself about a thing, Tony will help me. We'll take care of everything."

Tamara settled herself comfortably on the chaise, and Lorna returned to her office to get a notebook. When she returned, she pulled an easy chair closer to the chaise and said, "Now tell me where all the dinner lists are filed."

"In the second drawer of the filing cabinet next to the window."

"Fine. I'll pull out the lists and choose the guests for our New Year's Eve party. I want it to be very special. Perhaps if I call today I can get Myer Davis to come with his orchestra. I'd like to get those tiny little tables they use at the White House, cover then with floor length cloths in different colors, and put topiary trees of fresh roses on each table, like a tropical night club. We'll have two open bars and waiters passing lots of champagne. What would you think of crepes with all those different fillings?"

"That sounds wonderful. . . ."

"Poor dear, I'm sure no conversation about food sounds wonderful to you this morning. Do you have The Crepe Man's number? Time is so short, I'd better do some of this phoning today."

"Yes, the number for the caterers and extra help and florists and equipment are in the first blue folder in my desk, bottom drawer, left hand side."

"I'll find it. Now, do you feel up to riding in a car? I'll call Tony and see if his driver is free to take you home."

Tamara began to protest, but Lorna had already reached the phone and was connected immediately to Tony.

"But dear, she's not feeling well at all, she's really quite ill—no, she absolutely can't drive herself—her car can stay in the driveway. Yes, I told her that too."

Lorna turned toward Tamara and said, "Tony says you should see a doctor if you're not better by tomorrow."

Then she spoke into the phone again. "My driver has gone to the market with the cook—okay, send him here as soon as he returns from the bank. No, she's in my bedroom now. Don't worry, I'll stay with her until your driver gets back." Lorna hung up the phone.

Several weeks later, Tony, Lorna, and Tamara were seated together in the library, eating lunch from trays. "The most amazing thing that's happened," Tamara said with laughter in her eyes, "was when one of your erstwhile friends called me and carried on this lengthy conversation with me. She went on and on about everything, then she casually began to discuss your New Year's Eve party. After about five minutes, she blatantly offered me a mink coat if I would see that an invitation was in the mail that afternoon."

"No! Oh, no!" At first Lorna had looked astonished, then she laughed heartily.

"I hope you invited her and accepted the mink coat, for God's sake! We'll sell it and split the profit, Tamara!" laughed Tony.

"Yes, we'll pay the bills for the party with the proceeds! That's what we'll do!" added Lorna.

"All joking aside, it's too damn bad Betty Beale wrote about the party in advance. It makes it difficult for us. You must be more careful, Tamara, when you are talking to her. Don't let her trick you," Tony admonished.

"I've always got my guard up when I speak to those horrible press women, but she had heard about your party from so many different sources, I couldn't deny you were having one."

"Nevertheless, Tamara," Lorna said, "I'm absolutely firm about coverage of the party. This is a private party the Dandolos are giving. We will be paying for it, not the Italian government. There is absolutely no reason for press to be present. My God, can't they think of a better way to spend their New Year's Eve?"

"Perhaps if you let half of those people who are clamouring for invitations know that there will be no press, they won't be interested in coming," Tony suggested. "The biggest reason for coming is to read about yourself being there the next day in Maxine or Betty's column."

"Well, you know what my friend Barbara says," quipped Tamara sarcastically, "I don't care what they say about me, as long as they spell my name right!"

"That bitch!" issued from Lorna's lips.

"Lorna! Such language!" Tony feigned shock.

"You know how she affects me! There are a few others like her in this city, but I have a visceral reaction to that blonde witch!"

"I get the feeling she doesn't like you much either," Tony laughingly rejoined.

"It's a cinch she'll never get invited to this embassy," Lorna added.

"And would you believe she thinks that's my doing! She has no idea you loathe her too!" Tamara added.

"That's because my darling Lorna is the perfect lady. She's always gracious to Barbara in public—the whole time she's digging her fingernails into my hand to pull me away from her!"

"Hasn't she accosted you for an invitation to the party, Tamara?"

"No, after she heard about it, she decided to give one herself. But I imagine she's having a lot of trouble attracting her usual stellar crowd."

"No," Lorna sighed, "she won't have a bit of trouble. On New Year's Eve people party hop."

"But you can bet they'll be here at the stroke of midnight! This embassy is still the chic place to be, thanks to you two lovely ladies!"

By the time New Year's Eve arrived, Lorna had come to the reluctant conclusion that her idea of having a party had been a bad one. She had forgotten how tiring the month of December could be, with hundreds of gifts to select, Tanya's school programs and social events, and the strain of attending two or three parties a day for weeks before Christmas. But to complicate matters further,

Tamara had been sick most of the month. It was doubly frustrating to Lorna because she never knew when she could count on Tamara to show up, and even on the days she came, she lacked her usual energy and good spirits. Tamara was continually despondent and was visibly loosing weight. It crossed Lorna's mind several times that Tamara could be pregnant, but if that were the case, surely Tony would take care of it. Lorna could not be angry with her. Instead, she felt a growing concern, almost maternal in nature. But when she witnessed Tony's anxiety over Tamara's poor health, she remembered the good reasons she had to hate this woman.

But on the morning of New Year's Eve, Tamara arrived at the Embassy more chipper and rested than Lorna had seen her in weeks. The two women worked together with the floral design artist supervising the arrangement of huge numbers of spring flowers and topiary trees. They held a last conference with The Crepe Man to discuss the logistics of serving the two hundred guests they expected to jam the dining room and ballroom precisely at midnight. They finally had lunch themselves in the upstairs sitting room, balancing trays on their laps. Lorna sipped her sherry, then decided she would be especially nice to Tamara.

"I must say, it's good to see you looking and feeling so much better. I've been terribly concerned about you. Has your doctor given you any idea what's been the matter?"

Tamara gingerly picked over her cottage cheese and fruit salad with her fork, and then said, "I guess it's been a virus that has hung on and on, or maybe the beginning of an ulcer. I may have an upper G.I. next week if the symptoms don't disappear."

"Well, thank God you're better! I hope you will enjoy yourself this evening. Everything seems under control finally, doesn't it?"

"I think so. I can't think of anything we've overlooked. The only thing that troubles me is the possibility of press trying to crash the party and the probability of others—you know the people I mean—walking in uninvited."

"That can't be helped. We aren't the White House, after all, and I'll not employ a bouncer at the front door."

"Did I tell you that at the party last month, the one for the Secretary of Commerce, one of the newswomen pointedly asked me if we had invited everyone who was present. I didn't have the heart to tell her the truth, so I lied and said yes."

"I didn't have the heart to embarrass that little old lady, but I must tell you I saw her at the Embassy of France the other day, at a tea. She was walking around the table with a large pocketbook, and when she thought no one was looking, she put food in her pocketbook. Poor soul—probably the only food she eats is at the parties she crashes."

"Well, in that case I'd like to know how she can afford to live in The Shoreham West."

"I don't know. I feel sorry for her. We mustn't hurt her feelings. She's a harmless old lady."

Tamara looked at her watch. "Don't you have an appointment at Arden's?"

"Yes, at two. Oh my goodness, it's ten minutes to two! I had no idea it was so late. Well, Tamara dear, there's nothing more for you to do. Why don't you go home and take a rest—tonight will be a long night."

"Yes, I'd like that. What time do you want me to come back this evening?"

"The party begins at ten, so I should think nine would be soon enough. Are you bringing a date?"

"No—there's no one special in my life right now, and if you're going to have a date on New Year's Eve, it really should be someone special, don't you think?"

"You'll like some of the men here. Isn't that handsome bachelor from the Corcoran Gallery coming?"

"No, I don't think we invited him."

"Oh. Well, I must be off. See you this evening." Lorna walked quickly to her bedroom to gather up her coat and bag, and reflected that Tamara would have a bevy of special men in her life if she would only get over Tony. It was stupid for a single woman with so much going for her to waste her life on a married man—an Italian politician at that!

Well, I'll not feel sorry for her! It serves her right!

"You've outdone yourself again!" exclaimed Tony as, her arm entwined in his, they descended the marble staircase which was decorated with hundreds of potted tulips and daffodils. "This is the best this embassy has ever looked."

At the bottom of the staircase Bruno and Tamara awaited them.

"It's beautiful, wonderful! Thank you, thank you, Tamara!" Tony enthused.

"You look fantastic in green. I do think it's your best color." Lorna said to Tamara as they went through the motions of kissing one another in greeting at the bottom of the stairs. "Happy New Year to you."

"Would you like a drink, Mr. Ambassador?" asked Bruno.

"Yes. Yes, indeed. Let's all have some champagne!" Tony offered Tamara his other arm and said, "Now show me everything and give me my instructions."

They walked first into the ballroom. The rug had been removed and the parquet floor had been polished until it reflected the twinkling lights of the two enormous chandeliers overhead. The Myer Davis orchestra was setting up at the far end of the ballroom, to one side of the entrance to the solarium. Around the oval dance floor were placed several dozen small organdy-skirted tables, and on each table sat a miniature topiary tree of fresh yellow roses, surrounded at the base by colorful, deliciously fragrant vigil lights. Hundreds of candles twinkled throughout the room.

"You're not going to leave the lights on, are you?"

"No, no. We'll turn them off as soon as everything is ready. The ballroom will be lit only by candlelight. Come see the library and solarium."

They did not make it back to the dining room before the first two guests arrived. Bruno switched off the lights and answered the door. The party began.

It was about an hour and a half later that Tony whispered to Lorna, "Could you come into the library for a moment?" A few seconds later, she excused herself and joined Tony.

"What is it, darling? Is something wrong?"

"Tamara has become ill again. I took her upstairs to our bedroom, but a few moments ago I sent her home with the driver. I'm quite concerned about her. But I wanted you to know so you wouldn't look for her. Is everything going all right?"

"Yes, I think so. Poor girl. I wonder what's wrong? It's the strangest illness!"

"Yes. It must have been the champagne that upset her stomach. I wonder if she's developed an ulcer?"

"That's a possibility. We'll go visit her tomorrow and see how she's doing. But the party seems to be going fine, don't you think?"

"Yes, everyone seems to love the orchestra. You were right. Davis is worth the expense, every penny of it. When will you begin to serve the crepes?"

"Not until after midnight. Everyone realizes we won't serve until then. And the men are passing tons of hors d'oeuvres. I'm sure no one is hungry— Tony, relax! Why are you so nervous? This isn't like you!

"Is there plenty of champagne?"

"Yes. There are over sixty cases in the wine cellar. And at least one hundred bottles on ice. There's plenty of everything. Perhaps we should get back—"

"Yes, yes. Let's dance."

"I'd love to!"

The New Year's toasts were finished and lines of people had formed in front of the four chefs cooking crepes. In the ballroom, a rock band was substituting for Davis while his men took a break. Tony was smoking a cigar and chatting with Sargent Shriver and Senator Hubert Humphrey when Bruno approached him in the library, signaled him for his attention, and then told him in a loud whisper, "Mr. Ambassador, there's an urgent phone call for you in the pantry. It's the police, and they insist they must speak to you now."

Tony followed Bruno to the pantry, stunned.

"Yes, this is Ambassador Dandolo" he shouted into the phone, against the noise of the hundreds of guests and the rattling of dishes in the kitchen. "Yes, yes, I know her, she's my wife's secretary— no! My God! My God!—can they save her? But I have hundreds of guests here, a party—really? Oh

God! Yes, if you insist, I'll come. I'll be there as fast as possible, and tell them to do everything, spare no expense. Which hospital did you say? I'll be there. Tell her I'm coming now."

Bruno had stood by his side as he took the call, and when he hung up the receiver and turned to Bruno, he felt his cheeks quiver in anguish.

"Mr. Ambassador, what is it? What's happened? Are you all right? Here, sit down, sir."

Bruno helped him into a wooden chair at the table where the servants ate their meals. Tony's head fell down onto his arms on the table and he fought against his need to weep.

"Can I get you anything, sir? Should I call Mrs. Dandolo?"

"No!" he exploded. Then, his voice lowered, he said, "Bruno, a dreadful thing has happened, but Mrs. Dandolo must not know. Please—please ask Bill to pull the car around to the kitchen door. And—wait, before you do that, do you know Dr. Williams, do you recognize him?"

"Yes, sir."

"Good. Please go ask him if he will come into the pantry to see me. And also ask John Evans—you know, the tall black lawyer."

"Yes sir, right away, sir."

Tony sat trembling, thoughts and terrifying images racing through his mind. Yet he knew he must steel himself for the horrible scene that awaited him at the hospital.

The doctor walked into the pantry first.

"Henry, I don't know how to begin. A terrible thing has happened. Lorna's secretary—you know Tamara, don't you?"

"Yes. What happened?"

"She slit her wrists. She's at the emergency room—they're trying to save her. The police called me. I've got to go over there—would you go with me? Maybe you can help—"

"Yes, of course. Does Lorna know?"

"No, we mustn't tell her—not until tomorrow, not until this damn party is over with—oh John, thanks for coming!" he exclaimed when John Evans walked into the pantry. "I think I'm going to need the advice of an attorney. A terrible thing has happened. We've got to leave immediately for Georgetown Hospital. There's been an accident. Bruno, is the car out back yet?"

"Yes, sir, I was coming to tell you—"

"Let's go!"

"Wait," Dr. Williams interjected, "I think John and I should tell our wives we've got to leave for a while. There's no telling how long we'll be gone."

"Yes, yes—but don't alarm Lorna, please."

"I'll speak to Jane, John. She'll be happy to take Adele home, if we can't get back soon."

When the three men were finally in the back seat of the limousine, Tony cleared his throat and said, "I must explain something to you men. You're my good friends and you're professional men, and I must rely on your long friendship and your ethics not to divulge what I've got to tell you."

Both men nodded, signaling agreement.

"Tamara—ah, Miss Thompkins—and I have been having an affair for some time now." He looked at their faces, expecting to see expressions of shock or at least surprise at his revelation. They both nodded their heads in understanding, but no trace of surprise was visible.

"Ah, she very stupidly—carelessly—is pregnant. I don't know how, I thought she was protecting herself—American women generally do—I never asked her. She wants me to divorce Lorna and marry her." He threw up his hands in despair. "But I can't, surely you men understand that. It would ruin me in Italy! Besides, I don't want to divorce Lorna."

"What's happened to Tamara?" Evans asked in a businesslike voice.

"She tried to kill herself tonight, slit her wrists. The police say she's asking for me. She's already told them about us!"

"Oh, shit!" Evans groaned.

"Why didn't she get an abortion?" Dr. Williams asked.

"Because I didn't want her to. Does that sound crazy? That's my son. I couldn't let her kill it. I told her to have the baby and raise it—that I'd settle several million dollars on them both. She'd be a wealthy woman for the rest of her life."

"And?"

"She acted like maybe she would—honest, you've got to believe she never even hinted that she'd do a crazy thing like this. I'm shocked, I don't know what to think. It's my fault—"

"Wasn't she at the party earlier this evening? I vaguely remember seeing her—a green velvet dress?"

"Yes. She seemed fine today. Then she drank some champagne and got sick again. I sent her home. She's had terrible bouts with nausea. Lorna thinks she had a virus and tonight I hinted it might be an ulcer."

"Lorna knows nothing?"

"Of course not! If Lorna even suspected such a thing, she would have gotten rid of Tamara long ago. We've got to keep her from knowing, somehow —you men have got to help me. We can't let Lorna find out. She's innocent, so unsuspecting, she could never live with the thought that I'd been unfaithful. We can tell Lorna that Tamara is having a nervous breakdown."

Tony saw the strange looks on both men's faces. "Well, you don't think she'd forgive me for this, do you?" he demanded.

"Lorna would probably be most understanding," Henry said quietly. "I think she will have to be told. After all, if Tamara has already told the police the whole story—"

"God damn it, Lorna will not be told!" Tony thundered. "That's the one thing I'm determined to prevent."

"Take it easy, man, take it easy. C'mon, we're almost there. Now calm down, and let Henry and me do the talking. Henry, you handle the medical details and I'll handle the police and the newspaper men."

"Newspaper men!" exploded Tony, aghast.

"Yes, reporters will surely be there. Our only hope is that they won't be the same men who cover the diplomatic beat and won't recognize you."

"Why don't you wait in the car, Tony, while John and I go in and check out the situation?" Henry suggested quietly.

"Good idea," John agreed.

"But she's been asking for me, she's been delirious or something . . ."

"I'll find a way to get you in to see her while John is distracting the reporters."

"Thanks—I mean, I really don't know how you feel about this whole mess. There wasn't anyone else I could ask to help."

"Sure, don't worry, we'll take care of everything. Okay, it's only a block from here. Tony you look terrible. Calm down! She'll be okay, I'm sure."

Chapter Eight

Shortly after noon on New Year's Day, the front doorbell unexpectedly rang. Bruno admitted Dr. Williams carrying a black bag. Lorna heard his voice from the library where she was reading. She rushed out to greet him.

"Henry? What brings you here today? And where did you disappear to last night?"

He ignored the second question, but answered the first, "I've come to see Tony. He called me about an hour ago."

"Oh! I didn't even know he was awake. I didn't hear him come home last night, and when I tried to wake him a couple of hours ago, he said he wasn't feeling well, so I let him sleep. But I didn't realize he needed a doctor. . . ."

"Don't be alarmed, I don't think it's anything serious. Probably an upset stomach."

He ascended the staircase, led by Bruno, and

Lorna returned to the library, but could not concentrate on her book. Instead, she picked up her needlepoint and listened for the returning steps of the doctor. It was more than an hour later when she heard his soft steps on the foyer floor. She ran out of the library, anxious to speak to him before he left. "How is he?"

"He's really quite all right. His pressure is a bit high. I've given him a mild tranquilizer. Ah—he's waiting to talk to you. He asked me to send you right up."

As he opened the front door to leave, he said, "Call me later if you want to. Or if he needs me."

Lorna flew to Tony's bedroom, her heart pounding with trepidation. When she entered, Tony was looking out the window, dressed in a maroon silk robe.

Lorna deliberately tried to make her voice sound calm. "Henry told me you wanted to speak to me about something."

"Ah—yes. Sit down, dear."

She sat down in the large brown armchair he used for reading. Then she waited for him to begin. He had turned back to the window. Finally, not able to bear the tension any longer, she asked, "Are you feeling badly, darling? Is it your stomach?"

He turned to her, wiped his forehead in a gesture of despair, and sat down on the edge of his bed, facing her. "I—I don't know where to begin. We've been having—Tamara and I—I mean, this—this love affair."

Lorna felt her stomach muscles constrict involuntarily. She fixed on her face a look of impenetrable seriousness. She would not let him upset her. Nor would she let him know she had known it all along. But why was he telling her now? He was waiting for a reaction from her, but she would not give him that satisfaction. She deliberately said nothing; she did not urge him on with his story.

He looked at his slippered feet. He picked up the fringed sash of his robe and smoothed it between his fingers. "For about six months now I guess." He waited for a reaction from Lorna, either facial or audible. Her face was like a stone. There was no movement, not even in her eyes. She looked squarely at him.

Finally he gasped out, "For God's sake, Lorna, say something!"

"What would you like me to say, Tony?" she asked in a quiet monotone, enjoying his agony.

"I don't know." He stood up and walked back to the window and looked out. "Well, aren't you shocked?"

She ignored his question. "Why are you telling me this today, Tony?"

"Ah, yes. The emergency last night. The reason I left the party—well, she slit her wrists. She's in Georgetown Hospital."

"Oh, no!" Lorna was stunned out of her stubborn determination not to show any feeling. "How is she?"

"She's okay. Today. I mean, she's going to live." He sat down on the bed again.

Lorna swallowed the lump in her throat and regained her composure, her monotone. "What precipitated the suicide attempt?"

"She's pregnant."

Lorna heard an involuntary *oohh* escape from her lips. So this, then, explained the month of nausea. Morning sickness. Quickly, she contemplated what Tony's next move would be, but she said nothing. She waited, watching him suffer.

He cleared his throat. He looked at the carpeting. "Would you . . ." His voice trailed off.

"Would I what?"

"Would you consider—Lorna, I hate like hell asking you this! You've got to understand—"

"Yes, I'll give you a divorce," she answered cooly.

"No! God, no! That's not what I was going to ask you." Suddenly he was on his feet, pacing back and forth in front of the chair she was seated in.

"What were you going to ask me?" she intoned so quietly he could barely hear her voice.

"Would you—adopt the baby and raise it—as ours?"

"No," she answered abruptly.

"But why not? Why not? I've always wanted a son! And you can't have any more children." He said it accusingly, as if it were her choice.

He continued to pace the floor as she watched him calmly. Finally, she added, "Does Tamara want to put her baby up for adoption?"

"No. She wants an abortion if I won't marry her. But I forbid her to have an abortion! Can you imagine deliberately killing my child?"

"In this case, it would probably be the best thing for both Tamara and the baby. Unless, of course, you want to marry her."

"Just like that! You'd consent to a divorce just like that?"

"Yes."

"Our marriage means so little to you?" He read the unspoken answer on her face. "Oh, my God! Oh no, no." Suddenly Tony was down on his knees in front of Lorna. "Please, Lorna, don't even think of leaving me! You mean more to me than anyone in this world! I love you! You're the only woman I've ever really loved! Tamara was a terrible, stupid mistake. Believe me, darling, nothing like this has ever happened before."

Lorna was disgusted with his carrying-on. She

pushed him away and stood. "It seems to me that this discussion is a bit premature. Our primary concern this afternoon should be for Tamara. She must be suffering terribly. And Tony, the decision about whether or not to have the baby must be her decision. She is the one who will have to raise the child, or make the decision of giving up the baby, if she has it. If I were her, I would get an abortion. But that is her decision. We must give her moral support in whatever she chooses to do. Are you sure her life is out of danger? How many months pregnant was she?"

"I will not hear of an abortion! That's my child you are calmly talking about murdering!" he thundered, enraged anew.

"In that case, you should consider marrying her and sharing the responsibility of parenthood. You can't have it both ways, Tony."

"Why can't we do it the Italian way? Always, always when this kind of thing occurs in Italy, the wife adopts the—the baby and raises it as if it were her own."

"Perhaps a hundred years ago that was the tradition. But I am not Italian, and I will not do it! Don't ask me again."

Tony walked back to the window, silenced momentarily by the hatred and finality in Lorna's voice.

"I think Tamara loves you a great deal, Tony. Not that you deserve it. Nevertheless I'm sure she does. After all, she wanted to get pregnant—at least unconsciously."

"I don't believe it. It was an accident!"

"Accidents like that don't happen. Not these days. Not to a woman in her twenties who has been around. No, Tony, Tamara wanted your baby because she loves you and because she was willing to gamble that it was the one way she could take you away from me. She wants to take my place as the Contessa Dandolo—and I can't say I blame her. It looks like a nice life. And she figured out that the way to win you would be to give you the male heir I can't give you."

"You make her sound so—so calculating. She's not like that. You don't know her as well as I do!"

"Obviously not." Lorna laughed sarcastically. "But I understand women. And every woman is calculating where her love life is concerned, if not consciously, then unconsciously. No, it is no accident that she is pregnant. You might say, being vulgar, it's her ace in the hole."

"Lorna!" His furious voice followed her out the door. "Where are you going?"

"I'm going to the hospital to visit Tamara. She needs to know I don't hate her. She needs to know how well I understand." To herself she added, *She needs to know what a bastard you are*!

"Don't you dare go to that hospital—don't you dare! I forbid it!" Tony followed after her, shouting into her bedroom. Lorna disappeared into her dressing room for a minute, then emerged wearing her sable coat and carrying her pocketbook.

"I'm not going to let you go to that hospital. I forbid it!"

Lorna looked at Tony with all the coldness she could muster. "Tony, don't you ever, for the rest of your life, presume to tell me where I can or can't go. Now, get out of my way!"

Tony moved backwards, stung by her steeliness. She walked past him toward the staircase. He followed after her. As she reached the first step, he called in a pleading voice, "For Christ's sake, don't tell her—don't tell her you offered to divorce me! Please don't tell her that, Lorna."

Lorna looked back at him from the first landing. "Why? So you can continue to use me as an excuse for not marrying her?"

She walked down the steps through the pantry, and out the kitchen door. A few moments later, Tony heard her start the motor of her Ferrari.

Later, as she drove back toward the embassy immersed in thought about Tamara and Tony and Tanya and herself, she could no longer supress her tears. She wept for all of them and the ways they had hurt one another. It was as if they were riding an emotional roller coaster, with no end in sight, no stopping point. If only they could get off it and begin anew. . . .

I should have paid more attention to my mother when I was growing up. She recognized evil and sin when she saw it. "People should stay amongst their own kind, shouldn't try to be something they're not," Corinna had said. *I never should have married Tony. I don't belong in his world. I don't understand his thinking or his values.*

She tried to put herself inside Tamara's mind. She truly loved Tony, of that Lorna was convinced. And she wanted his baby, she wanted to be a mother, she'd wanted it for a long time. Now she was pregnant by a man she adored—and he had forbidden her to get an abortion, and he wouldn't marry her. What incredible pressure! No wonder she had tried to kill herself.

The simple solution, the one that will make everyone happy—except Tanya—is for me to give Tony a divorce. I despise him!

But he wouldn't consider a divorce, Lorna knew well enough. Crazy as it sounded, in his own arrogant way, he still loved her. No that wasn't it—he was concerned about his political career back in Italy. That was the real reason. That bastard!

But then . . . he thinks of me as his creation, almost his very own flesh and blood. How many times has he said to me, "You've come a long way, baby. Just think what you were when I met you, a poor girl from the provinces . . ." and I believed that! For God's sake, where's my self respect? The only thing Tony ever did for me was send me to the hairdresser, buy me clothes and jewels, send me to a make-up artist, buy me a palace to live in. Now's the time to leave him. After all, I'm the injured party. . . .

In some ways she didn't blame Tony at all. Tamara was probably a wild woman in bed. And there was Tanya to think of, who loved her daddy so much. It would be best for her if they stayed together.

Lorna couldn't make up her mind with any sense of determination. She vacillated, trying to picture her life without Tony, without the privileges of being the Contessa Dandolo. But most of all, she thought of Tanya's heartbreak. For her sake they must try to work something out.

It was after four when she pulled into the embassy driveway, turned off the motor, and walked into the kitchen. Tony was sitting alone at the servants' table with a nearly empty bottle of Scotch and a glass. He was still in his maroon silk robe, unshaven, his hair uncombed. His slumped shoulders and general air of disarray was the picture of their marriage.

Tony had suffered what felt like a lifetime of anguish since Lorna left for the hospital. At first his anxiety had been over what Lorna might say to Tamara about giving him a divorce. Then the even greater anguish of imagining life without Lorna and Tanya took over.

For all her coolness, her inscrutability, her aloofness, Lorna was still the woman he loved. Maybe that was why, because she was essentially unknowable. There was a mystery to Lorna he would never fully grasp. It was as if she were withholding something from him, as if there were a part of her she would never let him possess. She couldn't be more different from Tamara—wild, warm, fun-loving Tamara. His pussy-cat, his tigress. God, how he loved that woman!

Then he began to marvel at his emotions, at how he had let himself get into this mess.

Hell, after all the meaningless affairs he'd had, Tamara was going to be just one more. Every man in Italy had a mistress. For that matter, it seemed that every man he'd met in Washington—senators, ambassadors, presidential candidates—all played around. He'd never promised Tamara anything—other than some good sex.

And that was all she had expected—at least in the beginning. How did they know they'd come to feel this way about one another? How was it possible to love two women, to be obsessed by two women at the same time? He couldn't give up either of them . . . yet, he'd have to. Lorna would demand nothing less. Her pride was hurt. She'd demand that he give up Tamara—or she'd leave him.

Shit, she'd never leave him. She'd never give up her title, her palazzo, her fancy arty friends, her jewels. She'd never part with her position in the world. . . .

His thoughts were running in this direction when he poured his fourth scotch-on-the-rocks and looked up to see Lorna walk into the pantry.

"Tony . . . you look terrible."

"I . . ."

"Where is Tanya?"

"She's gone out with Rosina. No one is here. Just us . . ."

Tony looked so totally disheveled, so vulnerable and pathetic, that Lorna forgot her hatred for him for a moment, walked over to him, and pressed his forehead to her breasts. "Oh, Tony . . . I'm so sorry . . . all this has happened . . ."

"Darling . . ." He reached for her hand. "You can't feel as awful as I do. I'm so sorry. I've hurt you . . . and others. I love you, Lorna. Please believe me, I love you."

"Tony, don't . . . you mustn't. We'll work it out."

"Can I fix you a drink, darling?"

"None of that stuff, but I'll have a sherry . . . and let's go into the library. I hate standing here."

"Yes, of course." He took the Harvey's Bristol Cream down from the cupboard and poured Lorna a big drink. Then he took her by the elbow and guided her through the door, across the foyer, and into the library, wondering what pound of flesh she would extract from him.

"Let's talk for a while. Let's try to sort things out, and do the best thing for everyone."

"Yes, of course," he responded meekly.

"Tamara and I agreed that I would get a new social secretary. She is going to Florida to live. Her parents are there now. I guess she isn't going to get an abortion, though she still has about four more weeks to decide."

Tony turned away from Lorna so she wouldn't see the grief in his eyes at the mention of an abortion. *God, please don't let her do that*, he prayed silently.

"You should make some financial arrangements for her, Tony."

"Yes . . . right away . . ."

"And then I want you to give me your solemn oath that you will never see her again."

Tony nodded in agreement.

"And you must promise me that you will never make any attempt to get in touch with her or the baby. Just provide for them financially. Tamara will take care of everything else. She is very competent. She'll be a good mother. And if you leave her alone, she'll probably find a good man and get married and have a chance for happiness."

Tony said nothing. He looked at his feet, then up at the two Van Eyk oils over the mantlepiece.

"Tony, promise me you will never see her again. Say it."

He cleared his throat, then in a weak voice said, "Lorna, I do promise you. I won't see her again. You are absolutely right. We must make a clean break of it. It's best for her, she'll get over it. . . ." His voice had begun to crack and he was afraid he might begin to cry again, betraying to Lorna how great his anguish was at the thought of never seeing Tamara again, of never seeing his son. For he was positive the baby she was carrying was the son he so dearly wanted.

"You know, Tony, I love Tamara too. I guess that sounds strange to you, but I don't blame her, I blame you. You got her into this mess. You played with her emotions—"

"I did not play with her emotions!" he interrupted angrily. "At no time did I promise her anything."

"But you let her fall in love with you. You encouraged her. At any moment you could have stopped it, and you know it. No, Tony, as long as I live I will blame you for this, not Tamara." Lorna put her glass down on the table. "Now I think we've ended this discussion. Let's go upstairs. You shave

and shower and get dressed. I've discovered a
wonderful restaurant out in the country, way out
MacArthur Boulevard. . . .

While they dressed, they chatted amiably, careful
of one another's feelings, tiptoeing around dangerous subjects. An artificial politeness crept into their
manner. Lorna joined Tanya in the sitting room
while she ate dinner from a tray, watching her
favorite cartoon on the television. Then Lorna read
her a story, kissed her soundly, and called Rosina to
come upstairs and take over for her.

Tony stopped to tickle and hug his daughter, then
they left, looking for all the world like two lovers
going out for New Year's Day dinner. Snow was
falling softly as they drove out toward the Potomac,
and the countryside began to glisten like a winter
wonderland. A warm fire greeted them in the
cocktail lounge of Old Anglers Inn. Tony ordered a
bottle of champagne "to begin the sixties" and then
a fine burgundy to go with the chateaubriand.
Andre, the maitre d' who'd recognized Lorna from
her solitary luncheons, escorted them upstairs to a
table for two from which they could look out the
window at the softly falling snow. It was a very
romantic setting for a couple who appeared very
much in love, a couple about to try again.

Tony arranged for his bank in Milan to deposit
five thousand dollars a month in Tamara's account,
officially to be considered a gift. He would pay all
the necessary taxes on the money. Tamara was
released from Georgetown University Hospital and
quickly left for Boca Raton, where her parents
maintained a home. There, in July, she gave birth
to a nine-pound son whom she named Alberto
Tompkins, after her father. He was the picture of
Tony except for one thing—he had bronze hair,

exactly the shade of Tamara's. His eyes were deep blue, and as time went by, showed every sign of remaining that color.

In most external ways, life continued the same as before for the Dandolos. They made the obligatory social rounds even though Tony had lost his enthusiasm for so much partying. "But never mind," he said, "personal feelings don't count in this business. Going to parties is part of my job." And so he went, sometimes accompanied by his wife, sometimes not.

Lorna increased her painting and decreased her social activities. She began taking courses and private instruction at the Corcoran Gallery. She considered a one-woman show, but didn't quite have the confidence for it yet.

And she tried to be a good wife to Tony. She tried not to remind or reproach him in any way for his affair with Tamara. Yet there were moments when she pondered it, and it hurt her deeply, and there were times when they were making love and she was trying desperately to respond—the way she imagined Tamara might have—and even as she did it, she knew it was terrible to try to be someone she wasn't. And there were times when she watched him sit quietly with a far-off look in his eyes, a sad look, a mood of despondency and grief, and she thought: *This is what I will have to live with for the rest of my life—the knowledge that he loves another woman and her baby, and I am preventing him from going to them.*

Lorna and Tanya didn't spend August in Rehoboth that summer. Lorna felt she couldn't leave Tony alone, since he was so depressed most of the time. Instead, she told him she wanted to go back to Florence, alone, in September, "only for a week," to see her favorite paintings—"food for my soul"—and her artist friends. Tony agreed instantly, thinking the change of scenery would be good for her. And he would spend his evenings playing chess with his cousin Michael, a Jesuit who was spending a year at Georgetown University as visiting professor of humanities.

Chapter Nine

It was the last week of September. The vast hordes of tourists had left Florence, departing for Japan, Germany and the United States. Lorna observed the brown robes of two Franciscan friars as they walked past her table on the sidewalk. Their presence reminded her again of Florence's medieval past, which was always and everywhere present. She sipped her cappuccino. A sense of relief, of deep emotional release, flooded over her as it had several times in the last two days. She was home again. In Florence. Sitting at a sidewalk cafe, sipping coffee and watching the Florentines resume their daily activity after siesta. It was three-twenty, and she had much more work she wanted to accomplish at the Archivio di Stato before she would return to her home.

Coming home to the villa had been a delightful experience. It was the first time in her years of marriage that she had ever come home alone. And it was surprisingly pleasant. She enjoyed the feeling that she was free to come and go as she pleased, dress as informally as she wished, and that no one—particularly not Tony—was going to criticize her relaxed attitude toward life. With Tony back in Washington, she had to play neither the role of Ambassador's wife nor the role of the Contessa Dandolo. In short, it was a pleasure.

Now she had the freedom to think—to think with no one influencing her from one day to the next. She needed to get away from Tony. Her bitterness had reached the explosive point.

Five more days of peaceful solitude, of long morning rides across the hills of Florence, stretched ahead. Then a quick shower, breakfast, and she would leave the palazzo for the Pitti or the galleries she loved. She had deliberately not called friends; that would only necessitate dinner invitations, luncheon invitations, cocktails, and soon she would not have time alone to think or to work. Nevertheless, she was inevitably running into people at the museums, old friends from her student days. And those people she was genuinely delighted to see. But she promised herself she would limit her socializing.

What a splendid afternoon, she thought, as she stood up from the small table. She didn't feel like going back to work. She'd walk instead. She began to walk down Via del Orinolo, turned right onto Via del Proconsolo and continued past the Bargello. It was always a pleasure to walk there, she mused; one's eye never tired of absorbing the scene, the cobblestones—hot today—the ancient architecture.

I'll run in here for a quick visit with St. John the Baptist, she said to herself.

She walked quickly through her favorite rooms, then returned to the sidewalk. She began to walk briskly, taking the shortest route. Suddenly, without having for a moment consciously realized she had been headed in that direction, she found herself standing in front of the building where she and Tony had first lived after their marriage. For seventeen months they had lived there in total bliss.

Yes, it had seemed total happiness at first, with only rare moments of frustration, she remembered. How rapturous their love making had been! How frequent! And how quickly their passion had been eroded by her pregnancy. But Tony had insisted on children immediately. He had wanted to produce for his parents a male heir to the Dandolo line. But now there would be no more children, only Tanya. No son to carry on the Dandolo name, no son to inherit the vast industrial complex, the huge estates.

She walked on down the street.

It had been only a few years after that—perhaps they had been married five years—when she realized vaguely, then immediately repressed the whole idea as unthinkable, that Tony was probably having an affair with someone else. Yet now, she thought, it was obvious that was exactly what was happening. The signs were unmistakable—sudden two- or three-day trips to Rome or Milan "for business reasons," a lack of interest in sex with herself—although in truth she had welcomed his lack of physical attention—phone calls to the palazzo which he had had to excuse himself and go into the library alone to receive. A private line in his study which only he answered. The servants were forbidden to answer that phone. And Lorna had never bothered to.

Why was I so blind all those years? Why? Why?

she wondered as she passed the pastry shop she had frequented that first year. *I believed so totally in his fidelity. He seemed to care so much for me, to be proud of me. He was always taking me here and there, showing me off. And who else was he simultaneously showing off in Rome and Milan? I wonder, is fidelity possible for a man like Tony? For any Italian? For any man? The vast majority of Italian wives are devout Catholics, faithful wives—shrews and dowdy they may be, but they are chaste. And that is, ultimately, Tony's conception of me.*

Again and again these days, she found her thoughts returning to her simple South Dakota childhood, to her mother. Perhaps mother was really right in believing wealth led to evil, sin-filled lives. Her mother had believed Celia's life sinful. Her mother, if she were still alive, would tell her she was being punished for having let Tony drag her down into his evil net. She never should have let herself be seduced by his charm and wealth and sensuality. It was sinful, all of it.

Lorna turned around and headed back toward the Pitti. Her musings had brought her back to a predictable and frequent state of depression and had ruined a beautiful autumn afternoon. She sensed herself getting closer and closer to admitting the possibility of what she had, until Tamara, considered impossible—that her marriage might end.

Somehow, sooner or later, she understood in her heart of hearts that Tony would have to know about Tamara's baby. He was simply that kind of a man. He cherished his daughter, Tanya, and he would cherish Tamara's baby. Yes, sooner or later, there would be another explosion in their lives.

* * *

While Lorna was enjoying her solitary vacation in Florence, Tony was strolling down Massachusetts Avenue with Peter Lisagor of the Chicago Daily News. It was a glorious September afternoon, made for walking. Suddenly Tony noticed a woman pushing a baby carriage turn the corner and head directly toward him. It was her shimmering copper hair that caught his attention—he had been looking twice at every woman with red hair since last January and hadn't been able to break the habit—and with a thud in his chest he realized that it was Tamara, less than a block away, and she had recognized him too. Tony couldn't hear what Lisagor was saying; he had lost all power of concentration and he couldn't think what to do except keep right on walking toward her. Should he recognize her? But of course, he couldn't walk right past her—and the baby, my God, the baby!

"What a marvelous surprise! Tamara, dear, this is Peter Lisagor. Perhaps you know one another." Lisagor and Tamara shook hands. Tony couldn't help himself; he had to look into the carriage. "And what have we here?"

"This is my son Alberto, Mr. Ambassador. He's almost three months old. Isn't he a little doll?" she asked nervously as she pulled down the blanket, exposing a fat little infant with deep blue eyes dressed in a pale blue knitted suit.

"He's . . . he's quite a little man! Looks just like his mother," Tony responded as he reached into the carriage and tickled his chin . . . "except he's fatter! You look marvelous, Tamara! Are you living here now?" He had to know, had to know how to reach her once he got rid of Lisagor.

"I'm back in my old apartment. I didn't like Florida that much. It was awfully boring after living here in Washington where everything happens. So Alberto and I decided it was time to come back."

"I really must be going," said Lisagor. "Got a deadline of three. It was so nice to meet you, Miss Thompkins, and that's a darling little boy you have there."

"Yes, I must be getting back too," Tony chimed in. "It was good to see you, Tamara. You look grand."

"Thank you, Mr. Ambassador. Mr. Lisagor." And Tamara pushed the carriage off in the opposite direction.

Less than an hour later, Tamara's telephone rang. Even before she answered it, she knew with a certainty who would be on the other end.

"Tamara, darling, I can't tell you how wonderful —to know you and the baby are okay. I'm so relieved. God, how I've missed you!"

"I wondered . . ."

"Oh, darling, I've missed you so, you'll never know. But I thought it would be best for you if I left you alone, gave you a chance to find someone else. . . . Have you?"

Tamara laughed. "Are you asking me if I've found another man? Don't be ridiculous! I've been busy with your son."

"I'm so glad. I know it's wrong. I shouldn't be, but God damn it, I love you so much, Tamara. I can't tell you how many times I've almost gotten on a plane to Boca Raton. . . ."

"I would have loved that. I wondered . . . how you could stay away."

"I didn't sleep a wink during the whole month of July worrying, wondering if you'd given birth yet, if you were okay. Tamara, I really don't want to start up again, but could I see you tonight, just to-night . . . ?"

"Tony, I'd love that, but what about Lorna?"

"Lorna is in Florence, alone."

"Oh . . ."

"Just let me come this once. I promise you that after I've held you one more time, and held my son . . ."

"Come over for dinner. I'll expect you at seven."

"Wonderful!"

When he arrived, he was newly overwhelmed with her radiance. She greeted him in a lavender negligee and robe, trimmed in lavender maribu. Her long red wavy hair swirled around her creamy, freckled face. Her emerald eyes blazed with dizzying love for him. She was wearing the diamond and emerald earrings he had given her to celebrate the one month anniversary of their affair.

He kissed her soundly, then kissed her again.

Tony and his cousin Michael, dressed in his black suit and Roman collar, retired to the library where Bruno would serve them espresso and Cognac. Michael relaxed on the brown leather sofa while Tony stoked the fire—a sudden early autumn chill had descended on Washington. He put the poker down, sat in the club chair opposite Michael, and with an air of resignation said, "She's back, Mike. I spent last night with her. And the baby. A son, just as I wished. He's strong and healthy and obviously very bright. I can see it in his eyes."

"Ah ha! I knew there was some reason for this urgent dinner invitation. You wanted to confess!" Michael teased Tony.

"Hardly!" Tony lit his pipe slowly, watching Mike's face. "What I really wish you could do is convince Lorna to adopt Alberto—that's his name."

"I don't think there's a chance. I don't even think you dare tell her you've seen Tamara again. You're not going to continue seeing her, are you?"

Tony shrugged, then a sheepish smile crept across his face. "Hell, Mike, how can I not? She lives fifteen minutes away. And I need her."

"Holy Mother of God! Tony, you can't! Lorna's sure to find out. This is madness on your part, insanity!"

"I know it is." Tony looked like a beaten man as he slumped in the chair.

"Send her away again, Tony. Give her a chunk of money. Tell her to stay out of town. Either that, or resign the ambassadorship and go home. That's where you belong anyhow."

"No, no, I've thought about it and I want to watch my son grow up. I don't want to lose him."

"You mean you don't want to give her up. Tony, this is Mike you're talking to. I've known you forever. I read you like a book. And I've been hooked on a woman too—that's why I'm here in Washington, letting the dust settle back in Rome. Sometimes you just have to create a geographical distance to really end it."

"So what's new about an Italian having a mistress?"

"Nothing. If you can train Lorna to look the other way."

"We can be discreet."

"I wouldn't trust Tamara to be discreet. Remember, she's the lady who slashed her wrists while you were entertaining the *crème de la crème* of Washington society under your roof."

Both men sipped their cognac.

"What will you do when Lorna finds out you're seeing her again?"

"That doesn't have to happen."

"It will, mark my words." Michael stood up and began to pace around the library. "Lorna comes from a different background, a Christian fundamentalist one. She's obsessed with sin and evil and there's no room for confession and forgiveness. She told me she sees your whole life—all of this wealth and ostentatiousness—as evil."

"She didn't mind it when I was courting her."

"But her pride is damaged now. She's looking for an explanation of your behavior in the teachings of her childhood religion. What will you do if she demands a divorce and custody of Tanya?"

"I would never give her a divorce, you know that." He puffed on his pipe. "Besides, the truth is that I love Lorna. I would never give her up."

"You may have to make a choice."

"No, never!" Tony motioned toward the chess table. "Do you feel like a game?"

"Sure, why not?"

Chapter Ten

"I hate the thought of your getting on that plane with this little prince and leaving me, even if only for a few weeks," Tony said as he bounced his five-month-old son on his lap.

"That's really not fair of you," Tamara answered from the kitchen. "After all, you aren't going to spend Christmas and New Year's with me. If I stay here, I'll be all alone." She took the two crème-de-menthe parfaits out of the freezer, added two champagne glasses to the tray, and carried it back into the dining room. "And besides," she continued, as she seated herself, "my parents are so excited about seeing Alberto again. It's their first Christmas as grandparents, so you can imagine how proud they are."

"Ah, yes," Tony sighed, thinking how proud his own parents would be if they ever learned he had finally produced a male heir, a son to continue the

Dandolo line. But he could not tell them; they would never have the joy of knowing little Alberto. "Here, I'll open that," he said, reaching for the champagne, "if you'll relieve me of this little devil before he ruins my pants." Alberto had a lusty appetite, then spat up most of what he had eaten. At first Tony had been alarmed, but over the months Tamara had convinced him that it was normal for babies to spit up much of their feeding. Besides, it was obvious that the baby was thriving, getting fatter and fatter.

After he'd had a final kiss from his father, Tamara took Alberto into the nursery and put him on his stomach in his crib. He quickly found his thumb and Tamara returned to Tony, who was pouring the champagne.

"Exactly when will you be back?" Tony demanded, his mood sour.

"In time for all the inaugural festivities." She saw his face register annoyance, but she continued nevertheless. "I wouldn't miss it! Those Kennedys may not have won my vote, but they will really bring the glamour back to this town, like nothing we've ever seen."

"You're going to everything, then?" Tony was resigned, in a pained way.

"Of course. Wouldn't miss it."

"Who's the lucky guy?" He had never been able to reconcile the idea of Tamara's being escorted to Washington social events by various men, yet he knew it was the only solution to their arrangement.

"Bob White." She waited to see his reaction.

"The public relations guy? My God, Tamara, he's white-haired and bald. What do you see in him?"

"And also queer." She watched his face register relief with mischievious eyes. "I thought you'd like that, Tony. He's certainly no threat to you—and he's a good connection, even in this Democratic era. I certainly don't intend to miss all the highlights of life in Washington just because I'm hopelessly in love with a married man. A very important, easily recognizable, famous man, I might add."

Tony felt the intended sting of her remarks. Always, it seemed to him, their conversations returned somehow to the same subject—the fact that he would not divorce Lorna and marry her. Somehow or other Tamara managed to direct every conversation to "their problem," to remind him of how much he was hurting her.

"I love you, Tony," she said softly, reaching out for his hand. "Please don't ever doubt my faithfulness to you. I love you more than any man I've ever known, and . . . I can't even imagine a day when that won't be true."

He smiled at her in response, looking deeply into her liquid emerald eyes, experiencing again the agonizing feelings being with her caused him. His entire life these days was obsessed with trying to find a solution to the dilemma he found himself in. How could he bring together his two separate families, how could he claim his son, how could he manage to begin the long preparation Alberto would need for his future in the way his father and grandfather had prepared him? For he was determined that someday Alberto would take his rightful place as head of the Dandolo companies; someday this tiny baby would hold the world in his hands. He had to find a way to make that happen, and at the same time keep both the women he loved, Lorna and Tamara.

"Tony, there's something I need to discuss with you. . . ."

She brought him out of his thoughts by squeezing his hand and changing to her serious voice. "John Preston has offered me a job—director of special projects for the Republican National Committee."

Tony stared at her, dumbfounded, thinking that she couldn't possibly be seriously considering it. "But why would you even give it a second thought? Do you need more money? I'll increase your check."

"No, that's not it, darling. I don't need more money. What I need is adult stimulation. You don't seem to realize that I can't stay cooped up here in this apartment just taking care of Alberto all day long. I need to be with people, interesting stimulating adults."

"Hire a nurse. I'll be happy to pay for it. Then you can go to lunch with friends, go shopping—you can run around all you want to."

"No. That's really not the answer. I want my self-respect back. I want to be proud of myself again. I want to be doing something worthwhile."

"You consider some functionary job at the Republican Committee more worthwhile than staying home and raising Alberto right?" Tony's anger was growing, but he made a supreme effort to control it. "And what's all this garbage about your self-respect? Exactly what do you mean?"

"Being an unwed mother, having an illegitimate child, is not something one flaunts in polite society."

"Oh shit, Tamara, your private life is no one's business."

"And what would your Italian parents think of me, Tony? Wouldn't they consider me a common whore?"

"God damn it, Tamara, my parents don't even know about you—and that's beside the point anyhow. We love one another and that's what counts. And I'm taking care of you, you can't deny that."

"No, of course not. You're right. But if I had an important job, something to hang my identity to, I'd feel better about going out socially. I feel like some sort of shady lady, hiding out here in this apartment, not able to answer questions about the baby's father."

"If being Alberto's mother is such a burden for you, let me adopt him. As I've told you many times, I'd be delighted to claim him as mine and take over the whole business of raising him."

Her voice heavy with sarcasm, she answered him, "You are going to take him into your home, raise him as your son, as Tanya's little brother. And how does your fancy wife feel about that?"

Her eyes were blazing with fury.

Now it was Tony's turn to pat the back of Tamara's hand, to calm her temper. "It would take some time to get Lorna to agree to it, but if I thought you'd agree to adoption, I know I could persuade her."

"And the minute I agree to that, I can be sure I'll never see you again—right, Tony?" She abruptly stood from the table and began to carry their dirty dishes to the kitchen.

He was stung by her anger, but recognized the truth of what she had just said, and knew he was being deliberately baited. "Tamara, darling, how can you imagine that? I love you! Haven't the last four months convinced you of that? My God, I've risked everything by coming to see you so often."

"Where are you tonight, my love?" she responded with immense contempt.

"I'm playing poker with Carl Rowan and his buddies." He grinned, thinking of all the covers he used, and all the mental time he spent concocting stories to mislead his staff and Lorna. Then he stood and followed Tamara into the kitchen, where he took her in his arms. "My darling, this is supposed to be our Christmas Eve and here we are fighting again. Come, see what I've bought you for Christmas."

They walked into the living room carrying their champagne glasses to the sofa where Tony had deposited his small shopping bag of presents. He reached into the bag and brought out a long flat box, wrapped in now-familiar silver Tiffany paper. He handed it to Tamara with a big smile, certain it would cool her fiery temper. "Merry Christmas, darling."

Tamara hesitated, and Tony quickly said, "You must open it now. I want to see your eyes when you open it."

Quickly, she opened the package and gasped when she saw an inch-and-a-half-wide bracelet of square-cut emeralds and diamonds. "Oh my . . . oh my, it really is beautiful!"

"Next time you feel yourself lacking in self-respect, just put that bracelet on and flaunt it in front of your friends. And now, as the mother of Alberto Dandolo, you must accept this for safe-keeping."

Tony handed Tamara an envelope. She opened it and found a stock certificate for ten thousand shares of Dandolo Enterprises made out to Alberto Dandolo. Her pleasure in the gift to her son was short-lived when she realized that it was meant for him only if she changed his name to Dandolo—if she let Tony adopt him. But she said nothing. She simply smiled weakly at Tony and said, "On behalf of the sleeping prince, I thank you. As always, you have been very generous, Tony . . . very generous with your wealth."

The implied criticism was clear. "And not with my time. I'm sorry, Tamara. God knows, I'd do anything to work out this crummy situation. I know how frustrated you must be. Just give me more time. I'll think of something. I do love you—you don't doubt that, do you? I love you so much. . . ." He burrowed his face into her neck, then kissed her long and hard.

The next evening, Christmas Eve, Tony spent at home with Lorna and Tanya. All the servants, with the exception of Rosina who had stayed to serve them a light supper the cook had prepared, had been given Christmas Eve and Christmas Day off to be with their families. For Tony, being alone with Lorna and Tanya without any official duties to distract him always turned out to be a mixed blessing. True, he enjoyed his little princess more with each passing year. She had become an unusually gifted conversationalist; Tony had begun to suspect, and Frances Borders at Beauvoir School had confirmed, that she had a superior mind. She excelled in every subject, but what was even more impressive to Tony's way of thinking was her interest in and grasp of world events. She watched the evening news shows on television, and when Tony gave her the chance, she ardently discussed the election, the Kennedys, even the civil rights movement in the United States. Tony had been so impressed with her knowledge of these American political happenings that he had begun to bring the Italian newspapers home from the Chancery and encouraged Tanya to read about the politics of her own country as well.

It had occurred to him that she might be losing her facility in the Italian language. Lorna had reverted to English since they had been in America.

To compensate, Rosina and Tony both made it a point to converse with Tanya in her native language. But she had no chance to use the written language.

More and more often, he was considering Lorna's idea—that Tanya would someday be an executive in the Dandolo family enterprises. But it was preposterous! No woman had ever played a significant role in his companies. No, it simply wouldn't work. Tanya should grow up and become a wife and mother like his own mother, Catarina. She would be on a pedestal, above it all. She would never have to work a day in her life; she would simply reign over the household and the society of her peers.

She was sitting next to him on the sofa in the family room upstairs at the embassy. They were watching the Walter Cronkite evening news, waiting for Lorna to finish dressing. Tanya was already dressed in a smocked, sky-blue velvet dress, her long black hair fastened up on top of her head in a mass of curls with tendrils dripping here and there. She was the picture of feminine beauty and innocence—it was hard to believe that behind that sweet face there lived a brilliant, incisive mind. Tony took her hand in his and held it gently; she smiled up at him and he felt great love from her glowing eyes.

"And that's the way it is, Christmas Eve, 1960. Good night." Cronkite finished the show and Tony turned the television off.

"Daddy, can I go to the inauguration at the Capitol?" It was immediately obvious to Tony that this was a serious request, something she had been waiting for just the right moment to ask him.

"I . . . I hadn't thought of that, my darling." He hesitated, then, not wanting to disappoint her, he added, "Well, let me see if I can work it out. I'll speak to the protocol office next week and see if I can get three seats."

"Mommy probably won't care that much about going, so if you can't get three seats, maybe I could go in her place."

She had thought this out very carefully, he mused, and she was probably right. It wouldn't matter that much to Lorna, who probably saw it as a chore. "I'll have to check that out. The State Department might be offended if you attended rather than Mommy."

"But she gets to go to the ball and all the other parties, and she'll just be bored with President Kennedy's speech, and I want to take my tape recorder and record it so I can listen to it forever."

Suddenly it hit Tony. His little Tanya had developed an infatuation with the handsome American president-elect. "My goodness, it sounds to me as if you've fallen in love with John Kennedy!" he teased gently. "Don't you think he's a bit old for you?"

"I like older men," she responded calmly, smugly, but he couldn't miss the mischievious glint in her eyes. Now she was teasing him.

"Would you like to meet the President?"

"Gosh, Daddy, can you arrange that?" She was completely surprised and very excited at the thought that her daddy might have such power.

"I might be able to. But you must be patient. Soon, I'm certain, the prime minister will want to come to pay his respects to the new president. I would imagine—oh, sometime within the next six months. I'll see what I can do, my darling . . . and who is the lovely lady coming in this room?"

Lorna was walking toward them, a vision in wine

velvet by Valentino, her favorite designer. The gored skirt accentuated both her small waistline and her beautiful legs. Her long chestnut hair was swept back into a french twist; pearls and diamonds glowed at her throat and earlobes.

Tony gave a low wolf whistle to signal his appreciation.

Lorna grinned at both of them and asked, "Is this or is this not a real Christmas dress? Isn't it wonderful?"

"It is wonderful! But only because the woman inside is so wonderful. Come . . ." He stood and took Lorna in his arms for a big hug and affectionate kiss.

"Now do we get our presents?" asked Tanya, who had been for weeks patiently awaiting this moment, trying to guess the contents of the beautifully wrapped packages which had arrived from Florence in a large package from her grandparents and had been immediately placed under the eight-foot tree.

"Darling, we must do it correctly. First the champagne, then the presents, then dinner. Do you agree, Lorna?"

"Yes."

"And do you think this little princess should have champagne on Christmas Eve?"

Lorna laughed at Tony, for she had long since given up the fight. Tony would raise Tanya in his custom, not the teetotaling tradition of her South Dakota forebears.

"Mommy, let's pretend that we're back in Florence, just for this evening. I wish we could have gone home for Christmas. I wish we could be with Grandma and Grandpa, and go to mass at San Lorenzo."

"Next year, I promise, no matter what, we'll go home for Christmas," Tony said as he popped the top of the champagne bottle.

"We'll hold you to that, darling," answered his wife.

They settled down to open their gifts from the senior Dandolos—an alligator bag from Gucci, a ruffled silk confection of a blouse from Valentino, and a set of sweaters from Missioni for Lorna; a very thin gold watch from Bulgari inscribed on the back from his parents for Tony; and for Tanya three hand-made dresses, six books of Italian history (she had asked her grandmother to send her books on Italian history and politics), and a very dainty set of diamond earrings, a diamond pendant, and a tiny gold-and-diamond bracelet from her grandfather.

"One of the things I hate most about your being ambassador, Tony dearest, is how little we get to see of those wonderful people. I love your parents so much!"

Tony nodded in agreement, but said nothing, knowing how truly fond his parents were of Lorna and thinking how hurt they would be if they knew of his affair with Tamara. It was one of those things which kept him away from his parents, a feeling that if he exposed himself to their close scrutiny they would somehow guess his perfidy, as if it had in some indefinable way changed him.

"Maybe they'll come and visit us soon," Tanya announced hopefully.

"Now it's my turn to play Santa Claus!" Tony enthused as he began to pass out presents to Lorna and Tanya. "Go ahead, open them up, but save the envelope to last," Tony directed Tanya.

"I'll start with the biggest, because the best things come in small packages, so I'll save the best for last—right, Daddy?" The first package was two books: a large Italian language dictionary and an Italian thesaurus. "Ah—for my writing, Daddy?"

"Right!"

She began to open the small box, one which obviously contained a piece of jewelry. At first she was mystified when she saw the ornately engraved, antique-looking, gold heart-shaped locket, a little larger than a quarter. Quickly, Tony explained.

"I asked my mother to send me that locket. It belonged to my grandmother, and since there were no girls in the family, no one has worn it since she died. My grandfather gave it to her when they were engaged. Mother has been saving it for you, Tanya, until she felt you were old enough to wear it and appreciate its great sentimental value to our family. Last time I was home, I told her I felt you were ready now."

Tears had formed in Tanya's eyes, and when she looked at her father she saw that his eyes were misted over too. He had been very fond of his grandmother and had told her many wonderful stories about her. "Oh, Daddy, I love it so! Can I put a picture of you and Mommy in it now, on top of these old pictures?" she asked as she rushed to his arms to kiss him.

"Here, let me fasten it on you. You can wear it to midnight mass tonight. Grandma will smile down from heaven on you." His heart was bursting with love for his young beauty. He glimpsed Lorna's unaccountably sad eyes, watching them, and remembered that she had no family, none at all but the two of them. "Darling, aren't you going to open yours?"

"I was enjoying the two of you . . ."

"Wait, I have one more from Daddy!" Tanya insisted, loving the spotlight, unwilling to relinquish it quite yet.

"Indeed, you must open the envelope," Tony responded, anticipating her delight.

"Fifteen thousand shares of stock in Dandolo Enterprises! Wow! Does that make me rich, Daddy?"

"Yes, sweetheart." He grinned. It had become a matter of pride to him that he treat his legitimate daughter and his illegitimate son equally. He had spent many hours in thought during the past six months trying to figure out how he would someday make his son head of his empire without cheating his daughter. He had hit upon the idea of creating stock certificates which could only be issued to members of his family. Someday, his son Alberto would be the president of Dandolo Enterprises, as he himself was now, and would draw a large salary in addition to dividends on his stock. Tanya would never need to work a day in her life; she would simply draw an income based on her ownership of a certain number of stock certificates. He would give her certificates every Christmas, every birthday, for every milestone in her life. And he would be sure she would draw an income roughly equal to what Alberto would someday earn, which meant he would have to give her more shares than he gave Alberto, always with the understanding that Alberto would someday take his place at the helm.

Lorna looked carefully at Tanya's stock certificate. "Tony, I didn't think there were any stock shares—is this something new?"

"Yes, it's an idea I've had in my mind for some time. Last time I was home I discussed it with Dad and our accountants, and it seemed to make sense . . ." Even as he attempted his feeble explanation, he realized that Lorna had figured it out.

"I don't understand. Why does Tanya need stock certificates? Someday she will own it all." Lorna let the question hang in the air, realizing with a deep pain in her chest exactly what Tony had done. He was creating a procedure whereby that bastard of Tamara's . . . She winced and turned away from Tony and Tanya to give herself a chance to recover her equilibrium.

"Darling, it's only an accounting procedure."

"Never mind. It's your business, Tony, not mine. Now, Tanya I have some gifts for you. This one first," she said as she handed her daughter a large box.

"Oh, I love it! I love it! Alexandra's mother made her a sweater like this one, only in red!" she exclaimed as she held up the handmade royal blue angora sweater Lorna had made. Then she kissed her mother soundly on the cheek.

"And here is one more package—my favorite books when I was a girl. It's so difficult to buy for you, sweetie, because unlike most girls your age, you don't like dolls at all. When I was your age I would have loved a doll collection."

"Oh, Mom, I'd much rather have books," she said as she gleefully unwrapped three books— *Little Women, The Wind in the Willows,* and *Golden Treasury of Poetry.* "Oh, I can't wait to begin."

"I'm sure it will take you all of one week," Lorna joked, a bit scornful of her daughter's intellectual turn of mind.

"There's only one thing I wanted I didn't get," Tanya said as she surveyed the wreckage of the wrapping paper scattered on the floor.

"And I bet I know what that is too. I tried, darling, honestly I tried—but that mean old mother of yours positively forbade me to buy you a television for your room. Says it's a bad influence." Tony's eyes sparkled as he looked at Tanya on the floor and then back at Lorna seated like a queen in the wing chair. "Well, maybe if we both work on her, we can convince her by the time of your birthday."

"Now it is my turn," announced Lorna as she began to open a package she knew was from Bulgari. Tanya moved over to her side to see the surprise.

A sapphire-and-diamond necklace with cabochon sapphires the size of large olives surrounded by diamonds, with matching drop earrings, glistened on a black velvet lining.

"My goodness, Tony, what's the big occasion? I've never seen such huge sapphires!"

"Do you like it?" he asked quietly, searching her eyes for a more honest response.

"It's beautiful—truly spectacular, darling." She looked up at him and he saw that, as he had hoped, she was deeply touched.

"Oohh, Mommy, can I try them on? Can I wear them someday, maybe when I make my debut or something? Are you going to wear them to the inaugural ball? Oh, I can't wait to tell Alexandra! Her mother is wearing plain old diamonds."

"Whoa, there, little princess. You mustn't brag about your mother's jewels to your friends. That's a sure way to make enemies, not keep friends."

Tanya pouted, not liking it when her father reprimanded her—something he seldom did. She believed he thought she was perfect—she had him wrapped around her little finger, Rosina said. If only she could manipulate her mother the same way. . . .

"Your father is absolutely right. You must not talk about our wealth to anyone; that would be simply awful."

"But Mommy, you didn't answer me. Are you

going to wear them to President Kennedy's inaugural? Maybe he will ask you to dance."

Lorna grinned at her persistence. "Yes, I suppose I will. I'll have to get Valentino to create a dark blue velvet strapless gown with a matching cape, trimmed in ermine. What do you think, Tony?"

"Sounds gorgeous, but you'd better call him first thing next week. There's not much time."

A year has passed, thought Lorna as she sat with her knitting in the library on New Year's Day, *and we are exactly where we were last year at this time. Except that Tony doesn't know that I know he's back with Tamara.*

It had come as a jolt out of the blue to her the past week. She had received a call from the bank telling her that the embassy household account was overdrawn. Once a month, Tony's office deposited the household money in an account which Lorna managed, and only she could sign checks on that account. Tony was personally responsible for all other money spent by the Italian embassy in Washington. He kept the embassy checkbook from which he drew the household allowance locked in his desk drawer in his office.

Lorna had been mortified by the call from the bank and had promised to check it out immediately. She left her upstairs office and walked across the solarium through to the ambassador's private entrance to his office. He was not there, but his desk was unlocked, so Lorna took out the checkbook to ascertain if the monthly deposit had in fact been made. There, hidden under the checkbook, were two pictures—one of Tamara holding a chubby baby boy with red hair, but otherwise the image of Tony, and a second picture of only the baby. Under the picture was a note in Tamara's handwriting: "To my dearest love, I will love you always. Merry Christmas."

Lorna had dropped into Tony's chair, so shaken was she. Her body suddenly felt hollow, as if it had been drained of all its organs. Then it became a wind tunnel, and a hurricane was blowing through; her head began to pound, and tears formed behind her eyes. She couldn't think, couldn't sort out what was happening for what seemed like hours.

She picked up the picture of the two of them again, staring at it, willing them both to die, then ashamed of her thoughts. She realized suddenly how much that little boy must mean to Tony. He had so much wanted a son when Tanya was born. She knew Tamara must have had her baby by now, but she had never wanted to know for sure . . . and now . . . he was adorable, so like Tony must have been. . . .

God, I hate that woman! I hate Tony too. I hate them both. They will find no forgiveness this time! They have both betrayed me a second time. And it hurts even worse than the first time. I should have expected it. Why was I stupid enough to hope he would give her up?

Not knowing how to deal with the subject, and having forgotten why she had opened his desk drawer to begin with, she quickly replaced the pictures and the checkbook and fled from his office, feeling somehow like a thief, somehow dirtied by the ugly reality of their lives. She fled back through her solarium, across the ballroom, upstairs to her private bedroom where she quickly undressed and took a long shower to clear her head.

At the end of the shower, the one decision she had made was that she would not confront Tony with what she knew. She would wait and watch and let him suffer a bit. Now she understood his avid love of poker these days; she understood the lavishness of those Christmas sapphires; perhaps she even understood why he didn't want to go home this Christmas. . . .

Having made the decision not to confront Tony, she found it increasingly difficult to hold her tongue when she saw him despondent and unable to concentrate on a book he was pretending to read, easily irritated as he had been throughout the holidays. It was as if his personality had changed; he had a public facade of joviality and brilliance which he displayed only when they went out, and a morose, introverted, slightly hostile attitude toward her and the servants. Only Tanya was immune from his impatience these days; everyone else was an irritant.

"Do you feel like going for a walk?" he asked as he wandered into the library, carrying a cup of coffee.

"Oh no, it's so cold out today."

"I'm restless. That book is difficult to get into. . . ."

"Mmhh," she responded, thinking that if she were trying to lead two lives, she'd be unable to sit still too. *You've made your bed, Tony boy, now you lie in it, as my mother would say!*

"God, Lorna, I don't know how you can sit so long and knit. It's so mindless, so boring . . ."

"Knitting is very theraputic. It helps me think things through."

"And what do you need to think about so much?" he said with sarcasm.

"I'm thinking about us, about our lack of communication these days."

"What the hell do you mean, our lack of communication! Shit, Lorna, I'm here practically around the clock. If there's something you want to communicate, out with it!"

"It's nothing."

"God damn it, Lorna, you started this. Now tell me what's on your mind!"

With a sigh, she put down her knitting, the better to concentrate on his face. She would, after all, confront him with what she knew. "I had a call from the bank about the household account, I told you. . . ."

"Yes, I took care of that. A foolish mistake on the part of Geoff. But what's the big deal?"

"I went to your office to see you. You weren't there. I opened the drawer where you keep the embassy checkbook . . ." She saw his face register that he knew what was coming, that he knew exactly what she had seen. She didn't bother to finish her explanation.

Tony dropped into the sofa, put his hand over his forehead, and for an instant she thought he was about to cry. Then she heard an anguished moan.

"God, Lorna . . . I'm so . . . sorry. I'm sorry you found out like that. Why didn't you tell me immediately?" He looked up at her, anguish written over his face.

"I needed time to think, to calm myself."

"I see. And now?"

"I don't know. I don't know what we can do, Tony. I don't know if we can ever be whole again. There was a time when I hoped—I thought you would keep your promise." Lorna felt hot tears begin to trickle down her face.

"I love you, Lorna. You must believe that. I've been so obsessed with trying to deal with this that I can scarcely concentrate on anything else."

"You can't give her up, then?" It was both a question and a plea.

"God, I'd like to. I've tried, you can't know how hard I've tried. I've promised myself . . ."

"But you can't, can you, Tony?" She reached over to the coffee table for a tissue, her voice becoming stronger.

"I . . . I don't know. It's the boy. He's so wonderful. I love him just as much as I love Tanya." He stopped suddenly, realizing he had said the unforgivable, then continued, "Do you hate me for that, Lorna?"

"Yes. Yes, I do, Tony. I hate you for that." She picked up her knitting, the better to concentrate, to let him suffer as he well deserved.

Tony's hand flew to his forehead again. She clicked her steel needles in rebuke. After what seemed like five minutes, he gained control of himself and dared to look at her directly. She met his eyes coolly. "I want a divorce."

He stood, both to regain his dominance of her and to force himself to control his emotions. "No. I will never give you a divorce. That is not the Italian way."

"We aren't in Italy. We are in America."

Suddenly he could no longer control his pent-up fury. "You'd like that, wouldn't you? You hate me so much, you'd like to ruin my political future, disgrace my family—can you imagine what it would do to my parents if we got divorced?"

She said nothing in response, but only continued her cold-blooded knitting.

"You pretend to love my parents, yet you would hurt them like this. And what about Tanya? Think of what a divorce would do to that poor child! My God, Lorna, you must be crazy!"

"Tony, it is 1961. Lots of people get divorced,

even Catholics. I'm sure you could get some of your fancy church friends in Rome to give you an annulment if you pad their pockets enough."

"I will not give you a divorce and that is final!" He stormed out of the room, leaving Lorna by herself, but not for long. He barged in a few minutes later, a drink in one hand.

"Lorna, I will make you an iron-clad promise that I will never see Tamara again if you will accept Alberto into our home and raise him as our son. I absolutely swear to you that I will never see her again. Now *that's* the Italian way! These kinds of things happen all the time, and the children are raised as members of the family."

"No. I told you a year ago that I would not do that. And I will not."

"Then you'll have to accept things as they are. I will continue to see Tamara and my son. And I'll be as discreet as possible. I won't embarrass you, and I promise that Tanya won't be embarrassed by it. But I will not give Tamara up unless you agree to adopt Alberto. That's my final word on it."

"And what if I divorce you, if I sue you for divorce in the American courts?"

"Go ahead and try!" he shouted at her. "You won't get a thing. Not a dime! And don't even try to get custody of Tanya. I'll fight you to the bitter end, and don't forget I've got the resources to get the best lawyers."

He paced back and forth in front of her, his steps keeping time with his angry words. "By God, Lorna, I swear to you that if you try to divorce me, if you try to ruin me, I'll make the rest of your life miserable. I'll follow you to the end of the world. I'll never let you have any peace. I love you, I want you for my wife, and I want you to stop being such a puritan and try to be a bit human. Try to understand that my love for Tamara and Alberto in no way detracts from my love for you and Tanya. Why can't you simply accept the fact that I love you all and I will take care of you all?"

"You'll be hearing from my lawyer this week."

"And that will be the worst mistake you'll ever make. How do you propose to live without my supporting you? I hardly think you're young enough to go back to modeling!" he sneered.

She did not answer him, having decided to keep her own counsel.

"Lorna, you wouldn't do that. You wouldn't give up all this—this life style. You wouldn't give up life in Florence."

"I haven't had much of that lately, have I?"

"I've told you repeatedly—one year more and I'll be ready to go home."

"Will you be taking your mistress and her bastard home?"

"You bitch! That's what you are, a heartless bitch!"

She ignored his last outburst. "You also promised me a year ago today that you would give up Tamara. Your promises don't mean much."

"Yes, well, let me tell you that if you even try to leave me, I will cut you off with nothing. You'll never see Tanya again, and you'll have no home and no money! Do you understand?"

Lorna looked up at him, a cool smile on her face. Even as she nodded her understanding of his position, a plan began to form in her mind.

Chapter Eleven

Later in the day, a deep depression set in. Lorna moved about in a trance, refusing to think about her next move. She busied herself with Tanya for a few hours, and after that she impulsively began to clean out her closets, throwing all the clothes she never wanted to wear again in a pile so that Rosina could give them to her friends. Then she cleaned out her drawers, weaning herself from old sweaters and blouses she had worn for ten years or more. "Less is more," she told herself. How can one woman possibly need this many clothes? It's obscene. Our whole life has become obscene.

As dusk changed to evening, Lorna realized she was too nauseous to attempt to eat with Tony and Tanya. She asked Rosina to prepare steaks for them and serve them in the library in front of the television. They would both love that and wouldn't miss her at all.

She remained cloistered in her bedroom, looking at the double doors that had always stood open between her room and Tony's. Suddenly, with a vehemence that surprised even her, she shut them soundly, fastening the bolt at both the top and bottom. She turned the key in the lock and said to herself, "That ends that!"

She collapsed into her wicker rocking chair and picked up her knitting. Within moments she had to stop, for her tears were falling on the silk yarn. She put it down, wrapped her arms around herself tightly, and gave in to the grief that consumed her.

The locked doors were not lost on Tony. "If that's what she wants, that's what she'll get," he told himself as he prepared for bed. "All she is doing is driving me farther into Tamara's waiting arms, stupid woman that she is . . . . Oh hell, it'll blow over in a few days. She'll unlock those doors."

But months went by and Lorna did not unlock the doors.

Only Rosina, Lorna's personal maid, knew about the locked doors. And she discreetly said not a word to anyone in the household. Rosina was deeply attached to Lorna, having come to work for her when Lorna was a young bride learning Italian and learning how to cope with a large household and five servants. Rosina loved Lorna with the devotion many Italian servants had to their mistresses. Fifteen years older, and schooled since birth in the ways of the aristocracy, Rosina had not been surprised when she first heard from Bruno of Tony's female diversions; she had been surprised and deeply offended on behalf of Lorna when she realized that the ambassador was having an affair with an employee of the embassy—and an American at that! The whole situation was made worse by the fact that Tamara was supposedly Lorna's closest confidant and personal secretary. After catching a glimpse of "the lovebirds" getting into Tamara's Mercedes one afternoon eighteen months before, Rosina had lost all affection and respect for the ambassador. Her loyalties were firmly and irrevocably cast with Lorna—and with the sassy little princess they both loved.

As far as the rest of Washington was concerned, from their closest friends to the embassy staff to the State Department, nothing had changed with the Dandolos. They attended all the major parties together, smiling and brilliant and "with it." Tony soloed at the larger cocktail parties, but then Lorna had frequently sent him out on his own in the evenings, as did many of the other ambassadors' wives.

Only Lorna—and Rosina—knew that he finished those evenings at Tamara's apartment, and after a while, Lorna began planning on those evenings, consoling herself in her Georgetown studio, painting works which became more spontaneous, more abstract, more hard-edged. The emotion she might have spent berating Tony poured into her art; the paintings became individualistic, intense, evocative. Her love life, meanwhile, became dry and sterile—that part of her life, she told herself without regret, was over forever.

"So how have you settled it with Lorna?" Michael asked Tony as they finished their dinner at The Jockey Club.

"I told her that if she filed for divorce, I'd take Tanya away from her."

"Tony! You didn't!"

"Oh, of course I didn't mean it. I wouldn't do it.

What do you take me for, a heartless bastard? But she doesn't know that, and the threat worked. She's calmed down. She hasn't mentioned divorce in months. She just locked the door between our bedrooms."

Michael looked at Tony's sad face, suddenly drained of his usual exuberance. "I'm sorry, Tony. I know that must hurt."

"It's a terrible mess; it really is. There are moments when I wish I'd never met Tamara, but then I think of Alberto and I can't feel that way."

"Well, I'd have to say you're paying for your sins right here and now."

"Yes. I guess I am. Let's get the check."

Tony, deeply hurt by Lorna's continuing indifference, spent more and more time with Tamara, both in person and on the phone. Their love bloomed with a deeply satisfying emotional intimacy. Tamara seemed to open herself up totally, giving and receiving love with total abandon, nothing withheld. Together they watched their love child develop. He sat up, he crawled, he laughed and cooed, and finally, when he was nine months old, he stood up, and Tony felt his heart nearly burst with pride—where had he been when Tanya had done all these miraculous feats? Oh yes, he had been totally wrapped up in the family businesses. He barely recalled those milestones, barely recalled Lorna's delighted tales of Tanya's precociousness. But now, with Alberto it was different, everything was different. His visits became daily, sometimes twice daily occurrences. Alberto had become an obsession with him, the focus of his life—and Tamara relished every moment of it.

* * *

The plan that had been slowly forming in Lorna's mind began to take firm shape. She accepted Tony's word that he would cut her off without a dime, that he would mobilize the best lawyers and prevent her from keeping Tanya, that as an Italian citizen she could not divorce him in an American court of law. She secretly consulted Marvin Westerman, an old-line conservative Washington lawyer, and he confirmed what Tony had said: an American divorce would not be recognized in Italy. Divorce was not permissible under Italian law. When families separated, the father retained custody of the children. The cards were stacked against her as long as she continued to believe she was subject to Italian laws.

But, she reasoned, she was first an American, born and bred, and raised a God-fearing Protestant, too. She would simply take Tanya and disappear into the backwoods of America. They would create new identities for themselves, live in a secluded small town, pretending to be a bereft widow and her child. Tanya would grow up enjoying a simpler rural life, much as Lorna had grown up in South Dakota.

In late spring, when she was supposedly at her studio, taking no one into her confidence, Lorna began taking long drives into the Maryland and Virginia countryside, looking for the right small town they could evaporate into. In late June she found it. Woodstock, Virginia, was a small town off Route 80 between Washington and Roanoke, a town with decent public schools, a hospital, a public library, even a craft shop where Lorna could buy her oil paints and canvases, and sufficient accessible stores so that they would hardly ever need to leave Woodstock for anything—and if that need arose, they would go in the direction of Roanoke, not Washington. Driving through Woodstock, Lorna spied several small homes enclosed by white board fences, their green lawns enhanced by spring bulbs and forsythia and "for sale" signs! It was exactly the kind of rural, non-threatening atmosphere she wanted for herself and Tanya—a place big enough that everyone wouldn't feel they had to know your business and life history, yet small enough that a woman alone could manage.

She returned to Washington and began to solidify her plans. She presented herself at Arlington's motor vehicle office for a driving test, since she would need a driver's license for identification. She presented a birth certificate from South Dakota giving her name as Lorna Brown, though she explained to the clerk, "I always use Laura." She applied for and received a social security number. The next morning she cashed a check from the household account for a thousand dollars at MacArthur Liquor, where the embassy normally placed large orders. She took the cash to the Alexandria National Bank and opened a personal checking account in the name of Laura Brown, giving a post office box in Alexandria—which she had arranged for the day before—as her mailing address.

She then took six of her Valentino ballgowns to a thrift shop and sold them, depositing the money in her account. Week by week, she siphoned money from her household account and deposited it in the bank; she deposited all of her personal allowance of fifteen hundred dollars a month in that account, being careful to cash the checks first and deposit cash so the deposits could never be traced. Before long, she had a nest egg of ten thousand dollars.

In late July, she took another trip to Woodstock, and with the help of a real estate agent who believed he was assisting a widow whose husband had

recently died in a small plane crash, she signed a
contract to buy a white frame rambler with three
bedrooms and two bathrooms. The *pièce de résist-
ance* for Lorna was the small garage in the back
yard. There Tanya could have the pony Lorna had
been forced to give up at the same age—something
both Lorna and Tanya had looked forward to when
they returned to Florence. The third bedroom
would serve as Lorna's studio. She arranged settle-
ment for the last week in August, telling the agent
she would be paying cash for the forty-seven thousand dollar home. Somehow, in the meantime, she
would raise the money, even if it meant selling
Tony's Christmas sapphires!

The following week, Lorna arrived at an agreement with the Kingsman Art Gallery at the foot of
King Street in Alexandria. They would be the
exclusive agents for her paintings, which she would
market under the name of Lorna Dandolo because
they had already been signed that way. She turned
eighteen of her best canvases over to the gallery, a
parting which tore her heart out. She was anguished
to relinquish her private visions of Venice and
Florence and Rome, and she was apprehensive that
no one would appreciate the hardest—and she
believed the best—work she had ever done.

Finally the day arrived that all this frantic hidden
activity had been leading up to, the day when the
Contessa Lorna Dandolo would revert to her former self and become Laura Brown, and with her
eight-year-old daughter Tanya, renamed Tracy,
would disappear from the Washington scene. Tanya
knew nothing of her mother's plans for her new life.
Only Rosina had been told, and for the past four
days Rosina had frequently been seen wiping tears
from her eyes with the handkerchief she kept in her
bosom for such emergencies.

When Lorna had first taken Rosina into her confidence, the woman had been horrified; she protested vehemently that Lorna should never, never give up being the Countessa Dandolo. Only after many hours of soothing reassurances from Lorna did Rosina finally acquiesce to her mistress's wishes and begin to secretly pack her personal belongings.

Catching a glimpse of Rosina's tears, the ambassador had stopped her in the upstairs hall to inquire if someone in her family back in Italy had died or was sick. At first Rosina shook her head no, then realizing that she had to give him some explanation, she told him—"God forgive me!"—that her sister's son was dangerously ill. Then she ran to her bedroom to weep some more.

Lorna had convinced Rosina that she must remain at the embassy—as "my eyes and ears,"—and continue to keep Lorna apprised of the ambassador's activities—"especially with that Thompkins woman!" It wasn't so much that Lorna needed a spy, but that she knew she could not offer employment to Rosina, whereas Tony could.

The "escape," as Lorna had come to think of it, had been set for a week when Tony was scheduled to be in Italy confering with the Prime Minister. She thought he would probably take Tamara with him since she herself had declined his invitation to accompany him, pleading the beginning of Tanya's school year at Beauvoir. Lorna had thought the plan through, considering even the minutest details, and had determined to give all the servants off that Saturday, something she frequently did when Tony was out of town, so they could honestly say that they didn't know where she had gone, and none of them would have participated in her escape. She had, however, enlisted the aid of Rosina's husband Manuel, a man who worked days at IBM as a repair mechanic and evenings as a waiter for Ridgewell's.

Lorna had asked Manuel to rent a small U-Haul trailer, which she would attach to the back of the Chevrolet station wagon she had purchased the day before with the money she had received from selling her Ferrari three days previously. Manuel would then help her pack the U-Haul with her clothes and books, her canvases and her beloved Monet, and Tanya's clothes, books, and toys.

Finally, at three in the afternoon, just as Tanya was returning from a month-long trip to the beach with Alexandra, Lorna opened the wall safe in Tony's bedroom and removed all the jewelry he had given her during their marriage. She knew he carried well over a million dollars worth of insurance on it, though she understood she would never receive anywhere near that much for it when she tried to sell it. Never mind, she thought, it would be their security, Tanya's and hers, during the coming years. The jewelry and the Monet—and her growing talent as a painter—would be their future. That, and all the love she could lavish on the little princess who was bounding up the marble staircase even as Lorna closed the safe and zipped up the bag containing the jewelry.

"Mommy, Mommy—look how brown I am! And look at all the stuffed animals I won at the beach!"

Lorna bent down to kiss her sun-browned daughter on the forehead, thinking she had grown another inch in the last month. "You look wonderful— my goodness, you look like a little peasant child in Italy, one who works the fields. Grandma Catarina definitely would not approve!"

She listened to Tanya's enthusiastic tales of life at the beach with only half her mind, thinking with the other half how saddened Catarina and Emilio would be by the action she was about to take. After a few moments she said, "And now I have a surprise for you. We are taking a trip this afternoon." She watched surprise and dismay register on Tanya's face.

"A car trip?"

"Yes, darling, a long trip into the country."

"But I'm tired of riding in a car! I want to watch television and talk to Rosina and sleep—couldn't we do it tomorrow instead?"

"No, darling, we must go today. Don't worry, you can sleep in the car."

Suddenly Lorna realized what she had forgotten to pack—a television set! Quickly she went to find Manuel to tell him to take the television out of the family room upstairs. After all, Tanya would want to watch her favorite news shows, and there would be precious little money to spend on things for the house.

Tanya fell asleep the minute they left Washington, thereby putting off for a few more hours the ordeal that Lorna was dreading most—telling Tanya that she would never see her father again, telling her that her father preferred to make a life with Tamara and Alberto.

Not until she had passed Winchester and turned onto Route 80 did the muscles in the back of her neck begin to relax. Her throbbing tension headache eased. The panoramic view of the Blue Ridge Mountains activated her artist's eyes, and she was amazed anew at the different shades of green Mother Nature had devised for the enjoyment of mankind—yellow-green, deep hazy blue-greens, gray-greens with only an occasional intrusion by man in the form of a silo or home or barn. It was a beautiful part of the country she had chosen to flee to, and even as she continued surveying the vast canvas nature had spread out in front of her, beauty for as far as the eye could see, she began to realize that she had accomplished her mission. *She had succeeded in leaving Tony and taking Tanya with her.* As she congratulated herself on her courage and brazen efficiency, she realized that it had, until this moment, only been a fantasy her mind had been weaving. In the deepest part of her being, she really had not expected to succeed.

The thought struck her that it was as if she had been planning suicide, knowing all the while that someone would save her at the last moment. But no one had stopped her.

She pushed that thought from her mind. She told herself that leaving Tony was the most honest thing she had done since she had met him. She had never belonged in his world, in his family, and it had been the height of presumptuousness on her part to imagine that he would want her forever, that she would somehow satisfy him. Hadn't her mother always taught her that people who tried to remove themselves from the station in life they were born into came to no good end? Her mother had been right about that and a lot of other things too.

How could she ever have believed in Tony's fidelity after seeing how her father had deserted her mother? Wasn't that lesson enough? Surely her father had once loved her mother with the kind of ardor Tony had felt for her during their courtship, but she would never know for sure. She understood suddenly that Tanya would remember only the cold indifference of the past months, could never know the rapturous bliss of their lives together before she was born.

Children can only imagine the good parts of their parents' marriages, she mused; *they can remember the arguments, the ugliness, but they can only imagine the good feelings. Until they fall in love themselves—and then they hope, as I did, that what they saw of their parents' lives was a distortion. When they fall in love themselves, they hope that their parents were once that lucky, once that happy.*

Are we destined to repeat our mistakes from generation to generation? My father left my mother, left me to grow up under her stern influence, and now I'm taking Tanya away from Tony.

But that thought, if pursued, would be too painful. It would demand of Lorna a different course than she had set out on. She thought instead of the pride her mother had instilled in her. That pride—Tony said her "German pride" was the least attractive part of her personality—kept her honest, preserved her personal integrity, helped her keep her identity intact. *Far better,* she told herself, *that I live decently, if poorly, and raise my daughter to my set of values here in rural America, than continue to live a lie with Tony—and expose Tanya, in the process, to the decadence of wealth and power. She has seen too much of it already.*

The most important thing I must teach Tanya is not to rely on any man, either for her financial security or for her identity. She must learn intellectual discipline, she must have a profession, she must always have financial independence. Because all men are users. All the men she had ever met or observed were lecherous bastards, willing to bed anything in a skirt with never a thought to the consequences.

As she turned off the highway for Woodstock, she thought with grim satisfaction of the tidy little home that awaited them—white shingles with green shutters, a wonderful screened porch, a white picket-fenced yard bordered with roses, delphiniums, big black-eyed Susans, even a few hollyhocks nestled against the garage which *Laura*—their new names sounded good to her—planned to turn into a stable for *Tracy*.

Ah, but telling her the long tragic tale—that will be a horrendous task.

Chapter Twelve

Twilight was filtering into the ambassador's office. It was an unseasonably hot, muggy day with not even the relief of a thunderstorm predicted. Ambassador Dandolo had spent the late afternoon at a briefing at the State Department. Walking back to the embassy had been a mistake; it was simply too hot. But he had wanted to be alone, to concentrate one more time on the disaster his personal life had become. Now, perspiring and dejected, he took the key to his desk from his pocket and, for the hundredth time, read Lorna's letter, trying to fathom what it was he had not understood about her, what it was that had caused him to make the fatal error of believing she would never leave him.

Tony,
  When you return from Italy you will find that I have taken Tanya and left you. Please do

not try to find us, as it will only make matters more traumatic for Tanya. I am determined that neither of us will ever see you again. I am determined to save her from the ugly, sinful, hypocritical life you are willing to immerse us in.

My only regret in leaving you is that it will hurt your parents deeply, and over the years of our marriage I have come to love them as if they were my own parents. They are good people, loving, generous, and understanding of their fellow human beings. I admire them tremendously, as I once admired you.

My admiration and love for you, to my great sorrow, have turned to contempt and hatred. I can no longer stand to be in your arrogant presence; I am pained at the thought of your touch; I find myself left with nothing but contempt for your millions. In short, I despise you.

I will raise Tanya away from the corruption which wealth and power bring, in the way I was raised. I understand now how right my mother was about so many things, especially about the sin and evil which always accompany glamour and great wealth. Tanya will become an industrious, God-fearing, independent woman. Have no fear—her future will be a wholesome, happy one. I intend to devote my life to raising her to be the kind of woman I most admire—a sensitive, hard-working, middle-class American.

You will discover that I have taken only those things which are rightfully mine—my clothes, my jewelry, my paintings and the Monet, and my car. Until such time as I can make a living with my art we will live from the proceeds of the sale of my jewelry. You see, I have given much thought to this decision since last New Year's Day. I have carefully planned every step, Tony, and you will never find us, that I promise you.

Lorna

Well, she was right about that. She had covered her tracks well. Not one of the servants cracked under questioning, and he had interrogated them singly and in groups, over and over again. Rosina, whom he had suspected of being an ally of Lorna's, had spent that Saturday with Cecilia the cook, shopping all over Washington—the two women even had their department store receipts to prove it. So the servants knew nothing; they had not participated in her escape. And yet, she must have had someone help her.

He had thought of using the State Department to help find her, but had not done it out of fear of a scandal. So, too, with a private detective. If the story wasn't leaked to Maxine Cheshire or Betty Beale or Ymelda Dixon, it might be leaked to the press in Italy, and that would have far-reaching implications not only for his political career, which was almost over anyway, he feared, but even for Dandolo Enterprises. Once he had accepted the fact that Lorna was gone, and Tanya too, his main preoccupation had been to keep the whole scandal as quiet as possible.

It had been messy, of course, explaining to Beauvoir School after the term had started that he had sent Tanya back to Italy to school; not only had the school authorities been angry, but they had extracted a partial tuition payment from him. He had sent it along with a sizable contribution to their building fund.

Then there was the matter of Lorna's disappearance from the social scene in Washington. At first, he made excuses, saying she was in Italy or visiting relatives in South Dakota. But gradually people stopped asking after Lorna, and gradually he realized that the rumor mongers had done their work and people somehow understood that they were separated. No longer did invitations come addressed to "Ambassador and Mrs. Dandolo." One hostess had recently phoned him at his office to inquire if there was some "special friend" he wanted to bring to her dinner.

After that call, he had slowly come to understand that people in Washington must know about Tamara and his relationship with her. He wondered if she was behind it, if she had managed to let people know that she was his mistress. Perhaps she even told them that she would soon be his wife. He wouldn't put it past her. Well, he would never marry Tamara, that was for sure. Lorna, after all, might not be able to make it alone, she might come back to him . . . Oh, shit! He knew better, why did he continue to fool himself? If she'd been able to manage this long, her stubborn German pride won't let her admit defeat and come back. He might as well realize that. And yet . . .

He slammed the desk drawer shut, locked it, and stood preparing to leave the chancery for the residence. A wave of dizziness followed by nausea overwhelmed him, so strong that he was forced to sit back down. "Must be the heat!" he muttered to no one. Or maybe it was this sickness, this—this depression he couldn't seem to climb out of. . . .

God, I've made a mess of my life! How could I do it? How could I have misjudged her so? How could that poor little orphan from South Dakota have given up all this—all this "decadence," as she would say! When she first saw it all that summer in Florence, she wanted it so badly she could taste it.

Christ, every man I know has someone on the side. I had to marry the one woman who wouldn't tolerate it, who couldn't handle the affront to her pride.

He glanced at the picture of himself, Tanya, and Lorna, taken on the front steps of the embassy the day after they arrived. It had been taken by the butler with an instamatic camera, but it was a wonderful picture. It captured their immense joy at being there, their spirit of family and youth and love—and excitement. It had been the beginning of a whole new era in their lives—or so they had felt at the time. But it had ended in disaster.

He was overwhelmed with a feeling of fatigue, a tiredness which followed him around day and night. He woke up tired, lacking the energy to get out of bed and work his way through the routine his life had become. He couldn't concentrate, had no energy for the intellectual debates he once loved, no time for small talk with the embassy staff. He was a failure, a total and complete failure—in his personal life, and now in his professional life. He had become a walking zombie.

His eyes lighted once again on the picture, on Tanya's upturned face and her blue eyes blazing love and excitement. "God, child, how I would love to have you here on my lap this minute," he said aloud. He so wanted to be to able to bury his head in her dark curls, to smell her clean young smell, to nuzzle the soft part of her neck, to feel her love for him. . . .

"Goddam it, I hate Lorna too! How could she have taken that child from me, how could she have deprived us of even seeing one another again! She should be put in jail, arrested for kidnapping! God damn her! I'll never forgive her."

He had finally told his parents what happened on his visit home in April. They had been horrified, furious with him for not having used every possible means of investigating Lorna's disappearance and tracing her. He had told them his fear of scandal and they had mocked him, scandalized instead that their son had not moved heaven and earth, sources legal and illegal, to find his wife and daughter. Then he had told them of Tamara and Alberto, and gradually, after days of argument and bitterness, they had come back to where they had started, trying to understand, trying to be compassionate for Tony's dilemma, but urging him, nevertheless, to try to find Lorna if only to offer financial support. They had come to realize, as Tony had, that the marriage was finished. But they could not understand how their honorable son, with all his wealth, did not insist upon supporting his wife and daughter.

And of course they had been right. He knew it then, knew it now. Shit, he'd be delighted to give them every penny he had, if he could only have partial custody of Tanya!

In February, he had had his first clue as to their whereabouts. At a dinner party, Pamela Brown had told him that she had seen paintings by a Lorna Dandolo—"Could it possibly be your wife's work?"—in a gallery in Alexandria. The next morning, Tony had been sitting in his limousine outside the gallery on King Street when Sylvia Preston arrived to open the door. He had taken one look at the softly colored impressionist renderings of street scenes in Florence and had at once recognized canvases Lorna had painted during the first years of their marriage.

"How did you get these paintings?" he asked the startled gallery owner.

"The artist brought them to me. Why do you ask?"

"I know her—I mean, she's a friend of mine. I didn't realize her art was for sale . . ." He stumbled a bit. "Actually, we're related, but I've lost track of her. Do you have an address or a phone number where I might reach her?"

"No, I don't. When I sell one of the paintings, I send a check to her lawyer, Marvin Westerman in Washington. He forwards the checks to her. I really don't know how to reach her, I'm sorry." Mrs. Preston was both flustered and embarrassed at her inability to answer the questions of this obviously important dignitary.

Slowly, Tony walked from painting to painting, seeing with fresh eyes how good Lorna's work really was, how she had captured the essence of the street scenes, how she had transformed everyday life into something like music. Her own jubilant love of life—alas, now forever gone—came through, creating a mood of freshness and hope.

"I'll take them. I'll take them all. How many are there? Do you have any others?" he demanded of the astonished woman.

"My goodness!" she gasped, then gaining control of her excitement, she responded to his last question. "I have three more upstairs."

"I'll take those too."

"But you haven't seen them . . ."

"That's okay. I want everything she paints, everything you can get from her. And you must not tell her who I am. You absolutely must not let her know who is buying her art. I will make it very much worth your while."

After that, he had sat down in the gallery office, carefully giving Mrs. Preston instructions about shipping the art to his home in Florence. It was to be crated, shipped, and insured at his expense. And every canvas she got her hands on in the future was also to be shipped directly to Florence. "Just send me the bill." And then he wrote out a check for ten thousand dollars for Mrs. Preston, telling her that would be her annual fee for serving as his agent. He wanted every canvas painted by Lorna Dandolo, and with a wink to Mrs. Preston, he suggested that Mrs. Dandolo might increase her prices in view of the tremendous demand for her work.

Those negotiations finished, he directed his chauffeur to take him to Marvin Westerman's law office. He breezed past the secretary, saying he knew Mr. Westerman would see the Ambassador of Italy immediately.

"Westerman, I want to talk to you!" he demanded as he sat himself down, uninvited, in front of the lawyer's desk. "I want to know where I can find Lorna. Now, don't bother to deny you know anything because I've just come from Sylvia Preston's gallery in Alexandria, and I know you receive checks and forward them to her."

"Mr. Ambassador! You don't believe you can barge in here and expect me to betray your wife, do you?"

"Shit, Marvin, don't be a horse's ass! What the hell are you doing? Why didn't you come to me with this foolishness of Lorna's? I'm a reasonable man. We could have worked out something which would have served Lorna better—well, better than you are obviously serving her."

"I'm afraid, Mr. Ambassador, that it was my obligation as her lawyer to carry out her wishes. She told me exactly what she wanted, and I've tried to carry out her wishes."

You stupid prick! Tony thought to himself, but then realized he had to cool down. After that he tried cajoling Westerman, threatening him, even bribing him, but Westerman steadfastly refused to disclose Lorna's address or phone number.

"I will tell you one thing, Ambassador. They are well and seem to be quite happy and content."

Tony considered that for a moment. Maybe he would have a tail put on Westerman. Maybe he was Lorna's lover. "When did you see them last?"

"Last month. I drove—I mean, I met with Lorna to discuss some business matters and turn over a check to her."

"I see. Well, if I can ever . . . if Lorna needs anything—anything for Tanya—will you let me know?" Tony was angry with himself afterwards for betraying his softness, his concern for them. Why the hell hadn't Westerman prevented Lorna from committing this folly? And why didn't he give Tony her address?

If only he could see them again, he could make it right, he could fix things. *If not, he would at least kidnap Tanya and take her back to Italy!* Yes, deep in his heart he knew that if he ever found them, that was exactly what he would do. He would steal Tanya away from her mother and keep her as his own forever, exactly as Lorna had done to him.

Tony stood again, waiting for the dizziness again. But it didn't come. He walked to his secretary's now deserted desk and opened the top drawer. He picked up a piece of his personal stationary and an envelope and walked back into his office and sat at his desk. He picked up a pen and began to write in a nearly illegible longhand:

Dear Marvin,
    Enclosed is my personal check for fifty thousand dollars. Can you find a way to give this money to Lorna without her knowing it is

coming from me? I know she won't accept it if she knows it is from me, but I want to be certain she is well provided for and has everything she needs to provide a good life for Tanya. I will not attempt to find them—at least not now.

Please stay in touch with her, and with me. My apologies for any behavior on my part which may have been offensive to you. I am sure you realize I was quite distraught that day in February when I visited your office. Best personal regards.

Sincerely,
Anthony Dandolo

He wrote out the check, enclosed it with the letter, and carried it to his chauffeur, Adam, for personal delivery to Westerman. It was the longest letter he had hand-written since he was in school.

The last week in August, Tony was summoned home for meetings with the Prime Minister. He returned early in September.

Adam seemed on edge when he picked the ambassador up at Dulles airport. As he pulled the car into the circular driveway in front of the embassy, Tony spotted Tamara's Mercedes out front. Bruno opened the door.

"Welcome, Mr. Ambassador. How was your trip? And how are your parents?"

"Everyone is well, Bruno—but the trip was tedious. I'm glad to be home."

"Yes, sir." He took Tony's raincoat from his arm, and reached for his briefcase.

"No, that's all right. I've work to do yet tonight. Is that Miss Thompkins' car out front?"

"Yes, sir, she's waiting for you upstairs with the little tyke."

"I see," Tony responded, trying not to show his surprise and pique. Tamara knew he didn't want to flaunt her in front of the servants, damn it!

He nevertheless rushed up the steps. Seeing Alberto was exactly the tonic he needed right now.

He looked for her first in the family sitting room, then discovered her propped up in Lorna's bed, reading a book.

"Tamara, what the hell—"

"Tony darling, surprise!"

"Goddam it, this is a surprise. What do you think you're doing?"

"Tony, I'm sick of seeing you wallow in despair, grieving over someone who isn't even dead. I decided to take charge of your private life. I've brought Alberto and he's in the bedroom down the hall, and we're going to be a family—and you are going to cheer up and become a man again. See,"— she pointed to the double doors connecting to his bedroom—"I've opened the doors between our rooms."

He was so stunned at the boldness of her actions that he sat down on the end of the chaise, momentarily speechless, overwhelmed, against his will, at her poignant beauty as she sat confidently beaming at him in her sexy lavender negligee.

"Tony darling, we need one another," she purred as she climbed out of bed and walked toward him. "I love you, and I've missed you so this past week."

"I love you too, darling," he said. And it was true, he realized as he took her into his lap and kissed her softly. "And I've missed you . . ." He kissed her again, then held her at arm's length. "But however much I might want you to stay here, you've got to move out tomorrow."

"Tony, I won't."

"Hear me out, darling. This is a horrible breach of diplomacy. In the eyes of my government and the U. S. State Department, I am a married man. You must leave tomorrow morning."

He kissed her soundly, then continued, "But I've decided to resign my post and go back home and run the businesses. Dad's getting too old for all that, and now that he's no longer in the Chamber of Deputies, he can't seem to just retire, so he's head-over-heels involved—and, well, I think it is time I went home. They are both getting up there in years."

"That's wonderful. I can't wait, I love Italy. And it is time Alberto got to know his grandparents!"

She was so certain, so positive that he was including her in his plans for the future. What had he ever said or done that would lead her to believe . . . ?

"Will you get an annulment so we can be married?"

He didn't answer her, just looked into her deep green eyes, wondering all the while what gave her such incredible confidence, such self-assurance.

"I mean, really, Tony," she went on, "I don't think your parents will be too happy with you if you move me into your home without benefit of matrimony."

"Are you certain that is what you want, Tamara? Are you absolutely sure you want to be tied to me for the long haul?" He was deadly serious, wondering if she had really thought through all the implications of marriage to him.

"There isn't a shadow of a doubt in my mind, Tony. I love you more than I've ever loved anyone in the world. And I think it is time you properly acknowledged your son and we made a proper home for him."

"Yes, I suppose . . ." At least he should do that right, Tony thought, without any enthusiasm at all for the idea of marrying Tamara. The magic had simply gone out of his world, the fire out of his love for her—as if Lorna's leaving had destroyed everything he had ever cared about, had destroyed his very ability to feel anything. Maybe that was what he hoped to recover by returning to Italy for good. Maybe he would regain his lust for life.

"When will your resignation be effective?"

He looked at her calculating face. Already she was imagining herself as the Contessa, the mistress of his domain, of his wealth, of his position in Italian society and business. Well, he'd try to get an annulment, though he didn't have much hope.

"I plan on asking the Prime Minister to relieve me by June first. Nine months should be enough notice. Hell, we may even have a new government by then."

Tony continued to attend official functions alone, but he turned down every invitation he could get away with, and when he felt it necessary to entertain, he did it with stag luncheons and large seated dinners with no hostess. He would not breach protocol to the degree that Tamara might have wished, and understanding his sense of propriety, she accepted the situation. Soon enough, she told herself, she would be his wife.

The measured calm of their daily lives was shattered in April when Tony's father died suddenly of a heart attack. He flew home to console his mother and preside at the funeral. He spent ten days with his mother afterward, long contemplative days remembering the wonderful times they had enjoyed as a family. When he returned to Washington, he begged Catarina to come with him, but she assured him that she would be fine, and would anxiously await his return for good in June.

Emilio's death brought one surprise. Instead of leaving his estate to his only son, as Tony had always anticipated and as the Dandolos had done for generations, he had left it to Catarina. His action puzzled Tony, knowing that his father could never have doubted that he would have showered every luxury on his mother during her lifetime. A new will had been drawn only two months before his death, signaling a recent change of heart. Somehow, it had something to do with Lorna's disappearance. Tony was certain of that.

But, he rationalized, it was of no consequence. He had more money of his own than he'd ever spend in a lifetime. He certainly didn't need his father's. Yet, it was curious . . . .

The packing had been going on for two weeks now, and Rosina knew she had to move quickly if she were to fulfill Lorna's wish. Wanting to do something to demonstrate her contempt for Tony and Tamara, Lorna had asked Rosina to steal the two Van Eyk oils from the library. She knew they were part of a triptych, one panel of which had been lost through the centuries, and she had some idea of their fabulous value. Besides, it would be a good thing for Tracy to own someday, a piece of her Dandolo heritage.

Rosina had been assigned by Bruno to pack the books in the library. She packed hundreds of books in the boxes provided by the moving company, then she carefully wrapped the knicknacks in tissue, then newspaper, and placed them in boxes filled with styrofoam bubbles. It was a simple matter, then, to remove the two small paintings from over the fireplace and wrap them in plastic, then in newspaper, and place them in a box which she would transfer to her car during the afternoon siesta when all the other servants were resting.

As she packed the knicknacks, she came to the silver-framed enlargement of a photo taken the day after the Dandolos had arrived at the embassy. Five-year-old Tanya looked so lovingly up at her father, with such pride in her-father-the-ambassador. "I'll just tuck it away in my purse," she thought. "Someday the child will love having it. It's not right what Lorna's doing, keeping that child away from her father. It's just not right . . . yet he has been such a bastard to them both . . . ."

Late that afternoon, Bruno informed her that the ambassador wanted to speak with her in his office. Wondering how he had already discovered her theft, she walked shyly and guiltily into his office.

"Sit down, Rosina, please."

She saw both kindness and embarrassment in his eyes. Perhaps he didn't know.

"I have prepared a strong letter of recommendation for you. You should have no trouble getting employment."

"Thank you, Mr. Ambassador."

"I'm truly sorry you won't be going home with us. You've always done a fine job, but of course I understand. When you married Manuel, I realized you wouldn't come back to Italy. He seems like a fine man. I like him."

"Thank you, sir." Her eyes wandered to his desk where she saw a copy of the same photo that was hidden in her purse. "That's fine," she thought, "Now you both will have one, you and Tanya."

"Rosina, since you won't be coming home, and

since you haven't taken time to look for a job yet, I want you to have a little something to tide you over." He reached for an envelope on his desk, and as he handed it to her he continued, "I don't know if you will ever have an opportunity to see my wife and Tanya again . . ."

She felt her stomach tighten. So he still believed that she had been involved in Lorna's leaving.

". . . but if they should ever get in touch with you, if they should ever need anything, you *do* have my address in Florence, don't you? You will write me, won't you Rosina, if they need anything?"

"Yes sir, Mr. Ambassador, if ever . . ." She had to stop and wipe her eyes with her apron. The tears were streaming down because she saw how much he loved them and how deeply grieved he was. "Yes, sir, I'll be sure to write you."

"I'm sorry. I—I didn't mean to upset you, Rosina. I know you loved the Contessa very much." He stood to dismiss her. "I thank you for—for everything, Rosina, and I wish you and Manuel the best of everything."

Rosina wiped her eyes again and backed out of the ambassador's office, trying to escape before she broke down completely and betrayed Lorna.

It wasn't until she arrived home that night, unpacked the two paintings from her car, and collapsed onto her sofa that she remembered the envelope the ambassador had given her. In it she found a ten-thousand-dollar check made out to her and labeled on the left-hand corner, "severance pay."

Chapter Thirteen

JULY 4, 1963—WOODSTOCK, VIRGINIA

Rosina and Laura rose from the dining room table and moved to the wicker sofa on the screened porch. They had finished eating a midday holiday meal of barbecued chicken, corn-on-the-cob, potato salad, and watermelon. Rosina and Laura had prepared the festive meal; Tracy and Manuel were, by tradition, the clean-up crew.

Rosina and Manuel, having no other "family" in the Washington area and sensing Laura's need to keep in touch with what was happening back at the embassy, had taken it upon themselves to be regular visitors at the Brown cottage on holidays and long weekends.

Laura welcomed them with effusive greetings, each time making them promise to come back soon, firmly setting the date. The distance that had once separated the two women, that between employer and servant, was slowly disappearing. They were united in their need for one another, in their shared past, and in their devotion to ten-year-old Tracy.

This time Laura was especially eager to have her private chat with Rosina, to catch up on what had happened since their last visit to Woodstock on Memorial Day. At that time, hearing that Tony was leaving for good, Laura had suggested to Rosina that she might consider "lifting" the Van Eyck paintings during the pandemonium of packing.

"After all," she had confided, "he doesn't give a damn about art, and they are the most valuable pieces he brought from home. Besides, it would be nice for Tracy to have them someday."

Rosina had smiled her agreement, hoping she would be able to carry it off. Now, with great pleasure, she unpacked the two paintings and presented them to Laura. "I had a few nervous moments when the ambassador called me into his office that same afternoon I stole these, but he hadn't noticed. He had called me in to give me a letter of recommendation and a large bonus."

She began to open her purse, "I'd like to share it with you, Laura." It was still hard for Rosina to call Laura by her name after all the years of addressing her as "Contessa," but Laura had insisted, time and again, that they were now "family" and she simply had to drop the title and abide by her wishes and call her Laura and call Tanya by her new name of Tracy.

"Absolutely not! You deserve every penny for all your years of service. And besides, we are doing fine. My paintings are selling surprisingly well. I can't seem to turn them out fast enough. No, don't worry about us. Tracy and I have everything we need. I've even started a savings account for her college education."

"That's wonderful," Rosina beamed at her former mistress, thinking how truly resourceful she was, amazed at how well she had adapted to the role of full-time mother and housekeeper without any servants.

"Now tell me about your new job. I want to hear how Mrs. Merriweather Post manages her many houses."

The women gossiped about life back in Washington until Manuel and Tracy rejoined them, announcing that the kitchen would pass anyone's inspection.

"Thank you both, and now it is time for you to exercise your pony, don't you think, Tracy? Besides, there are some business matters I want to discuss with Manuel and Rosina."

"Yes, Mother."

The child was quick to obey without voicing any objections. The fire had gone out of her personality; her sparkling laughter had been replaced by barely veiled hostility toward her mother. Something had changed drastically in her, Rosina thought as she watched Tracy mask her feelings toward her mother. But her eyes were furtive, guilty-looking; she could not seem to look anyone directly in the eyes. It was an unsettling development. Rosina wondered what had gone awry between mother and daughter. But then, most mothers and daughters had difficulties as the daughter grew up. It was too bad, but it happened.

"I wanted Tracy out of earshot while I explained a decision I made last week which affects the two of you," Laura began. "I probably have imposed on your friendship—and I wouldn't have done it, except that I couldn't see any other way. . . ."

Laura nervously smoothed back her hair into the bun on the back of her head before she continued,

"Remember the lawyer, Marvin Westerman?" As Rosina nodded her head, Laura continued, "He has been helping me with matters lately, legal matters and investment advice, that kind of thing. He insists I must make arrangements for a legal guardian for Tracy, in the event anything should happen to me, so I have drawn up a will in which I name the two of you her legal guardians. I hope you don't object. . . ." She studied their faces for a reaction. They seemed to want further explanation.

"Of course, nothing will happen, but he insisted that I make a will. So I have named you to be her guardians until she is twenty-one. It's just a precaution—to prevent Tony from getting her."

"Don't you think," began Manual in a soft, concerned voice, "that she really should go to her father and his people if something were to happen . . . ?"

"Absolutely not! She must never see him again! How can you even suggest such a thing, Manuel? After he took—that woman into my bed in my bedroom, how can you even suggest that Tracy be exposed to that—that filth!"

Even Rosina was surprised at the depth of fury in Lorna's outburst. She reached for her husband's hand, patted it as if to soothe him, then said to Laura, "Don't worry, of course it's all right. We don't object at all. But it will never come to pass. You will live to be ninety and we will dance at your grandchildren's weddings!"

"I'm sorry," apologized Manuel. "It was thoughtless of me."

Laura had regained her composure. She smiled at Manuel to reassure him, then with a mischievious voice, she said, "Haven't you heard there is no fury like a woman scorned? Well, let me tell you, it's true!"

All three laughed, and the moment passed.

Several hours later, after a snack for the road, Manuel and Rosina prepared to leave for the three-hour drive back to their Bethesda home in the suburbs of Washington. They kissed and hugged Tracy, who seemed especially reluctant to have them leave. At the door, she looked at Manuel with a silent plea, then said, "If only Mommy would let us have a telephone, I could call you and tell you when I win ribbons at the horse shows. And I could tell you what books I want, too."

"You really should consider getting a phone, Laura. After all, in a few years the boys will be calling," Manuel teased as he bent down to kiss Tracy.

"It is so lovely not to have a phone. I can't tell you how much I love the peace, the serenity. And I really don't feel the need for one. When I do, I use the pay phone at the grocery." She paused, then added, "Not having a phone is a kind of liberation. . . ."

When they had driven away, Tracy said to her mother, "See! Even they think we should have a phone!"

"There will be no more discussion of that subject, Tracy. Do you understand?"

"I hate you, mother!" Tracy screamed, and then ducked to miss her mother's hand which was aimed for her cheek. She ran into the house, into her bedroom, and slammed and locked the door in defiance.

Laura, stunned once again by her daughter's growing hostility, felt her eyes mist. Then, with a determined gait, she forced herself to march toward the kitchen.

*   *   *

Tracy flopped down on the bed, pulled the pillow out from under the spread, and buried her face in it, wishing for all the world that she could die. Life was not worth living. Every day seemed to be more painful than the one before, each day she hated her mother more, then hated herself for hating her mother. If only her father would come and rescue her.

Ever since arriving in Woodstock, since her mother had told her the unbelievable story that her father had a second family, an "illegitimate family," and that he no longer wanted them, no longer loved them, had taken Tracy out of his will, and never wanted to see her again—"or he wouldn't have done this!"—she had felt a growing anger, not at her father, but at her mother. This reaction, when she thought about it, was illogical and she grew more confused with each day. A part of her simply did not believe her mother's story, but she could do nothing to prove it was a lie. Her confusion and growing hatred for her mother left her in a constant state of anxiety; she bit her nails to the quick, she broke out in horrible rashes, and some mornings she awoke to discover that she had wet the bed.

Her only salvation was school. She had been so far ahead of her classmates in the public school at Woodstock, due to her previous private school education, that the principal had talked her mother into allowing Tracy to skip a grade; though she was only ten, she would be entering the seventh grade in the fall. Even so, she led the class in every subject, and the principal, feeling she needed additional stimulation, had arranged for a very special woman, an "old maid" by the name of Sheilah Case, to work with her at the public library on an advanced reading list.

At first, Miss Case had stuck to business and counseled Tracy on books she might enjoy, books that would help prepare her for high school and college. Eventually, however, Miss Case began to ask her personal questions, sensing her basic unhappiness.

Tracy answered in clipped sentences, supplying only the factual information Miss Case seemed to want.

"Do you have any brothers or sisters?"

"No."

"What does your daddy do?"

"My father's dead."

"Oh. I'm sorry. When did that happen?"

"He died in a plane crash several years ago."

She obeyed her mother faithfully in matters such as these. She repeated all the lies her mother had coached her in, fearful that if she didn't, the worst would come true—her father would take her away from her mother and put her in a home for "wayward girls," and she would never see her mother—or her father—again.

Although she answered questions when asked by persons in authority, she volunteered nothing, and she made no close friends, brought no playmates home, and went to no parties or social events. Her best friend was her pony Bingo, and her two satisfactions in life were reading and riding her pony in shows. At least, those two occupations met her mother's rigid standards of what was suitable for her.

Being newly poor was another bone of contention between mother and daughter. Laura had become determined that Tracy would grow up knowing how to take care of herself in a world without servants. She created a schedule of housework the child would help her with, which began with keeping her

own bedroom immaculate. Even before she arrived
at the breakfast table, her bed must be made, her
clothes put away, and her books on the bookshelf.
After breakfast, Tracy had the responsibility for
washing up the breakfast dishes and feeding her
pony. Then she was excused to go to school. Three
afternoons a week she was permitted to go to the
library and meet with Miss Case, but on the other
two she had to come home immediately to help her
mother with housework. On Tuesdays, she ironed
her own clothes and her mother's, showing each
garment to her mother and repeating the process on
those pieces which did not meet her mother's
approval.

"Knowing how to care for your own clothes is
crucial for a woman. Someday, when you work in
an office, you will thank me for this discipline."

On Thursdays, she vacuumed the house and
polished the furniture while her mother cleaned the
kitchen and bathroom. Saturday mornings they
bought groceries and feed for the pony. Saturday
afternoons and Sundays Tracy was permitted to
ride to her heart's content and read.

Tracy hated the housework, and vowed that
someday she would be rich enough again to have a
maid; her mother, sensing Tracy's frustration, used
the opportunity to once again lash out against men.

"Never trust a man, never depend on a man,
Tracy. They'll let you down every time. My mother
learned it, and now I've seen it again. You must
make something of your life, you must be independent, you must be able to walk away from a man at
any time. . . ."

It was speeches like this that made Tracy wonder
if her father had kicked them out or if Laura had, in
fact, done the leaving. But when she thought that,
she couldn't imagine her mother leaving that glori-

ous house, all those servants, those beautiful clothes and jewels which were nowhere in evidence in Woodstock. Tracy wondered what Laura had done with all her clothes. She wore nothing but jeans and shirts these days. Her hair was never as pretty as it once had been, and she never touched make-up. Laura looked twenty years older than she had when they left Washington only a year ago; she was grotesquely thin, and many were the mornings that she greeted Tracy with swollen, red eyes. On those mornings Tracy felt she had misjudged her mother, that her father probably really did have a second family.

Then again, there were moments when mother and child felt very close, when for a few hours Tracy felt a deep love for her mother. These were the times when Laura put down her paint brush or her book and they sat for hours drinking iced tea and talking about Laura's girlhood and her career as a New York fashion model. Tracy asked questions and Laura didn't flinch from answering, telling Tracy of her love for her own father, of the pony she had lost when he left them, of her strict grandmother and even stricter mother.

"At the time, I hated their restrictions, but now from the vantage point of being your mother, Tracy, I can understand what they were trying to protect me from. Of course, in those days, living in South Dakota, I couldn't even imagine the opportunities you will have as you grow up. You must make something of your life. You must be financially independent."

Over and over again that was Laura's theme. Laura's mother had been hurt by her father, who had left her for another woman. And then Laura had been betrayed by Tony, who prefered Tamara.

"You see, if I had come from a background of

financial security, I never would have been swept off my feet by Tony in the first place. It was all that incredible wealth, that art . . . And his parents were truly wonderful people."

"And I didn't have the education you will have someday, something which always made me feel inferior. It's an awful feeling to be lacking in something that everyone around you has. It destroys your self-confidence. Yes, Tracy, you must have the best education possible. I'm saving money every week so you will be able to go to any college in America. It's up to you to get the grades and do the work once you get into college."

At times like this, Tracy could not hate her mother, could not doubt her love. She knew that everything her mother was doing was aimed toward creating a better future for her. But still she missed her father dreadfully. And for some strange reason, when she tried to conjure up feelings of hatred for him at what he had done to her mother, she could not feel that emotion. Try as she might, she could not hate him.

Laura was putting the finishing touches on a small watercolor of a covered bridge she had sketched at Bryce when she heard the doorbell ring. It was mid-afternoon, a Wednesday, and she was expecting no one. She brushed a wayward strand of hair from her face, wiped her paint-stained hands on a damp rag, and went to the front door.

As she approached the door, she could see it was a smartly dressed woman, and as she got to the door, her stomach lurched and her heart began to pound frightfully. Terrified of the consequences, she was nevertheless impelled to open the door.

"Catarina! Catarina—my God, what a surprise!" And as if there were not a world of conflict separating the two women, Laura impulsively wrapped her arms around the older woman and held her close while tears began to form in her eyes.

"Lorna, oh Lorna dear, how are you? Let me look at you!" Laura, expecting censure, heard only love in Catarina's voice.

"How . . . how did you find me?"

"I hired a detective—no, dear, Tony is not with me. He doesn't even know I'm in the United States. He thinks I'm in Monaco with Princess Grace and Ranier."

Relief flooded over Laura. She was not afraid of Catarina, and they would have a lot to catch up on. "I'm so sorry about Emilio . . . I heard about his death. He was a wonderful man."

"Yes, he was a wonderful husband. I have good memories. . . ."

"Come, let's go out on the porch. It's cooler out there, and I'll make some tea." Laura led the way to the screened porch, her mind racing. Why had she come? What did she want? Had she come to take Tracy away from her? She excused herself and went to the kitchen to put the kettle on, then returned to the porch.

"Is Tanya here? I tried to arrive when I thought she would be home from school."

"No, she goes to the library on Wednesday afternoons. But I expect she'll be here by five. How long can you stay?"

"I promised the driver we would return to Washington this evening."

"Then you must stay for dinner with us. Tanya will love seeing you."

"Lorna, I don't know where to begin. I came to see you because I wanted you to know how sorry I am about how everything has turned out, about you and Tony. Both Emilio and I have been deeply grieved about all this. I can't tell you how awful it has been for us, not knowing where you were, if you had everything you need . . ."

"But you can see that we are fine. We live simply, the way I was raised. We—we have everything we need."

"Money?"

"I sell my paintings. They are selling well, and—I guess you can't tell from looking at me this afternoon—but I'm really very happy, doing what I love most." Laura felt self-conscious about her jeans and dirty tee-shirt; her hair needed washing and she looked a mess. She smoothed back her hair again, and as she did so, she realized how dirty her hands were. "You caught me at a bad time. I shower and dress every afternoon before dinner. Believe me, I don't always look this terrible."

"I shouldn't have arrived unannounced—but you have no phone? Is that right, dear?"

"Right. We don't need one and quite frankly, I'm happier without one. I don't have many visitors."

Laura went to the kitchen to get the tea and returned with a tray. "I wish I had some sherry to offer you, Catarina, but I don't keep anything like that in the house."

"Don't worry, dear, this will be fine."

Catarina accepted a chocolate chip cookie and a cup of tea. She smoothed a paper napkin out over her purple knit skirt and recrossed her Gucci-clad feet. Laura marveled at how wonderfully chic and sophisticated she looked, how youthful for her sixty-odd years. "Catarina, you look simply marvelous in spite of everything you've been through. I'm sure it has been a difficult time for you."

"Yes, it has. I don't know which gives me more grief, Emilio's death or what happened between you and Tony. I've always been very fond of you, and I wish there were something I could do to make life easier for you. You certainly don't have to live like this. . . ."

"It's my choice. It really is, believe me. I prefer Tanya to grow up with a different set of values than what she would have had with Tony. I guess that must be hard for you to understand. . . ."

"Do you really intend to keep her from Tony forever?" Asking the question had cost Catarina a lot, a lot of pain and pride.

"Tony told me that he would take Tanya away from me, that I would never see her again."

"Lorna, surely you don't believe that!" Catarina had raised her voice in shock and disbelief. "That was an idle threat, made in anger. Whatever else Tony is, he is not cruel. He would never have deprived his daughter of her mother!"

"He said he would. I had to take him at his word."

"It must have been in the heat of anger. Believe me, Tony loves you. He loves you still, in spite of all you've done." Catarina paused, then added, "And he loves Tanya too much to deprive her of a mother."

"Will you tell him how to find us?"

"No, my dear, I won't. I will respect your desires in this. If this is the way you want things, I guess—"

At that moment, the front door slammed and Laura knew that Tanya was home. Again, her heart began to pound furiously.

"Mom, whose car is that out front, the big black one with the chauffeur?"

"Come out onto the porch, dear. We have a guest."

Tanya rounded the corner and looked for a long second at her grandmother. "Oh Grandma—I knew you'd come, I knew it!" She ran to her grandmother, who rose to greet her. They hugged, kissed, then hugged again. Both grandmother and granddaughter had tears streaming down their faces.

"Now sit down, here beside me, and we'll catch up. You are so beautiful—my goodness, a real princess! If only your daddy . . ."

"Oh, I'm so glad you came, Grandma. You can see Bingo, you can see how well I ride. . . ."

As they chatted about school, her pony, her life in Woodstock, Laura got out her camera and began to load film. "I'm so impressed with the resemblance between the two of you, I'm going to do a painting. I rarely do portraits, but this will be an exception." She took dozens of pictures of them while they talked, pictures from every angle, capturing every conceivable emotion, even while Catarina told Tanya of her grandfather's death.

When it became time for Laura to prepare dinner, she invited them into the kitchen so she could participate in their conversation. Later, as the three of them dined on tuna fish salad, fresh green beans, and brownies—made by Tanya—the conversation turned to a future visit.

Catarina, fully comprehending the depth of Lorna's determination to keep father and daughter apart, suggested that she come back next summer for a month at the beach. "How about that beach in Delaware—if you will get us a house, Lorna, I'll pay for it, and the three of us will have a vacation together, just the three of us."

"Mmhh," Laura responded, trying to determine if Catarina really would keep her word about not letting Tony know where they lived.

"That's a wonderful idea, Grandma, I can't wait. That's a great idea! We can ride bikes together on the boardwalk in the morning . . ."

Catarina laughed at the idea of herself on a bicycle, patted Tanya's hand tenderly, then said to Lorna, "You will make the arrangements, Lorna?"

"I'll see. Now Tracy, darling, why don't you show your grandmother what a splendid little helper you are and clean up the kitchen while we finish our coffee?"

"Yes, I must be leaving soon. I do want to get back to Washington tonight."

"You won't tell Tony . . . about us, then?" Laura ventured when Tracy was out of ear shot.

"No, Lorna. If that is the only way I can keep in touch with you and my granddaughter, then I won't tell Tony where to find you. But you must promise that if there is ever anything you need for Tanya, you'll write to me."

"It's a deal!" Lorna sized up Catarina once again, thinking that she was trustworthy, then impulsively asked, "Have you met Tamara yet?"

"Yes, I have." She paused, as if to consider what she was about to say, then went ahead, "Lorna, when Emilio had a serious mistress—and it happened twice during our years together—and each of them had a child by him, I was very deeply hurt, as I'm sure you have been. I know what you feel. But I chose to handle it differently because I knew how deeply he loved me, and I knew nothing would ever take him away from his son Tony. So I ignored the situation, pretended it didn't exist, refused to discuss it with anyone. Eventually the passionate affairs ended, as all such affairs do. But then there were the children to consider. We did what Italian families of our class have always done and settled a trust on the mother and the child. And then we continued our lives together as if nothing had ever happened. For me, that was the solution. I don't regret it. If I had to do it over again, I would do it the same way. You see, I always loved Emilio. I never for a moment stopped loving him, and I knew he felt the same. And I wasn't about to let another woman have him permanently. He would never have left me."

Catarina paused, looked deeply at Lorna, then added, "I don't believe Tony would have ever left you either, Lorna. I'm convinced of it."

Laura walked to the screen and looked out at her rose bushes. "I couldn't live that way, Catarina. I tried for a year, knowing about Tamara, suspecting they were back together. But I couldn't live that lie. I couldn't stand to have him touch me, knowing he might have spent the afternoon at her apartment . . . . I just couldn't live that lie." She paused to wipe away the tears which were beginning to run down her face. "And I didn't want Tanya exposed . . . to that kind of hypocrisy."

"I understand," the older woman said softly. "What is right for one person at one time and place is not necessarily right for another person at a different time and place. The only thing I wish—I wish there was some way we could have Tanya in Italy, perhaps for a couple of months a year. . . . I do love her so! Let her visit us for my sake, Lorna."

"No, I'm sorry . . . I can't," Laura responded, knowing that if Tanya ever went to her father, she would never return to Woodstock. *She* wouldn't want to.

"Well, I'm sorry—sorry you don't trust me enough. But I must be going."

"Yes . . ."

"Perhaps you would grant an old lady one last wish. Could you possibly bring yourself to part with that wonderful portrait of Tanya in the blue dress? I would love it for my bedroom."

Laura was immensely flattered that her mother-

in-law wanted one of her paintings for the Villa
Dandolo, that one of her paintings would hang in
the same room with Fragonards and Tiepolos. "Yes,
yes, of course you may have it. I'd be honored."

"And will you do two portraits of the two of us?
I'd love to have one to remember this afternoon by.
It has been a good visit for me."

"Yes. It will be your Christmas present from us!"

Tanya came back onto the porch, beaming at her
grandmother. "It's spotless. Your Nella couldn't
make a kitchen shine better!" Then she realized
that her grandmother was preparing to leave. "Oh, I
wish you could stay one more day. I wish you could
watch me ride in the show on Saturday."

"Not this time, darling, but next summer we'll
have loads of fun at the beach. Now give me a big
hug and kiss. . . ."

Her last words to Laura as they parted were,
"Don't worry about your secret. I'll protect it. I am
leaving a happy woman, and I have what I came
for—the comfort of knowing that the two of you
are all right. Now, keep in touch—and make those
plans for the beach!"

Tanya lay awake long after her bedtime that
night, positive in her heart of hearts that her father
would arrive any day now to reclaim them. If her
grandmother could find them, so could her father.
She began to plan the essays she would write for
him. When he arrived—he would probably come
before the first snowfall—she would surprise him
with her knowledge of world events.

*What has Lorna done that she must punish herself
so much for?* Catarina wondered as the limousine
left Woodstock and sped out onto Route 80. *What
incredible self-flagellation! To live like that, to let
herself go to pieces. My God, she looks sixty years*

old! What would Tony feel if he saw her now? But that child, that adorable Tanya, is something else again. What a charmer, what a beauty she is going to be! It's such a shame she won't grow up with us in Florence . . . somehow, somehow, if it's the last thing I do on this earth, I'll find a way to bring her home.

She began to scheme, knowing that she must play her cards very carefully and cautiously. Lorna was a desperate woman, perhaps—probably, in fact— mentally deranged. The first step was next summer at the beach. If that went well, if she could get Lorna to trust her . . . then perhaps a visit could be arranged for the following Christmas.

But then there was the problem of Tamara and Alberto. Tony was adamant that his son would not be snubbed by Italian society. It would be a tricky matter to have Tanya and Lorna visit the Villa Dandolo, especially during the holidays when they did so much entertaining. But somehow, she would get Tanya back to Italy where she belonged.

Chapter Fourteen

Laura Brown packed up her three remaining watercolors and the two small oils that hadn't sold. All together, it had been a good Sunday at the Bryce Mountain Ski Lodge. She had sold nine small watercolors and three small oils, all scenes of the surrounding area done during the various seasons of the year, nostalgic small town scenes. They were the kind that sold to the folks who journeyed deep into the Shenandoah Valley, mostly people who lived and worked in large cities but came to Bryce in the winter for skiing. Each weekend they filled the condominiums and chalets, swelling the ski lift lines so that one had to stand in line twenty minutes for a five-minute run. But they loved her art, and that was all that mattered to Laura.

She carried the remaining watercolors to her car and put them in the back seat, then sat down in the front seat for a moment to count her checks. She had made thirteen hundred dollars that day. Not bad! And this was the art she created exactly for that purpose, a fast dollar. Her better and larger canvases she still sold at the gallery in Alexandria.

She put her wallet in the glove compartment and got out of the car and locked it. Then she took her skis from the top of the car, got her boots out of the trunk and went to the ticket booth. Now she would reward herself with an evening of skiing.

She rode to the top of the mountain, looking down at the ice-covered runs. She decided to ski down the most treacherous run, White Lightning. It was the least crowded, and though it was very narrow, it was nowhere near as difficult as the skiing in the Italian Alps at Cortina d'Ampezzo, where she and Tony had honeymooned.

How she had loved skiing with Tony! He had been a wonderful teacher, so patient and so proud of her daily improvement. Year after year, she had improved. Even now, after all the bitterness and hatred, she found herself looking back in utter amazement at the wonderful times they had had, at the love they had felt for each other and for their darling little toddler who had begun skiing when she was only two years old.

The first years of her marriage, she recalled, had been sheer heaven—learning to ski, learning to manage a magnificent home, learning to buy clothes, spending time with artists in the art world of Florence. Tony had been totally indulgent—she could have anything she wanted, go anywhere, bring anyone home for dinner. He had quickly understood that Lorna craved the stimulus of artists, even though they weren't his cup of tea. He had welcomed them, put on his best manners, and only occasionally retreated to his study upstairs.

"Ah, yes." She sighed aloud. "We had something wonderful in those early years."

These were the thoughts pleasantly roaming through her consciousness when a reckless skier, not looking ahead, hit her from behind and sent her flying off the trail headfirst into a pine tree. The impact burst her skull. She died instantly.

PART THREE
Tracy

Chapter Fifteen

"Rosina, I need your help!" The girlish voice, ringing with nervous anticipation, called from the upstairs bedroom.

"I'm coming!" Rosina answered as she put down the sweater she was crocheting and ran up the stairs. She had positioned herself in the small den at the bottom of the staircase, waiting, hoping to be called upstairs.

"This dress is magnificent, but I'm afraid I need help. It's so hot, I can't bear to think of perspiring in this gorgeous dress!"

Rosina began buttoning the four dozen buttons on the white tulle ruffled ballgown that she had found for Tracy at Garfinckel's. It was a designer original—frightfully expensive for a high school senior, but Rosina believed that it was exactly what Lorna would have wanted for her precious daughter. If there was ever a daughter who deserved the best, it was Tracy. What a wonderful child she had been through all her high school years, never a moment's trouble, Rosina mused as she finished the last button. "Now let me look at you."

Tracy turned around and smiled lovingly down at Rosina, then planted a kiss on her forehead. "Thank you for finding such a wonderful gown. I love it."

"You look like a movie star, more beautiful than Elizabeth Taylor! Oh, if only Manuel were here right now, he would be so proud! I must take pictures of you before Eddie arrives."

"Only two more minutes and I'll be ready."

Rosina sat on the edge of Tracy's canopied bed, watching her slip into her white heels, put her lip gloss in her white beaded evening bag, and touch up her hair. "Would you like to wear your mother's pearls tonight? They would be lovely with that dress."

"No, they're much too valuable. Someday I will, Rosina dear, but not yet." She re-checked the backs of the fake pearl earrings she had purchased at Korvette's—they would do just fine for now. "Okay, I'm ready for your famous instamatic."

Both Tracy and Manuel teased Rosina about the pictures she was forever taking. Manuel had asked her if she was afraid that at some future time she would be asked to account for everything that had happened in Tracy's life, but she had answered that she wanted them for herself, for the day when Tracy was grown and gone and she would want to relive every wonderful moment of being her foster mother.

Though it had come about through a tragedy, it was nothing less than a miracle for Rosina to have Tracy, even for a few years, as her "adopted" daughter. Rosina and Manuel had already been in their late forties when they met and married. Children of their own had been out of the question, so they had pursued the American dream instead. They had risen from the servant class they had been born into in Italy to the mainstream of middle-class America. They had become citizens, and Manuel had continued his job at IBM while moonlighting as a waiter for Ridgewell's. Rosina had worked for a while, but after Lorna's death Mr. Westerman had convinced her that the proper course would be to pay herself a salary out of Lorna's estate, exactly what she would have made working for Mrs. Merriweather Post, and stay home to be a full-time mother to Tracy. Nothing could have pleased Rosina more.

Tracy preceded Rosina down the staircase, carefully holding up her ruffled skirt.

"If only your mother could see you tonight! She would be so thrilled."

"Oh, I don't know. I think she would be more pleased to see me in a debate tournament or on stage. There were times when mother spoke with great disdain for social life."

"Yes, but don't forget your mother was a great fashion model, one of the most famous. She had respect for beauty."

"It is my father who should see me tonight!" Tracy said defiantly, knowing Rosina hated it when she spoke about her father.

The doorbell rang, announcing Eddie's arrival. Tall, blonde, and Irish, he arrived bearing a nosegay of red sweetheart roses. "Wow! You are gorgeous! That's some dress. Jeez!"

Tracy rushed to the refrigerator to get his boutonniere, and pinned it on his lapel with fumbling fingers. Then the two of them posed patiently for Rosina's camera. Not a word was said about a curfew as they hurried out the front door; it was Tracy's first real date, and she had only accepted Eddie's invitation because Manuel had insisted. Tracy, strangely for a girl her age, had no interest in boys whatever. She had held herself totally aloof from high school social life, going out rarely, and then only in crowds. In the process she had earned herself the reputation of being a snob, though in truth, as Manuel had told Rosina, she was terrified of boys. Her mother had seen to that! And Manuel had accused Rosina of reinforcing Tracy's fear of boys.

She didn't seem afraid of Eddie tonight, Rosina thought as she picked up her crocheting and sat down again in the rocker in the den. Eddie seemed like a nice young man, and he'd been hanging around Tracy like a sick puppy dog for two years now. It was good that she finally gave him a chance. They even looked nice together, he so blond and fair and tall, and she almost as tall, with that jet-black wavy hair. Like her father and grandmother's.

How time flies, five and a half years already, and now she's almost ready to leave. A joy she's been, an absolute joy!

Rosina's mind flashed back to Lorna's funeral. The five of them had been so bereft, so alone, so cold that blustery dark day at the cemetery. The child had been flanked by her Great Aunt Celia on one side and by the lawyer, Westerman, on the other. Rosina and Manuel had stood just behind them as the priest had intoned the final words of commitment to the earth. Rosina worried about Lorna's immortal soul. She had not been to church since leaving Tony. The child's religious education had ceased entirely, something which Rosina had immediately corrected after getting custody of her.

Bitter arguments had preceded and followed the burial. Celia wanted to notify Tony, wanted to ship Lorna's body to Italy for burial. She also felt that Tony should have custody of his daughter, arguing that he would raise her in the appropriate setting, in keeping with her illustrious birthright.

Westerman, who had always been a bit in love with Lorna, argued, along with Rosina, that Lorna's greatest wish had been that Tanya never see her father or "that woman" again. It was inconceivable that Tanya should go to Florence and grow up in his household, and they had Lorna's will to prove their point.

Manuel felt that Celia might be the answer. Perhaps she could take on the chore of raising Tanya. But no, she was getting on in age, had never had a child, and certainly could not take responsibility for raising a teenager in New York City.

Tanya's feelings were taken into consideration. She barely knew her great aunt, having seen her only rarely before her mother's death. But Rosina had always been there, her mother's devoted servant since the second week of her marriage to Tony. Rosina's love for Lorna was legendary, her devotion complete and unswerving. And Rosina clearly wanted this child to mother. It seemed the right solution at the time, and it had been Lorna's wish. So Westerman arranged for Manuel and Rosina to be Tracy's legal guardians and, as he himself and Rosina had been named executors of Lorna's estate, he made all the necessary financial arrangements, setting up a trust fund which would be accessible to Rosina as needed, and to Tracy when she turned twenty-one.

Poor Manuel. All the responsibility for funeral arrangements had fallen on him. Then, in spite of his doubts, he had become a foster father. Unlike

Rosina, he had always felt it was wrong. Tracy should be with her real father; she should be raised in Florence as an Italian heiress, not as an American in a middle-class immigrant family. What could they do for her in the way of culture that could compare to what her father could do for her? He was determined, Rosina knew, to reunite father and daughter as soon as Tracy reached twenty-one. And she dreaded that day. It hung over her like a dark storm cloud.

It was hard for Rosina to understand what Tracy felt for her father. She rarely mentioned him—in fact what she had said this evening was astonishing, that he would like to see her in her prom gown. Her father had always appreciated her intellectual precociousness. But of course, she had been an outrageous flirt with her father, and he had adored taking her places, seeing her all dressed up. When Rosina remembered Tracy's personality as a child and compared it to her personality during the five years they had had her, she was very troubled. Tracy had changed dramatically from a fun-loving, coquettish child to an extremely introverted, almost insecure, young woman.

The first few months had been the worst. She had been thin and wan, distracted, unable to read or even ride her beloved pony. She had lost interest in everything, and frequently Rosina had found her crying alone in her room. Rosina had provided the only comfort she knew—warm, cuddling, affectionate love, accompanied by endless stories about her parents and her early childhood. These times always ended with upbeat, optimistic thoughts about Tracy's future, about how she would make her mother "in heaven" proud of her achievements, how she would carry on in the way her mother would have wished. She would be brave, strong, and dedicated. She would fulfill her mother's dreams for her. It was, Rosina reminded her, her solemn obligation.

Rosina's tender loving care worked its magic. Over a time, Tracy regained a small sense of security and became comfortable at her new school. By June, her grades were high again and she was preparing for the spring and summer riding shows. Rosina became a full-time "horse-mother," driving Tracy all over the Washington area to horse shows.

It was that summer that Manuel had introduced Tracy to the Library of Congress. It was easy enough to drop her off once a week at the Library, meet her for a picnic lunch on the Capitol grounds, and then pick her up on his way home. The first time he had given her a complete tour, shown her how to find the books and magazines and newspapers she wanted, and she had taken to it like the bookworm that she was.

The following summer, he had an even better idea—she should get a head-start on high school by learning to type during the summer. Tracy had hated the whole idea at first, then warmed to it when she imagined herself a great television reporter preparing for her evening news show. She agreed, Manuel made the arrangements, and Rosina did the driving every day. By the end of their second summer together, Tracy was not only a crack typist but she was also the grand championship winner of the Washington Bridle Trails Association show at Meadowbrook Stables.

Tracy discovered her true métier when she tried out for the drama club in high school. As a freshman she was chosen to play Anne Frank in *The Diary of Anne Frank*, and that triumph was followed by the role of Miriane in *Winterset* her sophomore year. She snared the leading role of

Laurie in *Oklahoma* away from a beautiful blonde during her junior year by wearing a blonde wig during try-outs, and now she was rehearsing for *My Fair Lady*, which would open in two days. Rosina and Manuel had tickets for all four nights of the musical's performance and had already placed an order for a copy of the taping of the opening night.

But the theater was not really "her bag," Tracy had told them, nor was modeling, even though she enjoyed being part of the teen board at Saks Fifth Avenue. What was most important to her, "to my future," was her work on the school newspaper and the debate club. She had declined being editor because she preferred to do interviews, and using Manuel as her go-between, she had managed to interview four United States senators and three foreign ambassadors for special columns in the paper. These people had agreed to the interviews after Manuel had done a superb job of serving as the butler at their dinner parties. And in every case, they had been astounded at the brilliance of "Manuel's daughter." She came well prepared and asked them precise questions which weren't always easy to answer.

It was New Year's Day of her senior year— Rosina would always remember the scene—when Tracy had confided to them her intentions.

"I am going to be the next Barbara Walters. Someday, I am going to be the most famous female television journalist in America, perhaps in the world!" She had not said it to brag or to call attention to her talents. She had stated it as a simple fact, a statement of her determination, of her tunnel-vision dedication to a particular career path which no one would dissuade her from.

Manuel gave her arguments: it would be a highly competitive field, it mattered more who you knew than what you knew, it was a precarious existence, you could be on top one day and fired the next. And being a reporter was no life for a woman! He had all kinds of reservations, and he expressed them vehemently, but he never said, "I don't think you can do it." He had watched her perform for five years now, and he knew she would do anything she set her mind on. But, as he had confided to Rosina, he didn't want her to suffer the heartbreaks that were inevitable with a career like that. He wanted her to go through life with no heartbreaks at all, sheltered by her father's money and place in Italian society.

"It will never happen like that, Manuel. She hates her father. She will never take a dime from him!"

"Only because you and her mother have poisoned her mind."

"That's not true. I've never said one bad word about her father."

It was the only continuing, recurring argument that marred their marriage. They both loved the girl with an enduring devotion, as if she were their own. But Manuel continued to believe that she would be better off with her father, and sometimes he even made plans to get in touch with Tony, but he never carried them through, mainly because he couldn't bear to deprive Rosina of her "daughter." Rosina knew all this and spent many hours planning the inevitable conversation she would someday have with the Count Dandolo. She would summon up her new-found American courage and tell him a thing or two!

Rosina put her needlework down and went into the kitchen to fix herself a cup of tea. Her home gave her such pride; who would ever have dreamed that a servant girl from southern Italy could live in America in such splendor? Well, it wasn't really splendor, not by Italian or American standards. But it was a wonderful three-bedroom home that they had bought new four years ago and furnished with carpeting, modern furniture from Woodie's and all the latest laborsaving appliances. She even had instant boiling water at her sink! America was really a wonderful place to live. Tracy would be better off as an American.

She heard the garage doors open and realized that Manuel was home. She walked to the door to greet him.

"She was beautiful, so beautiful!" Tears formed in her eyes.

"My God, what did you expect? You silly thing, don't cry! Why are you crying?

"*Cara mia*," he began as he wrapped his arms around her to comfort her, "I know you don't want to let go. You are probably holding on tighter than a real mother would, but it is for *her* sake . . ."

"I know, I know. You've explained it. But couldn't she stay home her freshman year?"

"Rosina, we've been over it again and again. She's a wonderful student, a wonderful girl. You've done a good job. But this is not Italy. It's America, and she must have a normal social life. And she won't have that unless she leaves us and lives by herself."

"But it's so cruel, turning her out like this. . . ."

"We are not turning her out. We are simply suggesting that she take an apartment of her own when she begins college—or live in the dormitory or in a sorority house. She needs to develop the social side of her personality. Now tell me, how did Eddie look tonight? I like that young man."

"He looked wonderful. They looked good to-gether."

"Look, Rosina, we have a whole summer to work this out. Don't be so upset. I know you'll get to see

her a lot, probably every weekend. Smile, please?"
And he tilted her chin up toward his so he could
kiss her lips. "I love you," he whispered quietly as
he put his arm around her waist and guided her
toward the stairs.

Two evenings later, Tracy sat alone in the dressing room of Walter Johnson High School. She loved
the quiet and gentle disorder of the backstage two
hours before curtain time; she loved having the
time all to herself, the dressing room her private
domain until it was filled with noisy students
getting ready for opening night. She had discovered
it her freshman year and had always insisted that
Rosina drop her off two hours before curtain time,
even though the cast call was only an hour before
curtain. It was here, in the quiet of the massive
dressing room with its racks of costumes and
makeup lights and musty odors, that her fantasies
and dreams took shape. And from those early
fantasies had come her goals, her purpose in life.

She put the original-cast recording of *My Fair
Lady* on the small phonograph—Rosina had reminded her that her father had given it to her for
Christmas when she was six—and hummed
absentmindedly as she began to cleanse her face
with cream. She began to prepare her mind for the
coming performance. She deliberately cleared it of
any thought and let the music wash over her.

"*. . . Does enchantment pour out of every door?*"
Enchantment. Somewhere in the back of her
mind, buried deep in her memory, she knew what
enchantment felt like—riding on the back of her
daddy's shoulders eating an ice cream cone, feeling
his strong hands on her ankles. That had been so
long ago. That was happiness, paradise. She vaguely remembered happiness. The memory was like a

butterfly which grazed your cheek, then wafted away before you could catch it. She couldn't quite grasp and hold on to the feeling of being loved, adored even, by a mother and father who loved each other too. Her vague memories of that glorious world were a dream that hovered over her life, a dream she would give anything to find again.

Somehow, even if it took a lifetime of effort, she would recapture that world. Intuitively, she knew it would take her own effort. That's what this evening and the next three nights were all about—for a few brief moments at the end of each act, and then at the end of the performance during those curtain calls, she would feel the unconditional love of the audience. It was a moment almost as wonderful as the happiness she had once experienced, as glorious as the life she had been born into, a life which had evaporated without explanation when her mother had stolen her away from her father.

During those horrible dark days after her mother's death, she had brooded on what had happened to her, on how they had both abandoned her. At first, she felt she had done something wrong herself; then in recent months she had come to realize that it had happened to her, that her parents had wronged her grievously, though perhaps unintentionally. And every day of her life she had prayed desperately for her father to come for her, to find her as her Grandmother Catarina had found her. But it was to no avail. She had never heard a word from him.

Bless Rosina and Manuel! How stalwart, how loving they had been. Through long hours of weeping, Rosina had comforted her, had held her and let her know how cherished she was. Then Rosina had told her, over and over again, that her future was her own choice. What had happened had happened;

it was over with. She should concentrate on her blessings. She had a fine mind, a beautiful face, and every opportunity America had to offer. She could have the finest education money could buy—her mother had made sure of that before she died. "Through your own efforts, you can create a wonderful life for yourself. It's up to you." This was Rosina's refrain over the years, and it was beginning to look as if she had been right.

Gradually the fog lifted, and an idea had begun to form: she would someday be a television star, either an actress or a newscaster. She began to watch television with a different kind of concentration and a talent for analysis developed. High school opened new avenues for her developing talents. She had participated in any and all dramatic events, joined the debate club, and began to write for the school newspaper. She had decided to keep the options open, as between acting and newscasting, but she would become a television personality. Just as quickly as possible.

She developed a protective outer shell, like a mollusk. She resolved that she would never again let anyone bruise or injure her feelings. She convinced herself that the fame and money she would earn as a great television star would somehow provide her with the happiness she remembered. She became certain that money had something to do with her mother's lost happiness and with the jolly, loving man her father had been.

Her mother's brainwashing had not been able to destroy her memories of her father. He had adored her, petted her, pampered her, and had never scolded her. He had loved her unconditionally, and it was that kind of love she wanted to recapture. It became mixed up in her child's mind with fame and money, and with a clarity she would always remember, it had flashed across her mind one day as she rode in the fields along the Potomac, that fame and money equalled love and happiness.

After that day, her personality began to change in subtle ways. She developed a special kind of discipline. She concentrated on her goals, took on those assignments which would propel her toward her television career, and let the rest of the world pass by. She had no time for social life or boys. To tell the truth, she sensed she was not yet ready for that heady atmosphere. Popularity at school meant not a wit to her, because it had no connection with the fame and money she coveted.

In addition to her more academic pursuits, she became a student of makeup, clothing, and styles and fads in entertainment. She read *Variety* every week.

"Oh, so loverly sittin' abso-bloomin'-lutely still!"

What fun it was to act with a British accent, she thought as she deftly applied mascara to her already long black lashes. *If only Daddy were in the audience. . . .*

It had been her recurring fantasy, awake and asleep, that one day the curtain would go up and he would be sitting sixth row center, his eyes glazed with pride, awaiting her opening number.

But he doesn't even know where I live or what my name is now . . . although I know everything about him. . . .

Manuel had introduced her, perhaps unwittingly, to the Library of Congress. At first she had concentrated on books and articles about the entertainment industry. She had read *Theatre Arts* and *Variety* and even the *Wall Street Journal.* Then one day, purely accidentally, she had discovered the international newspapers. Quickly, she had gravitated to the Italian papers, and the third week she read *Italia*. There, on the inside of the front page, was a picture of her father! He was being interviewed about his investments in South Africa and the climate for development in the Third World countries. After that, she read the Italian papers and periodicals from cover to cover, frequently reading about her father and his banking and industrial activities. Then, during her junior year, he had been elected to the Chamber of Deputies. She had felt a bitter mixture of pride and hatred; she had put the paper down and run to the ladies' room to wipe her tears away. How she wanted to write to him! But it would have been a betrayal of her mother, a betrayal of Rosina and Manuel.

And then one day, after she had asked for the Italian *Vogue*, a magazine she had begun to read once a month, she saw Tamara, Tony, and her step-brother, Alberto. Tamara was resplendent in a magnificent ballgown, and around her neck was a magnificent necklace of robin's egg-sized emeralds surrounded by diamonds. Her green eyes blazed from the picture, and on her perfectly manicured hands Tracy saw a huge emerald and diamond ring. Her father's hand rested lightly on Tamara's shoulder, the possessive gesture of a man for a much-cherished woman.

She had slammed the magazine closed, run from the library and walked for miles through Washington, tears blurring her vision, her legs and feet aching. Finally, in sheer exhaustion, she had collapsed on a park bench.

"So . . . Mother wasn't lying after all. He has another family . . . he loves them . . . he doesn't want me."

After a while, she gathered herself together and

returned to the library to wait for Manuel to pick her up. She did not go back again. Her love affair with the Library of Congress was over.

Since then, she had been obsessed with the idea of getting revenge on behalf of her mother. She would become world famous, rich and powerful—then she would find him and tell him how she hated him, how he had destroyed her life. She would expose him to the world for the despicable man he was. . . .

But no . . . this frame of mind would never do. She must get herself in the mood to be Eliza Doolittle.

The door to the dressing room opened, and Gene McMahon, the drama coach and director of the musical, stuck his head in. "Tracy! I wondered if you were here yet. I didn't hear your record playing."

"I've been here for a while, you know me. . . ." She smiled weakly.

"Yeah, well, I want to wish you good luck. I know you're going to be great. We're sold out, and we've got some people here from American University's Drama Department, like I promised you!"

"Gee, thanks. That's great Mr. McMahon. Do you think you can get them to come backstage so I can meet them?"

"I'll sure try—you know that!" For a moment the coach seemed embarrassed, even awkward. Then he added, "Okay, kid, break a leg!"

If there was ever a teacher's pet, I'm it, she thought. *I've been his favorite since* Anne Frank, *and he's always bent over backwards to give me every chance. I hope I have that kind of luck in college.*

McMahon had tried to talk her into attending the

American Academy of Dramatic Arts in New York. But she had told him her dreams, and he had been unable to convince her that she should put all her eggs in one basket and work toward being an actress. She was determined to keep her options open.

He and the debate coach and the journalism teacher had spent hours with her, poring over college catalogues, unable to agree among themselves which was the most appropriate school for her. She had gone along with their discussions, knowing all the while that she would stay in Washington and attend the American University. After all, it had a fine communications department and the Washington area presented ample opportunity for on-the-job training, with five television and a multitude of radio stations.

Besides, if she stayed in Washington, there was always the remote possibility that her father might find her. . . .

The dressing room was filling up now with the rest of the cast members, all acquaintances of hers, none of them close friends. She knew they felt admiration and a begrudging respect for her; she also knew they would stab her in the back if she faltered even once. She began to hum scales to warm up her voice.

The auditorium had filled up, the show had begun, and Walter Johnson High School's version of Rex Harrison was finishing his opening number: "Oh, why can't the English learn . . . to . . . speak!"

Tracy stood quietly waiting for the cue to her entrance, concentrating on the mood of her initial appearance. She sauntered onto the stage, muttering her best "ooohhww," holding the action still for a moment until the initial applause died down— Manuel and Rosina had imported their very own claque for the occasion—and almost unconsciously letting her eyes scanned the sixth row center. . . .

He wasn't there.

Chapter Sixteen

Tracy had spent the three summer months working as a "gofer" at WUBS, the Washington affiliate of the United Broadcasting System. Exactly as it was with her print interviews for the high school paper, it had been Manuel who had opened the doors for her.

He frequently served as the butler at Ben Stanton's home when Stanton and his wife entertained. One night in May, when Stanton was paying Manuel for the evening's services, Manuel asked Stanton if he might speak with him a moment about a personal matter.

"Of course, Manuel. Please sit down," he said as he himself collapsed into a leather rocker and began to take his tie off.

"I have a beautiful foster daughter who is determined that she will have a career in television. She is enrolled in the American University Communications Department next fall. She's an honor student and a drama star, too. I've been trying to talk her out of a television career because I think it's a terrible career for a woman—too competitive, too dirty . . ."

"Yes, I quite agree."

"But she's determined. I thought if she could work with you this summer—a messenger job, you know, whatever errands you need done—she might get a better feel for the awful grind, the pressure."

"I'm sorry Manuel. We don't have the budget to hire summer help, and if we did, we'd have kids standing in line."

"It wouldn't be necessary to pay her. She could be an intern. She doesn't need money. Could I send her over to see you, just for fifteen minutes?"

Ben sighed, resigned to the fact that he couldn't say no to this decent, struggling immigrant. "Sure, sure, I'll be delighted to meet her, but I know right now there is no way we can pay her."

"Understood." Manuel stood, his mission accomplished. "Thank you, Mr. Stanton. This is a great favor you are doing me." The smile broadened on Manuel's face, and Ben decided he was delighted he had agreed to meet the girl. No harm could come of it, and he could count on this man for the next twenty years to handle the dinners that were so important to his career to perfection.

"Have her at my office in Spring Valley at nine sharp on Monday. Okay?" Stanton stood up and shook hands with Manuel in what was clearly a dismissal.

That weekend, Manuel took Tracy out and bought her a secondhand Chevy so she would have transportation back and forth during the summer.

He was that confident that Stanton would want her once he saw her.

Stanton was expecting a high school senior to walk into his office, awkward, nervous, probably with a bad case of acne. Instead, a poised, tall, stunning young woman dressed in a tailored navy suit, wearing three-inch navy pumps, and carrying a matching bag entered his office. He had planned on remaining seated, but in the sudden presence of such radiant femininity, he quickly stood and extended his hand, saying redundantly, "Hello, I'm Ben Stanton."

Tracy flashed him a smile that indicated both respect for his television stardom and her enthusiasm at meeting him. "You're even better looking in person! I don't believe it!"

"Ah, well, television is not a flattering medium. One's faults are always maximized."

"I'd never noticed any faults. You are simply more—overpowering, I think is the word—in person."

"Well, thank you." Her flattery had reduced him to a blithering idiot, but he loved it nonetheless. "Please sit down."

He began by reiterating to her that they had no money to pay her, that it didn't seem right to have someone work for them without pay. She countered by saying that he could consider it a tutorial experience for her. She should actually be paying him tuition. She was certain she would learn much by being physically present in the studio, even if she was only emptying wastebaskets.

How could he answer her? How could he tell her that her physical appearance, the radiance of her smile, would be a terrible distraction to the cameramen, to the production assistant who was an incurable womanizer, to literally everyone in the studio? So instead of telling her all the thoughts flooding his mind, he inexplicably invited her to stay for the afternoon's show and then "have a bite to eat across the street with me."

She not only spent the morning at the studio, sitting in the control room while the show was done live, but she also took notes. She tried to think of all the ways she could help him.

The show Ben Stanton co-hosted with raven-haired Maureen Kelly was one of the most popular daytime shows aired in Washington. Called "Today's Journal," it was one of the first "magazine" format shows, which combined news and entertainment. Stanton handled all the "hard" news and interviews with key personalities in fast-breaking stories. Maureen did many of the "soft" interviews, especially if there was a woman's slant involved. And on most shows they teamed up for an interview with a national celebrity, a book author, a movie star, a member of Congress or the cabinet, or an international diplomat or celebrity.

The show aired live every weekday; it was the most popular midday show in Washington, yet they had a small staff. Clearly, Tracy told herself reassuringly, they could use an extra pair of hands, eyes, and feet. She would give anything for the opportunity to work for them for free for the summer. She had to convince him!

Stanton began their lunch by ordering a martini. Then he sat back and looked at the sophisticated woman who was offering to run errands for him. "So tell me, how do you think you can help us?"

"I can type, take shorthand, answer phones, conduct pre-interviews, read books for you in advance and prepare questions for your interview, and in a pinch I could help with makeup." She paused to think if she had left anything out. "Also I can make coffee and serve it, carry in breakfast and lunch. And I can give you a critique every afternoon at six over your first after-work drink!" She flashed him a wicked smile.

He grinned at her audacity. "How would Manuel feel about that?"

"Only your first drink. After that I disappear, you can count on it."

"How were you planning on dressing for the job?" She looked at him with a puzzled expression, so he decided to level with her. "Quite frankly, you look too good, too glamorous. You're too much of a threat to Maureen. She doesn't like to have competition on the set."

"But I won't be on-camera."

"No, but you will be in the same offices all day long."

"How should I dress? You tell me."

"Like a high school girl who has been hired to be a gofer. No high heels, not so much make-up, and"—he paused to let a teasing smile spread across his face—"can't you do something to your face so you won't be so beautiful?"

For the first time that day, Tracy blushed, realizing that he was joshing her.

"Well, you don't have to look ugly, but for God's sake don't come in here looking like you do today. Four different people thought you were a movie star here for a guest appearance. I've never had so many questions."

Tracy followed Stanton's instructions about her appearance, and within a week she had won Maureen over. Maureen became an ideal, something to aspire to, and Tracy found herself obsessed twenty-four hours a day with the show.

Within two weeks she had so insinuated herself into the team that they gave her several books to summarize and prepare questions about for the co-hosts. She read the books during the evenings, thereby saving valuable studio time for learning all she could about the business of television production. She overcame her inclination to shyness and forced herself to have a beer with the crew, staying after work to go out with them for a quick deli sandwich.

Her main attention, however, was focused on Ben and Maureen. Realizing that although they were of equal public stature, Maureen probably had more clout with the owner of the station—it was rumored that she was his mistress—Tracy lay awake nights trying to figure out small ways to please her. She went along with Maureen to the hairdresser to brief her on a book while she had her hair cut and blown dry. She volunteered to take her clothes to the cleaners one day when Maureen spilled coffee on her jacket. And Tracy observed every item of clothing Maureen and the other female broadcasters wore. She began to keep a daily journal of their clothes, and long after Ben and Maureen had left the studio, Tracy stayed to watch the activity in the newsroom as the local news team prepared for the evening news.

All the studio personnel knew her by her first name by the end of the first month; no one questioned her right to be wherever she happened to be in the studio, and she had begun to position herself in the control room next to the "boss," Ted Ryan. Charmed by her enthusiasm and quickness of mind, he answered all her questions and was rewarded by her sincere words of thanks and radiant smiles.

At the end of the first month, Ben called her into

his office, shut the door, and told her that he had managed to get a salary for her. "It's not much, but you have been so marvelous that Maureen and I went together to Mr. Albertini and pleaded your case. From now on we can pay you seventy-five dollars a week."

"That's . . . that's incredible. Oh, I love you, Ben!" In her enthusiasm, she hugged and kissed him as she might have hugged Manuel.

"Hey, hey—that's okay, kid. You don't have to love me, only keep on with the good work." He moved backward, trying to avoid the physical contact she had initiated. "And don't forget, I'm a lecherous old man. Avoid me whenever possible and we'll continue to work well together."

Later that night she replayed the scene over and over again in her imagination. What had he meant? Was it possible that a television star like Ben Stanton found her sexually attractive? Impossible! No way! She was a child; he was old enough to be her father. It was absurd. Yet he had said it, and he had seemed vaguely embarrassed. True, she could have thanked him in a more professional, adult way; she should not have been so carried away. Yet it was so wonderful to know they liked her, to know they needed her and wanted her to stay—enough to pay her!

Ben didn't call her into his office often after that, and she spent most of her time with Maureen, running errands, helping Maureen choose clothes, greeting a guest because Maureen wasn't out of make-up yet, generally being Maureen's private assistant as well as a researcher.

The summer was over quickly, and even as she packed up the few personal things she kept in her desk and prepared for the "going-away" party the crew was holding for her across the street at the deli, she knew it had been the happiest summer of her life—well, at least the happiest summer she could remember. She had been part of a team, and she had been building toward a future for herself, for the day when she would have a show to host, when she would become a Maureen.

Ben walked into the office she shared with several researchers and said: "I've come to escort the most beautiful errand girl television has ever had to her party!"

"Oh, Ben, how can I ever thank you? I've learned so much this summer!"

"So Manuel's plan didn't work quite like he had hoped." Ben eased himself into the chair by her desk. "You loved every minute of it, didn't you?"

Her face told it all. She positively thrived on the hard work and the frantic atmosphere.

"I've come to make you an offer you can't refuse. How about working part-time for us during the school year?"

"I'd love to! Oh, you can't imagine how I've dreaded today—leaving the show, leaving you and Maureen. But . . ."

Sensing her hesitation, Ben drummed his fingers on the desk. "Well?"

"I don't know. Do you really think I can handle a full load of classes and work part-time? And with the show in the middle of the day . . . well, I don't see how it would be physically possible."

"We've thought about that. Maureen and I had dinner last night and discussed this, and we decided that you could be invaluable to us if you'd simply continue to handle all the books. You can do it at your convenience, and drop the summaries and questions off on your way to class. If we have other special needs that you can work into your schedule, we'll let you know. And of course, we'd welcome your critiques."

This last comment was a bit of a jibe. Tracy had been outspoken in her objection to some of the guests who had been given "free air time," and she had let her feelings be known. In retrospect—and after some of the ratings had come in—Maureen and Ben had begrudgingly admitted that she had some sort of sixth sense for what would play well and what would bomb. They had come to trust her instincts and judgments, which was remarkably on target for a seventeen-year-old student.

"How many hours a week do you want me to work?"

"Doesn't matter. Whatever you can spare from your studies. I've told you, kid, those classes are going to be a waste of your time. You're going to be bored out of your skull. You won't learn one thing you haven't already learned a hundred times over this summer. You could probably cut all the classes and get an A on the exam."

"Yeah. Well, there's also history and econ and English . . . Can I have three weeks off to get started in college? Then I'll come back and help,out whenever I can."

"Sounds good. We also decided we want you back next summer." He stopped to savor the wonderful look of surprise and gratitude that illuminated her eyes. "And now, my lady, let us go to your party!"

As he ushered her across the street to the party, his arm around her waist, she remembered the time she had impulsively kissed him and wondered if what she was feeling in her stomach was related to that.

* * *

Tracy had thought fondly of Maureen and Ben as she packed her clothes to move out of Manuel's house. She felt affection for them, a feeling she had never had for anyone besides her foster parents. Her "mentors" had become the predominant influence in her life, and watching their program each day had become a necessity. She missed the excitement of the studio, the thrill she always experienced when the set was hushed in anticipation of air time, and the floor manager was giving the signals: "three minutes to air," "two minutes to air," "one minute to air," and finally the seconds were counted off, and the magic began. Whether she was in the control room or on the floor, her stomach always lurched when Ben opened the program. It was a moment she yearned for, the time when she would be on the set, on-camera, instead of only a part of the production team. But then she stilled the pounding of her heart, reminding herself, "I'm only seventeen. But someday . . . someday soon."

"What a magnificent color! I love it!" Tracy bent down to kiss her foster mother. She had opened a large box containing a raspberry mohair sweater that Rosina had lovingly made for her as a special "going-away-to-college" gift. Actually Tracy had not gone far from Manuel and Rosina's Bethesda home; she had simply packed up her clothes, her phonograph, and her clock radio and moved five miles away to a furnished apartment in Chevy Chase.

Given her own choice, she would have preferred to remain living with the couple who had loved her and lavished such wonderful care on her since her mother's death. But Manuel had insisted, carefully explaining to her that their ways were "from the old country" and that though they loved her dearly and hoped she would visit at least once a week, they wanted her to live in her own apartment, "so you can have the kind of social life an American college girl should have." Tracy understood, though he never actually said it, that it was her lack of interest in boys that had made Manuel so determined to move her out of their home. Perhaps he felt she was ashamed to bring boys to their home, but that was ridiculous!

"So tell me." Tracy grinned mischievously at Rosina. "What did Manuel think of Kristy?"

Rosina hesitated, determined to say the right thing. "He thought she was . . . charming and obviously very smart. And he's glad you've found someone quickly with the same interests. We're really very pleased."

Tracy had met Kristy Trenton, a gorgeous, sun-browned blonde with twinkling silvery-green eyes and a sparkling, irreverent wit while the two of them had sat nervously waiting for their first meeting with the head of the communications department at American University. They were struggling over their schedules, trying to decide which history and economics classes to take. They discovered that they would be together in two classes—the Fundamentals of Television, and Broadcast Journalism I. From that, they launched into a discussion of where they were living and when Kristy mentioned that she was apartment-shopping, Tracy quickly invited her to meet her for lunch after their conferences were over. "I have a two-bedroom apartment, and I'm looking for a roommate. Maybe we could work something out."

Tracy later told Rosina that she had known at the end of that first lunch that they would become friends, even if they didn't become roommates. It was the first time in her life that Tracy had felt such instant rapport with another person. Perhaps, she told herself, it was because they both had similar career goals, and they seemed so equal. Both were obviously extremely attractive and both had been the "stars" at their respective high schools. The envy that Tracy so often felt on the part of other girls did not come from Kristy; there was only a mutual respect. They both took their dreams seriously and neither of them doubted for an instant that they would succeed.

There were also differences. Kristy was very much "into boys," as she said, and she had been homecoming queen as well as the drama star of her high school in Michigan. She had a great sense of fun and was clearly dedicated to enjoying her college career, whereas Tracy was serious and barely knew how to have fun. For her, studying and writing and working were pleasure. Kristy also had a sense of humor, a knack for practical jokes, and a way of seeing herself objectively as others might see her, and then poking fun at that image of herself.

That Kristy came from wealth was evident three days later when she moved into Tracy's apartment. She carried in her colored television, her four-speaker stereo and collection of records, and her portable hairdryer. Then she began to bring in her clothes.

Tracy had never seen such clothes—dozens of cashmere sweaters, wool skirts and slacks, three ballgowns, and half-a-dozen "dinner-dresses." And then there were dozens of designer jeans and blazers and even a red fox fur "battle-jacket"! As Tracy oohed and aahed, Kristy poked fun at her father, an executive at General Motors, who was determined she would be the best dressed co-ed in Washington.

"He wants me to find a John Kennedy, the way Jackie did! He could not care less about my television career; all he wants me to do is marry rich—'Maybe a congressman or senator!' he says. Wouldn't he love to tell that to his friends back at General Motors!"

While Tracy watched Kristy unpack, she thought of the sensible wardrobe she had accumulated over the summer—blazers, oxford shirt-type blouses, tailored slacks and skirts, and a few sweaters and scarves. All of her clothes had been bought with television in mind, with how they would look "on-camera." And she had been lucky enough to acquire a role model and tutor during the summer.

At Kristy's insistence, Tracy began to date. "You can't just study and work. You've got to have some fun! And besides, Kevin is a doll. Six-foot-three, a real hunk of man." Kevin was the first of many men, mostly seniors or graduate students, whom Kristy "fixed-up" with Tracy. Usually they doubled with Kristy and her latest love, her newest "grand passion."

Tracy had been more than a little shocked to discover that Kristy had been "doing it" since she was sixteen. But after listening to Kristy rave about the joys of being in love, the fabulous times she had spent in bed, all described in luxurious graphic technicolor for Tracy's delight—and perhaps to arouse her envy—Tracy herself began to feel that maybe she had been missing something important.

One night, as they were dining on omelettes and a carafe of chablis—Kristy believed in wine with dinner—Kristy began a double-barreled attack on

Tracy. "John told Ned you're a chill, and he's getting sick of waiting for you to put out. Mind you, darling, I'm only quoting your lovely law-school idiot."

John was the nicest of all the men Tracy had met since beginning college, but even he bored her much of the time, and although he had a magnificent physique and wonderful eyes, she couldn't feel toward him the way he said he felt toward her. One night, he had even suggested that someday they might marry! Imagine!

"You know, love, someday you're going to lose it. I don't know what you're waiting for—why you're missing all the fun."

It was a discussion they had had several times before. Kristy considered Tracy's virginity excess baggage, almost a social disease.

"I'm waiting to fall in love, that's all," Tracy responded quietly.

"Yeah, well, that's fine. Of course." Her voice dripping with sarcasm, she continued, "You don't think I fuck just to be fucking, do you? I love them first." Kristy loved to watch Tracy's face when she used four-letter words. "But the trouble is"—she stopped, grinned mischievously—"I fall in love with someone new every month."

"I've noticed." Tracy couldn't suppress a smile, thinking of all the times Kristy had come home to announce "This is it. This is the grand passion I've been waiting all my life for. No more fucking around. I'm going to marry (John, Ben, Sam, Ricky, etc., etc.)!" Three days later, she would be following some other gorgeous guy around the campus.

"You know what you need, Tracy. You need lessons in how to have fun, in how to relax. You're always so uptight, so tense—like right now! Hell, I'd like to get you drunk once, to see if you could let your hair down."

Tracy considered what Kristy said and realized that there was some truth to it. But that's who I am—can I change who I am?

"I was daydreaming about you today in econ class. That jerk who teaches it is such a bore, I can't pay attention for two minutes. Anyhow, I was thinking that John and Ned and I would all be doing you a great favor if we taught you about some of the finer things in life. Like getting stoned. Getting drunk. Getting laid. We'd be doing you a real favor. . . ."

Kristy stopped as she saw Tracy's eyes mist over with tears. "Hey, I'm only joshing you! Don't take me seriously—don't cry. Oh, Jeez, I'm sorry, I wouldn't hurt you for the world, Tracy. I love you!" And she wrapped her arms around her roommate to stop the tears.

Tracy was crying because she knew much of what Kristy said was true. Even Ben and Maureen and the crew had commented at various times on her seriousness, her inability to relax and have fun. Was it so visibly apparent to everyone? She had goals to achieve that would take work, and there was no time left for play. Hadn't that been her mother's message to her? Surely Rosina and Manuel had constantly reinforced it. Well, not Manuel so much, he had wanted her to date.

"You've done me a lot of good, Kristy. At least I'm dating every weekend now. That's more than I ever did in high school."

"Yeah. And I've got you drinking one glass of wine. Now if we can just get you into bed with a real live man before half the guys on campus decide you're a lesbian—hey, don't hit me, I'm only teasing!"

It was the week after Thanksgiving when Professor Stanley McDivit, the head of the communications department at the university, stopped Tracy as she was leaving his class and asked her to drop by his office that afternoon. He was a magnificent-looking man, a sort of Marlboro cowboy type in turtleneck and tweeds, smoking a pipe. All the females in the department had a crush on him.

"Yes, of course. What time?"

"I'm free at two if that suits you."

"I'll be there," she responded as her pulse leaped in anticipation. She grabbed a candy bar out of a vending machine instead of stopping for a proper lunch, quickly delivered three book summaries to Channel 2, and raced back to the campus, hoping to find a parking space near McDivit's office.

She raced into his office, slightly breathless but on time. He continued talking on the phone while he motioned to her to sit down. He finished the conversation, then turned his full attention on her.

"Tracy. Thanks for coming. I've been wanting to get a little better acquainted, to find out if the rumors about you are true."

Stunned, she blurted out "What rumors? I can't imagine—"

"Don't be alarmed. They are all positive. For instance, I've heard that you spent the summer working as part of the production staff for 'Today's Journal.'"

She nodded assent, and then began telling him about her experiences at WUBS, responding to his gentle, probing questions. "Have you ever been on-camera?"

"No." She thought a minute, wondering where all this was leading. "Can I ask you, sir, what this is all about?"

He finished lighting his pipe, sat back in his swivel chair once again, looked at her intently from his deep brown eyes, and then quietly began, "The communications department is going to produce a public affairs program after the first of the year, on PBS. We're going to do the whole thing—the staffing, the camera work, the research, the whole ball of wax. And I've got to begin now to choose the on-camera talent."

His appraising eyes never left her face.

"What kind of a show? What format?"

"It will be similar in format to 'Meet the Press' and 'Face the Nation.'" He watched her nod her instant familiarity with the format. "Because we are here in the nation's capital, I think we can attract members of congress, diplomats, business leaders, members of the cabinet." He paused to let her ponder the implications. Then he continued, "Mind you, there will be no open tryouts. The department has decided to invite those students who show the most promise of having a future on-camera to try out for the position of moderator and panelists. We'll rotate panelists so that the best students will have the opportunity to appear several times during the year."

"I see." Her heart was thudding—could he hear it from where he sat? Was he going to invite her to try out?

"Since you've never appeared on camera, I think you and I need to spend some time getting you ready. When I think you are, we'll make a tape. Six members of the faculty will decide who the moderator will be for this coming semester, based solely on taped pieces. Then we'll staff out the rest of the show and be prepared to tape our first show right after the New Year."

He waited for her response, but she was still trying to believe what he had implied, that she was being invited to try out for the moderator slot.

As if he could read her mind, he said, "You are the only freshman being invited to try out."

She felt her face flaming. She wanted to hug him and scream her joy to the world, but she contained her enthusiasm and said quietly, "Thank you for your vote of confidence. When can we begin rehearsing—oh damn, Professor McDivit, I'm so thrilled I could kiss you! Thank you so much! This is like a dream for me." She began searching in her bag for a tissue.

"There's one wrinkle. If you are chosen as moderator, I would expect you to devote all your free time to this. You'd have to quit your job at 'Today's Journal.' You might want to think about that."

It didn't take her a second. On-camera opportunity could not be passed up, not even for Ben and Maureen. Besides, she could always go back to them in the summer.

"No problem, sir. I'd quit in a minute for an opportunity to be on camera."

He smiled broadly. "I thought you'd see the possibilities."

They set an appointment for the next afternoon and she left his office after thanking him profusely one more time. She was dying to find Kristy and share her good news, but then she was jolted by the realization that Kristy would be envious, and with good reason. She calmed herself by going home and writing pages and pages in her diary. Ever since her mother died, she had kept a diary, a sort of letter to her mother telling her the good and bad things of her life, the hopes, fears, and anger. She had no intention of ever doing anything with the diary, but she instinctively knew that it was a form of therapy for her, a place to vent her emotions.

A week later, Professor McDivit shot a fifteen-minute film of Tracy and promised her he would notify her as soon as the faculty made their decision. She fell asleep every night imagining the possibilities, thinking of how she would invite Ben and Maureen to watch her, planning her future. She dreamt about it, and then she woke up thinking of it. She lost five pounds without trying; she was too nervous to eat.

The last class before Christmas break was over. She lingered behind, picking up her things slowly, hoping he would approach her. Sure enough, he walked toward her as the last student was leaving the class.

"Time for a cup of coffee?"

"Sure!"

She struggled to be casual during the walk to the student union, trying hard not to ask the question that was almost bursting from her lips. When they were seated at a table for two, in a corner where no one could eavesdrop, he lit his pipe and then slowly began.

"I've something to discuss with you."

His somber voice told all. She hadn't made it.

"The faculty has selected Kevin White to be the moderator of 'College Forum'." He waited only a second, saw the disappointment in her eyes, and watched her trying to disguise it.

"I didn't think a freshman—"

"You didn't let me finish. You were their second

choice. In my eyes, you were the only choice, but they couldn't seem to buy the idea of a female as moderator of what they hope will be a very serious public affairs show."

He puffed on his pipe, silencing her with his hand.

"You will be the permanent panelist."

"What do you mean, exactly?"

"You will be on every show. You will be the toughest questioner, and you will help me with the research and briefing the other panelists. Not only will you be part of the on-camera talent, you will be listed in the credits as a research assistant."

She beamed. Her eyes began to tear and her palms were sweating, but she was speechless.

"I take it you agree."

"Agree? I'd have to be an idiot not to. What a magnificent opportunity! I promise you, I'll do a great job for you!"

"You'll have to quit your job."

"As long as I can be on-camera, I'll do anything. I'll stand on my head and do handsprings."

He laughed, then got serious again. "Our first taping is set for January 5, and the guest is Senator Hubert Humphrey. I'm hoping you'll pull together all the research by December 27. We'll need two briefing sessions before the show, so if you could meet with me during Christmas break, I'd appreciate it."

What a wonderful Christmas she would have— with a project like this to work on, to dream about—and this wonderful man to work with. The thought crossed her mind that he had created the position of permanent panelist especially for her, but she quickly pushed it to the back of her head.

"A couple more things—go to Saks the day of the

taping and have Mahin do your hair. She will know exactly the look I want. And do you have a tailored suit you can wear, and a blouse with a feminine ruffle around the neck?"

Tracy nodded, knowing Rosina would love the opportunity to take her shopping for her television wardrobe.

Again, as if reading her thoughts, he said, "If you're going shopping for new clothes, bring them here on approval and we'll look at you through the eyes of the camera. I want the most flattering colors on you, and I want you to look very softly feminine in a tailored suit. Do you get what I mean?"

She was astounded at his overwhelming personal interest in her. It seemed as if he was intent on creating his own star.

"And as your pay for all this hard work, I will arrange for a set of tapes to be made for you. Who knows, someday your appearances on 'College Forum' may be the stepping stone to a real television career. At least, that's the idea."

She couldn't resist it another moment. She reached for his freckled, hairy hand which was resting on the table, squeezed it, and said, "I'll never forget this, sir, it's the greatest thing that's ever happened to me. I'll never be able to thank you enough."

"Whoa, whoa—we haven't even done the first show yet! You may grow to hate me. I can be a mean son-of-a-bitch under pressure." He paused and relit his pipe while she sipped her coffee, once again ashamed of her outburst.

"I'm going to be relying heavily on you because you've had more real-life studio experience than any of the others, and I'll bear down hard." He saw a question form in her eyes. "Yes?"

"This is probably silly, but why? Why are you giving me, a freshman and a female too, this opportunity?"

"Simple. I recognize a star when I see one. Someday I'll be able to tell my children that I gave you your first chance in television. Oh, one more thing, you can drop the 'sir'. We're colleagues—sort of—now."

After that she raced home and inscribed those words in her diary in royal-blue ink.

Chapter Seventeen

"Five seconds to air."

The countdown began. Cardboard signs passed in front of them. 4 . . . 3 . . . 2 . . . 1 . . . 30 seconds . . .

The floor director pointed at Kevin White, and the announcer began speaking while one camera focused on Kevin and Senator Hubert Humphrey. The second camera, back a few feet from the four panelists behind their desks, was poised, ready to begin with Tracy. The voice-over began:

"From the nation's capitol, The American University proudly presents the first in a series of exchanges between national and international leaders and America's young adults on issues of crucial concern to us all. Welcome to the first edition of 'College Forum'."

WHITE:

"Good afternoon. My name is Kevin White. Welcome to 'College Forum.' We are very honored to have with us for this first program a man who holds the record for the most appearances on shows similar to this on the commercial networks. Former Vice-President Hubert Humphrey, currently a member of the Senate from Minnesota, has appeared on "Face the Nation," "Issues and Answers," and "Meet the Press." We are extremely pleased that you could make time to join us here today, Senator."

HUMPHREY:

"Thank you, Kevin. I'm delighted to be with you young people here today."

WHITE:

"And now meet our student panelists: Tracy Brown . . ."

Tracy smiled a broad smile for the camera. It would be her last calculated smile until the show was closing. The camera came in for a close-up on each student, then panned them all as Kevin said:

"And now for the first question, back to Tracy."

After twenty-eight minutes of questions and answers, Kevin once again turned to Tracy for the last question.

"Senator Humphrey, what is your position on granting amnesty to those young men who fled the country to avoid going to Vietnam?"

Humphrey answered, "Not yet. Not while we still have troops in Vietnam. Which brings me to a point I've been wanting to make here today. I'm for the immediate withdrawal of our troops. It's taking Mr. Nixon longer to withdraw our troops than it took us to defeat Hitler. Had I been elected in 1968, we would now be out of that war. I repeat that pledge."

The announcer came back on while the camera continued to film the students and Humphrey. Kevin turned to Humphrey and said, "You'll probably find this hard to believe, but Tracy is a great fan of yours. In fact, our problem in preparing for this show was that no one wanted to ask tough questions."

Humphrey laughed and looked at Tracy, who finally flashed him one of her characteristically radiant smiles, affirming what Kevin had said. "Well," Humphrey said in a loud voice, "if that's how Tracy treats a friend, let's hope she interviews Nixon soon!"

Everyone laughed, the tension of the telecast was broken, and the floor director signaled that the cameras were off. They were free to move about the set.

Professor McDivit joined them from his perch in the control room. There was much handshaking and congratulations all around. They posed for pictures. Tracy took it upon herself to walk Senator Humphrey to the door, explaining all the while that she had to make her questions tough to keep the audience from knowing he was really her first choice for President.

"Listen, you're terrific. You'll go far in this business. Why don't you come down to my office and meet my gang? If I can break away, we'll have lunch."

"I might take you up on that, Senator. Bye, now!" And as he waved farewell, she remembered the time when she was a small child, and he had joined her parents for a Sunday afternoon luncheon at the embassy. She had sat on his lap. She had a picture of this scene in the scrapbook Rosina had stolen for her when her father left for Italy. But she couldn't bring herself to tell Humphrey this; she could not take a chance on revealing her real identity to anyone, for the sake of her beloved mother. Then she thought of Rosina and Manuel and Ben and Maureen. She had alerted all of them to watch. She must run and call Rosina.

The last television show of the spring semester was over, exams were finished, and as a celebration Stanley McDivit had invited the student panelists and the staff and crew of "College Forum" to Mr. Smith's, a popular food-and-dancing emporium in Georgetown. During the season, they had been fortunate enough to get most of the Democratic presidential candidates on their program, and the last guest had been George McGovern that afternoon.

Kristy Trenton, who had appeared on the program twice as a panelist, was now dating Kevin White steadily. The two of them supported George McGovern and were elated with the telecast. Tracy, as usual, had gotten her digs in.

"That was dirty pool, Tracy, telling McGovern his welfare reform proposals would cost the taxpayers $72 billion. Where did you get that figure anyway?" asked Kevin.

"You notice McGovern didn't dispute the figure, so there must be some truth to it. He probably calculates it even higher, if he's bothered to figure it out." She sipped on her Scotch and soda, then continued. "I'm telling you, Kevin, the American people are not ready for such a radical shift to the left."

Kristy took up Kevin's argument. "I resented

your characterization of his proposed cuts in defense spending and space exploration policies as 'national suicide.' That's a great exaggeration."

"It probably doesn't matter who the Democrats nominate," Stanley McDivit offered. "Nixon will be re-elected. He's got the initiative. Trips to Russia and China, a solid economy—and the Democrats in disarray."

"Oh, how can you say that?" groaned Tracy.

"Because much as I dislike the man, he'll probably win again." McDivit placed his pipe on the table, took Tracy's hand in his, and said, "Let's dance."

Her heart jumped at his touch; then, as she looked at his twinkling brown eyes, she felt her face begin to glow. *I'm glad it's dark in here*, she thought as she made her way to the dance floor.

He took her in his arms with great authority, as if she belonged to him already, and without missing a beat he kissed her forehead softly, then tucked her head beneath his own in such a way that his lips continued to graze her temple. Their bodies melted together and they danced as one person.

She told herself that she should make some attempt at conversation, but she could think of nothing to say. She could only think about how wonderful it felt to be in his arms, to have him take possession of her body the way he had dominated her mind during the past seven months.

They danced through one entire song without saying a word to each other. When Tracy opened her eyes, she saw that he had moved her to the other side of the dance floor, where none of the others could see them. The music began again immediately, but not before she had a chance to look him squarely in the eyes and see that he was feeling the same overwhelming emotions she was. Quickly, she looked away, burying her face in his coat, willing him not to stop holding her.

"I've been struggling to keep my hands off you all year, Tracy, and now, the last night, I'm making a fool of myself." She smiled weakly up at him, feeling dizzy and unsure of what he meant.

Then he gripped her body with a new fervor, and with mingled delight and horror she realized that he had a huge erection. How embarrassed he must be, she thought, but then, at long last, she allowed herself to acknowledge that he was sexually attracted to her. It hadn't been her imagination! But how could it be? This sexy, sophisticated, older, incredible man—how could he be turned on by her? *Oh God, don't let him stop! I love him! I love him!*

The music stopped for a moment, then the band swung into a fast number. McDivit grinned at her, a boyish, sheepish look on his face, and muttered something she could barely make out about the best intentions of mice and men.

Tracy summoned up a new boldness of spirit. Feeling the power of having a man in her thrall, recognizing the delicious feeling of it, she began to flirt openly with him as they danced around the floor. With her eyes she told him she loved him over and over again, though not a word passed from her lips.

Abruptly, he took her hand and led her off the floor toward the door. "Let's get a breath of fresh air."

She was terrified. He seemed angry, brusque.

Outdoors, they walked up M Street toward Wisconsin Avenue. He said nothing, but held her hand tightly.

After what seemed an eternity, he said quietly, "I'm leaving for Wisconsin tomorrow morning."

"Oh," she responded weakly, her heart breaking in a million pieces.

"I spend every summer in Wisconsin with my two children."

"Why do they live there?"

"Because my wife is institutionalized. Mental illness." He paused to let that sink in, then continued, "Our children live with her parents in Madison. I teach there during the summers and spend lots of time with the kids."

"I see." But her heart wanted to cry out, *It's not fair! I finally fall in love only to find out he's married!* Then a demanding inner voice told her she had always known it; it was no surprise.

He stopped walking, and with both hands he turned her gently toward him. He lifted her chin with his hand, forcing her to look him in the eyes. "All that I've told you doesn't change the fact that I've fallen in love with you, my Tracy, my darling. I'm going to spend the summer trying to straighten out my heart. But right now . . ."

He held her face in both his hands, gently, lovingly. Slowly he bent to kiss her. Stunned, she felt his gentle, then demanding mouth, and she felt herself kiss him with great fervor, though she had willed herself not to respond. Once, twice, then after a long look in her eyes, he kissed her a third time, this time wrapping his arms around her body and holding her as closely as he could without crushing her bones.

"I haven't felt like this in twenty years. I don't know what you've done to me—you've bewitched me!" He kissed her forehead one last time, then admonished her to go quickly back to the restaurant, to the ladies room to repair her makeup.

But even after she had fixed her makeup and returned to the table, she continued to feel light-headed, both enamored of and furious with him. At last she knew what love felt like—at last a man she would willingly give herself to, a man she could trust, loved her. And he was leaving her the next morning. He wasn't even going to give her the chance to make love to him—which at that moment she wanted to do more than anything else in the world. It occured to her that she could beg him to take her home that very night and forget about tomorrow morning—take her home and teach her the wondrous joys of lovemaking.

But there was no way she would verbalize that. No, if and when it happened, it would be his doing.

He didn't ask her to dance again that evening, but left her sitting at the table with the others, who seemed so juvenile and uninteresting by comparison. He made it a point to dance with every female in their group. Bitterly, she wondered if he got an erection with each of them; then she chastized herself for letting her imagination run away with her.

Each time he returned to the table, she pointedly ignored him, but when it was time to leave, he bent down and told her he was taking her home. He gathered three other students into his car and they made their way through Friday-night traffic toward Spring Valley. Though she was seated next to him in the front seat, not a word passed between them until everyone else had been dropped off.

They drove the short distance to her apartment in silence. When he stopped the car in the parking lot, he reached for her hand.

"Tracy, I apologize for what happened tonight. I got carried away. I can't explain it. I'm usually pretty self-controlled. But the idea that I won't be seeing you every day, that I'm going away tomorrow—well, that and the Scotch, and your seductive beauty—I should be strong enough to resist. It won't happen again."

She stared down at their hands, unable to look squarely at him.

"I don't want you to be frightened. You won't be will you?"

"No."

"We must concentrate on what is important, and that's your career—making you a star!"

She felt the tears form in her eyes. She willed them to stop, but instead they spilled over and began to run down her cheeks.

They fell on his hand.

"Tracy, don't cry. I wouldn't hurt you for anything in the world—you realize that, don't you?"

She shook her head, but could not speak. She felt abandoned, as utterly abandoned as if he had died.

He reached for her head and pressed her forehead against his chest for a long moment, waiting for her sobs to subside. "I'm so sorry I've upset you like this. Can we talk about it? Can we talk about how you feel? It might help."

"I . . . I wish you weren't going away."

"I wish that in my heart, but in my head, my darling, I know it is the right thing for me to do. For both of us."

"I'm going to miss seeing you every day. It's a long time until September."

"When September comes, we probably should try not to see one another every day. It would be asking for trouble. I'm nearly twice your age, Tracy, but I'm still only a man, a man with very strong desires. We must be careful next fall."

But I don't want to be careful, I want to have an

affair with you! a voice inside her head raged at him.

"Tell me what you're thinking."

"I can't."

"Why? Don't you trust me? I've shared my innermost feelings—to my horror—with you tonight. Now you be honest with me. Why are you so upset?"

"Because . . . because I love you, you dope! Can't you see it, haven't you felt it all semester long?" Then her sobs took over her body again and she leaned against his chest, burying her face in his jacket. For a long time they sat like that, his hands stroking her hair, trying to soothe her with his touch.

"Let's spend the summer concentrating on other things," he said. "You've got your job to keep you busy. I won't be quite so busy, but the children will occupy much of my time. We'll let it rest, then talk about things again next fall. Okay?"

She wondered what he meant. Was he giving her a reprieve? Was he opening the door a crack? Was there a chance he might permit this love between them to grow?

As if he could read her mind, he said, "I hope you know what you're asking for, my darling. A love affair with a married man twice your age would be insanity, but God knows if I'll be able to resist you. Now, let me get you inside."

When they reached the entrance to her building, she asked him, "Will you write to me? Or call me perhaps?"

"No."

Again she was desolate, destroyed.

"But . . ."

"No buts. I want you to fall in love with someone

else this summer. Someone your age who is single."

"Oh, go to hell!" she said angrily, then walked away from him toward the elevator.

Chapter Eighteen

There were those who claimed spring was the most beautiful time of year in Washington, but for Tracy it was undoubtedly the fall that stirred her senses. The air began to smell crisp and cool after the sultry, polluted heat of summer; the campus was abuzz with incoming freshmen; the bookstore was newly crowded. There was an air of anticipation about everything and everyone.

She dumped what felt like ten pounds of new books onto the back seat of her Chevy, climbed in herself, and turned the key. An idea popped into her head. It would be fun to run by Stan's office and see if he was back from Wisconsin. Classes began tomorrow, she thought, surely he must be back. And she had so much to tell him!

The summer had begun badly with his leaving, but had quickly picked up when she resumed her job at WUBS. She was a bit of a mini-celebrity at first because of her appearances on "College Forum." She had so endeared herself to the production staff the previous summer that they had become her own private fan club. The floor crew treated her to dinner at the deli her first evening back at work.

Being an errand girl was quite a comedown after spending the semester on-camera. Ben and Maureen recognized the problem and promised her that she would be permitted to make three mini-appearances during the summer season, assisting one of them with a book-and-author interview. To her delight, she not only received fan mail after each appearance, but Mr. Albertini, the station owner, stopped her one day on the set to tell her he had enjoyed her appearances immensely.

He continued the conversation by asking her about her education and her plans when she finished at American University. Then he told her, "I'd like the right of first refusal, so to speak. Come see me when you graduate. I'll see if we can find a slot for you on the evening news show." She tucked that promise in the back of her head, hoping he wouldn't forget it when the time came.

As a parting gift, Ben and Maureen presented her with a tape of her three appearances on "Today's Journal," and it was this tape she was aching to play for Stan.

Now, as she knocked on his door, she felt her stomach crawl with fear. Perhaps he wouldn't love her anymore. He had probably forgotten last spring's emotion.

"Come in!" a gruff voice answered.

She bounded in the door, grinning from ear to ear, and deposited the tape on his desk.

"Well, hello! What's this?"

She planted a kiss on his brow, then sat down across from his swivel chair and told him nonstop about her summer experiences, ending with, "I had this sudden urge to see you, and thought I'd check to see if you were in today!"

"You look incredible, a real sight for tired, lonely eyes." Realizing what he had said, he quickly changed the subject. "Let's go look at this tape."

Forty minutes later, they emerged from the studio. "Tracy, let's have dinner and talk. I've done a lot of thinking this summer, and I think I know exactly how to manage your career."

Her career wasn't foremost on her mind at that moment, but she would grab any excuse to spend a few more hours with him.

"The real dilemma is," he began after they were seated and had ordered drinks, "that you've got to finish college before you can sign on with any news organization. You know what you need to know about television, but you still need the history and economics and sociology and science—the perspective all those courses will give you. And you've probably worked long enough with 'Today's Journal' to learn what you can from that."

"But we're going to do 'College Forum' again this year, aren't we?"

"Yes. The first show is in three weeks. Are you ready for this?" He stopped long enough for the suspense to build. "I've got Kissinger lined up for it!"

"Wonderful! I can't wait!"

"I thought you'd like to get your nails into him. It should be a great challenge—for both of you. By the way, he's requested three tapes of the show from last year. Seems he's never watched the dragon lady in action, but he's heard about you."

"I can't wait!"

"Which reminds me of something else I've been thinking about this summer. You must guard against letting your partisanship show. That is one of the primary rules of broadcast journalism. You must be fair, independent, and not abrasive."

"What I'd like to be is a female Dan Rather!"

"Yeah, well that's exactly what I'm trying to warn you against. He's going to get into trouble sooner or later for being too anti-Nixon. You wait and see."

They each sipped on their drinks, then he said, "I want you to concentrate on journalism courses this year instead of television. Sooner or later, and the sooner the better, you need to get out there with the rest of them and prove yourself as a newswoman. I mean, cover the courthouse, the police station, the traffic accidents, the whole ball-of-wax that makes up the evening news at a local station."

"I had an idea along that line this summer," she jumped in to volunteer, "that I would like to get your opinion on. I want to do interviews—you know, like Oriani Fallaci. Perhaps I could get published in the *Washingtonian*, or the *Atlantic Monthly*. Publications like that."

He looked at her with mild astonishment playing around his eyes. "That's what I like about you, Tracy. No lack of self-confidence or ambition." He puffed on his pipe, looked at her closely, and added in a soft voice, "You know, my love, success brings success, but it doesn't necessarily bring happiness."

"What's that supposed to mean?" She was angry suddenly, and also puzzled.

"How's your social life been this summer?"

"What business is it of yours?"

"It's not my business. But I'm curious."

"I haven't had time for any social life this summer," she nearly spat out at him.

"I was afraid of that. You're working too hard. You need more fun in your life."

"My work is my fun. When I'm not at the studio, I watch every TV public affairs program. And when I'm not watching, I'm reading."

"So I have no immediate competition."

"No, but I do. Your wife and children."

"Sounds to me like you have a lot of pent-up anger at me. I am sorry you feel that way, Tracy. I don't want it to get in the way of the work we have to do together." She didn't respond, but took a big drink from her Scotch. She was livid.

"I suggest you take a good look at the law students, the medical students, the graduate students—and find yourself a lover."

"Yeah. Well, I'm glad to know that's what you want me to do. At least we've cleared that up." She took another big drink. "But of course it's easier said than done. I've yet to meet a man on campus who interests me."

He puffed on his pipe, moved his drink so the waitress could put his dinner plate down, then looked up at Tracy, in control of his own emotions once again. "Who are you going to interview first?"

"Would you believe Federal District Judge David Bazelon?"

"Hey, that's terrific! Do you have an appointment?"

"Yes—this weekend, three hours on Saturday at his Watergate apartment. And I'm taking my camera and tape recorder."

"Good for you!"

The Kissinger show was over, and the last panelist had left the studio when Stan walked into the conference room where Tracy had briefed the other panelists before the telecast began. She was gathering up her research material, especially carefully this time because she was planning on doing an interview with Kissinger for the *Washington Journal.* He had agreed to it before the telecast and confirmed their appointment afterwards; she was thrilled at the prospect.

"That was quite a coup, getting him to agree to an interview, especially after the way you grilled him."

"Terrific, isn't it! I'm so excited!"

"That makes three things we have to celebrate this evening. Your Bazelon article, your Kissinger date. And my thirty-eighth birthday!"

"Today is your birthday? I wish we had known—the panelists would have loved to celebrate it with you."

"I don't want their company. The only person's company I want this evening is yours."

Oh God, here it goes again, she thought, as her heart began to thump loudly in her chest.

"I've made reservations for two at the Old Angler's Inn if you feel like a ride in the country."

"That sounds lovely. But I'd like to go home first and change."

"Of course. Meet me at my house at seven?" He wrote down the address and handed it to her.

She quickly gathered the rest of the materials into her briefcase and fled to her apartment. What did this mean? They actually had a date, a real date, didn't they? Had he reconsidered? Oh, if only she could read his mind the way he seemed to read hers!

As she luxuriated in a warm bubble bath and shaved her legs—be prepared for any eventuality, she told herself—she fantasized how she would seduce him, how she would simply force him to take her into his bed that evening. She dressed in a new scooped-neck white angora sweater Rosina had made for her and a black wool skirt; she wore her mother's opera-length pearls and matching earrings for the first time. Deep in her heart, she had always known she was saving those pearls for a very special occasion. Tonight was that occasion.

"You smell wonderful, absolutely delicious!" he exclaimed as he walked her to his car. "I've never noticed you wearing perfume before."

She flashed him a coy smile and said, "Only on dates."

He opened the door for her and continued to hold her hand until she was comfortably seated. As he walked around to the other side of the car, she thought how magnificent it was to be with a real gentleman, a man who cherished her.

She snuggled close to him as they drove out MacArthur Boulevard to the century-old restaurant. She wanted him to understand clearly that she felt they were together as potential lovers, not as professor and student, mentor and protegée.

"Good evening, Dr. McDivit, so nice to see you again," Andre, the maitre d', greeted him as they walked into the old stone restaurant. The smell of pine logs burning, the nostalgic voice of Juliette Greco on the stereo, and the shadowy profiles of other loving couples silhouetted by dozens of glowing candles, caused Tracy to marvel at the absolutely perfect setting Stan had chosen for the long-awaited seduction. Surely he had the same idea in his mind.

Andre seated them on a deep, musty-smelling velvet sofa near the fireplace. "Your champagne will be right over. I have it cooling."

"Thank you, Andre." Stan turned his attention to Tracy. "I took the liberty of ordering champagne, and dinner also, ahead of time. I think you'll like it."

"I know I will," she answered as she snuggled closer to him. "What a wonderful lover's hideaway this is. Do you come here often?"

"Maybe once a month. It's always been my favorite restaurant in the Washington area." He brushed a wayward curl back off her forehead. "But I've never been here with anyone so beautiful before."

The champagne arrived. The waiter showed the label to Stan—"a very good year, sir"—and promptly began the tasting ceremony.

"Fine!" Stan pronounced.

The waiter poured some champagne into a fluted crystal glass and offered it to Tracy. Her mind traveled backward in time, and she seemed to get a fleeting glimpse of her father offering her a sip from his glass—it must have been New Year's Eve or some other grand occasion. He had been so dashing, so handsome and suave.

Stan held his glass toward hers and said, "I want to toast television's next superstar, and . . . our love."

She clinked her glass against his, hearing his words reverberate unmistakably. Hadn't he just said it? Hadn't he just confirmed her rampaging wish that they should be lovers? It was almost too good to believe. She felt she should hold her breath, cross all her fingers and toes. . . .

After a long speechless moment, she found her voice and quietly asked, "You've changed your mind then?"

"I'm not sure my mind is even working. I had a thought about you this morning when I saw you working Kissinger over before the show—by the way, you'd better be careful around him, he is known to like beautiful women—and I had this sudden revelation that you are the kind of woman who always gets what you set your heart on. There are women like that, you know. They have a tenacity and a sort of charisma that seem to open every door for them. You are one of those, Tracy. It will take you far." He saluted her with his upraised glass, then sipped from it.

"Into your bed?" she boldly asked as she mischievously grinned into his velvet-brown eyes.

"Aahh . . . time will tell. . . ."

"And this will be a victory for me—but not for you?"

"You can't stop interviewing, can you? You can't stop analyzing and simply enjoy the moment."

"I'm sorry. Forgive me. Kristy is always nagging me about things like that. Both of you are right."

"Which reminds me. Will Kristy miss you if you don't go home tonight?"

That's it, she thought. *He's committed himself. There's no turning back now.* "No, she'll think I'm staying overnight with Rosina and Manuel. I do that every now and then. Besides, Kristy spends most nights at Kevin's."

He lit his pipe and nodded his understanding of the Kevin-Kristy situation.

"Tell me about Rosina and Manuel. I've never met them. You didn't invite them to our party last spring."

"They are my legal guardians and I have lived with them since my mother's accident. I guess they are sort of foster parents." She paused, wondering what else she could say about them. "They are good people and have been very good to me."

"Are they relatives?"

"No. They were close friends of my mother, and

she had no other family except an aunt in New York City, and that's no place to raise a teenager, they decided, so I ended up with Manuel and Rosina."

"Your father?"

"My father was killed in a plane crash when I was small." She lied easily, glibly. She had told the same lie so many times it felt like the truth. Besides, in a way, he was dead. Dead to her.

"Strange . . . I never realized what a traumatic childhood you've had. I somehow imagined you had been born into a wealthy, aristocratic family—perhaps European nobility."

"Whatever in the world made you think that?"

"I'm not sure. There's something about your looks, about your carriage, your obvious refinement. It's as if you've been to a finishing school. There's something so out of place about you. When you use a four letter word, it's so out of character. . . ."

"That's crazy. I grew up here in Bethesda. I've never been to Europe!" Suddenly on the defensive, Tracy was horrified that he had so nearly guessed the truth.

At that moment, the waiter returned to escort them up the circular wrought-iron staircase to the dining room. Their conversation ranged far and wide over their dinner of chauteaubriand bouquetierre and Caesar salad for two. When the raspberries with Amaretto were served, it took a more intimate turn.

"You asked me a question earlier this evening, Tracy, and it deserves an answer—or at least some discussion. You asked me why I had changed my mind."

Her stomach cramped, fearful that he was about to change his mind again.

"I've given our case a lot of thought. Having an

affair with you will be a joy for me, darling, but it could be a disaster for you. I keep trying to think about what is best for you, and part of me feels very strongly that this is an awful idea. I'm married—and I want you to understand that if Myra ever gets well enough to come back home, then this will have to end. I will never leave her; you've got to accept that."

She nodded her head, agreeing with him, though in her heart she heard a vicious voice say, *I hope she never gets well!*

"And I'm too old for you. You should be having an affair with someone much younger."

"Isn't there something to be said for experience?" she asked him with a throaty laugh and a suggestive wink.

"You are incorrigible! Absolutely corrupt! So much for my innocent European princess fantasy!"

"Indeed. That was a stupid fantasy."

"I've got a few more things to say on this subject. This will not be an exclusive relationship. You are free to date other men—and I hope you will. And I am free to see other women."

"Wow! And you call me corrupt! You're so very married, but you have a string of mistresses, is that it?"

"I didn't mean that. Of course I don't. But I insist that you see others. Otherwise—otherwise, when the day comes that it ends—and that day is inevitable—you won't be so bereft."

"You know, nothing has even happened yet. You sure are laying a heavy load on me. I don't know, maybe it isn't such a good idea. Let's get the check and go. Meanwhile, where's the ladies room?"

Tracy felt as if she had been hit in the stomach after a heavy meal. She raced down the winding staircase into the ladies' room and vomited her dinner. Why had he done this? Why had he spoiled such a beautiful evening by telling her he was going to date other women? He was an absolute cad! *I hate him!*

She sat down and leaned her head against the wall. Too much champagne, too much wine, too much Amaretto, too much heavy conversation. She sat there for a few minutes, letting her mind go blank. Then someone knocked on the door, and she answered, "I'll only be another minute." She stood up, applied some lipstick, ran a brush through her long black hair, and screwed up her courage for the evening still ahead. What the hell, she thought, if he's still willing, I am. I've got to lose my virginity someday, and he's my first choice.

They drove back to his house without talking, simply snuggling close and letting the warmth of their bodies and the haze of the champagne soothe them. He parked in the driveway and came around to her side of the car to help her out, then led her into a living room filled with modern abstract art and a multi-speaker stereo playing a Tony Bennett recording.

"Is that a record or the radio?" she asked, suddenly very nervous.

"A tape. I use very large tapes and do my own recording. This one plays for several hours. All Bennett and Sinatra. Especially selected just for you."

"For me?"

"You are Italian, aren't you?"

"Oh—well, I guess I'm lots of things—German, English, Italian, American."

"I don't know why, but I've always thought of you as Italian." He had finished fixing a fire in the fireplace, and now was standing directly in front of her. "Are you having second thoughts?" He tilted her chin upwards, forcing her to look him in the eyes.

"No. Are you?"

He didn't answer her in words. Instead he bent to kiss her lips, softly, tentatively at first. Then, without touching her otherwise, he kissed her ferociously. Her hands crept up to the back of his neck and she held on for dear life as she felt currents of heat surge through her body. All thought of restraint and ladylike behavior fled from her mind. He wrapped his muscular arms around her and his hands caressed her back, moving up and down, molding her body into his, forcing her to feel the effect she was having on him. His hands traveled down her back again, and he cupped her buttocks and pressed her pelvis into his own. For a long moment they stood suspended, swaying to the soft crooning of Sinatra, feeling the heat of their bodies mingled with the scent of the burning pine cones and cedar wood. Then, in a hoarse voice, he said, "If it's not too warm, let's try the rug."

In front of the blazing fire, on top of champagne-colored carpeting, lay a sumptuous fur rug. Stan gradually lowered her toward it. He slipped off her black pumps, massaging her feet for a fleeting moment, then moved toward her. He kissed her again, devouring her mouth, while his hand traveled over her body. It grazed her hip, traveled across her flat stomach and up to her breast. He cupped her fullness with his hand, feeling the rise and fall of her breathing. Then his fingers traced the hard, erect nipple, teasing it to even greater fullness. Each touch sent new currents racing through her body, already a pulsing instrument, crying out to be taken even further toward ecstasy. As her body strained against his hands, her mouth became the aggressor, the seeker of pleasure.

"You don't really need all these clothes," he murmured as he gently lifted the white sweater up and over her head. Then, as if in the same movement, he unfastened her bra and slipped it off, exposing her naked beauty. She saw the pleasure in his eyes and proudly offered them to his hungry lips. She was overwhelmed by a feeling of vulnerability, and at the same time awestruck by the sensations coursing through her heated limbs.

"You are beautiful, so beautiful," he sighed as he began to unfasten her skirt.

It was further than she had ever gone with any man, and as this thought crossed her mind, she realized it was as it should be. She had never been willing to give up that inner core of herself; she had never trusted a man before. She trusted Stan with her life, with her soul, with her entire being. She could open herself inside out for him, and she would intuitively understand everything that was expected of her.

He stood to undress, hurriedly unbuttoning his shirt, laying his trousers on the sofa, never taking his eyes off her creamy body, which now lay exposed before him. He devoured her with his eyes, and every place they paused, she felt flickering sensations, a vibrant tingling she had never before experienced. Then he removed his shorts and for the first time in her life she saw a fully aroused man. The sight of him both terrified her and aroused her even more. She felt a sudden desire to touch that shining, gloriously pink tumescence.

Tentatively, she reached for him and he let her explore with her fingertips, lying still for a moment to savor the exquisite sensation. To her own surprise, she enjoyed touching him as much as she had enjoyed his touching her. Impulsively she bent her lips to him. His hands flew into her hair and she felt his passion even to the roots of her hair. Then suddenly, as if he could tolerate her fondling not a moment longer, he moved her roughly back down on the rug and began to tease her body with his kisses.

With rough hands, he parted her thighs, his mouth searching for that delicate bud, and with a flickering tongue he brought her to new heights of anticipation. She was coasting, then soaring through a sea of explosive clouds; she felt the pressure building up, up, up even more until she thought she would burst, that her entire body would erupt in one volcanic cataclysm. And then it started. Up from the soles of her feet in ripple after ripple, which became tides of convulsive spasms, her body wrenched and gasped and wrenched again, and from a distance she heard herself cry out, "Oh yes, oh yes, my darling, oh it's so wonderful, don't ever stop, don't ever stop . . ."

He pulled away from her and was quickly on top of her, demanding entrance. She raised her body, now a blooming instrument of passion, now on fire with her love for him, and reaching downward she guided him inside herself. But it was not that easy. Realizing the problem, she arched her body again, willing herself to open out to him, and as he pushed for entrance, she willed herself to relax and make it possible.

It worked. He entered her and began the ancient, age-old, thrusting, pounding, thrusting. Her body met his rhythm, her spasms tightening around his spear until he gave one final thrust, cried out in delight, then lay spent, his face in her tangled hair.

Even after his spasms stopped, hers continued. She reveled in his pleasure, understanding that giving love is receiving love. Finally she comprehended the power and glory of being a woman; she understood what Kristy had been trying to tell her; she felt whole.

After a while they made love again, then showered and sipped on a bottle of champagne he had in the refrigerator, talked into the wee hours with her sitting naked on his lap. When they were exhausted, they slept in his big bed, their bodies entwined as if their very lives depended on continuing physical contact.

She awoke to the sound of birds outside the window. He was asleep, and as she looked at his face with its weather-born wrinkles and the beginnings of crow's feet and furrows in his forehead, she thought of the new knowledge she now possessed. And she knew that, in spite of his best intentions and his lofty language, she now belonged to him and he to her. This was no casual affair for either of them; there would be no other men for her, just as she was certain that he would need no other woman. She would be enough for him; she would take care of him, satisfy his every romantic fantasy, fulfill his most gargantuan sexual appetites.

It was several weeks later—several glorious weeks of daily lovers' trysts and meals and meetings—that he casually asked her, "Tell me, darling, since we're telling our whole life histories to one another these days, who was your first love?"

She had known that someday he would ask her. Didn't every man have an innate curiosity about his woman's previous sexual experience, especially her first? Yet, knowing this, she had never prepared an answer.

Watching her hesitate, he said, "You don't have to sugarcoat it. I'm not judgmental, and I do live in the present century."

"What would you think if I told you that you were the first?"

"I'd say you're a damn quick learner!"

She smiled fully in response. "You mean I'm that good?"

"Darling, let me tell you—you were born for the bedroom! You are the best!"

"Must be because I've had a good teacher."

"But you won't tell me who it was . . ."

"I just did."

He let the subject drop then, and she knew he didn't believe her. Perhaps it was just as well; he would feel guilty if he knew she had been a virgin. Kristy was right; it was a lot of useless baggage. But she was glad she had waited until he came along.

Their love blossomed and grew amidst their disappointment at the re-election of Richard Nixon, and then through a season of fairly tepid telecasts. Never losing sight of his determination to make Tracy a star, he set about teaching her everything he knew about television journalism. He made reading lists for her and discussed the books with her as she read them. He spent long hours with her going over magazines, discussing the clothes and hairstyles that were the most telegenic.

One day, he sat her down in his living room with a checklist in front of him and began giving her his appraisal of her strengths and weaknesses.

"You write well, you look terrific, and you communicate well on television. You have a real knack for ad-libbing, which is important if you ever want to be an anchor. You can be counted on in emergencies and under fire." He paused to relight his pipe. "What you need to work on now is your ability as a journalist. You must hone your story judgment, learn how to 'smell' a story. Can you recognize something that will become a story? And can you run a staff?" He paused, then continued, "Actually, I think you could probably do that very well, considering how you've handled the other panelists the past two years.

"And you've also got to work on off-the-camera skills, such things as inner-office politics. Don't forget the little smart, politic things like asking a cameraman about a sick child. Get to know the secretary of the station manager, give her a Christmas present. Because you are a woman and a threat to all other women, this is even more important for you than if you were a man."

"These are good tips for a few years down the road, Stan, but what should I do this summer?"

"I've been thinking. How about going to Albertini and asking him to make you a fill-in summer reporter for the evening news?"

"He'd never do that."

"Don't be so sure. After all, reporters take vacations, too, and usually during the summer months. You could offer to cover any beat, to substitute for any reporter on vacation. I'll splice together a special tape of your performances on 'College Forum' and take him copies of the Kissinger interview, the Bazelon interview, and the interview with Golda Meir. He can't help but be impressed with your news sense."

"I wouldn't even know how to get an appointment with him."

"Easy, darling—you call his office and ask for one."

As April turned to May, Tracy began to think about the coming summer with dread. Stan was probably going back to Wisconsin to be with his

children, though he hadn't mentioned it. He tried
to avoid all mention of his wife and children. Once
she had begged him to go with her to a concert on a
Sunday afternoon. After saying "no" calmly twice,
when she asked a third time he told her what she
didn't want to hear: "Sundays are reserved for
Myra. I visit her every Sunday at Sheppard Pratt."

Seeing the hurt in her eyes, he admonished her,
"Tracy darling, I told you at the outset that this
would be difficult. I have a wife who is ill. For her
sake, I want her well. She is showing improvement.
When she is well, she will come home, and our
relationship will have to end."

The rest of that day she walked around in a fever
of hatred for him, recognizing the whole while that
he was right and she was wrong. If it hadn't been an
obscene idea, she would have gotten down on her
knees and prayed to God that Myra would never get
well. Thoughts like that were wicked. Nevertheless,
she could not banish them from her head.

To her surprise, Mr. Albertini granted her an
appointment for the day after she called him. She
took her "ammunition," as Stan had called it, and
dressed in a bristol blue-silk dress for the interview.

After listening to Tracy present her carefully
thought-out and clearly articulated idea, Rick
Albertini sat back in his chair and smoothed his
sparse gray hair over his ears, giving himself time to
develop a response.

"I don't know. I'd have to try the idea out on the
news manager, Mr. Kook."

"I understand."

"But it's not a bad idea. And I don't have to play
your tapes—I watched you last summer, and I'm
fully aware of the high regard Ben has for you." His

eyes traveled up and down her body, mentally undressing her as he calculated what it would take to make her happy.

She said nothing, not wanting to break the spell her physical presence had so obviously created. She would let it work to her advantage. Stan, without knowing it, had taught her much more than he knew.

"I'm sure Ben and Maureen expect you back this summer. Have you spoken to them yet?"

"No. What I need at this point is to broaden my skills as a newsperson, and the only way to do that is to cover the news."

"Yes. I see. I suppose you are right." His eyes were riveted on her legs, which she recrossed for his added pleasure. "Well, let me think about it and I'll speak to Mr. Kook about this idea. I'll tell you what, leave those tapes with me for a week—in case Kook hasn't seen you." He stood up, signaling that the appointment was over.

"It's good to see you again, Tracy. You look wonderful; you get more beautiful with each year— if that's possible." He put his hand under her elbow in a possessive way to guide her out into his outer office.

"Thank you so much for your time, Mr. Albertini."

"Nonsense. It's always a pleasure to see you, Tracy. I'll call you within a week. If I don't, you call me."

Two days later, he called her to tell her she was hired, at one hundred fifty dollars a week. She would be the "roving" reporter and all-round floater during the summer months. Two hours later, Ben called to complain that she hadn't gone through him to make the appointment, saying he felt she owed him that courtesy. She pleaded that she hadn't wanted to bother him with her personal needs. But she learned a lesson—don't step on the toes of a mentor. Don't burn bridges. Finally, after listening to him harangue for twenty minutes, she insisted he let her take him out to dinner to apologize and to celebrate. He accepted; they kissed and made up. She had learned her first lesson about office politics.

Tracy began work at the WUBS evening news the day after her final exam, giving herself no time at all to brood over Stan's departure for Madison. Three days later, exhausted, but with a new kind of pride in herself—she had appeared on the evening news interviewing the county attorney about a rape case for four minutes—she marveled as she stood in the shower washing her hair that she hadn't thought of Stan once that day, so busy was she with her new career as on-the-spot newswoman. She loved it. If ever a person had chosen the perfect career, she was that person.

By the end of the summer, not only had she appeared on nearly every evening's news, but she had created a special piece—"Window on the World"—which aired every Friday evening for ten minutes. It was an idea she had one morning in the shower—she got her best ideas in the shower, so she began taking two a day! Washington was filled with foreign embassies, and in many cases the ambassadors spoke fluent English. But most Washingtonians never had any benefit from their presence in the city. Tracy devised a format which interspersed film clips from the country with new film she shot at the embassy and an interview with the ambassador and his wife. It was a clever mix of international culture and human interest, and the feature became a great favorite with the viewing audience. When the summer was over and it was time for her to take her leave, both Kook and Albertini suggested that she try to continue the Friday evening piece during the school year.

They didn't have to ask her twice!

Unbeknownst to her, Stan arrived back in Washington two weeks before the fall semester began. He watched her on ten broadcasts before he called her.

"You're back!" She gasped. "Did you listen to the news tonight?"

"Wouldn't miss it. Your voice was too high-pitched during the fire coverage."

"But I had to scream over all the noise in the background."

"I realize that. Just be conscious of your tendency to get high-pitched when you are excited, that's all. I love you, darling. Did you miss me, or have you found an exciting new lover in the diplomatic corps?"

"You've seen 'Windows' then?"

"Yes. It's brilliant. A terrific idea and well executed. My protegée is talented, but what else did I expect?"

"Are you at home?"

"Yes. All alone. And lonely."

"I'll be there in fifteen minutes!"

"Drive carefully."

"You be sure the champagne is cold and Sinatra is singing!"

They resumed their love affair with all the passion of the previous spring. It bloomed and grew amidst the unfolding tumult of The Watergate scandal.

"I told you all along, McDivit, that Nixon was

behind the whole break-in. You didn't believe me! Now admit it, Mr. Professor, which of us has the best nose for a story?" She made her demand, pounding on his hairy chest to punctuate it, as she entwined her leg in his.

He lay with his arms above his head, flat on his back, looking at her naked beauty, enjoying her fury. He couldn't suppress a grin. "I always knew Nixon was capable of masterminding the break-in, but I didn't think he was that stupid."

"It was stupidity and arrogance! He's the most arrogant son-of-a-bitch in the world. And to think the American people were stupid enough to elect him president. That's what's shocking."

"Since you are such a stunning prognosticator of world events, where will it all end? Will he resign or will he be impeached?"

"I don't think he'll ever resign. They'll have to impeach him."

"I disagree. I think if the evidence really becomes incontrovertible, he'll resign."

That morning, March 1, 1974, the Watergate grand jury had charged that seven former associates of the President "did combine, conspire, confederate, and agree together and with each other to commit offenses against the United States." Tracy had told Kristy that Nixon was behind it. She had never wavered from that position, and now it was becoming clear that Nixon had played some role in the conspiracy. Every time Stan had tried to get a member of the Nixon Administration on "College Forum," Tracy had fought him, saying that they didn't deserve air time. McDivit had told her time and again that she was letting her personal prejudices alter her professional judgment. It was their one continuing argument.

But that morning in March, Stan had something

else on his mind, and he was trying to figure out how to break it to Tracy.

After they were dressed, he sat her down with a cup of coffee in the living room.

"There is something we need to discuss."

With chilling certainty, she knew it was about his wife. "I spent yesterday afternoon out at Sheppard Pratt. It is likely that Myra will be well enough to come home in a few months. You must begin to prepare yourself."

The look that had taken hold of her face caused him to stop in mid-sentence. Quickly he moved beside her on the sofa and picked up her hand. "I've tried to prepare you, my darling. I don't want you to be hurt. . . ."

"But you love her more than you love me—that's it, isn't it, Stan? I guess I've always known it deep down."

"No. That's not quite right. I loved her first. I married her when we were young, and we had two children together. That love, that prior commitment, has to take precedence over my love for you. It isn't a question of love; it's a question of responsibility."

She dug into her purse, searching for a tissue for the tears that were forming.

"I'm so sorry, Tracy. We will always have wonderful memories . . . and we'll have a few more months together."

"And then?"

"I'm not sure. But if she is well enough to separate from her doctor, I'd like to take her to Madison and try to start over there."

She looked at him, thunderstruck. "You mean—you mean you'd move away? For good? You wouldn't come back next fall?"

"No. I think it would be the best thing for both of

us. A clean break. It would be hard at first, but eventually . . . ." He had to stop talking because he too was crying, weeping over the beginning of the end of their consuming passion.

After that morning, Tracy carried a dark cloud over her everywhere she went. Every time she was with him, she hovered in fear that before this meeting was over he would break the bad, the worse news: his wife was well, and she was coming home.

She hated herself for the pettiness of her character; she despised her own greediness for his love, his time, his total commitment to her.

To make her life even more of a shambles, Albertini had cancelled her weekly "Window on the World" piece to make more room for coverage of the Watergate hearings. She had one more reason to hate Nixon; he had managed to pre-empt her very own television show.

On May 24, Special Prosecutor Leon Jaworski asked the Supreme Court to intervene on the question of his power to subpoena material from the President. The issue must be settled promptly, he declared, before the Court adjourned for the summer. That same day, at dinner at The Old Angler's Inn, where it all began, Stan McDevit ended their affair by telling Tracy that Myra was coming home that weekend, and they would be leaving for Madison immediately, where he had accepted a position for the following year.

Devastated, Tracy looked up from her espresso to ask, "What about my career? The career you were so delighted to be managing?"

"I've taught you—or tried to—everything I know about broadcast journalism. And in many ways you've surpassed me. You have it all—you have that special something we call 'star quality.'

There's nothing more I can do for you. Except love you from afar."

She took to her bed. She cried and screamed and wept and shouted obscenities at him. Kristy found her three days later when she came home to pick up some clothes. Immediately understanding the situation—it was what she had always predicted would happen between Tracy and Stan—she encouraged Tracy's anger and grief. She also changed her plans and stayed in the apartment, day and night, caring for Tracy around the clock.

Kristy was tempted to call Rosina, feeling Tracy needed a mother's love, but Tracy vetoed it, saying there was no reason "to expose them to the sordidness my life has become."

For seven days she grieved, realizing she hadn't been so wretched since the death of her mother, knowing that Rosina had nursed her back to life that time, but not wanting Rosina to know about her illicit affair with a married man. How could she ever understand or forgive her? No, she got exactly what she deserved, exactly what she had asked for.

After seven days of talking her heart out to Kristy, it got to the point that Tracy was constantly defending Stan while Kristy was blaming him for abandoning her so suddenly and cruelly.

Kristy, an experienced woman in matters of the heart, consoled her with the assurance that "time heals everything," and "this too shall pass," and "what you really need is a new lover. We must find you a new lover."

"Shit! What I need is a good job. I'm going to pull myself together, go see Mahin at Saks, and then go seduce Albertini!"

They both laughed, and Tracy hugged Kristy and said, "Thanks for sticking with me when I needed you. It's more than that shit from Wisconsin had the decency to do."

"Now you're getting smart. The best antidote to a broken heart is to hate him, hate him, hate him! Take it from one who knows."

Chapter Nineteen

Tracy didn't have to call Rick Albertini because Phil Kook called her first.

"Hi, kid! How are you?" He didn't wait for her response to his opening, but went right on, "Vacation season starts in two weeks. I need you, same as last year, if that's okay with you. When can you start?"

"Would the day after tomorrow suit you?"

"Hey, yeah! Super."

"Can we resume 'Windows'?"

"Nah, too much Watergate to cover. But I'll give you good assignments, scout's honor. And more money. Albertini okayed it today."

"Great! see you Wednesday."

Shortly after the Fourth of July, Rick Albertini called her into his office. After the usual pleasantries, he invited her to accompany him to New York City the coming weekend to an "industry meeting."

While he proffered the invitation, his eyes roamed over her body.

"You know, I think you're getting too thin. I noticed it last night on the news, but it's even worse when I see you in person. Anything wrong?"

"No. Hard work, running around, I guess."

"Well, a weekend out of town will be good for you. Can you arrange it?"

Her mind did dozens of calculations in a split second. It was a command performance, coming from her employer, wasn't it? It could be simply a nice gesture on his part, but that wasn't likely. *He wants to get me into bed.*

It had the potential for turning into an ugly situation. Did she really want this at this time in her life? She looked up at him and assessed his potential as a lover. He was not sexy, exactly, yet there was a sexy aura about him. Was it his wealth, his power, his control over her future? Or was it just the glamour of a weekend in New York— something she had yearned for since she fantasized over the scrapbook of her mother's modeling days. Rosina had told her that her father had courted her mother in New York City, that it had been the most glorious time in their lives together. New York beckoned her like a magnet. And here was her chance to see it with a multi-millionaire, a powerful, sophisticated, distinguished-looking man who was probably even older than her father.

"I'd be delighted to accompany you, Mr. Albertini. Do you have a schedule of events so I can decide what kind of clothes to pack?"

"Oh, bring dinner dresses. In fact, bring the most glamorous evening clothes you own. Suits will be fine for the daytime." Suddenly he reversed himself. "On second thought, don't bring any evening clothes. I'll send you over to my friend Kay at

Martha's. You may as well begin to spend some of your ten-thousand-dollar clothes allowance."

Tracy looked at him in amazement. She had never heard anything about a clothes allowance, though she knew Maureen had one.

"Did Kook forget to tell you? We give each of our female reporters a small clothes allowance—it's one of the perks of being on-camera. Makes all the other females around here envious as hell!"

Even as he was talking, she wondered if he had invented this explanation.

"We'll be staying at the Park Lane. It's a wonderful new hotel on Central Park South."

"Fine. When should I be ready?"

"We'll go up in my plane, leave about noon. Meet me here at ten Friday morning with your suitcase."

His invitation set Tracy on a flurry of shopping, since she didn't even own a proper suitcase. After considerable thought, she went to see Rosina.

"I'd like to look over Mother's jewelry and see if there are some pieces I could take this weekend."

"That's good. I'm so glad you've finally gotten to the point where you'll consider using her things. She would have wanted her famous television daughter to have them." They went to the bank, and Tracy selected a few gold pieces and a delicate sapphire and diamond bracelet with matching ring and earrings.

"I'm going shopping Friday afternoon in New York," she explained to Rosina, "and I'm going to try to find a royal blue evening gown. Something very simple but slinky."

Rosina beamed her approval, so pleased was she with the way this beautiful young woman was developing.

* * *

They drove to Page Airways in his chauffeured Rolls, flew to New York in his Lear jet, and were met there by a stretch limousine. She could barely contain her excitement at finally seeing New York City, but she was careful not to reveal to Rick—he had begun the trip by insisting that she stop calling him Mr. Albertini—that she had never been to New York City before.

She tried to appear disinterested while he registered them, having assumed that he was registering them as man and wife. She was taken aback when the concierge opened a suite for Rick and informed her that her room was next door. As he installed her in her room, he showed her the air conditioning control, the television control, and then pointed out the locked door which, if unlocked on her side, would join her room to Rick's suite.

"*Hah! As I suspected*, she thought, but she was delighted that she would have at least some privacy.

They lunched in the magnificent, mahogany-paneled dining room that overlooked Central Park. Then Rick sent her to Martha's, explaining that he would go for a workout at the New York Athletic Club. "When you return, you will find that I've arranged for Pablo to come and do your makeup, and Carita will do your hair for this evening."

"Mr.—Rick, that's tremendous! I've never had a real make-up artist do my makeup. What a treat!" At the same time she pretended to be thrilled, she wondered why he was so intent on making her over. First new clothes, then a new face and hairstyle! *Well, that's television*, she told herself—*all cosmetics.*

She arrived back in her hotel room late that afternoon having had her first experience of being rich. Kay had been expecting her, for Rick had called her and told her exactly the kind of clothes he wanted Tracy to buy. Seven evening gowns were hanging in a dressing room awaiting her, as well as fourteen cocktail dresses and several outfits suitable for the camera. Kay had advised her, told her some of the dresses were not right for her, and had encouraged her to buy more than she needed for this one trip. When she had made her selections, Kay had announced that they would tighten the buttons and check over the dresses to make sure everything was right. They would be delivered to her room at the Park Lane no later than five-thirty. She left having no idea how much of her ten-thousand-dollar allowance she had spent; Kay had assured her that Mr. Albertini had directed her not to discuss price with Tracy. "And he's the boss, right?"

When Pablo and Carita were gone, she slipped into the blue silk matte jersey dress she had chosen. Strapless, with a sheared top that followed her curves sensuously, it fell in a long straight column from her hips to the floor. With it she wore silver shoes, a printed silk chiffon scarf, and her mother's jewelry.

She looked at herself in the full-length mirror and was excited and pleased by what she saw. "So this is what it's like to be rich. But then, anyone would look like a movie star after the afternoon I've had."

Her phone rang and she quickly answered it. Rick's quiet voice brought her back to reality. "I've ordered some caviar and champagne to begin the evening. Whenever you are ready, unlock the door and come in."

"Okay."

"How did you like my friend Kay?"

"She was wonderful. I think you'll like her choices."

"I can't wait."

Sooner or later, she would have to unlock that door and walk into his suite. And once that door was unlocked, there was no turning back. Oh, shit! Once she got on that plane, there was no turning back.

Rick immediately pronounced her "magnificent" and clearly was bowled over by her radiance. In the limousine he looked carefully at her bracelet and commented on the quality of the sapphires. She felt some explanation was necessary.

"All of this is my mother's jewelry."

"She has superb taste. I'd like to meet your parents sometime."

"My mother is dead . . . and my father is also."

"Oh, I'm sorry. Have they been gone long?"

"Yes. Since I was a little girl. I was raised by foster parents in Bethesda."

"I see." He picked up her hand and held it in his, as if to comfort her.

Fifteen minutes later, she was pinching herself to see if what she was experiencing was real or simply a wonderful dream. She had been introduced as "my secret weapon" to Dan Rather, Barbara Walters, Pauline Fredericks, Walter Cronkite and Mike Wallace. She had never realized it would be that kind of evening! And they had been curious about her; it showed in their eyes. They appraised her looks, wondering if she was a threat, competition, or only one more beautiful woman.

Between the first course and the second, Rick invited her to dance. After gathering her in his arms, he whispered to her, "How does it feel to be the most beautiful woman in a room full of stars?"

"Oh my! That's a bit of an exaggeration!"

"Not at all. I met Lambert in the men's room and he positively raved about you! You've taken this crowd by storm. One of the guys asked if you weren't 'too beautiful,' too much of a distraction for news."

"So how did you answer that?"

"I told him you would be our biggest money-maker within three years!"

"You must know something I don't, then."

"I know that as soon as you graduate from college, we are going to have something special for you, something that will really put you on the map and make me tons of money."

"Ratings and money. That's what this business is all about, isn't it?"

"That's exactly right. And the sooner you realize that and forget any idealism you may have, the better off you'll be. Television is a cutthroat business, and it *is* a business! It must show a profit, and the bigger profit the better. I'll bet they don't teach you that in your classes."

The evening was magic for her, and it was only after they got back into the limousine that her anxiety about what was expected of her returned.

When they reached their rooms he asked her, "Did you bring your key?"

She fumbled in her bag for it, and he took it from her to open her door. "You were lovely this evening. I was very proud to be your escort."

"Thank you. It was a real thrill, meeting all those people."

"Good night, Tracy." And he kissed her forehead.

She walked into her room, surprised and feeling strangely let down. Her bed had been turned down, a chocolate mint lay on the pillow, and she noticed that the adjoining doors had been nearly closed so that only an inch remained opened. She wondered what she should do about the door—close it and lock it, or just leave it the way it was? She decided to leave it the way it was.

She undressed, put on the pair of men's pajamas she always slept in—actually, they were an old pair of Stan's—and crawled into bed. She wondered what Rick was doing, what he expected of her. . . .

He had surprised her several times that day. She had imagined that he would try to get her into bed even before they had lunch. He hadn't. And his overwhelming generosity surprised her. Back at the station he had a reputation for being tight, but it certainly didn't seem that he was.

As she continued to think about him, she began to realize how disappointed she was. She had actually been looking forward to the long talks that went with an affair. That was what she wanted of one, really—a best friend, a mentor, an older man to confide in. She turned out her light and saw light from his room coming through the door. *He's still awake; maybe he's waiting for me to come in.*

Impulsively, she picked up the phone and asked for his room. She heard the phone ring through the door, then his quiet, well-modulated "Hello."

"I—I was wondering if you might like company. . . ."

He cleared his throat. "Yes . . . that would be delightful. But only if you want to come in. I've ordered a brandy. Should I make it two?"

"Yes."

She walked slowly toward the adjoining doors, her heart thudding so loudly she felt he could hear it. He was seated in a Queen Anne wing chair, reading a leather-bound book. He looked up at her, noticed her pajamas, and a smile spread over his face.

"Is this the latest in high fashion sleepwear or is this what college girls wear these days?"

She sat down on the sofa facing him, tucking her legs underneath her. "When I was packing, I realized that I didn't have a proper negligee, but it was too late by then to do anything about it."

"That can be remedied easily. Bergdorf's is across the street and they have lovely lingerie. But I must say, you look quite fetching."

Room service knocked on the door; he motioned her to stay put, accepted the tray of drinks at the door, signed for them, and closed the door, securing it with a chain.

He offered her a brandy and toasted her future career. Then, all seriousness, he asked her, "Why are you here, Tracy?"

The bluntness of the question shocked both of them.

"I mean, why did you accept my invitation to come to New York? I'd like to talk about that— clear the air, if you will. I think it is important that we understand each other."

"I guess . . . because I wanted to get to know you better." She tested that response for honesty and realized it was exactly on target. For four years she had been aware of his presence in her life; she had been thrilled every time she passed him in the hallway and he spoke to her. She had been ecstatic when he commented on her performances. To be invited to spend a weekend with him, even if it did include obligatory sex, was a big deal!

"Did you imagine that I wanted to take you to bed?"

His bluntness continued to catch her off guard. Surely he wasn't queer!

She blushed and admitted it with a nod of her head.

"I do. You imagined correctly. But that's not the only thing I wanted. I wanted the company of a very intelligent, very perceptive, very *young* woman. A young woman who has caught my eye for the past four summers. You know, Tracy," he said as he crossed his knee, "you are younger than my two daughters. I keep asking myself how I would feel if one of my colleagues in the industry tried to seduce one of them at the age of twenty-one. Am I right, are you twenty-one?"

She nodded, hoping he would never learn the truth, that she was only twenty. "I came willingly, Rick, hoping that we would become friends, hoping that I could share the glamour of your life, if only for a weekend. I don't think any harm will come of it."

"Did you imagine you would lose your job at the station if you didn't come?"

"I thought about it. But I don't really believe you are like that. I trust you more than that."

"Good. I want that very clear. If you'd like to go back into your room right now and lock the door, I give you my word of honor that it will never affect your career. If you stay, we will have a wonderful weekend getting acquainted, and perhaps many more. But let me warn you—if you have an affair with me, it will not help you advance at the station. You need to know that too. You will be a great television star, Tracy, regardless of what I do or don't do about your career. I'm in the business to make money, not to make stars. If I can make money on your rising star, I will. Understand?"

Again she nodded her head.

After that, they talked a long time about the industry, gossiped about the people she had met that evening, and about Watergate. It was when he said, "Tell me about yourself, I want to know everything," that he moved over to the sofa and began to caress her body.

The next day was even more glamorous than the first had been. He began by taking her to Bergdorf's and buying her lingerie. Then he took her to the flower-filled Le Grenouille Restaurant for lunch. They spent the afternoon at the Frick Museum and then went to the Plaza for tea.

Dinner and dancing on the Waldorf Roof elicited the confession from her that her parents had been there years before, when they were courting. On Sunday they explored Madison Avenue, Fifth Avenue, and the Central Park Children's Zoo. After dinner at Le Cote Basque, they drove to La Guardia and flew back to Washington.

But before he kissed her good night at her apartment, he had invited her to spend the following weekend at his home on the Eastern Shore, where he kept his yacht.

Tracy's senior year began without the familiar support of Stanley McDivit, but with the news that she was to be the moderator of "College Forum," which would be taped every Friday afternoon. Her first thought, strange for her, was how that would affect her long weekends with Rick. She hadn't realized until then how much those weekends with him meant to her.

Kristy was formally engaged to Kevin White, who was now an evening news reporter for a Philadelphia station. They were to be married after Kristy's graduation. Kristy was not at all pleased with Tracy's new love affair, except for the fact that Rick was enormously wealthy, his one saving grace in her eyes. "Why can't you fall in love with someone your own age?"

"I'm not in love with him. I told you that. But we

do have wonderful times together. He's my best friend, next to you, Kristy. He is a really nice man."

"Yeah, and he's almost old enough to be your grandfather, for Christ's sake!"

After that conversation, Tracy didn't bring the subject of Rick up again, but rather concentrated their conversations on Kevin and other things.

It was two weeks after the beginning of the second semester when the phone call came that would radically change her life. She had spent Christmas and New Year's with Rick at his home in Palm Springs, the first time she had not spent the holidays with Manuel and Rosina. They had been hurt, but surprisingly understanding.

"Ben Stanton is calling you," his secretary's crisp voice informed her. *That lady doesn't like me*, Tracy thought.

"Hi ya, beautiful! How soon can you get over to the studio? I've got news for you—my God, have I got news for you! You'll shit in your pants, you won't believe it!"

"If it's that exciting, Ben, can't you tell me over the phone?"

"Shit no, I've got to see your face on this one."

"Okay. I'll be there in fifteen minutes, if you promise no cameras. I haven't washed my hair in two days."

"You women are all alike, always worrying about your hair. No camera. Hurry up."

Minutes later, she walked into his office. Maureen was there also, waiting for her. Both Ben and Maureen looked immensely pleased with themselves.

"First the bad news," Ben began. "Maureen has decided to leave us for the greener pastures of Hollywood. You guessed it—she's to be co-anchor of the evening news in Los Angeles. Rumor has it that she's being compensated at the rate of a quarter of a mil!'"

"How wonderful!" Tracy gasped as she rushed over to hug Maureen. "Congratulations."

"Now for the good news," Ben continued. "You, my beloved pet, have been unanimously chosen to replace Maureen as my partner on 'Today's Journal'."

"Oh, my God!" Tracy said quietly, stunned beyond words. "I—I—oh, my God! Me? But—but I have to finish school."

"Your first appearance is scheduled for March 1. You'll have to work something out with the university, go to school at night or something. Maybe they'll give you credit in your communications classes for the show. Play tapes for them or something."

"I don't believe it!" she gasped again.

"Hey, kid, don't take it so hard! It's good news, like I said."

Phil Kook came walking in at that moment carrying a tray with champagne and glasses. "Congratulations, young lady. I hate to lose you, but I guess it's to a greater cause."

Before she left, Rick Albertini sent word that she should stop in his office; he wanted a few words with her.

"First, may I offer my congratulations," he began as he kissed her cheek. "I want you to know this is not my doing, Tracy, it was a decision arrived at by Ben and Phil Kook and Maureen. They were unanimous in their recommendation to me. They came to me with the idea, and it took me twenty-four hours to make up my mind that I agreed with them. You will boost the ratings of 'Today's Journal' more than anyone new we could have brought in."

"Thank you. I appreciate your giving me such an incredible opportunity!"

"It's going to mean some changes, changes in our personal lives." He sat down behind his desk and looked down at his nails as if he was assessing his manicure. "We can't be seen together anymore, not in Washington or anyplace else."

She looked at him with puzzlement written on her face.

"You will be an instantly recognizable celebrity within months, perhaps even weeks. When you walk into a restaurant, heads will turn, people will ask for autographs. I don't want your reputation blemished in any way."

"But you aren't married . . . I don't understand."

"I am your boss. And people in the industry will be only too eager to say that you slept your way to the top. I don't want anyone to ever be able to say that about you. I certainly don't want to give anyone ammunition. No, my darling, much as I hate to say it—and believe me I've been struggling with my own feelings of selfishness during the last twenty-four hours, too—much as I hate to do it, it's done. You will be the new co-host of 'Today's Journal.' We will remain the best of friends, but we will no longer be lovers. I'm sure in no time at all you'll find someone more appropriate, someone your own age."

"I see." She understood his logic, knew he was right, but also knew she would miss their quietly marvelous times together.

"How much money do you think you should make?"

"I—I have no idea. It's such a marvelous opportunity. . . ."

"Sixty-five thousand. With a few added perks. I'll

give you a six-month contract. At the end of six months, we'll negotiate. You probably ought to get yourself an agent by then. Tell you what, for every point we go up in the ratings, I'll add ten thousand to your base salary."

"What happens if the ratings go down?"

He looked out of the window, then at his cuff-links. "If the ratings go down," he said in a steady, cool voice, "you may have to look for employment elsewhere." He paused to let that sink in. "As I told you once, a long time ago it seems, I'm in this business to make money. And there is a direct relationship between the ratings and my profit margin. Keep that in mind."

"I'll do my best." She hated it when he turned so cold, so indifferent toward her.

"If you do, the sky is the limit! I want to offer my congratulations again." He walked around his desk, raised her to a standing position and kissed her long and hard.

Graduation was over. Cameras were flashing all around, and Tracy stood amid the crowd still in her black cap and gown, signing autographs. Presently, her "special fans" found her—Rosina and Manuel, Ben, Phil Kook and his wife, Rick Albertini—who that day had presented a cash award to the university communications department—and Kristy Trenton and Kevin White. Albertini had invited them all to his home in Wheaton for a celebratory dinner in Tracy's honor.

She had managed to graduate *summa cum laude* by taking evening courses and final exams in her television courses, even though her mind had been on nothing the past three months but her daily television appearances. At first the ratings had dropped, but Ben had assured her that it always happened when a steady, popular figure was replaced. Then, on the seventh week, they had begun to climb. By the tenth week, the ratings were one point above what they had been before Maureen left, and now with thirteen weeks behind her, Tracy was pleased to note that they were three points up. Albertini was delighted and told her so every week when he told her the latest ratings.

She tried to keep up a running conversation with her friends even while she signed the programs for a few remaining fans. Suddenly she felt a tap on her shoulder and heard a familiar voice.

"Can I congratulate the big new star of 'Today's Journal'?"

Her stomach cramped and she turned to see the man she had been trying to forget—Stanley McDivit.

After a quick kiss hello and introductions all around, Tracy extricated herself from Stan's attention to quietly ask Rick if she could include him in the dinner party that evening.

"Of course, my dear."

Several hours later, while they drank champagne in the cherry-paneled library of Albertini's country estate, Misty Meadows, McDivit cornered her alone. After explaining that he had been in Washington to see about a federal grant for the communications department back in Wisconsin, he said to her, "As I watched you receive your diploma, I found myself wondering if you've ever taken the time to survey where you have come from—from that errand girl at WUBS four summers ago to the leading new star. Life is very short, and success is sometimes even shorter, especially in the world of television. Take the time to look at your accomplishments and savor them. Take the time to feel good about yourself."

As she listened to his wise words, she found herself also listening to her heart. Had he changed? Or was she seeing him with new eyes as a result of her relationship with Albertini? She couldn't put her finger on it, but something was different in her visceral response to his presence.

Her anger toward him had totally abated. There were moments in the middle of the night when she could think back on their love and realize that it had been a wondrous blending of innocence and passion. Though he had been the first lover to break her heart, she understood that he had given her a glorious sexual initiation. She wondered if all her subsequent lovers would pale by comparison.

The eerie sensation of watching herself in the presence of her loved ones continued unabated through the dinner. At one point she caught Rick's eye, and he winked at her, his affection and lingering love and pride showing through. Then she glanced at Stan and saw that he had just seen the exchange between herself and Albertini. *He knows*, she thought, and felt her face turn crimson.

Then another thought struck her. Everyone I love, everyone who loves me, is here tonight for this dinner.

Everyone . . . except him.

Chapter Twenty

At that precise moment, across the Atlantic in Florence, Count Anthony Dandolo pushed back his massive leather chair, closed the large leather journal in front of him, put down his pen, and stood to stretch his legs. His calves were cramping, probably the result of a potassium deficiency resulting from his twice-yearly attempt to lose the extra ten pounds which were the inevitable result of his life style. Losing that ten pounds was necessary in order to maintain the youthful appearance and vigor of which he was inordinately proud. He liked to look at himself naked in his dressing room and tell himself that he looked no different than he had thirty years earlier.

At fifty-three, he was at the height of his intellectual powers. And because of his discipline, his love of riding and skiing, he had maintained the girth and the muscle tone of a younger man. True, his hair had begun to gray at the temples, but as Tamara—and other women—told him, it merely added to his sex appeal. A sex appeal enhanced by his power and immense wealth.

As he turned around to walk to the window— the swans below on the lake were his favorite moonlight sight, a restful scene which magically disolved his middle-of-the-night tension—his eyes stopped on the large portrait of his mother Catarina with his daughter Tanya. The resemblance was strong between the two of them, and their blue eyes seemed to stare accusingly out of the painting, silently begging him to try to find Tanya.

Ah mother, mother, I hear you! Won't you ever give me any peace? He walked quickly to the window. *Tanya is twenty-one now*, he thought as he looked down at the terrace, remembering scenes of gay parties and dancing. *It's been, let me see, thirteen years since Lorna left. Tanya was eight then. If only . . . if only I could know for certain that she doesn't hate me. I couldn't bear that rejection on top . . . on top of mother's. . . .*

Catarina Dandolo had died three years before in a small plane accident. She had been on her way to Milan to participate in the quarterly board of directors meeting of the family corporation. She had surprised the family after Emilio's death by becoming very active in the business. She had insisted that she be included in major discussions and decisions. At the time, Tony had resented her lack of trust—didn't she think him competent to manage her affairs? Hadn't he been giving it his full time and attention?

In truth, that hadn't been the case at the time. He had been giving most of his time and attention to being a politician, a member of the Chamber of

Deputies. God knew, Italy had a host of internal problems—labor unrest, the highest inflation rate in Europe, productivity down and absenteeism running at fifteen percent. Then there was the problem of Japanese and German surpluses competing with Italian manufactured goods. *Thank God for the Americans*, he had found himself thinking in those days, *those Americans who buy our fashions, our leather goods—yes, thank God for the ostentatious Americans.*

He looked back on his time as ambassador as an unmitigated disaster, capped by the disappearance of his wife and daughter and followed by his mother's stern disapproval. Ultimately, she had disinherited him. Not that he had needed her money. But it had never ceased to hurt him that his mother had bypassed him and left her entire estate, including the Villa Dandolo and all its furnishings, art collection, and her jewels—to his daughter Tanya!

Tanya! Who had been lost to him now for these thirteen years.

And though he had a fine, strong son, Alberto, to inherit the businesses—and perhaps his political position as well—it never ceased to annoy him that his mother had wanted so desperately to prevent Tamara from becoming the mistress of Villa Dandolo, such was his mother's hatred for the usurper.

In spite of his mother's will, in spite of his unceasing love for her, he had contrived to gain control of the Villa, telling himself that if his father were alive, it would never have happened that way. Emilio would have wanted to continue the tradition of passing the villa from father to son as it had always passed down through the generations.

His mother had not only left the villa as her

bequest to Tanya, she had also left Tony a note telling him of her trip to America, telling him how she came to possess the startling portrait of Tanya which now graced the library. And she had left Tony the address in Woodstock, Virginia, where she had visited Lorna and Tanya, with the admonition that he go over there and renew his relationship with his daughter.

"It has been six years since I visited them," she had written before she died, "and all attempts to communicate with Lorna have failed. Perhaps I frightened her, though God knows I promised her I would not tell you their whereabouts. I intended to keep that promise. But I have lost track of her, and the detectives seem unable to come up with anything. I urge you, Tony, for the sake of Tanya, to search with all the resources at your disposal, and to bring her home where she belongs."

In the aftermath of Catarina's tragic death, and the bitter knowledge that his mother had essentially disinherited him because of his relationship with Tamara, he had chosen not to attempt to find Tanya. Rather, because his mother had named him trustee for Tanya, he had moved into the Villa with Alberto and had made their home there for three years now. The Church had not granted him an annulment and he was glad; he hadn't really wanted to antagonize his mother further by marrying Tamara. So he had adopted Alberto, acknowledging him as his legal son and heir. He had rewarded Tamara with a beautiful villa of her own in the heart of Florence and an unlimited allowance for jewels, clothes and travel. She had everything she could possibly desire, except the title Contessa— and the respectability she lusted after.

For generations, this library, his favorite room in the palace had been the private domain of male

Dandolos. There they kept their ledgers, their passionate journals. Portraits and pictures of weddings, christenings, and political happenings adorned the faded wine-colored, silk-upholstered walls. There Tony adjourned when he couldn't sleep, like tonight, or when he wanted to be alone to think; when he wanted to be alone to reminisce about his life and his women, to savor his victories or nurse his wounds. It was a room filled with the ghosts of all his years, a room that stirred his senses and challenged his integrity, a room that he found himself spending more and more time in with each passing year.

Is this what they call a mid-life crisis in America? he wondered as he slumped in the worn leather wing chair. *It's time we had this reupholstered*, he thought as he looked down at the arm rests. More and more these days, his mind returned to America. Perhaps the time had come; perhaps the wounds his mother had inflicted on him had healed sufficiently that he could chance a trip to America. Perhaps he could find Tanya. She would be twenty-one by now, probably a junior in college someplace in the states.

He wondered if Lorna had taken her back to South Dakota to live, perhaps thinking that she should discover her American roots. God knew, Lorna wanted to disassociate herself from him totally; otherwise how could she have chosen to live in a backwoods place like Woodstock?

And yet, every time he thought of making a journey to America, he talked himself out of it. There was the press of work, his work in Italy and in Indonesia and Thailand and Hong Kong. Life had changed radically for him after returning from America.

The post-war recovery and reconstruction had

been nearly complete when Tony left for Washington in 1958; by the time he returned to Italy in 1961, industrial development had created a boom of prosperity unequaled in Italian history. The prosperity was followed, predictably enough, it seemed in hindsight, by a recession. Nevertheless, his companies had flourished, as had all of Italy. Industrial production had doubled, exports had doubled, and the per capita income had dramatically increased. In a nation with two million artisans accounting for one tenth of the national income, Tony and others like him had begun to capitalize on the manufactured goods, of highest quality, which would become status symbols throughout Europe and the United States.

While Tony created opportunities for the artisans, he also began investing in the third world. He created Dandolo International, Ltd., for the purpose of building an infrastructure in primitive countries. He began building bridges and roads, but soon he expanded his company's capability to build dams, airports, canals, shipping ports, railroads, hospitals, hotels and universities.

He told himself that he was an international "social worker" of sorts, advising other governments and peoples. Nevertheless, his eyes remained riveted on the bottom line—profit.

He sometimes told himself that in expanding Italy's industrial base abroad, he was continuing the work of his hero, Enrico Mattei, who after founding Ente Nazionale Indrocarburi (ENI), had been killed in a mysterious air crash in 1962. Many Italians suspected that the American CIA had engineered his death, but Tony continued to believe that the culprit was one of the international oil companies. Mattei, who had made Italy one of the first Western customers for Russian crude oil, seemed to get a particular thrill out of fencing with Middle Eastern oil sheiks and defying the international oil cartel.

It had been Tony's desire to investigate the circumstances of Mattei's death which had led him into his first construction deal in the Middle East. Since that time in 1962, he had returned numerous times and had collected both friends and enemies in the oil capitals of the world, but he had never been able to gather convincing evidence that Mattei's death was a direct result of his penchant for annoying the Arabs.

While keeping a close eye on developments abroad, Tony had also attempted to use his considerable prestige to restore some clout to the Italian government. To no avail. The Italian people continued to view government with a deep-seated mistrust. They prefered instead to live their lives surrounded by family, distant cousins, business friends, and clients. It was the ancient way, the way that had well served generations before them. Prime ministers would come and go—and they did often during the postwar years—but family would always be there. Italians would not look too carefully at their government; they didn't need government, in spite of American sentiments to the contrary. They had family. They would conduct their lives and solve their problems as they always had; they would rely on *la famiglia*.

Tony fingered the brass nails on the edge of the arm chair while his eyes scanned the photos on the nearby wall: his father meeting with Roosevelt, his father with Stalin. He looked at another set of pictures: there, between Toscanini and Mattei stood the beautiful Lorna. It had been taken on her first visit to Villa Dandolo. Oh, how gorgeous she had been then, how cool and regal and mysterious . . . .

He stood up to get closer to the picture, as if to understand something about her basic nature which had eluded him then. A wave of deepest love swept over him, followed abruptly by anger. How dare she deprive his life of her radiance? How dare she walk out on him? And take his little princess . . . . He pulled a handkerchief out of his robe pocket and mopped his brow, a sudden cold sweat having overcome his normally disciplined emotions. The deep smoldering blueness of her eyes had been passed on to Tanya, but with a variation. Lorna's eyes were nearly the color of ripe blueberries. Tanya's were closer to bristol blue.

He closed his eyes and tried to summon up how Tanya would look at twenty-one. Classic beauty, a nearly perfect profile, he imagined. *I hope she doesn't get too tan*, he thought, remembering her fair white skin, the color of egg whites with the hot blush of roses in her cheeks when she got angry or was especially happy.

He wondered what Lorna had told Tanya about their marriage, about him. No sooner did this thought flicker across his consciousness than he found himself angry again, then felt unsolvable grief well up inside his chest.

If he had his life to live over . . . if there was any one thing he could have changed, he would never have begun that affair with Tamara, he would never have hurt his beloved Lorna. But, he reassured himself, how could he have known she would react so—so radically? Who would have believed she would walk away from everything he had given her, from what he had made her?

But to carry on with this line of thought was to

deny his lasting love for Tamara and for Alberto, a young man even a father had to admit showed great promise.

"Oh, shit!" he sighed aloud and collapsed back into the wing chair.

But one can't relive one's life. We must go on, we must continue. He turned his chair to study the more recent pictures: himself with President Kennedy in Paris, himself with President Richard Nixon. Tamara was strangely absent from any pictures in this room, he realized, and wondered if his unconscious was preserving this one room pristine and pure from her, as if there was also a piece of his soul she hadn't inhabited, a piece of himself that he was saving for Lorna and Tanya— and Catarina.

Sooner or later, and probably it should be sooner, he thought, he must go to America and find her. He hoped Lorna hadn't poisoned her mind with all that women's lib crap, but he suspected she may have. *I hope she won't hate me . . . too much.*

Quietly, tentatively, the door creaked open and Tony saw Tamara's robed figure hovering on the other side of the threshold. He had almost forgotten she was spending the night, as she so often did, in his bedroom. He stood to greet her.

"Tony . . . Tony, it's four in the morning, darling. Are you all right?"

"Yes, my love. I'm fine. A bit of insomnia. Seems it comes with age, and I've begun to feel very old." He walked toward her, put his arm around her waist and steered her back toward his room.

"I'm always frightened when I awaken here and you aren't beside me."

"You should be used to it by now, I suffer insomnia so much."

"I'll never get used to waking and finding half the bed empty. I love you, Tony."

"And I love you, my darling. Let's see if we can't get some sleep between now and eight, shall we?"

The two of them closed the door as they prepared again for bed in Tanya's Villa Dandolo.

Chapter Twenty-One

WASHINGTON, D.C.—1980

The camera panned the stage while the actors and actresses took repeated curtain calls, then cut to the audience to show the black tie patrons giving the cast a standing ovation, then back to the stage where the head usher was presenting a bouquet of roses to Marguerite Petrus.

Voice over:

Is this what all the effort has been for, this magic few moments of applause, of recognition for a job well done?

The film clip over, the camera focused on Tracy Brown on the familiar set of "Today's Journal."

"That was the scene last night at the Arena Stage, and today we have in the studio the two stars of *View From the Bridge*, Marguerite Petrus and Jon Mori."

Tracy launched the interview which would conclude the five-part mini-documentary, "Theater in

Washington: The Last Twenty Years." It had been her brainchild, her production from beginning to end; it was typical of the kind of special programing she had initiated on "Today's Journal" and it was part of the reason why the show had become the biggest money-maker of any locally produced daytime show in Washington.

It was Friday afternoon, the end of another grueling week behind the lights and cameras. It was the one day of the week when Tracy permitted herself the luxury of a drink and a decent lunch after the telecast was concluded. She was on her way out of her office, headed for lunch at The American Cafe and after that a quick shopping trip to Saks Fifth Avenue, when her secretary buzzed the intercom twice.

"What is it, Sally? I was on my way out the door."

"I'm sorry, Tracy, but I've got this man on the phone who says he's the president and owner of Pacific Cable Company. He insists he must talk to you right now, as he lives in Hawaii. His name is David Bowen."

"Shit!" She was exhausted and annoyed. Why couldn't her secretary lie once in a while and say she wasn't there? She picked up the phone from her standing position by the desk. "Hello, this is Tracy Brown."

"Thank you for taking the call. I understand you are on your way out to lunch, but I need to meet with you, and the sooner the better. My name is David Bowen, I'm the owner of Pacific Cable Company. I've been watching you this week, and I'd like to discuss the possibility of your coming to work for Pacific Cable."

"That's very kind of you, Mr. Bowen, but you should get in touch with my agent."

"Wait a minute. You haven't let me finish."

"But—"

"I'm going to make you an offer you can't refuse, but only if you agree to meet with me in person with no agent involved. At least at the outset."

"No, Mr. Bowen, you know that's not how it's done."

"Miss Brown, I'd like to suggest that you call Senator Dan Inouye for a recommendation. I guarantee you he will vouch for my character, he's known me for a dozen years."

"I'm sorry—"

"Meet me tonight for dinner at *Lion D'Or* at eight. I promise you, you won't regret it. And in the meantime, check me out with the Senator."

She was so hungry she thought she might faint. She had to get rid of this guy and get something in her stomach. On the other hand, something about his arrogance, his determination, intrigued her, and she almost wanted to go to dinner just to see the man who belonged to that voice.

"I've made other plans."

"Cancel them. Our dinner tonight will be the turning point in your life."

Her plans were to take a bubble bath and curl up in bed with a good book. She was continuously exhausted. She had planned to spend the entire weekend holed up in her apartment reading and recuperating and storing energy for the coming week. But she found herself wavering. He sounded interesting. Arrogant, demanding—and interesting.

"Very well, I'll meet you there at eight."

"Great! Till then."

During lunch and later on her shopping expedition, she replayed the conversation in her mind, hearing again his deep resonant voice. *I must be*

some kind of idiot to have accepted that invitation!
But when she returned to her office she placed a call
to the Senator, she was put through immediately
and briefed the senior senator from Hawaii on her
dinner date.

Senator Inouye told her that Bowen was young,
very wealthy, formerly a newscaster in Los Angeles,
who had invested wisely in television properties
and other real estate, and was now creating what
would ultimately be a major cable network serving
the west coast, Hawaii, and the Pacific Islands. In
short, he was legitimate.

She dressed carefully, wondering all the while
why she had been so turned on by his voice. She
wore a new black knit suit by Adolpho. The
Chanel-style suit was trimmed in a black and silver
braid and worn with a matching silver camisole.
Perfect for a Friday evening dinner, she thought as
she brushed her dark hair loosely around her shoulders and sprayed *Madelaine de Madelaine* perfume
generously on her neck and clothing.

She was greeted by the maître d', who recognized
her on sight, as did all Washington restaurateurs.
"Mr. Bowen is waiting for you, Miss Brown."

He stood to greet her at the corner table for two.
"I'm so glad you decided to come," he said warmly,
before he bent to kiss her hand.

She couldn't take her eyes off him. Even after she
had been seated for several moments, she continued to stare at him. Suddenly she realized that he
had said something to her and was waiting for a
response.

"I'm sorry . . . I didn't hear."

"I said I hope you like champagne."

"Yes, I love it. It's my favorite drink." Still she
was in a state of shock. He was the sexiest, most
compelling man she had ever seen. She felt her

heart would burst out of her chest; she would never be able to carry on normally with this man. His good looks were totally intimidating.

He held up his glass to toast her. "To a great future, to us, to Pacific Cable, and to the future star of its news department." He saluted her with his glass. Obviously, he was going to offer her the anchor position.

"Whoa, you're moving too fast for me, Mr. Bowen—"

"Please call me David, and I'll take the liberty of calling you Tracy."

"Of course." *Damn him*, she thought, *he's totally disarming, and he's determined to retain complete control of this conversation.* As she was preparing to ask him to tell her about his cable company, he took the words out of her mouth.

"I've brought a financial report and copies of our current programming plans, as well as our projections five and ten years down the road. I figured you would probably have time to read them over the weekend. The most important thing you need to know is that our programming is specifically geared to the tastes of people who live on the West Coast and Hawaii and in the Pacific region. I intend to dominate that market within ten years."

"You have no lack of ambition, as Senator Inouye said."

"Ah, you checked me out."

"I never meet strangers for dinner."

"Yes, of course." He paused to sip on his drink, never taking his eyes away from hers. "I'll bet you get lots of invitations, though."

She returned his mischievous look with what she hoped was a mysterious one of her own. "I get invitations from marines stationed at Quantico, and from United States Senators, and from cabinet officers. But I don't accept them."

"They aren't offering to advance your career. They're after something else."

"Possibly."

"For sure. You can relax, Tracy, my interest in you is strictly and solely professional. You can help me make money. Otherwise I wouldn't be wasting my time and money here tonight."

She nodded her head, indicating that she understood his terms, but she nevertheless felt let down, disappointed.

During dinner, he offered her the position of anchor for the evening news. She didn't accept, so he sweetened the bait by telling her she could do as many "specials" as she had the time and ideas for, and when she asked about staff, he told her to let him know what she felt she needed. "You will have complete control over the specials, both editorial control and staffing."

She savored that for a moment, thinking that back at WUBS she didn't even have the power to hire her own research assistant. Ben had managed to retain control over all personnel decisions, as well as have final editorial control over the content of her mini-documentaries. "You would give that much control to someone as young as I am?"

"You may be young, but you've had ten years of studio experience and six years of appearing five days a week for two hours. That's a pretty impressive record." He paused, then continued, "I have the definite impression that you are the brains behind the mini-documentary I've been watching this week."

She quietly nodded her head, realizing he knew much more about her than she had dreamed.

"That's the kind of quality and innovative programming I'm looking for. That's what it will take to lure an audience away from the networks."

"How much control will I have over the evening news?"

"That's my own baby, my special domain, my pride and joy. And I maintain very close supervision over that. But I've also got a damn good news department head, Rob Manson. You'll like him."

He began to pressure her for a date when she would come out to Honolulu and look over his operation, meet his people. She had never been to Hawaii, and the idea of visiting the island paradise —at his expense—tickled her, even though she felt great doubts about ever leaving her job at WUBS or Washington, the hub of the news world. Deep inside herself, she had a nagging doubt that she could even handle the job he was offering her. But then, she thought, as she listened to him describe the technical aspects of his cable operation, Stan and Ben and Rick had always had more confidence in her than she had had in herself. Perhaps David was right. Perhaps she could be a successful anchor.

When a scrumptious desert of raspberries, blueberries, and blackberries with a sabayon sauce was served, he poured more champagne in her glass and asked, "Dinner tomorrow night? After you've had a chance to read the material I'm going to give you?"

She wanted to accept, she didn't want the evening to end—but this discussion was so ridiculous. She wasn't going to go to Hawaii!

He saw her hesitation and added, "You name the restaurant. Tell me where."

"There's a lovely old restaurant out in Potomac. I haven't been there in years, but it's wonderful on a cold winter night."

"You're talking about the Old Angler's Inn?"

"You know it, then?"

"It's one of my favorite hideaways in Washington."

They ate dinner together Saturday night and again on Sunday. By the time he left her at her apartment on Sunday evening, she had agreed to fly to Honolulu in April and spend two weeks looking over his operation, seeing Hawaii, and considering his offer. The one issue which had never been raised was her salary. Somehow she felt it would be wrong for her to bring it up. If she agreed to everything else—which was highly unlikely—he would have to negotiate that with her agent.

The seven weeks flew by. She barely had time to get her office set for her absence and buy cruise clothes for the tropical climate. It was the first vacation she had taken since joining "Today's Journal" in March of 1974. She had cohosted more than fifteen hundred shows without missing one because of illness or a vacation. She was bone tired, sometimes felt burnt out, but every Monday morning she was raring to go again. It was the perfect career for her.

David met her with three leis—orchids, carnations and plumeria. He guided her toward the airport exit where his chauffeur-driven, cream-colored Rolls awaited them. He narrated their drive through Waikiki, around Diamond Head, and into the residential neighborhood of Kahala. When they pulled up to the entrance of the splendid Kahala Hilton, the doorman greeted David by name.

They walked into the open-air lobby, resplendent with orchids of every color and variety and chandeliers that took her breath away.

He accompanied her to a suite of rooms overlooking both the Pacific Ocean and the beach leading to Koko Head. He took her to the glass doors where she also had a view of the golf course and the mountains. "See that house on the other side of the golf course, the white house with the blue tile roof?"

She saw the mediterranean villa he was pointing out.

"If you walk down the beach, past the golf course, you can walk right into the yard. I'll be waiting for you there tomorrow morning at ten for breakfast."

"That's where you live?"

"Exactly. Wait till you see the views!"

He kissed her on the forehead and left her to get some sleep after her long flight. She walked back to the door twice to see the villa he called home. *My God, he must be rich*! She slipped into her blue negligee and climbed into bed, where orchids awaited her on her pillow. From somewhere below she heard mellow Hawaian music and a beautiful tenor voice singing "Blue Hawaii."

After a breakfast of papaya and maple-butter crepes, David took the wheel of the Rolls himself and gave Tracy a leisurely tour of the city of Honolulu. Then, after a quick lunch, he took her on a tour of Pearl Harbor, escorted by the Admiral in charge of the base. Senator Inouye had made the arrangements, and she made a mental note to drop him a thank-you when she returned to Washington. After the tour, David took her back to the hotel and encouraged her to rest up because he had a big evening planned for her.

They ate dinner at Michel's, a wonderful French restaurant overlooking the ocean, then went back to the Kahala to see the Danny Kaleikini Show. It dawned on her as she listened that this was the music she had heard as she drifted off to sleep the previous evening. After the show, they adjourned to the nightclub next door and danced for nearly an hour. She realized as he held her closely that David possessed an animal magnetism that she hadn't responded to since she was in love with Stanley McDivit years ago. There had been no one in the intervening years who had touched her emotions or called forth erotic feelings in quite the same way. It would be tempting, she mused as she swayed to the guitars, to stay here and fall in love with David Bowen.

Perhaps the same kinds of thoughts were passing through his mind. Abruptly, he stopped dancing and led her back to their table.

After they were seated, he said, "One thing I don't do, Tracy, is screw around with my employees."

He was setting the record straight for her again.

She couldn't resist saying, "I don't work for you yet, and I probably never will."

"Let's talk about that. You haven't said anything all day about that. You must have some questions, some thoughts."

"I do, but they will keep till Monday."

He had told her on the way from the airport that he would take her sightseeing Saturday and Sunday, but on Monday and Tuesday he wanted her to spend the day with him at the studios. On Wednesday, he had arranged for his private jet to fly her to Mauna Kea on the big island of Hawaii so she could spend three days alone, in the sun, thinking about his offer. He wanted an answer on Friday. He also wanted her to spend the weekend with him at his ranch. He would pick her up Friday afternoon and take her there. Then on Monday they would fly back to Oahu and iron out any unsettled details. He wanted to be able to call her agent on Monday and get the contract written and signed by the time she left for Washington the following Saturday.

She had felt annoyed and a little pressured at the way he had organized her visit without consulting her. But then she remembered that he was, after all, paying for it, so she would do it his way, and graciously.

She finished her Amaretto and said, "I think it's time to turn in. It's morning back home!"

"Good idea. I'll be by at noon, and I'll bring a picnic lunch. Wear comfortable shoes and long pants, and bring a bathing suit."

He had planned a drive around the island, followed by a swim at his country club—an early evening, he said, "because Monday will be very busy."

Going along with his careful orchestration, she kept him company all day Monday and Tuesday, asking questions and making comments as the spirit moved her. She was pleased to note how receptive he seemed to her ideas and comments; he was eager for any innovation that would improve the quality of his programming, and budget didn't seem to be a problem. Clearly, she thought, as she looked around the studio and talked with the audio and video technicians, he had invested in state-of-the-art electronic equipment.

One thing disturbed her—the total subservience of his employees. They seemed to creep around almost in fear of him. Only two of the senior newsmen seemed truly at ease with him. There was no socializing between the boss and the employees. But then, as she pondered it during her flight to the island of Hawaii, she realized that Rick operated the same way at WUBS. He gave orders when necessary, treated Ben almost as an equal, and spent as little time as possible at social events. As her mind flitted here and there, measuring the possibilities for her own future, she found herself asking, *What do I want him for—an employer or a friend . . . or a lover?*

Many times during the next three days, as she lay on the beach looking at the waves and the palm trees and the other tourists, she summoned up his image in her mind's eye. He was so gorgeous! Tall and broad-chested—he had confessed to having been a baseball and soccer player in high school and college in southern California—his face was perpetually tan—not a dark tan, but a golden-copper tan. His deep brown eyes penetrated her own until she felt he was boring a hole into her mind. His dark brown, wavy hair looked silky rather than coarse—she would have loved to reach up and run her hands through his hair, and then bury her nose in it and smell his very essence.

There had been no sign of a woman's presence in his palatial mansion-by-the-sea, but the subject had not come up and she had not dared to ask. After all, he had told her twice that he was off limits as a lover. Too bad! Everyone should be with their lover when they are here in Hawaii, she thought as she turned over onto her stomach to even out her tan.

Is he divorced or widowed . . . or queer? No, that couldn't be. After all, he had certainly responded to her on the dance floor. *I wonder how old he is?* she thought as she dug her fingernails into the sand. *Kristy would think he was perfect: sexy, handsome, wealthy, and probably eligible. Even the right age. He couldn't possibly be more than ten years older than I am.*

When she thought of the offer he was making her—a truly incredible offer—she felt like a fraud. By late Friday afternoon she had carried on enough of an internal dialogue with herself to know she was going to turn him down. She could not bring herself to leave Washington, to leave the few friends she had in the world. How would she tell David that? How would she explain that she was turning down the chance of a lifetime?

I really shouldn't be taking up so much of his time. I should simply tell him here at Mauna Kea, before he wastes a weekend with me. It would be the honorable thing to do.

And yet she wanted the weekend. She wanted to see his ranch, see how he relaxed. She wanted to get to know him better. She decided to carry the charade a bit further.

She was not disappointed in her decision. When they pulled into the long driveway leading up to the ranch house, she breathed the air, fresh with the smell of ripening pineapples, and spotted galloping horses in the field. With the kind of instant clarity she had felt several times before in her life, she knew it would be a weekend that would change her life in some significant way.

After a dinner of beef barbecue, cole slaw, and fresh fruit, they adjourned to a cozy sofa in front of a roaring fireplace in the "great room." Even with the fire, she was chilly, so he went to the closet and brought an old blue bulky sweater for her.

The house was a surprise. In startling contrast to his mansion in Honolulu, this was a huge log cabin, rustic and plain, yet comfortable, and as she looked around she recognized the fine hand of an interior decorator. It was a cowboy's domain, but everything was in superb taste.

He sipped on his brandy, then set it down and picked up her hand and began tracing the veins on it with his forefinger. "Tell me why you've decided not to accept my offer."

Stunned, she blushed, looked away, then back at his face. His eyes were searching hers both for confirmation of what he had said, and at the same time hoping for a denial.

"How . . . how did you know what I've decided?"

"If you were going to join us, you would be bubbling over with ideas for specials, you'd be bursting with enthusiasm. Instead, I sense a sadness. I'm disappointed, but also curious."

Inexplicably, tears began to form in her eyes and roll down her cheeks. With his thumb he gently wiped them away, but still they came. He bent down and kissed her cheek right where the tears crested on her cheekbone. "Tell me," he murmured softly.

"I can't. I'm not sure I know. I don't understand it myself. . . ."

"Let me try to guess. You are in love with Ben Stanton and you want to stay in Washington with him."

"Don't be ridiculous! That's crazy. Besides, he's married."

"Lots of young women fall in love with older married men, especially if those men have helped them in their careers."

"No, truly, that's not it at all."

"Someone else?"

"No." She paused, wiped away another tear, then continued, "No, I'm sorry to say I'm not in love with anyone right now. But that's really not too bad. It's hard to combine a love affair or marriage with a television career. Too many problems, too much stress."

"I agree. It's one of the reasons I've never married."

"I wondered about that . . . about you."

"I've never married because I'm a selfish sonuvabitch and I know it. I want what I want when I want it, and no woman in this day of women's lib is willing to put up with that kind of relationship. Besides, I like to sample women the way a little kid likes to taste every different candy in a candy store."

"You like variety. And you don't like commitment."

"Yes, and I've always had lots of variety. No way could I ever be faithful to one woman. Knowing that, I simply enjoy my life and don't make any promises to anyone."

"Don't you ever want a family, children?"

"Yeah, sure. There are times when I think about that, especially on weekends like this. I'd love to come over here, shut the office out of my mind, and relax with a couple of little kids and a warm, loving wife. But that'll never happen."

"Sounds very seductive to me—your life style, what you could offer a woman—except for the infidelity part." They both laughed and he went to the kitchen to refill his glass of brandy.

"Can I bring you something? Wine, coffee, Amaretto?"

"How about a glass of milk?"

"Sure thing."

He returned to his place on the sofa, sipped his drink one more time, and then bent down and kissed her softly on the mouth.

"Aren't you breaking your rules?"

"If you aren't going to work for me, you're fair game!" he teased, then kissed her again.

She offered no resistance, thinking that she was

finally getting what she had come for. Then she found her hands in his hair, and discovered that it was as silky as it looked.

They made love, expertly and passionately, their bodies melding together as if they had always sought one another. Afterwards he carried her into his bedroom and deposited her on his fur-covered, king-sized oak bed. She reached to the bottom of the bed for a large blue afghan to cover her naked body, which was covered with goosebumps, then cuddled close to him. He played with her hair for a moment, then kissed the tip of her nose; he lay back on the huge pillow and said, "Tell me why you don't want to come to Hawaii."

She reached for his hand and held it tightly, then slowly met his eyes. "I don't even know why myself. I just have this very strong feeling that I can't leave Washington. I've got to stay there."

"You'll soon be bored with 'Today's Journal'. I'm surprised you're not already. You've been there so long, it must be routine by now. Don't you want to become a network personality, have a nationwide show?"

"Oh sure, but I keep thinking that's a long way in the future." She played with the golden brown hair on his arm. "The idea of my relocating has never come up before."

"Are your parents in Washington?"

"No . . ." She hesitated, and then realized she would take the plunge, she would tell him what she had never told anyone. "My mother is dead. She was killed in a skiing accident when I was ten," she stammered, then closed up.

David shifted his weight on the bed so he could nuzzle her neck while she talked. "Your father?"

"My father is an Italian count, a member of the Chamber of Deputies. He lives in Florence with—

with his mistress and their son." She had barely been able to say the words aloud. It seemed like disloyalty to her mother even now to admit that her father still loved "that woman."

Little by little over the next two days, he coaxed the whole story out of her: her mother's desertion of her father, her own broken heart when her father never came for her, her grandmother Catarina's visit, and then Tracy's disappointment when the trip to the beach never materialized. They interspersed lovemaking and horseback riding with all their quiet talks, and several times during the two days they spent together, David had to take Tracy into his arms to quiet her sobbing and soothe her tormented heart.

After their last long ride Sunday afternoon, they showered and dressed in preparation for their return to Honolulu. Tracy turned off her hair dryer, gave her long black hair one last flick with the brush, and turned to pick up her blouse off the bed. "I suppose I really should go back to Washington tomorrow. Do you think I can get an airline reservation at this late date?"

"Why should you go? You have no reason to rush back."

"But my being here is costing you a lot of money, and since I'm not going to work for you—"

"Have you heard me complain about money?" He put his arms around her, then lifted her chin so she had to look him in the eyes. "If you're tired of me, of making love to me, then you are free to go. If you stay, I promise you six more wonderful nights, and if I can possibly manage it, we'll spend Wednesday and Thursday on Kauai."

"You are certain you want me to stay?"

"Positive."

* * *

That glorious week—Tracy secretly thought of it as her Hawaiian honeymoon-sans-marriage—passed too quickly. Soon they were on their last trip to the airport, holding hands in the back of his car.

"You have six months to reconsider."

"Reconsider what?"

"Both my offers—becoming the star of Pacific Cable, with a starting salary of five hundred thousand, or becoming Mrs. David Bowen. I promise you great wealth, a splendid lifestyle, and lots of good love."

"But you aren't promising I'll be your one and only Hershey bar?" She grinned at him; it had become a private joke which she threw in his face at every opportunity.

"I never make promises I'm not certain I can deliver on. In addition to reconsidering these two options, I want you to think seriously about my two recommendations. You must go see your father. You must give him at least the chance to make amends. I'm sure he needs to see you as much as you need to see him. And secondly . . ." He hesitated, unlike him.

"Yes?"

"You should try to ski again. When there is something in life that you fear, you must run toward it, not away from it. That's a lesson my father taught me years ago, and it has served me well. Go to your father, resolve that problem before it destroys your life. And come ski with me. Then you will have nothing to be afraid of."

"I just might. Would you be my teacher?"

"No. But if you'll come to Aspen this winter, I'll hire you the best instructor in the West, and I'll take over when he's finished—every evening."

"Sounds wonderful. And I'll see you when you come to Washington?"

"Wouldn't miss it for the world. You can count on it."

It was only after the plane was airborne over the Pacific that she realized that in all their love-making, he had never said, "I love you."

Life back at WUBS did seem dull after her splendid two weeks in Hawaii. At first she said nothing to either Ben or Rick about David's offer. She did, however, tell her agent, and authorize him to sound out the networks for opportunities in Washington. He listened to her recitation of David's offer and insisted that she should accept what he was offering. "You can always come back to the mainland and join up with a network. But you're really crazy to turn down that salary."

She stood her ground and told him simply to keep his ears open on her behalf. When he stopped nagging her about accepting David's offer, she decided that he too surmised that it was a personal reason, like a lover in the Washington area, that was keeping her there.

Then one evening six months later, when she was attending a dinner for the Washington press corps with Ben and Rick, she told Rick about David's incredible proposition. She watched his eyes grow angry at the possibility that she might desert WUBS. She assured him she wasn't leaving—"not yet"—and that if she did leave him, it would be to cover hard news for one of the networks.

"That's your dream? To be a network correspondent?"

"To cover the White House would be a dream come true!"

"Hell, it'd be downright boring with Reagan as President!"

The subject was dropped and didn't come up

again for several months. Shortly after the Christmas holidays, Rick summoned her to his office.

"It seems I have a belated Christmas present to give you."

He looked pained even as he tried to smile and be pleasant. "Yes," he continued as she sat down in front of his mahogany desk, "the head of Network News for UBS has asked me to release you from your contract with us so that you can become the Washington correspondent."

Her face broke into a full smile, even though a voice inside her warned her that Rick was not happy.

"I guess I always knew it was coming. At least you'll be a part of our network, not someone else's."

"I'm thrilled! Thank you—thank you so much, Rick. I know you're behind this." She rushed over to him and planted a kiss on his cheek.

"Well, I'm not happy, not happy at all."

"But—you're my godfather! You've got to be happy for me!"

"Well"—a grin began to spread over his face—"I guess I am happy for you. I can always claim that I discovered you."

"When do I begin?"

"I don't know. I suppose as soon as your agent works out the contract. I told them I was paying you half-a-million. Figured the lie wasn't really a lie, since that guy Bowen offered you that. I suppose you'll be worth it to the network. They're looking for all the good women journalists they can find, and you're one of the best."

"My God! I don't believe it! Half a million dollars . . ."

"Hold out for six hundred thousand is my advice."

"I don't have that kind of nerve."

"Hell, why not? Bowen would top that if he thought he could get you to Hawaii. He told me so."

"He's a bit crazy. No one makes that much."

"Barbara Walters has been making a million dollars a year now for years, and you are better. Not as experienced, not a household name yet, but better. Your ratings here are fantastic, and as I told you years ago, that's all we look at in this business."

Tracy Brown signed a three-year contract with United Broadcasting System on February 5, 1981. The contract's language specified that she would be a "principal correspondent" for the UBS news operation and that she would handle "Washington based political interviews" for the UBS early morning news and variety show, "A.M. America."

PART FOUR
Tony

Chapter Twenty-Two

MILAN, ITALY—JUNE, 1983

Tracy stood on the opposite corner for a long time, looking at the huge office building across the street which took up the entire block. The product of the imagination of one of the leading architects of postwar Italy, the skyscraper appeared to be constructed of steel, black marble, and black mirrors. She knew those mirrors were actually enormous shaded planes of glass. The words "Dandolo Int." were carved above the massive entrance.

She gripped her briefcase tighter, took a deep breath, summoned up all her courage, and crossed the street with the light. It had taken her a long time to make the decision to confront her past, her real identity. She was now determined to carry it off with great aplomb.

She gave her name to the guard on duty at the security desk and permitted her purse and briefcase to be searched. "I have an appointment with Count Dandolo at four."

The guard nodded his head and picked up the phone, pushing one button as he did. "Your name, please?"

"Tracy Brown. I'm a reporter with the United Broadcasting System in the United States."

A minute later, a tall young man, dressed impeccably in a vested banker's suit, arrived to escort her to Count Dandolo's office. "My name is Mario Visconti. The count has asked me to assist you in every possible way during your stay in Italy."

He led her past a long bank of elevators to the one on the far left and turned a key in the lock on the wall. Instantly the door opened and they stepped in. Mario then pushed the PH button, and they sped to the top of the building, Tracy's ears registering the quick ascent with several popping sensations.

"Have you just arrived?"

"No, I flew in from Rome last evening."

"Then you've had a chance to see a bit of our city?"

"Yes, I spent the morning and early afternoon sightseeing, then I had lunch and people-watched. It was great fun!"

"Ah, you've only begun. I hope I will have the pleasure of showing you much more of Italy."

"Thank you, that would be very nice." So that means, she told herself grudgingly, that the count himself doesn't intend to spend much time with me! She wanted to ask him why he had been chosen for the honor of escorting the American television star around Milan, but then realized it was probably because his English was perfect and he was eminently presentable.

Mario escorted her into a large reception room which was presided over by a beautiful young woman sitting at a large glass-and-chrome desk. It seemed her only job was directing traffic in and out of the count's private office. The young woman, obviously expecting Tracy and a bit in awe of the television star whose reputation had not only preceded her, but for whom the count had made lavish preparations, asked her to be seated on one of the several beige suede upholstered sofas. "May I offer you coffee? Or perhaps tea?"

"No, thank you, I'm really not thirsty." Just nervous as hell!

"The count will be with you in a few minutes."

While she waited, she surveyed the reception room. It was larger than her entire apartment, she thought. And magnificent in an understated way. The floors in the hallways were beige marble, but in the large reception area they were covered with deep plush wool. The walls were covered in a textured wall covering which looked very much like the suede covering the sofa. Several glass-and-chrome coffee tables adorned the room, but the striking decoration, which the entire area served as background for, was the modern art. Huge canvases filled the walls; large sculptures in bronze, copper, and etched glass filled space which had obviously been designed exactly for that purpose. A few large green plants added the only touches of warmth. It was a cold, pristine environment, the kind of place where people spoke in whispers and telephones were muted. Then she realized what she was missing. Nowhere were there typewriters busily chattering away, nor was there a computer in sight.

She rubbed her hands together to warm them. They felt like ice, and her stomach was churning.

This is worse than waiting for the camera to roll, she thought as she checked her briefcase to be sure her tape recorder was inside.

At that moment a tall, distinguished-looking man strode quickly around the corner and into her line of vision. Her heart tumbled to her feet as she looked up into the eyes of her father, hoping against hope, against all her preparations to the contrary, that he would recognize her.

He didn't.

Instead, in a very formal European way, he bent to kiss her hand. She used the moment to regain her composure while she listened to his melodious, passionate voice sing her name.

"Miss Brown. What an honor it is that you have come across the ocean to visit with us!"

She stood, tried to find her voice, and finally managed to say, "I'm so pleased, Count, that you have agreed to this rather rigorous round of interviews."

"If it will help improve my Italy's image with your countrymen, then I'm all for it."

He took her by the elbow in a courtly but possessive way and guided her around the corner into his inner sanctum.

She gasped upon entering the room, overwhelmed by the view of Milan which spread out below them. Rather than taking the seat he had indicated, she walked over to the window and looked down. "This is . . . spectacular! When the cameras come on Monday, we must get this view."

"The weather is perfect today. Sometimes there are clouds obscuring the view, and some days I look out into a sea of clouds and it feels as if I'm in an airliner."

As she turned to the sofa he had initially indicated, she spied the paintings on the walls of his office. Again, she was speechless for a long minute.

"The . . . artist . . . those paintings, are lovely. Who is the artist?" she managed to get out, even though she already knew the answer.

"Those paintings . . ." Now he seemed at a loss for an explanation. ". . . were painted by my wife, Lorna Dandolo. These days, I believe she uses her maiden name professionally. You might have seen her work before; she is an American."

"They are lovely, yes, very nice." It was too soon to begin talking about her mother; she didn't want the series of interviews to go that direction yet.

She opened her briefcase, took out her tape recorder, and placed it on the coffee table, though she didn't turn it on. Then she took out a steno-graphic pad and a pen. Meanwhile, he walked toward a credenza at the other end of the room. "It's late, it's Friday, and this is only the beginning of our week together, so why don't we get ac-quainted first, before you turn on that machine. Will you join me in a glass of wine? Or perhaps some sherry?"

"Sherry would be lovely, thank you." She used the time while he was getting their drinks to look around the room again and decide on her opening tactics.

"Could we discuss my schedule and the ground rules a bit first?" he asked as he walked back toward her, gave her a glass of sherry, and sat down in a dark blue velvet club chair.

She nodded acquiescence.

"I thought it would be nice if you spent the weekend with us at our villa in Florence. We have horses—I understand you ride?"

"Yes. Sounds like you've done some homework, too!"

"Naturally. I probably know as much about you as you know about me at this point. I daresay I have a larger staff to do the necessary research."

My God, that can't be so! He can't possibly know who I really am. If he did, he never would have agreed to this charade!

"We'll show you Florence and you'll have a chance to get acquainted with my son Alberto. And then we can do the first taping there on Sunday, as you requested."

"Wonderful. I'd like to schedule the camera crew for two o'clock Sunday afternoon, if that's agreeable. That way, we will have the option of filming indoors or out, whichever seems more appropriate." Her hands were hot and sweaty, and her stomach reeled at the mention of Alberto. *Dear God, help me carry this off,* she prayed silently.

"Tuesday and Wednesday I have to be in Rome for nonstop meetings both days. You asked to follow me around during a typical week, so I've scheduled myself as if you weren't going to be with me."

"Fine. I'll alert the camera crews to be available all day, both days. Perhaps someone on your staff could assist me with hotel reservations."

"I've taken the liberty of doing that already. You can fly with me in my plane. And I've reserved two seats on commercial airlines for your crew. I've confirmed hotel reservations in Florence and Rome, and company cars for your use as long as you are in Italy."

"You've thought of everything. Thank you." He was an exceedingly thoughtful and pleasant man. *I can't help myself,* she thought, *I like him.*

This was going to be great fun, just as he had expected, Tony Dandolo thought as he studied the

American television star. He loved a challenge, he loved being interviewed, he loved reading his own press. And besides, it was good for Italy's image abroad.

"Now about that machine . . ."

"If you find it totally intimidating, I won't use it. But, you see, I have several sets of plans for these interviews."

"Yes, tell me about the format of your show."

"In addition to my daily pieces for 'A.M. America,' I do an hour special once a month called 'Windows on the World'. I do an in-depth interview, usually on location—both office and home—of a major international figure. We do two people each program, alloting half an hour to each."

"You are going to follow me for a week and turn it into half an hour?" Christ, he thought, what a waste of time!

"We will shoot seven or eight hours of film and edit it down to half an hour. But I will also be doing a separate piece for *The New York Times Sunday Magazine.* And there is also some talk of doing a ninety-minute film for educational purposes for our high schools to use. The film we shoot next week will be used many ways."

"I see. I guess that makes more sense, then." She is a very bright, very industrious woman, this one! And beautiful to boot!

"Again, let me reassure you, if you object to the tape recorder, I won't use it."

"I have no objection. If I want to tell you something off-the-record, I'll ask you to turn it off."

"Agreed."

"Where would you like to start? I ask you because I've told my pilot to be ready to leave for Florence at six. Even though you will be with us for the weekend, I do not intend to work, if you understand what I mean, after six on Friday night!" They both laughed, and Tracy sipped her drink, indicating by her smile that she understood the Thank-God-its-Friday feeling and shared it with him.

She planned on starting by discussing the history of his business enterprises. He told her to start her tape rolling, because it would be a long story. Then he sat back, savoring the opportunity to recall the many stories his father and grandfather had told him. While he talked, he watched her, unable to take his eyes off her lovely face. Her skin had the glow of sheer alabaster, reminding him of a marble of the Virgin Mary he had seen somewhere long ago. Her eyes were the deepest green he had ever seen; one moment they looked like priceless emeralds, then they sparkled like black opals. It was her enthusiasm, her total absorption in the story he was telling her, that caught him by surprise. She seemed enchanted with his family history—almost, he might imagine, with himself. She crossed her legs, and for a split second he saw the soft flesh of her inner thigh and felt a stirring in his groin. *My God, she is gorgeous! And I've got to be on my best behavior*!

At five thirty, just as he was really getting wound up, he glanced at his watch and said, "That's it for today, Tracy. Let's go get your bags and go to the airport. We dine at nine. I've invited three couples, something I frequently do on a Friday. You'll enjoy them."

The next morning Tracy slept late, then awoke to discover she was ensconced in a glorious blue-and-coral guest bedroom in the Villa Dandolo. For a while, she didn't move, but simply luxuriated in the incredible glamour of the pagoda-like four-poster bed and the scent of fresh roses; then she began replaying scenes from the evening before in her head. It had felt like a whirlwind; so many conflicting and tumultuous emotions had rolled around within her, and the necessity of keeping up pleasant chitchat with the dinner guests, the necessity of forcing herself to be gracious to Alberto—not to mention the necessity of making mental notes about things she wanted to recreate in her pieces on the Count—had added up to exhaustion.

She had forced herself to think of him as "The Count," rather than her father. It was a kind of trick, like putting horse-blinders on herself, that would force her to concentrate, or at least appear to be concentrating, on the reason for her trip.

·Deep in her heart she knew the real reason for her trip was to see her father again, to measure her own emotions toward him after she had given him a fair chance to demonstrate who he was and what he was all about. Then—if he passed muster, if he passed all the tests she would throw at him—she might let him know who she was. That was the part she hadn't thought through. What happened at the end of the week of interviews, next Friday?

She climbed out of the big bed and walked to the window and opened the draperies. Below stretched the magnificence of the estate—a mosaic terrace with a fountain in the center surrounded by ancient boxwood and holly, steps leading out to a small lake where swans, ducks, and flamingos were being fed by one of the groundskeepers. To the right she saw huge flower gardens, a large greenhouse, and in the distance several barns, possibly the stables.

At that moment, a door beneath her opened and she saw the top of Tony's head appear. He sat down at one of the round tables set with breakfast china and the butler immediately began to serve him.

Feeling that she was spying on him, almost a

voyeur, Tracy walked into the bathroom and began to fill the blue marble tub with water and bath crystals. As she lowered herself into the tub, she ordered herself to think through her emotions.

What about her halfbrother Alberto? Almost—almost but not quite—the spitting image of his father, with different coloring. Alberto was lean, trim, and had his mother's peaches-and-cream complexion, complete with the freckles and her red hair. But he was blessed with the blue eyes, just like her own, that Tony was so proud of in his family. Alberto seemed the perfect heir-apparent—obviously intelligent and well-educated, he had Tony's love for people. He could charm her, anytime, Tracy mused, as she remembered how he had tried to get her alone outdoors last night. If only he knew!

He looked and acted older than his years—he must be twenty-two or twenty-three by now—but he was so much more sophisticated than his American counterparts! He was being groomed . . .

She climbed out of the tub and picked up the phone to order breakfast. Then she wrapped herself in a blue satin and lace dressing gown and sat down at the desk to make notes in her journal. Before any of it escaped her, she must record her first impressions—and then match them with her feelings when she left the following Friday.

She picked up her pen and began, "The Dandolo men are enormously likeable. . . ."

She wrote for an hour before Alberto interrupted her with a phone call. "Can I interest you in a game of tennis?"

"I'd love it, but I didn't bring tennis clothes."

"No problem. Just tell me what size shoes, and I'll deliver the works in five minutes."

It was completely one-sided. Tracy was hardly in

Alberto's league, but at least it gave her a chance to get to know him. After the game, he took her into town for a sandwich at his favorite deli. He was, she noticed, becoming increasingly smitten with her. *This is great fun,* she thought. *I'm turning into quite a tease!*

When they arrived back at the villa, Tony was finishing a solitary lunch. "What would you like to see?" Tony asked, then before giving her a chance to respond, he said, "Come. I'll give you a tour of the grounds first, then a tour of the house. It's probably one of the most historic things you'll see on your entire trip!"

He gave her the grand tour and it was glorious, but her heart nearly stopped when he took her into his second-floor library. It was an enormous room, with two walls filled with ancient leather-bound books and two walls covered with pictures. One of the largest canvases was of Tracy with her grandmother Catarina. It was the twin of the one she had in her bedroom, the last painting her mother had completed before her death. Tracy remembered going with Lorna to the post office to mail it to Catarina.

Nervously, she let him lead her around the room, pointing out all the famous pictures—his father with Stalin, with Averell Harriman, with President Kennedy; himself with various European heads of state, with Queen Elizabeth, with the Shah of Iran and other Middle Eastern princes. She was dizzy; she desperately wanted to ask him about the picture of herself.

"And this is my wife, Lorna. See, here she is between Toscanini and Enrico Mattei. Wasn't she a beauty? She was a famous fashion model in New York. I'll bet you didn't know that, did you?"

Tracy shook her head, unable to find her voice.

"This picture was taken on her first visit to the villa. I'll never forget that weekend. She was the most beautiful woman at the dinner. I fell head-over-heels, and my father and mother adored her.

"Here we are in Washington. See Tanya! This is our little daughter. . . ."

Tracy held her breath. What could she say? How could she respond to his obvious enthusiasm and—she had to admit it—to the love that poured out of his voice as he looked at the pictures.

Finally, she found her voice and asked, "Where . . . where is Tanya now?"

His hand dropped down to her waist, and he gently guided her away from the pictures, as if it had suddenly become too much for him. "I don't know," he answered in a quiet voice. "I don't know where she is, and that is a very sad story. Perhaps, before you leave, I'll tell you about that . . . I."

She felt his overwhelming grief and thought her eyes were about to fill with tears. Quickly, she turned to the large portrait of herself with Catarina.

"Tell me about this painting."

"That is Lorna's painting of Tanya with my mother. It was a gift to my mother. When she died . . ."

Tracy felt her face register pain. Her beloved Catarina was dead. She had read about her death in the paper at the time, but it still grieved her to think about it.

"What's wrong, Tracy?"

"Nothing. I just had a pain in my stomach. I have an ulcer, and it's probably reacting to the pas-trami."

"Can I get you something, perhaps some medicine?"

"No, I'll be fine. Please continue about the painting."

"When mother died, she had this painting hanging in her bedroom directly across from her bed. Tanya was her favorite person in the whole world." Tony stopped, took his handkerchief out of his smoking jacket and wiped his brow, blew his nose, then continued.

"When I moved into the villa, I put this painting in this room. It's where I spend most of my time when I'm home, and with it hanging there, I almost feel I have mother and Tanya here with me. Forgive me, but I'm a very sentimental man when it comes to family. My family means everything to me."

Tracy suddenly had an idea. "Could we—would you mind if we used this room for the filming tomorrow? It's filled with your family history, and I think it's the perfect setting."

"You are the boss. It would be fine with me. But I was hoping you'd want to film in the garden."

"I'll do some shots there, too. Perhaps of you and Alberto walking, inspecting the swans—yes, we'll do film both outdoors and here. I'd like to have just you, sitting in that leather chair at your table; then we'll do some shots with you and me—perhaps you'll tell me some of the stories about the beginnings of Dandolo Enterprises—then we'll cut to Milan, then to Rome. . . ."

"Tell me your impressions of America. What did you feel toward us when you left to return to Italy?" Tracy asked as she put her soup spoon down. They were dining alone at a table set for two in the downstairs library in front of a window overlooking the lake.

"I was very impressed with your young President John Kennedy and his wife. They seemed to have captured the imagination of the younger generation. Yes, those were heady days for America. Of course, coming from Italy, and being so tremendously in debt to the Americans for rescuing Italy after the war, I had feelings of gratitude mixed with resentment for America's arrogance. One never really likes one's patron, not in life or in politics."

He placed his spoon on the plate and wiped his lips with the linen napkin. The butler stepped forward to remove the first course. Tony reached for the wine bottle to refresh Tracy's glass.

"Don't forget that my stay in America was a great personal tragedy for me. As I told you this morning, I lost both my wife and my daughter. I left a broken man."

Tracy was stunned by his description of himself, having let herself imagine over the years that he left happily with his new baby son and mistress.

"I probably shouldn't talk about it." He grinned mischievously. "You don't have a concealed tape recorder, do you?"

"No," she murmured, hoping he would continue. Now that she was fortified with two glasses of wine, perhaps she could handle whatever he wanted to tell her.

"I feel this need to explain it to you, I don't know why. Somehow you instill in me a willingness to open up. Perhaps that's one of the reasons you're famous for your articles. I've read them all, you know."

"I sort of imagined you might have."

"Yes. You can be a bitch too, I realize."

The butler returned and placed gold-and-cobalt china dinner plates in front of them, then began to serve veal Orloff and fresh asparagus. After he had poured the red wine, the butler retired and left them alone again.

"As you saw in the pictures, Lorna was a magnificent-looking woman. She had been a model, but her greatest love was art, both the history and study of art, and painting itself. After she left me, she supported herself by selling her paintings. I bought them whenever I could locate them, and I also sent her a substantial check once a year to be sure she had everything."

Tracy swallowed to hide her amazement. She knew her mother had sold paintings, and now she understood that the best customer had been her father. But she had no idea that Lorna had received a check for support. Perhaps he was lying, trying to sound good for the American reporter.

"Did you get divorced?"

"No, Lorna simply took Tanya and disappeared. I was shattered, couldn't believe it, kept thinking one day she would realize what a mistake she had made and come back."

"You didn't do anything to find her?"

"Not at first. I—I think I was afraid of myself, of what I might do. I have a ferocious temper, you see. I also have a tremendous ego, and I couldn't quite accept the fact that she had left me! Me! The person who had made her a countess, who had lifted her out of poverty, taken her away from her provincial childhood in South Dakota and made a veritable princess out of her. I mean, it was like a Cinderella story, for God's sake! And she walked away from it. She gave it all up! It made me so damn mad—I don't know, I might have done something terrible if I'd found her."

He sipped his wine, gathered his thoughts, and continued. "The worst of it was that she took Tanya. Under Italian law, the father always has custody of the children. We don't believe in divorce in this country; it's one of the fundamental differences between Italy and America. Divorce is too easy in America. Families fall apart when there's one argument, one infidelity. In Italy, the family is everything. More important than any government, more important than any other allegiance."

"Why did Lorna leave you?"

"That's a very sad story. If I could live my life over . . . my greatest grief, my greatest regret is that I . . . it's true I was a foolish, headstrong young man who imagined I could have everything no matter who I hurt. I fell in love with Tamara, who was Lorna's best friend, confidante, and social secretary. We didn't want to fall in love. We tried to fight it at first, but it happened." He paused to sip his wine. "And Tamara got pregnant with Alberto. Well, I don't believe in abortion. I don't want anyone killing a child of mine, not when I can provide handsomely for that child, not when I'm willing to accept full responsibility for that child. And besides, Lorna couldn't have any more children and I wanted a son." He sighed, resigned to admitting the truth. "I really wanted a son very badly."

It wasn't enough to have me as a daughter? You had to have a son to satisfy your male ego, your paternalistic pride? Tracy thought with resentment. But she hastened to ask, "So Lorna discovered the affair?"

"Yes. Tamara tried suicide and we split up. She went to Florida to live with her parents, Alberto was born, then she came back to the Washington area. I really don't understand, Tracy, why I'm telling you all this. . . ."

"Sometimes one needs to talk."

"Yes. The affair started again. I asked Lorna to adopt Alberto. She refused. That would have been the Italian solution to the problem, but Lorna had this rigid set of rules, a sort of Protestant attitude toward sin.

"In retrospect, after years of analyzing it in the middle of the night—you may be sure, Tracy, that I have my 'dark nights of the soul' and when I do, it's Lorna and Tanya that my mind turns to—well, I've come to believe that Lorna's mother had poisoned her attitude toward men even before I met her. Also, she never felt she really belonged here. She felt she was a sort of imposter, living this life of wealth and culture. She never got over her South Dakota roots, and she almost felt guilty for having so much when her ancestors had had so little."

"Did you talk with her about that?"

"No. I don't think I was consciously aware of it at the time. In fact, I really didn't think it through until after my mother came back from seeing Lorna and Tanya. She said something to me, something which started me thinking. Mother said, 'Lorna is living in such a way that it makes me think she is deliberately punishing herself for something. I can't imagine what she feels so guilty about.' That set me thinking."

"And?"

"I remembered that Lorna never let me go to South Dakota to see where she grew up, she never took me to meet her mother. She didn't want me to know, firsthand, her background. The only thing I get from that is that in the deepest recesses of her soul, she was ashamed of her family, her background. She had deliberately chosen to marry me, to accept my lifestyle. But some part of her felt guilty about her feelings toward her background and at the same time she felt inadequate to play the roles she felt I expected of her. She never got over that."

"Mmhh . . ." Tracy responded, groping for a next question to keep the conversation going. "Did Lorna ever remarry?"

"I don't know. After my mother's death, she left her entire estate to Tanya—"

Tracy gasped, put her fork down suddenly and looked at Tony, her eyes pleading for further explanation.

"Yes, she left the villa, all the art, her jewelry collection, and her stock in Dandolo Enterprises to Tanya."

"And you still didn't find Tanya?" she demanded furiously.

"No. Mother had traced them to Woodstock, Virginia. Then they disappeared off the face of the earth. Three years ago, I sent a private investigator to Woodstock, but there was no record of where they had gone, no forwarding address at the post office. The home they lived in has been sold three times since."

"So you have no idea what happened?" Tracy paused, then had a thought. "But what about the money—you said earlier that you send them money every year."

"Yes. I arranged with a lawyer, who I think was sweet on Lorna anyhow, to deliver a sum of money to her once a year. He has subsequently died, and a young lawyer in the firm forwards the money to Lorna. But when I tried to find their whereabouts, he pleaded client privilege. It seems Lorna has forbidden them to release that information to anyone."

"So you've given up trying to find them?"

"Not really. Every now and again, I stir myself and contact a detective agency. There was a maid, a woman who came to work for us in Florence shortly after we married. I've always suspected that she was in cahoots with Lorna. Several things were missing when we unpacked. I've always felt that Rosina took them to Lorna."

"Like what, for instance?"

"Well, there were two small oil paintings in the embassy library. Extremely valuable. Lorna loved them, and somehow they got lost in the move."

Tracy looked down at her plate to suppress the smile that she knew suffused her face. Those two paintings hung in her bedroom at the Watergate. Rosina had stolen them from her father. Good for Rosina!

"Where is the maid now? Surely you can locate her?"

"I don't know." Tony sighed helplessly. "I've lost track of her too. I suppose I could track her down with the help of the State Department and the immigration service, but something is keeping me from it. I don't know, but I think it is my fear of rejection."

"Rejection?"

"Yes. Tanya would be a young woman by now, a bit younger than you are. I don't know what Lorna has told her about me, about our marriage. I'm sure she knows about Tamara and Alberto. But I don't know how much she hates me." He pulled a handkerchief from his pocket, wiped his eyes, then looked directly at Tracy.

"Pardon me. I'm sure you're not used to seeing a grown man cry. Americans don't. But I do. We're talking about the most painful thing in my life. I would give anything to find my daughter. There isn't a day that goes by that I don't wish for her. But I don't think I could live another day if I found out that she hates me. That's what I'm afraid of."

Tracy found she had to look away to avoid his eyes; they were too sincere, too filled with agony. An agony she had it in her power to end.

"What about your mistress? Why didn't you marry her?"

"I tried, but I couldn't get the Church to give me an annulment. Oh, I adopted Alberto. The whole world recognizes him as my son and heir."

"Where is she now?"

"I took care of her for years. She lived in a beautiful villa in Florence. But she wanted respectability, so she married a member of the Chamber of Deputies three years ago."

"And so . . . you're alone?"

"For the moment, yes. Let's change the subject—enough of this personal stuff. Let me tell you about the museum I'm building in Kenya. . . ."

After that, they both forced the conversation to stay on a lighter plane. He was in the middle of a discussion of how Aldo Mora's assassination had changed his attitude toward security when Alberto reappeared, filled with anecdotes about the party he had attended.

"They missed you, father, and they told me to warn you that Tracy Brown is a devil!" Alberto announced, with a twinkle in his voice, believing that his father was more than equal to any American interviewer. Tony retired shortly thereafter, leaving Alberto and Tracy to feed the swans a midnight snack of cheese and crackers. Tracy excused herself as quickly as it was diplomatic to do so and fled to her bedroom to write in her journal.

First, however, she removed the cosmetic contact lenses that changed her eyes from blue to green, and she took off the dark auburn wig that hid her black waves. As she set the wig on its stand, she realized how wise she had been. Surely by now he would have recognized her.

Three hours later she was still awake, unable to relax, unable to stop replaying the evening's conversation against the talks she had had with her mother when she was a young girl.

Chapter Twenty-Three

After tossing and turning, then writing for two hours and taking a hot bath, she finally got out of bed again and paced in her blue satin dressing gown. She felt claustrophobic and longed, for some inexplicable reason, to return to the second-floor library and commune with her beloved grandmother, Catarina. She put on her satin mules, brushed her black waves off her face and quietly made her way down the hall to the library. The door was ajar, and the room was lit softly by a full moon. She walked to the painting and stood looking up at her grandmother's wise, forgiving eyes. For that was what she read in those eyes—forgiveness. And she realized that was an emotion her mother had put in those eyes when she painted the portrait. Had it been in the snapshots? Or was it an addition of Lorna's? Had Lorna been sending Tony a message?

"Beautiful, aren't they?"

Her hand flew to her face, and her stomach lurched as she turned to see Tony sitting in his leather chair, watching her.

"My God, you startled me!"

"I'm sorry. You startled me, too, when you walked in here."

"Oh . . ."

"So you couldn't sleep either, is that it?"

"I guess the . . . must be the jet lag . . . or the strange surroundings."

"Come, sit down." He motioned her to a comfortable wing chair across from him. "I'll fix you a brandy—or would you rather have Amaretto?"

"I'd prefer Amaretto," she said as she slid into the chair, eyes down, hoping that the darkness of the room would obscure the blueness of her eyes and the blackness of her hair.

"Since neither of us is getting any beauty sleep before the cameras roll, tell me about yourself, Tracy."

"I thought you'd done all that homework," she said with a soft laugh.

"But I certainly haven't researched your personal life. Are you married?"

"No. Too busy."

"So, you're one of those women's libbers, is that it?"

"I do agree with the feminists on many things, but I'm not an activist. I'm much too busy with my own career."

"Then there are many men in your life. Or just one special man?"

"There have been a couple of men who have meant a lot to me. But . . ."

"And now? Is there anyone special now?"

"Well, there is this one man. He's in the same business, television."

"I see."

"But he lives in Hawaii, so we don't see much of one another. For the last couple of winters we've gone skiing together. He has a home in Aspen, and I spend a week there."

"Will you marry him?"

"No. He's sort of like you, I think." She couldn't help herself; she wanted to tease him.

"Oh, in what way?"

"He has a proclivity toward wanting lots of women. He doesn't want to settle for just one."

"And you want fidelity?"

"If I decide to marry, which is unlikely, then I would expect fidelity."

Tony made no comment, merely sipped extra long on his brandy.

"It is highly unlikely that I will marry. A television career demands forty-eight hours a day and leaves one no time for a private life."

"And you are determined to continue your career? But of course, that was a stupid question. You've worked hard to get where you are, and of course you will continue. But doesn't there come a time when you've conquered all the worlds there are to conquer? Doesn't it ever get monotonous?"

"It hasn't yet," she said as she smoothed the skirt on her satin gown.

"I think sometimes that I lead my life in constant search of new challenges. And then there are some projects I just give up on."

"For instance?"

"I've given up trying to bring stability to the Italian government. And I've given up trying to explain to everyone else why and how our system works for us."

"Does it?"

"Yes, I think it does. After all, Italy is stronger

than it has ever been—in spite of a new president every few months or years."

"That's why I want to film in this room. The blending of family and government and history and antiquity and art. This room seems a synthesis of the country—warm and old and overflowing with tradition."

"Speaking of that filming, I'm going to escort you to your room so you can get some sleep." He stood and took her by the elbow; then, as they crossed the threshold into the hall, his arm dropped to her waist with a comfortable feel of affection. When they arrived at her bedroom door, he bent down and kissed her forehead. "Goodnight Tracy. You are a very beautiful woman."

With his free hand, he turned the knob and she fled from his warmth and tenderness before she blurted out the words on her mind: *I love you, Daddy!*

Tracy overslept on Sunday and was awakened shortly after noon by the butler, who phoned her to say that Gene Rogers, her cameraman, had arrived. She asked to speak to him.

"Gene, you won't believe this! I've overslept! Listen, while I'm getting ready, you begin to film shots in the dining room, the large reception room, and the library. Be sure to get the ceilings with all those gorgeous frescos. I'll be down in fifteen minutes."

When she arrived downstairs, she found him in the large reception room. "Have you ever seen anything like this house? Wait till you see the grounds."

Gene grinned at her from behind his camera. "Have you ever seen anything as beautiful as the Italian women?"

"I might have known!" She looked through the camera at the ceiling. "You know, as I was dressing I had this incredible idea—let me try it out on you. How about a weekly—or perhaps monthly—series on magnificent homes from all over the world, a sort of televised *Architectural Digest*, taking cameras into the homes, the owners reciting their history, sort of conducting the tour. I'd love to do that kind of show. I'd do this house and one of the Rothschild mansions in England, and Georgia O'Keeffe's home in Abiquiu, New Mexico, and R. C. Gorman's—can you imagine?"

"Sounds terrific. But didn't Edward R. Murrow do that before you were born? Hell, I'm only kidding. When do we begin?"

"Oh shit, Gene, you know how long it takes to get a new idea like that through the big chiefs. Even if they liked it and found a sponsor, it'd be two years! By then I'll be bored with the idea. Oh, well . . ."

Two hours later, Gene was filming the Dandolos as they conducted their tour of the grounds. They stopped to feed the flamingos and swans by the lake, Tony narrated a tour of the topiary gardens, and Alberto narrated a tour of the flower gardens and greenhouse. Then Tony took them into the house for a description of each major painting and the ceiling and wall frescos. He interspersed his narration with vignettes about his family, described the state of the villa when his exiled family returned after the American occupation (Tracy noted that he toned down his animosity for the viewing audience), and credited his mother with having restored the villa and grounds, patiently, over some fifteen years.

He then stunned Tracy by saying for the camera, "When my mother died, she left the villa to my daughter, Tanya Dandolo. We are taking care of it until such time as my daughter is ready to move into it." As the words pealed out of his mouth, Tracy realized that he was making a plea to his daughter in America, and that Tony had agreed to do this interview in hopes that his daughter would be watching back in the states.

My God, this is a terrible game I'm playing with him.

And then they moved upstairs to the library and Tracy prepared herself mentally to go "on-camera," to interview the count.

Chapter Twenty-Four

Tracy had turned down the count's offer of a tour guide, though she had accepted his offer of a car and driver. She wanted to be alone, to wander through the streets of Florence and try to see it through the eyes of her mother when she had first visited Italy in 1951. How had she felt then, and what had her reaction been to the Dandolo family and lifestyle?

That had been the subject matter she had set for herself when she began her stroll along the Arno, but her mind refused to cooperate. Instead, she found herself marveling at the news that she was a fabulously wealthy heiress, owner of one of the greatest private art collections in the world—not to mention the priceless jewels and home her grandmother had bequeathed to her. All she had to do was reveal her true identity to her father. But did she really want the responsibility of all that wealth?

Did she really want to play the roles, to live the life that inheritance would demand of her?

It would mean moving to Florence, to the Villa Dandolo, and becoming a part of the great hoard of international jet setters. She would become the much-photographed socialite attending charity balls, luncheons, dinners, races, polo matches, *ad nauseam*. It would mean fittings at the world's leading couturier houses, vying with all the other beautiful young heiresses to see who could collect the most fantastic clothes, the most magnificent houses—one would never be enough!—and the most spectacular jewels. A rat race in splendor! No, that was not for her.

But what about the option of becoming a major force in Dandolo Enterprises? Her father had said during the taping that sixty-four percent of the stock was controlled by his family, and he had explicitly mentioned his daughter as one of the members of his immediate family. She knew that if she revealed her identity, in view of his horrendous fear of her rejection, he would bend over backward to offer her any position she felt herself to be qualified for in the company. That option had some possibilities, she thought as she rounded the corner and turned onto the Ponte Vecchio.

One by one, the shopkeepers on the ancient bridge were opening their shops and stalls for the day. One jeweler caught her eye and invited her to inspect his wares. She politely looked, then shook her head and walked toward the sidewalk vendor selling juice. She asked for apple juice, then continued slowly down the ancient cobblestones. Her feet remembered being there before even if her head did not. A flood of memories passed through her, and suddenly it was as if she had been there only yesterday, a tiny girl walking with her mother, her grandmother, and Rosina. Yes, she thought, we came here every day for an ice in the afternoon after my nap! The clarity of her memory overwhelmed her—these were the streets and sights and smells of her own childhood.

Her mind turned back to the idea of working with her father, living in Florence, participating in the life of her family. It would be quite a challenge, the kind of challenge she thrived on.

But something bothered her about that idea—something having to do with identity. Was she Italian or was she American? Where was her real allegiance? For all these years, attending American high school and college, she had believed herself to be an American. Not for a moment had she questioned it. It was her mother's heritage. Yet now she wondered . . .

And wouldn't I be submerged by him, by his overwhelming personality? Do I want to work for my father? To live in his shadow?

The glamour of their lifestyle was extremely seductive, the kind of thing she might want to try out for a few years, always keeping her option open to go back to America and resume her television career. But her knowledge of the industry and her mind's strong bent toward common sense quickly convinced her that she could not take a few years' leave of absence from such a highly competitive business as the television industry in America and expect them to welcome her back with open arms when she tired of her jet set existence.

What about a television career in Italy? Could a career like hers be transplanted across the Atlantic? Did she want that? Was her Italian good enough? No, it certainly was not; she would have to do a lot of brushing up on that.

And what about her sense of the Italian cultural

and political scene? That was what made her so effective back home, her intuitive knowledge of what people wanted to know, what they wanted to see and hear when they sat down and flipped on the tube.

Suddenly she stopped still and brushed her hair off her forehead. She had just heard what her own mind was saying: "That was what made her so effective *back home!" In my heart of hearts, home is Washington. That is where I am most comfortable. That is where I belong.*

But it's not as easy as all that. You've got more things to consider. You can't walk away from such a fabulous inheritance.

Yeah, but neither do I have to make any decisions today. Nothing is going to happen to the villa or the art or the jewels today.

A lovely young woman was walking toward her pushing a pram.

And then there's Alberto to think about. Forgive me mother, but I like him. And my father seems healthy, robust in fact, for a man his age with his pressures. My God, how does he do it? How does he keep up with that monster conglomerate and practice politics at the same time? And yet he had time for me, time for these extensive interviews. Not once has he given me less than his undivided attention. Not once has he shortchanged me. In fact, his generosity has been amazing.

Alberto is the perfect son. Yes, Tony has everything a man could want—except peace of mind. He has created his own hell on earth, and I'm the person who could lift him out of it. I could give him peace of mind—but I want him to come to me! That must be my mother's German pride operating again. . . .

Would it be horribly unfaithful to you, mother, if I let him know?

But damn it all, he's guilty! He destroyed her, he ruined her life! It's his fault she left him, his fault she became such a hermit; it's even his fault she was killed in that miserable ski accident.

No. That wasn't fair. He had nothing to do with the ski accident. That was a freak accident and could have happened to her in Italy or in Switzerland, or any place. Lorna did love skiing. It was her one great enjoyment after she left Tony.

Tracy wandered into a residential neighborhood, a street of ancient tall townhouses surrounded by high brick walls. She saw a bench and sat down to rest her weary feet. She watched two young boys toss a ball back and forth under the watchful eye of a maid. Something about the scene was so familiar. . . .

Daddy loves me. He really does. It would be so wonderful to tell him, to see his face . . . but how could he do that to Mother? She must have loved him so, he must have been some sort of incredible god to her. What is it about men and their need for more and more women?

David's words—"like being a small boy in a candystore, wanting to taste each kind once"—reverberated through her mind. Why couldn't they sow their wild oats, do all their damn tasting, before they committed themselves to a woman in marriage?

He claimed he loved both women, Lorna and Tamara, at the same time. Was that possible? Did she still love Stan? Did she love David too? And perhaps—a love of a different texture—did she also still love Rick?

She listened to her heart for the answer. *Yes, I still love Stan. I will always love Stan. Or perhaps it's the memory of Stan and our love for one another that I love. No, that's not quite right. If he walked into my room tonight, I'd make passionate love to him. We could pick up where we left off without missing a beat. And David? Yes, I love David too, but I love him with my eyes open, with the knowledge that we will never make a lifelong commitment to one another. He told me that about himself, and I know him well enough to believe him and respect him for his honesty. And that, surprisingly, doesn't change the passion I feel for him.*

And if I can feel this way about men—love two of them at the same time, even though I'm only sleeping with one of them, and that only occasionally—then I should also be able to under-stand men, understand Daddy. . . .

No, that's not quite right yet. We must live moral lives. It's not right to hurt another person the way my father hurt my mother.

And yet it's not always possible to avoid hurting people. . . .

Her mind replayed the horrible scene when Stan McDivit told her his wife was coming home from the mental hospital, and they were moving to Wisconsin. Stan had hurt her instead of hurting his wife, and she had hated him for it for many months afterward. Yet, with years of hindsight now to reassess the situation, she knew that she had bene-fited mightly from her relationship with Stan. It had been her first experience with love, and he had guided her very gently through the pleasures and the pains. She would not exchange her memories of their love for the pain of their separation. And Stan had done the right thing—she had been young and strong, but his wife had been totally vulnerable.

The thing to remember, she told herself, was that her father did not leave her mother. It was her mother who had chosen to desert him and deprive her of a father while she was growing up, in spite of all the things that father might have done for her.

True, he had fallen in love with another woman, but he claimed he never stopped loving her mother. Did she believe that? Did it make any difference?

She glanced down at her watch, heard her stomach growl, and decided it was time to look for a sidewalk cafe and some lunch. Several blocks later, she found a small cafe that looked exactly right. She ordered soup and a sandwich, then began making notes for her four o'clock interview with Tony. She would pick up the car back at the hotel after lunch and see some more of Florence.

Tony ushered out the manager of his leather-goods factory, asked his secretary to hold his calls, walked over to the window of his small office in Florence, and looked out at the imposing dome of the Duomo. It was three blocks away, but as he looked down the narrow street toward it, he found himself thinking again of Tracy Brown. A striking, brilliant woman. A good match for himself, a challenge.

Be honest with yourself, you fool—she has bewitched you. Admit it!

It was that small inner voice which had been trying to erupt all morning during his business meetings. It had started nagging at him that morning when he was shaving.

The worst thing you can do is try to seduce her. American women, especially liberated ones like Tracy, resent that. Didn't you learn anything from Lorna?

Oh shit! I'm not going to try to seduce her. At least I don't plan to. . . .

You've told her too much, opened up too much to

her. You know she's a bitch, like all those media types. I don't understand why you tell her so much.

I hope she'll be discreet, use some judgment in what she writes about my private life. After all, I can't hurt Alberto, and I sure as hell don't want to hurt Tanya.

It was all the wine and brandy—and something seductive about that woman. She digs it out of me, and makes me feel so good about telling her everything.

He turned from the window and walked to his desk, opened a mahogany humidor, and removed a large cigar.

What the hell, it did feel good to talk about Lorna and Tanya. I never have the opportunity, and she seemed very interested, like she's some sort of psychologist or something.

Well, enough is enough! Remember that tonight in Rome. . . . But what a temptation—the rest of the week, just the two of us together in Rome!

He was startled out of his reverie by a buzzer. His next appointment had arrived.

"Just a few minutes," he answered, willing himself to turn his attention back to more important things. He spotted a picture of Alberto on his bookshelf. "Poor boy," he said aloud, thinking of the crush Alberto had developed on Tracy. He was so young, so unsophisticated, so relatively inexperienced in matters of love. If she was to be seduced, he said to himself, let it be by a man like him!

He pushed the button on his intercom and told his secretary to show Mr. Moravia in.

The late afternoon sun was glistening on the reddish-gold tiles of the Duomo when Tony ushered Tracy and Gene Rogers into his office. They had scheduled two hours with him, and Tracy had specified the general subject she wanted to discuss was the state of the Italian government. "A sort of in-depth philosophical discussion," she had said.

When the red eye of the camera blinked on, Tracy posed the first of her questions:

"Count Dandolo, would you give me your assessment of the stability of the present government?"

The count crossed his leg, relaxed, and began to answer. "Yes, Tracy, but first I'd like to review our recent history for your American viewers. . . .

It was after nine o'clock when Count Dandolo's limousine deposited Tracy at the Excelsior Hotel. He pleaded a political meeting as the reason for not escorting her to a proper dinner on her first night in Rome. She graciously told him that she certainly didn't expect him to babysit her during her stay. Nevertheless, she was disappointed when the bellhop left her in her room. Now what? she wondered. Do I get room service, or do I go downstairs to the dining room alone?

She decided that she would brave the world of Italian night life alone. After all, when would she be back in fabled Rome again?

She bathed and dressed in a blue silk dress, left her green contacts and auburn wig in her bedroom, and, feeling completely relaxed and ready for a good time, she left her room carrying a light sweater and a small bag.

She thought she detected negative vibes when she told the maître d' "one for dinner." He seated her against the wall at a table for two in the ornate dining room. As if to emphasize the fact that she was alone, first the waiter, then the busboy asked her if anyone would be joining her.

She was finishing her lobster when she first noticed a dark-complected businessman sitting three tables away. He was looking at her in a rather forward way, obviously trying to make eye contact at some distance. She looked away, then back—he was, she realized, devastatingly handsome, and he probably felt as alone as she did at that moment. He lifted his glass in a salute to her, and a moment later she was vaguely aware that he had summoned a waiter.

The waiter left his table and came directly to her. "The gentleman across the way would like to buy you a drink, *Signorina*. Are you agreeable?"

"Please tell the gentleman I would be delighted and ask him to join me at my table."

"*Si, Signorina*."

But not without a sniff of disapproval, she thought. If Ben could only see me now, picking up strange men in exotic dining rooms!

She watched a smile break out on the mysterious stranger's face as he quickly stood to join her.

He greeted her in Italian. She returned the greeting, then added in English, "Do you speak English? If so, I'd be more comfortable."

"Yes. My name is Pietro Bocca. I am from Milan, an officer in the Ferrari Corporation." He produced his business card and she introduced herself, not telling him her television affiliation, only her name.

"Are you in Rome on business or simply as a tourist?"

"I have been visiting relatives in Florence, and now I plan on seeing Rome for a few days before returning to America."

"Then you must let me show you Rome by night in a carriage. We will go see the Trevi Fountain, and you can make a wish. I understand they always come true," he said with a big twinkle in his eyes.

"That would be delightful," she responded, pleased that he had something on his mind other than rushing her upstairs to bed.

Chapter Twenty-Five

Thank God she wasn't on camera today, Tracy told herself as she leaned back in the large leather armchair, placed her steno pad on the conference table, and began to take notes on the bank meeting. Tuesday and Wednesday, she and Gene Rogers would follow Tony through his appointed rounds, taping those portions of the meetings he would permit. Meanwhile, Tracy would take notes to refresh her memory when she wrote the voice-over after they edited the film down to half an hour. She would also refer back to the notebooks when she wrote the articles she was planning.

The evening before had been great fun, an unexpected treat. She had seen the ancient monuments, the ruins, and the fountains of Rome by moonlight. Then Pietro had taken her on a tour of night spots. They returned to the Excelsior at three-thirty, exhausted and a bit drunk. He had made no move on her, had not suggested even that he walk her to her bedroom, but had left her on the elevator when he got off at the fourth floor. He had asked her to have dinner with him Tuesday night, and not knowing what Tony's plans were, she had accepted, with the mental reservation that she would cancel out if Tony had other plans for her.

Tracy forced her brain to focus on what was happening at the bank meeting, calling up her limited memory of Italian. Actually, she had surprised herself on the trip by recalling so much that she could understand nearly everything said in Italian if she really concentrated. Her ability to speak was limited, mostly by her inhibition and her pride.

The count was arguing on behalf of a multi-million-dollar loan to a company preparing to do business in Ghana. The loans he frequently sponsored to businesses doing construction work in third-world countries were usually met with dismay from the four conservative members of the board. But if he threw his weight behind the project, he could usually convince five of the members of the board to agree to the loan. He hated to be heavy-handed, but he firmly believed that the way to make money in the coming years was to invest in these countries. Besides, as he had told Tracy, he simply believed it was the right thing to do.

After the morning bank meeting, Tracy, Gene Rogers and a young assistant Gene had hired for the three days they would be in Rome, followed Tony to Al Vicario Restaurant where he was to meet with two Saudi Arabian shieks to discuss an imminent import contract. Tracy sensed immediately that her female presence at a business luncheon was a serious affront to the Saudis, and in spite of

Tony's diplomatic words, the luncheon was stiff and unproductive, except for the greater depth it gave to Tony's image.

Tony, as promised, had managed to coax the prime minister into letting her film a few minutes of their meeting, which took place early in the afternoon. After that they returned to Tony's office for a meeting with some labor leaders, then a meeting with four members of the Chamber of Deputies. Tracy enjoyed watching the Count—her father, she reminded herself with growing pride—manipulate each of these groups to his own point of view, for his own purposes. As the day wore on, she realized how seldom he referred to a briefing paper or asked a question of an aide. He carried around an amazing amount of expertise in his brain, it seemed. His greatest asset was not his knowledge of intricate details or statistics, but his ability to deal with people. As she listened, she found herself wondering how much of what was taking place had been staged for her ears, for her cameras, and how much of it would have happened anyway.

In addition to his charismatic personality, she marveled at his basic decency, a view which she had not had of her father before seeing him at work. Everything she had felt for him had been colored by her mother's anguish, by the way in which he had hurt her mother. Now she saw the public man, the man who counseled responsibility, negotiation, reconciliation, and occasionally took big chances. But, she noticed, when he took chances, it was with his own money, not with other people's money, not with government funds. With those funds he was strangely conservative.

A new image began to take shape: he was a leader of men, a moral man who believed in his country with every cell in his body, a man who had arrived at a stage in his life where his country meant far more to him than personal wealth, even if he did have more money than he could ever spend in his lifetime. What made him tick, she came to realize, was love of country and love of a challenge. Each new challenge, each person he came in contact with, was a challenge. He must woo and win that person; he must enlist that person in his causes. While he always dominated the meetings—even one-on-one conversations—he did it in a tactful, gentle way. He never raised his voice, never argued too loudly for his cause. He dominated in a quiet, strong, almost magnetic way. He would make a strong prime minister—perhaps just what his country needed. She must ask him about that later that night.

When the last meeting was over, the participants gone, he turned to Tracy and Gene. "Well, you two must have enough tape for five specials by now!"

"It's been wonderful. Thank you for letting us eavesdrop all day."

"Time for happy hour!" he announced as he opened the bar in his office and offered them a drink. Gene packed up his equipment and sent it back to the hotel via his assistant; then the three of them began "happy hour." After two drinks, they decided to adjourn to a favorite watering hole of members of the Chamber of Deputies. Tracy excused herself to cancel her dinner date with Pietro. They drank, then had huge steaks, and after dinner Tony declared that the evening was still young and invited Tracy and Gene "to see Rome in all her glory."

Gene begged off, pleading exhaustion; Tracy knew he had a date waiting. She decided to stay and enjoy her father, for she would have so little chance to be with him in the future—God only knew when she would get back to Italy!

They went to Cabala and Tony ordered drinks. The first show was over, and the second wouldn't begin for two hours. "In that case, let's dance a bit."

Tony took her in his arms, holding her as she had known he would, with all the masculine possessiveness his macho ego required. She felt wave after wave of sexual energy pass between them, and a little voice in the back of her brain began to tell her she was skating on dangerous ice.

She pulled away, noting a puzzled look in his eyes, but they continued the dance until the music stopped. When they sat down, he reached for her hand. She wanted to withdraw it from his reach, but couldn't quite bring herself to do it.

"I hate to confess it to you, Tracy, but you've bewitched me—I haven't felt like this since I met Lorna, a lifetime ago."

"But—but that's absurd!"

"What's absurd about it? You are a decent, serious, highly attractive and extremely intelligent woman. A man would have to be crazy and blind not to fall in love with you."

"That's ridiculous. You're . . ."

"I'm what?"

She blushed, then rushed on, "Old enough to be my father."

Quietly, his eyes momentarily cast down, he said, "I realize that. Don't think I haven't thought about it. Don't worry, child, I'm not propositioning you. I'm only telling you that you hold an enormous attraction for me. Let's go. Besides, there's something I want to show you back at my apartment."

Torn by rampaging emotions, she followed him

blindly out of the nightclub. He was taking her to his private apartment, there would be just the two of them, and he had told her he was sexually attracted to her. What should she do?

Well, he's not a rapist, I know that. And I won't let him touch me.

Still, she knew she was playing with fire. . . .

As they drove through the beautiful city, Tony pointed out landmarks from time to time, but did not revert to his previous seductive talk. They entered the building—"I built this seven years ago"—and he removed the key to his own private elevator to the penthouse apartment from his pocket and inserted it. They sped to the top, where the elevator opened directly into a spacious art gallery, filled with sculpture and modern abstract oils. But when they entered the living rooms, they took her breath away. White upholstered French furniture was arranged invitingly in conversational groupings; the walls were covered with white-on-white stripped silk wall covering, and the floor was carpeted in deep white plush wool. The color in the room was provided by eight large impressionist canvases. She knew without looking for the signature that they were all by her mother. Yet she did not recognize any of them; she could not remember her mother ever having created canvases so large.

"These paintings—are they by your wife?"

"Yes. They are her best, to my mind. She painted these during the first years of our marriage, before we left for the United States. I had them in storage, then decided this apartment would be the perfect showplace for them. Do you like them?"

"Yes. They are lovely, so full of happiness and serenity—the pure joy of living."

"Exactly. It gives me great peace of mind to come

here after a hard day at the Chamber and simply sit in the room and let my mind go blank. It's . . . it's almost as if Lorna is here with me."

"You . . . you love her still?"

"I don't think a person ever gets over that kind of love. Real love. I will always love her, till the day I die."

Tracy was silent.

"Can you understand that? Is there anyone you feel that way about?"

Tracy thought of Stanley McDivit. Quietly, barely daring to look at Tony's eyes, she answered, "Yes, I think I know exactly what you mean. Love continues, even after the relationship ends. Sometimes it takes a while to get over the hate. . . ."

"Yes, exactly! Come, there's something I want to show you." He led the way into what Tracy realized was his bedroom. She steeled herself for whatever was coming.

He took a large canvas, another one of Lorna's, off the wall to reveal a wall safe behind it. He turned the combination, took out a black leather case, and carried it to the dresser. Carefully, he opened the case.

Inside the case, she saw an exquisite diamond-and-sapphire necklace with matching earrings. And even as she stared at the necklace, with its seven sapphires the size of quarters—or robin's eggs!— she began to remember it. It was the gift her father had given to her mother that Christmas—that Christmas immediately before President Kennedy was inaugurated. The Christmas Eve scene played itself out again in her memory, a scene she had blocked out all these years. Tears formed in her eyes. She knew Tony was looking at her for a reaction.

"Beautiful! Absolutely beautiful . . ."

"They were Lorna's."

She almost murmured, *I know, I was there, I remember.* But she stopped herself just in time.

"She must have sold them because she needed the money. Anyhow, when my agent at Sotheby's called me about this necklace, I asked for a picture. Then I had it sent here so Bulgari could authenticate it, since he had made the necklace to my specifications originally. Sure enough, it was Lorna's necklace, so I bought it a second time."

"Why? Why did you want the necklace? Didn't it bring back bitter memories?"

"I wanted it for Tanya. Someday I want her to have these jewels. I want her to have everything which would have been her inheritance; I want her to have everything I can give her."

"And—and yet you can't seem to give her yourself. You can't bring yourself to go back to America and find her. . . ."

He left her side then and walked to the window. After a while she saw him reach in his pocket and pull out a handkerchief, wipe his eyes, and replace the handkerchief. "You think I should, then," he said without turning from the window.

"Perhaps that's what she's waiting for. She probably has as much pride as you and Lorna seem to have."

"I never thought of it that way. . . ."

She wanted to tell him. She wanted to pick up the necklace and claim it as her own, not because she coveted the jewels, but because the necklace was a powerful symbol of her father's undying love for her mother—and for her. But the moment passed.

He walked past her, back out into the living room, to the bar. He needed a brandy. Slowly, reluctantly, she followed him.

"I'm afraid I'm giving you the wrong impression

of me. I've broken down several times—that's not usually my style."

"Don't worry about it. I'll forget it immediately. Promise." She accepted the brandy snifter from him.

"Let's sit and enjoy these paintings."

The next morning Tracy felt surprisingly bright-eyed and bushy-tailed as she ate her breakfast on the run. It suddenly hit her that she felt so good because last night she had learned conclusively that her father loved her—that is, he loved Tanya. Troublesome was the news that he also loved Tracy Brown with a sexual love! She was beginning to botch this whole thing, she thought as she waltzed into his Chamber office and announced herself to the secretary.

The middle-aged blonde looked her up and down, then said, "Yes, he's been asking for you for the past half hour. Are you late?"

Tracy checked her watch. She wasn't late; she was five minutes early.

"Good morning!" Tony greeted her effusively. "My, you look good! I've got the television gallery passes I promised! My God, what a hassle."

Tracy sat down and accepted a cup of coffee he had poured for her. "I hope you won't find today too tedious. I expect to give a speech around eleven, and you can tape it if you wish. Then I've scheduled a luncheon with Valentino—I thought you might like that!" He beamed as he watched her face light up. "We sell the finest of our fabrics to him.

"This afternoon you can probably forget about filming anything. I've got loads of paperwork back here at the office, and no appointments of any consequence. Would you like my car and driver to do some shopping or sightseeing? I've made reservations for us at nine at Domus Aurea for dinner. I think you'll enjoy it."

"Wonderful. You've organized my day splendidly, as I've come to expect."

By four, however, she was exhausted from her week in Italy. She asked the driver to return her to the Excelsior, where she collapsed in bed until it was time to dress for dinner.

Flickering candlelight, the heady scent of roses, sweet violins, magnificent food and service—it was the perfect setting for romance. Tracy had developed two sets of antennae: one set for Count Anthony Dandolo, the sexy older macho man of every woman's dreams, and one set for her father. As she sat across from him on their third night in Rome, the idea that he was her father kept fleeing from her conscious mind. It was almost as if she had willed herself to forget it.

He was, she felt at that moment, the sexiest man she had ever come across. Was it his power, his wealth, his body? No, she told herself as she listened to him talk about world energy problems, it wasn't those extraneous things, it was his personality—his decency, his arrogance, his graciousness, his perfect manners, his brilliance . . . and his sense of himself, his firm grasp on who he was, on his power and his limitations. She loved him dearly, and she could see why any woman would fall in love with him.

"You know, Tracy, tonight is the first time since you arrived in Italy that you seem distracted. Am I boring you?"

He read her mind! "No, I think I'm beginning to be tired. I napped this afternoon, but it's been a big week, and it is catching up. I'm sorry. Please continue."

"No, let's dance instead."

She allowed herself to be led to the dance floor, as the small voice in the back of her head again objected.

"If I came to America, could I see you?"

"You mean—like a date?"

"Yes. We could have a nice dinner at your favorite restaurant. You could show me Washington. It's been a long time since I've been there. I'm sure a lot has changed."

"I don't—I don't know."

He suddenly held her at arm's length. "Tracy, do I repulse you? Am I so old that it's unthinkable that we . . . that you and I . . . ?"

"Yes. It's absolutely out of the question," she blurted out, not meaning for it to sound so mean and angry. "I—I lied to you the other day, I—I do have a man in my life, who means a lot to me. A special man."

"I see." He resumed dancing, daring to press his face against her forehead. After a few minutes, he said, "I have a question."

They pulled apart and she looked up at him. "Yes?"

"Why did you lie to me? Were you trying to get me to proposition you so you could humiliate me?"

"Oh, no, it never occured to me."

"Nonsense!"

"But—"

"You know me well enough to know that I would be helplessly attracted to you. You wanted to humble me."

They began walking off the dance floor. When they were seated, Tracy said with defiance in her voice, "There is never anything helpless about you. You are invulnerable, my dear Count Dandolo."

"Would you like to leave?"

"Yes, I think that's probably a good idea under the circumstances."

She retreated to the ladies' room while he took care of the check. Then his chauffeur drove her back to the Excelsior. Few words were exchanged between them. When the car stopped at the hotel, he smiled warmly at her. "I'm sorry, Tracy. Please forgive me for acting so stupidly, and for the harsh words."

Realizing that he had overcome his pride for her sake, she smiled back. "All is forgiven. See you tomorrow. Bright and early."

Thursday followed the pattern of the two previous days except that a huge barrier had risen between Tony and Tracy where before there had been warmth and a feeling of comradarie. They were distantly polite to each other all day long. Finally, at four in the afternoon, after Gene had pronounced it a great week and departed, Tony asked Tracy to step back inside his office for a moment.

Sitting on his sofa was a huge box, wrapped in blue paper and tied with a silver bow. "This is a gift I risked putting together for you. A sort of farewell gift. I say 'risked,' because I'm taking a chance on your reaction. I don't want you to think I'm attempting to bribe a member of the press."

"Tony! I wouldn't think that of you. You don't need to bribe anyone!"

"Good." He paused and straightened his tie. "I've put together a box of goodies—things Dandolo Enterprises manufactures. I hope I got the sizes right. I figured you were a size eight."

Her face broke into a smile. What a man he was! "Yes, I'm an eight. I see you are an expert at judging a woman's figure also!"

"My dear, all Italian men are!"

They laughed. Then he continued nervously, "Why don't you wait till you are back home to open the box, surprise yourself then. . . ."

"Okay."

He paced to the bar, then back to where she had sat down. "I want to say something to you, and I can't find exactly the right words. . . ."

"That's not like you!"

"Ah, no, it's not often that I'm so inarticulate . . . .Well, I want to apologize for any uncomfortable moments I've given you. But I want to say again what I said before—I've fallen for you. You've bewitched me. I wake up in the middle of the night wondering if I'll ever see you again, if I'll ever get over you, forget you—and I don't think I will. Don't be surprised if you find me on your doorstep someday soon."

She felt her face flush with embarrassment and wished he'd stop—and yet some part of her wanted him to continue.

"I'll say good-bye for now, Tracy. I've got to fly back to Milan tonight. I decided, since last night was such a disaster, that I'd get out of town and let you have your last night in Rome to yourself. Anyhow, it's been a wonderful week for me. I'll never forget it, and I'll be anxiously awaiting your videotape and articles." He handed her the box, forcing her to stand up to accept it and bid him farewell. As he walked her to the door, his hand found her waist. At the last possible moment, he kissed her cheek and gave her a quick bear hug. Then he shut the door behind her.

Tracy Brown fastened the seatbelt on the TWA 747. She was headed for home, for Washington. *Well, Mom, I think I really botched that one . . . I*

*don't know, he wasn't such a bad guy after all . . .
but I think somehow I evened the score for you. You
got your revenge, that's for sure!*

As the plane taxied down the runway and then
lifted above the Eternal City and headed home
across the Atlantic, Tracy allowed herself the luxury
of a few tears.

PART FIVE
Paul

Chapter Twenty-Six

The camera pulled back from Tracy and Senator Paul Benson, the sound went off, and the theme music began to play as the credits were superimposed over the picture of them chatting.

"I must say that you are as tough as I imagined you were," the Senator said, flashing her his famous boyish grin.

"And you, Senator, are as handsome and articulate as my assistant Sally told me you are. I hope I didn't get you in too much trouble with the leadership."

"Nothing we can't handle. When I get back to my desk, I'll have a note from the White House saying, 'With friends like you, we don't need enemies.'"

"It's really sad, isn't it . . ."

"Break" yelled the floor manager.

"Let me help you with that," Tracy offered as

Senator Benson fumbled with the microphone that had become caught in the fabric of his coat.

"Tell me," he said as she took the microphone from him, "what do you do for fun?"

"Oh—this! I mean, I don't really do much these days except work."

"Could I interest you in a nice quiet dinner some Saturday night soon?"

"I'd . . . I'd love that," she murmured as she looked again into his dark blue eyes. Sally had told her, "He's one of the wealthiest men in the senate, he's gorgeous, and he's eligible!" Tracy had looked at Sally's flushed face and had stopped herself from saying, "Why don't you go after him?" because Sally was already married. And she was such a convert to the state of matrimony that she was constantly suggesting eligible men to Tracy.

"I'll check my schedule and call you."

"Wonderful," she responded without meaning it. *He's too busy,* she told herself, *just like me.*

It was after Labor Day, three weeks later, before he called her, and when he did she had to turn him down because she was in New York negotiating a contract with her bosses at UBS. They had decided to add a female co-host in an attempt to lure some of the "Today Show" audience to "A.M. America." Tracy was more than willing to add being a co-host to her duties as Washington correspondent, but she wanted to remain in Washington, and it was a long-standing tradition for the show to originate in New York City. Her agent had gone back and forth with them for a week, and now she was to go to New York herself to let them see how unshakable she was.

The truth was that, in addition to her firm determination to stay in Washington for personal reasons, she knew she would be reduced to handling the "soft" pieces, the "women's pieces," even though no one dared to refer to them by that name anymore. Hard, tough interviews were her forte and she wasn't about to give that up for a more prestigious host job. She wanted to continue to cover the hard political stories, to interview members of Congress and the Administration. She'd made up her mind that she'd change networks before she'd leave Washington, and that was her bottom line.

Meanwhile, her agent, as a matter of principle, was trying to negotiate a higher salary for her. After four lengthy negotiating sessions over the weekend, she had left New York with things unresolved.

She returned to her Watergate apartment late Sunday night to find messages from Senator Benson and from Rosina. She called Rosina and set up a luncheon date with her for the following weekend, then called the senator at home.

"I just got in from New York City and thought I should call you tonight rather than try to catch up with you tomorrow."

"Too bad, it's too late. I was invited to a wonderful weekend at the River Oaks Horse Farm in New Jersey and since someone told me you loved horses, I thought you might like to go with me."

"Oh, I would have loved that!"

"What's next weekend like for you?"

"Mm . . . not too bad."

"Dinner Saturday?"

"I'd love it!"

"I'll pick you up at eight."

As she put the receiver down she felt a rush of exhilaration she hadn't felt in a long while. He *was* attractive, and if anyone could understand her busy life, it would be a man who was equally busy—and equally driven!

She walked to her closet and began to look through her cocktail clothes. What should she wear? It was the first date she had accepted in months.

Rosina walked shyly into the grand apartment, looked around again as if she were seeing it for the first time, kissed Tracy a second time, and hugged her a fraction longer. Then, with a mist of tears in her eyes and twisting an embroidered handkerchief in her hands, she sat carefully on the blue silk upholstered sofa. Tracy watched her thoughtfully, thinking that however well she and Manuel did financially—and they had a solid, if modest, income—Rosina would never get over feeling that she was an Italian peasant, a member of the servant class. It was reflected in the way she walked and in the clothes she wore—severe, plain clothes in black, navy, or gray. Nothing to call attention to herself.

And yet she was so conscious of Tracy's appearance, wanting her to be an absolute fashion plate. She was always urging Lorna's jewelry on her.

"You look wonderful, though I still think you're much too thin," she said, mother-like. "And last week even Manuel remarked about it when we watched you with Dr. Kissinger."

"You never miss a show, do you?"

Rosina blushed, grinned slowly, and said, "You know we couldn't love you more, couldn't be prouder of you if you were our own flesh. Your dear saintly mother would be so proud of you . . ." She wiped her eyes again with her hanky.

Why was it that every time Rosina visited her, she became so emotional?

"Rosina, I've made us a wonderful lunch. See! I

told you I would learn to cook! But first, could I coax you to try a glass of sherry?"

"That would be lovely, if you'd like that."

Tracy poured some sherry for both of them, carried a glass to Rosina, and sat beside her on the sofa, taking one of her hands in her own. "I've something to tell you, and I may as well start, so we can discuss it during lunch."

At first Rosina's face registered alarm, then broke out into a big smile. "You're going to get married!"

"Whoa! Slow down a bit. No, nothing like that."

Alarm again took its place on her face. If it wasn't good news, then she expected the worst.

"Last June, when I was in Europe, I visited my father." There, the worst of it was out.

"My God!" Rosina gasped, her skin turning ashen as the blood drained from her face and fear took over.

You have good reason to be afraid, Tracy thought as she watched Rosina, *but no, I wouldn't let him hurt you for anything. Not after all the love you've lavished on me.*

"Don't be alarmed. I didn't tell Count Dandolo who I am." A devilish grin on her face, she continued, "I disguised myself with a wig and contact lenses that made my eyes green. He never suspected."

"But how can that be?"

"He didn't know, I'm sure of that."

Rosina reached into her purse and fumbled around for her rosary beads.

"The reason I'm telling you this—Rosina, please don't cry, please don't worry. There is absolutely nothing to worry about."

"I . . . I was thinking of your mother. She will never forgive me. She made me promise never to let you see your father again. . . ."

"You know, Rosina—it's just possible, remotely possible, that my mother was wrong about that, that she was really wrong about denying her daughter a father."

"Don't say that! You mustn't say that! Your mother . . . your mother was a saint!"

"Rosina, darling, I know you loved my mother dearly, and I love her too, and I always will. But when a person dies . . . life must go on. Thank God she left me to two people as fine as you and Manuel. But I should have at least been given the choice of seeing my father once in a while, maybe for a vacation. . . ."

She watched Rosina break down into sobs. It was what she had expected. Well, Rosina would simply have to deal with it. She decided to let that theme alone.

"The reason I'm telling you this is that next week the network is going to begin advertising the next 'Windows' special, and I interview Count Antonio Dandolo on that special. I didn't want the advertisement to be a shock to you—and to Manuel." She paused to let it sink in. "Actually, I think it is one of the best shows I've ever done. There is a sparkle to it, a special chemistry."

"Are you going to see him again?" Rosina asked in a quavering voice.

"No. At least, I have no plans to see him again. He has absolutely no idea who I am, I promise you that."

"If he knew, if he knew about all those years. . . . The money—my God, the money—he might try to put us in jail!"

"Rosina, Rosina, don't be ridiculous! Why, if he knew about everything you and Manuel did for me, he'd be eternally grateful to you both, I know it." She put her arm around Rosina to comfort the badly shaken woman. "My father is not an evil man, Rosina, despite what you think of him. He is a very fair, very generous man."

Rosina began to regain control of herself. Tracy wondered if she dared ask about the money, since it so obviously was a source of guilt for Rosina. "Tell me about the money. What are you talking about?"

"After your mother left your father, he arranged through her lawyer to send her money once a year."

"Yes." She waited.

"After Lorna's accident, the lawyer decided it would be best not to inform the count of her death. That way, the money would continue, and we would have it to pay your expenses."

"That sounds reasonable." *Except that someone should have had the decency to tell my father about mother's death*, she told herself.

"They made me quit my job at Mrs. Merriweather Post's so I would be home to take care of you, and to make up for the lack of salary, Mr. Westerman paid me an annual salary of twelve thousand a year, until you left home for college."

"That sounds fine. Why are you so upset?"

"I always . . . felt guilty. Because it seemed like such a miracle for me to have you as a daughter . . . it was a blessing from God, and I shouldn't have been paid for it."

"But that's silly. You lavished money on me, bought me beautiful clothes, a car, furnished my first apartment—"

"All that was money from your father."

"I see." All these years she had been feeling grateful and indebted to the wrong person. It had been her father's generosity that had made everything possible.

"Does he still send money?"

"Yes. He increased the amount to one hundred

thousand years ago. So Manuel found a financial manager to invest it for you." Her voice began to lighten, and as Tracy looked hard at her she saw the beginnings of a smile. "Manuel says you are a multi-millionaire already. The money has been invested wisely."

"Let me understand this. You received a salary for caring for me, you spent some of the money directly on me, and the rest was invested for me. And you think my father is going to be angry?"

"He will destroy us." Rosina began to sound hysterical. "We helped your mother leave him. I stole paintings for your mother, very valuable paintings. Manuel even pawned your mother's most valuable jewelry so she could buy the house in Woodstock. If your father discovers all this, he will do something terrible to us."

"No, I won't let him," Tracy said firmly. "Not that he'd want to anyhow." Tracy thought of the immense cloud of terror and grief these two people had lived with for so many years. Somehow, she had to dispell that fear, that daily terror of discovery. "Rosina, do you still have all the rest of the jewelry?"

"Yes, in a box at the bank."

"Okay. I think you and Manuel should turn over the jewelry, and the investments and all the remaining money to me. And we must direct the attorney to send any money my father sends in the future directly to me. That way I alone will be responsible for my relationship with my father. The two of you have done more than anyone could have expected of you."

"Yes. I'll tell Manuel. He'll be so glad." Relief broke out all over Rosina. "He has wanted to turn it all over to you for some time now. He always thought we were wrong to keep you from your father. He will be glad if you see your father again, if you let him know who you are."

"Well, I'm glad I'll please one of you at least! Now, I think it is time we had lunch." As they walked toward the patio where Tracy had set a table for two, she saw a visible lightening in Rosina's step and in her mood. *I've done the right thing*, she thought.

The following Friday afternoon, Tracy stayed late at her office to compose a long letter to Count Dandolo. She had ordered a videotape of the special and she had saved copies of the two different magazine articles she had written about him. Now it was time to send them, and it would be simple politeness to enclose a covering letter.

Dear Count Dandolo,

Many times during the past three months, my thoughts have returned to my wonderful visit with you in June. I fell in love with Italy, with the art and the people and the bustling cities, and all the monuments and museums, and especially with the devilish Italian men! I even gained six pounds which, you may be sure, I promptly shed on my return to work— real work!

I am sending you a videotape of the show which will air in America next week. It is one of the best I have ever done. I trust Alberto will be pleased with the views of the gardens and stables. And I hope you will find the interviews to your satisfaction. After next week, Dandolo will be a household name in the U.S.!

Fall is the most glorious season of the year in Washington, should you ever make up your mind to return for a visit. And the World Bank and International Monetary Fund always meet in September. If your travels bring you this way, do look me up.

Finally, again I offer my thanks for a glorious week in Italy. Working is rarely so pleasant.

> Mi saluti tanto i suoi,
> Tracy Brown

She read it a second time, signed it, and placed the letter with the rest of the package to be shipped to his office in Milan on Monday.

Chapter Twenty-Seven

JANUARY, 1984—PHILADELPHIA

Tracy sat in the kitchen at the large oak table and watched Kristy White feed her two adopted children, sixteen-month-old Todd and four-year-old Sheilah. Much to Tracy's surprise, her old roommate Kristy had metamorphosed into the perfect suburban mother. She seemed totally delighted with her life, continued to be enthused with Kevin's career, and seemed not the least bit jealous of the spotlight that constantly shone on him. Even more surprising to Tracy was Kristy's dedication to monogamy after what could only be described as promiscuous college years.

The two women made it a point to get together twice a year, usually with Kristy playing hostess and her children much in evidence. Tracy didn't mind a bit, because it gave her a chance to glimpse firsthand the joys and trials of motherhood and to return to her own serene environment at the Water-

gate and congratulate herself on having withstood
Rosina's and Kristy's constant suggestions that she
should be getting married.

"It's getting late, you are over thirty! And you
certainly don't want to start a family after thirty-
five or six," had been Kristy's warning the previous
evening as they sipped brandy before the huge
stone fireplace in the "great room."

Kevin had risen in the ranks of local television to
become the highest paid local newsman and anchor
of the ninety-minute evening news. As such, he was
a much-in-demand Philadelphia celebrity. He and
Kristy had an active and very sophisticated social
life, "which gives me all the glamour I need,"
Kristy had assured Tracy.

There were times when Tracy envied her the lack
of pressure in her life, and other times when she
thought how nice it must be to come home to a man
who adored you and children who needed you. She
felt this way especially on holidays like Christmas
and New Year's and Thanksgiving—holidays she
incvitably spent with Manuel and Rosina, whom
she loved dearly but found rather boring company
after the first hour.

But this had been her choice, her decision. She
was the one who deliberately discouraged men,
who usually ended a relationship after a second or
third date. She told herself she didn't want anything
to interfere with her career. She had told Kristy that
the night before.

"My God, Tracy, how can you be worried about
something like that? Here you are, the female
co-host on one of the most popular shows in the
country, you make a cool million a year, and your
ratings are phenomenal. You can write your own
ticket. You could afford to take a few private hours
a week and cultivate a personal relationship. What

are you afraid of, for God's sake? Someday, mark my words, someday you're going to regret that you've wasted these years. Someday you're going to want grandchildren, even if you don't want children now!"

"You and Rosina sound like broken records on the subject."

"Look, you make more money than you'll ever spend. You work fourteen, sixteen hours a day. For what? Who do you spend your nights with? Who do you spend your weekends with?"

"Sometimes I think of you, Kristy, and wonder if you are as happy as you try to make me believe. Don't you ever miss having a career?"

"Hell, yes! I'm envious as shit when I see pictures of you in a magazine, when I watch you rip some cabinet officer to ribbons. By the way, you were especially good with Alexander Haig last week. But I think you could have been rougher on Cap Weinberger. I think he's a snake."

"But did you notice how many of the cabinet we've had? More than any other network."

"So I am envious, I'll admit it. Once in a while. Then I tuck Todd into bed and tell Sheilah a bedtime story, and I think about all that you are missing, and I wouldn't change places with you for anything in the world."

Tracy pondered what Kristy had said, taking note of the vehemence in her voice. She really seemed to believe it. "Do you think it would be possible to combine both, keep the show and get married and have children?"

"Well . . . you'd have to have awfully good help in the house and a husband who was willing to pinch-hit a lot of the time. I don't know, the pressures would be very intense."

"That's what I think. I don't see how anyone

could combine what I do every day with motherhood. Maybe marriage, if the man was really sympathetic, perhaps someone in the industry who really understood. . . ."

"Hey, whatever happened with Senator Paul Benson? Last summer I thought maybe something real was beginning to happen there."

"The problem is always the same—time. He has a heavy schedule and so do I. The chemistry is right, sometimes a wonderful kind of magic. But then something happens."

"Most likely you turn him off. You're afraid of a real commitment."

"That's one of the surprising things about you, your faithfulness to Kevin. I never would have believed it."

"Yeah. One of the benefits of sowing a few wild oats in college and high school is that it makes it easy to be faithful later on because you know for a fact that it doesn't get any better, ever!" Kristy put down her knitting and stood up to stretch. Then she offered Tracy another Amaretto.

"Haven't you even been tempted to try an affair?"

"Nope. Besides, both Kevin and I are too easily recognized. It would be impossible. And I have never met anyone who seemed exciting enough to take the risk." She poured more Amaretto into Tracy's glass. "So tell me, are you sleeping with the Senator?"

Tracy flushed, then thought, *what the hell, we're best friends. I can admit it.* "Once in a while, when we both have time for a long, leisurely evening."

"And how is it? Is he good?" Kristy grinned at Tracy. "C'mon, spill the beans, tell me!"

"Mostly he's tender and gentle and filled with humor. And then there are times when he's wildly passionate." She paused, then added in a slightly dreamy voice, "He's as good as I've ever had and sometimes I fantasize about throwing in the towel at UBS and living happily ever after with him. But I'm never sure—sure that it *will* be happy-ever-after that is. I'm not sure I want to compete with his first love, which is his career. I don't think I could stand to take second place—to anything."

"Look, you idiot, he's rich, he's good-looking, he's famous, and he'll probably go on to bigger and better things. I don't know what you are waiting for—you should grab him!"

Those words of Kristy's had reverberated in her mind all night, causing her to toss and turn and flail at the blankets in the huge antique four-poster bed. Much of Kristy's life appealed to her, especially the two adorable little ones, yet there was a part of her which would not seriously consider marriage. She woke up with a start at sunrise when she heard a rooster crow from an adjoining farm. *Mother would be opposed*, were the words on her mind. But she had to ask herself, *what is it that mother would be opposed to*? And a voice answered back, *Mother would be opposed to your marrying Paul.*

Chapter Twenty-Eight

"Ah, here comes the glorious Morning Star!" Mel Krupin exclaimed as Tracy descended the staircase. She presented her right cheek for the obligatory kiss, aware that all of Krupin's customers were watching. "Mike, you take Tracy over to Senator Benson. He's been waiting fifteen minutes already." Then to Tracy, with a wink, he said, "You'll have to drink fast to catch up with him."

Tracy followed Mike the few feet to the first banquette. Paul stood to kiss her lightly. When they were both seated and she had nodded hello to Dan Rather seated two tables away, Tracy asked Mike to bring her a Kir Royale.

"I was afraid you'd changed your mind. I'm glad you came," Paul said quietly.

"I'm not sure this is the right place for this discussion, Paul. . . ."

"I love you, Tracy. I want to begin by telling you

that I love you more than anyone in the world, and I do want you to marry me. Soon."

Tracy smiled weakly, warming to his gentleness.

Mike brought the Kir Royale and set it in front of Tracy with a great flourish. "And how about you, Senator? Another Diet Coke?"

Paul shook his head, then immediately turned to the reason for their lunch—a discussion of her father. "The first time the special on Count Dandolo was aired, I thought I recognized the picture of you, your mother and father standing in front of the embassy—that one over your night table that I asked you about the first night I stayed with you. Anyway, I was stunned, but I wasn't certain. Two weeks ago, when it was aired again on a Baltimore station, I recorded it on my VCR and I've watched it several times since. Yesterday I looked at the picture beside your bed. It's the same picture." He stopped to sip on his coke.

"I have the feeling it's a long story." He took her hand in his. "I also have the feeling that it has something to do with the way you feel about me."

She looked into his eyes and found compassion and love she had never seen before. This man—perhaps—she could trust. After all, she had trusted David, and it had been such a relief. . . .

"You must never tell anyone what I am about to tell you," she began, and it took her most of the rest of the afternoon to tell him her life story. Late in the evening at dinner, after listening compassionately since lunch, he finally said to her, "You haven't asked me for advice, but I'm going to give it to you anyhow. Until you make peace with your father, until you give him a chance to make amends for a horrible mistake he made when he was a young man, until you let yourself love him again, you will never find peace of mind. And you will never be able to bring yourself to make a commitment to a man."

She knew he was speaking of himself. Somehow, though he had said not a word about marriage since lunch, she knew he wanted that from her, and she found herself wondering what the connection was. Was it possible that he was right?

That night they made love, slowly and deliciously, savoring their new level of emotional intimacy, each delighting in the desire to find greater fulfillment in pleasing the other.

Finally, sated with food, drink, and love, they fell asleep entwined with hope.

Chapter Twenty-Nine

APRIL, 1984

Tracy walked into the kitchen, put her briefcase and two newspapers down on the table, poured herself a glass of iced tea from the pitcher in the refrigerator, and peeked at the casserole and salad her housekeeper Asun had left for dinner. Paul was planning on coming over about eight, after attending three cocktail parties. Since his discovery about her father, they had begun to spend much more time together. He left several changes of clothes in her apartment, and they tried to have dinner there at least three evenings during the week; then he treated her on weekends. It was a comfortable arrangement for both of them, and sometimes Tracy thought that they lived almost like an old married couple.

She went to her bedroom for a sweater and came back to open the patio door. The sun was already beginning to make its way behind the treetops and glass buildings of Rosslyn. The Potomac River shimmered in the late afternoon glow, and cars were beginning to slow to a crawl on the freeway below her balcony. It was her favorite time of day, and as often as possible she excused herself from her office and brought her briefing materials for the next morning's show home to study on the patio. She was interviewing Admiral Morgan Alexander the next morning and, next to the federal budget, she always found defense issues the most complex subject to interview a guest on. It was doubly complicated because she knew they could always hide behind a "security" screen and refuse to discuss material which was, in reality, a matter of political judgment. Alexander was very good at this, and she set out to find an opening wedge.

She had been working for a little more than a half hour when her phone rang. The doorman informed her that she had a visitor, "a very distinguished European gentleman who doesn't want me to tell you his name. He wants to surprise you."

With only a moment's consideration, her mind still back on European defenses and intelligence operations, she told the doorman to send the gentleman up.

She ran a brush through her hair and applied fresh lipstick. When the doorbell rang she opened it, not even trying to guess who it might be.

Count Dandolo, holding a huge bouquet of roses, smiled broadly at her, then reached for her hand.

"My God, Tony! I mean—Count Dandolo, what a surprise!"

"That's what I wanted. You look wonderful, as beautiful as ever! I wanted to thank you in person for the marvelous television program and the articles. My God, you are even more beautiful than I remembered! Aren't you going to invite me in?"

"Oh—oh, but—yes, of course." Her mind was swirling, she had to get her green contacts, her wig.

"What a wonderful apartment you have here. I never dreamt something so elegant existed in Washington. You know, when we were here in the fifties, there was nothing like this. . . ."

He laid the roses down on the dining table and walked directly onto the patio where Tracy had been working. She was frantically wondering what to do, what to tell him, when, almost to her relief, the phone rang. She excused herself, telling him to make himself a drink from the bar in the living room while she got the phone in the kitchen.

A female voice on the other end of the line asked her to hold for the President. Damn, she thought, this is going to take a long time, and I'm going to have to concentrate.

"Tracy, how are you? I've been meaning to call you for several days now to tell you personally that I'll do that special for you."

"Wonderful, I'm thrilled . . ."

Count Dandolo poured himself a stiff Scotch and turned to face the sofa. His eyes rested on the large canvas, obviously by Monet or one of his students, hanging above it. He walked slowly toward the canvas, looked carefully at the signature, then backed up again. *Strange, it looks so much like the painting I gave Lorna as a wedding present*, he thought. Then his mind jumped to the fact that Tracy herself looked different. He couldn't put his finger on it . . . the eyes—yes, that was it, her eyes were blue today! He thought they were green.

He looked around the apartment some more, applauding Tracy's taste in furnishings, then walked back to the Monet. It seemed to be the same painting. He would ask Tracy where she found it.

He could overhear her conversation from the kitchen well enough to know she was talking to the President of the United States, and that it seemed to be continuing.

He wandered down the hall, past the small library and into the bedroom, drawn by a painting visible from the hallway which looked remarkably like one of Lorna's. As he crossed the threshold into the bedroom, he saw the two small Flemish oils, the missing Van Ecyk paintings. He sat his glass of Scotch down on the dresser, feeling himself trembling.

He walked, mesmerized, toward the head of the four-poster bed, toward the long-missing paintings. His mind was beginning to dare to hope. . . . He looked for a long moment, then slumped down on the bed, a devastating feeling creeping over him. *Tracy Tanya Tracy Tanya* burbled through his mind. Then his eyes wandered to the picture framed in silver, sitting alone in the place of honor beside her bed. He picked it up and looked at himself, his Lorna, his Tanya . . .

Tracy said good-bye, feeling relief and trepidation flood over her. She walked into the living room. It was empty. Suddenly, she knew. She knew he had walked into her bedroom. She walked quickly to the door and saw him slumped on the bed, the picture in his hand. She walked into the bedroom, stopping herself at the dresser to regain her equilibrium. He sensed her presence and looked up at her, grief and questions in his eyes.

"Daddy . . . Daddy, I . . ."

He put the picture down. He stood and she ran to him, threw her arms around him and embraced him with the passion she had wanted to show him that night in Rome. "Oh Daddy, I'm so glad you've come. I'm so glad you've come to find me. It's been so long . . ."

"Tanya, my darling. Why . . . why didn't you tell me?"

They hugged and they cried and they didn't even try to talk intelligently for a long while. Presently, he wiped his eyes and said, "We both need a drink—a good strong one," and they walked with their arms around each other back into the living room.

For two hours they talked, Tracy trying to tell her father her whole life story in as compressed a form as possible, Tony simply reveling in having found his lost beauty and overwhelmed at her story, at the realization that his Tanya was the famous American television star. And most of all, he was overwhelmed and grateful that, in spite of everything, she had a huge reservoir of love for him—love mixed with forgiveness, mixed with questions.

"Oh, Daddy, we have so much to talk about! You must stay for a long time. Will the bank meetings really take up a lot of your time?"

"In the daytime, but then you have your show to do."

"But evenings and weekends—how long can you stay?"

"I'm sure I can stay at least two weeks, maybe a month—however long, it doesn't matter. I'll make the arrangements tomorrow."

"Wonderful. I want you to meet Paul—oh, he'll be here in a few minutes. I almost forgot. Daddy, I hope you don't mind, but you're going to be introduced as my father in a few minutes! Do you think you can handle that?"

"With the greatest joy—the greatest joy I've felt in years and years. You can't imagine how happy I

am this minute. But I must confess, I'm not ready
to share you with any young man, not yet. I hope
this is not serious. . . ."

Then he saw from her eyes that it was serious,
and he quickly said, "I'm only kidding. I want to
meet your young man. Then we'll send him away
for a month so we can get reacquainted."

Paul arrived a few minutes later, astonished at
the developments he had hoped for. He felt he was
an interloper in a very dramatic, very emotional
reunion, but Tracy insisted he stay for dinner and
they stretched the casserole and salad to feed three.

It was the wee hours of the morning before Tracy
would let the two of them depart. Paul was to drive
Tony back to the Madison Hotel, and then was
going home himself, as Tracy had her usual five
a.m. call the next morning.

"I really don't expect to sleep much tonight," she
said as she kissed Tony good-night, and he assured
her that all the wine she had drunk would take care
of that.

But she slept like a baby that night, and awoke
with a happiness she hadn't felt since she was a
child. He had come to find her. He loved her and
she loved him in return.

She spent her hours at the station in a cloud of
love, feeling nothing could go wrong ever again.
Her mood was so dramatically altered that her
producer asked her if she was suddenly "in love."
"Yes indeed!" she replied gaily, thinking of both
her father and Paul.

She looked forward to their evenings together as
if he were a favored beau, dressing to please him,
flirting outrageously with him as she had done
when she was six years old. She teased him about
having fallen in love with her in Rome, and he
scolded her for having tricked him, then they both

laughed at the memories of those hectic days. She poured out the details of her life and told him shamelessly of her love affairs, a small voice in the back of her mind reminding her, even as she told him, that she might not have chosen those particular men as lovers if she had had a father to come home to.

The subject she couldn't let go of, she couldn't hear enough about, was his feelings for her mother. On the second Saturday morning after his arrival, she drove him to her favorite spot in all of Washington—Great Falls in Potomac. She had made it a point to retreat there many times during the year for long walks, to see the seasons change up close, to practice her rusting photographic skills.

They walked down the long path and came to rest at a place where she liked to sit and watch the water career off the rocks. They sat on the boulders. Tracy picked up a dry leaf and began tracing the veins with her fingernail.

"Tell me, Daddy, is the love you felt for Tamara different from the love you felt for mother?"

"In so many ways! I loved your mother with a love that made no judgments. When I think back on my feelings for her, I realize that it was a one-sided relationship. I had her way up there on a pedestal. She was different from any woman I had ever met—regal, cool, distant. I was never able to breach that distance. We never achieved what I would call real intimacy. She kept me at arm's length, as if there was some part of her I wasn't to be allowed to know, to penetrate. It annoyed me, but I think it was also a part of her fascination for me. She was a challenge."

"Mother was so beautiful. I don't understand how you even looked at another woman."

"Ahh, those were the Kennedy years. That was a

special time in Washington, a permissive, almost licentious time. The atmosphere in Washington, at least among the men, permitted anything, in fact applauded womanizing. Everyone was doing it."

"That's no excuse."

"Of course not. But let me tell you how it felt at the time. We had always heard in Europe that Americans were prudish, puritanical, Victorian, especially in matters of sex. When we arrived here, I quickly saw that was certainly not the case in the Kennedy Administration. It seemed the more outrageously they behaved sexually—I mean group sex, wife-trading, all that sort of thing—the more the American people loved the glamour they had brought to the White House. I was observing it as an outsider, weighing everything I saw and heard and sensed against everything I had heard before I left home. Well, let me tell you, Washington at that time was as hedonistic as anything I've ever seen in Europe, even among the idle rich, the jet set. It was fascinating, and at the time seemed very glamorous. Every man I knew in Washington had a mistress. Some had several, and they all loved to boast about their exploits."

"So you joined the crowd."

"Not exactly. Not quite like that. Tamara was a beautiful, talented woman, your mother's best friend and confidant. We worked together for a long time before anything happened. Oh, I won't tell you that the sexual attraction wasn't there from the start—it was, but we tried to overcome it, to rise above it. Then one day the temptation simply became too much for both of us and we found ourselves in bed together. Tamara was instantly accessible in ways your mother never was. She was a master of instant intimacy—the kind I needed and wanted from your mother. She had an understanding of the male ego that Lorna never had. I viewed our relationship as a passing, though nevertheless meaningful, love affair. It would build to a certain level of passion, then gradually die away, which in my experience has been the course of all love affairs."

"Except it didn't go away."

"Because Tamara was clever enough to get pregnant." Tony stood, walked over to a tree, picked a piece of the drying bark off, and began to massage it between his fingers. He looked back at Tracy and she saw that he was deep in reverie, almost lost to her.

"I'll never know if Tamara knew that Lorna couldn't get pregnant, if she knew how deeply I wanted a son, someone to carry on the family's ancient name, to take over the businesses. Maybe she knew, maybe she didn't. In any event, she got pregnant. She told me she wanted an abortion— well, Tracy, darling, you'd have to understand how strongly I felt about that. No child of mine was going to be murdered, not when I could give that child everything."

"Not when that child might be a *son*. . . ."

"It wasn't just that. I truly believe I would have felt exactly the same—hell, I did. I didn't know Tamara would have a son, but I wanted our baby to live, to have all the benefits I could provide." He dropped the piece of bark, walked to the railing, and stood contemplating the falls.

After a few minutes of deep thought, he turned and came back to where Tracy was sitting. "She tried to kill herself on New Year's Eve. Lorna discovered our affair, and I sent Tamara away to Florida with plenty of money. We agreed the affair would end, completely end. Then after Alberto was born, she got terribly bored in Florida and came back to Washington. One day we ran into each other on the sidewalk, when she was pushing the pram with Alberto in it. Well, seeing that little baby destroyed my resolve. I went to see her that afternoon, and it all began again. Inevitably, I suppose, Lorna found out. But even if she hadn't, the feelings Lorna once had for me had been destroyed. She had begun to hate me. Love turned to hate is an awful thing to live with."

"Why didn't you get a proper divorce?"

Tony sat down beside Tracy and reached for her hand. "I refused to face the fact that Lorna might really leave me. I couldn't tolerate the idea, couldn't bear to think about it. I loved Lorna, always loved her more than I loved Tamara. I never entertained for one second the fantasy of spending the rest of my life with Tamara. I would always have provided for her financially, but I really believed that Lorna and I would return to Florence and live out the rest of our days there, and that Tamara would ultimately marry some man and live happily ever after here in Washington. I figured that when Alberto was an adult, he would come to Florence and assume his rightful place in the business."

"Did you even discuss a divorce?"

"Yes. Lorna asked me for a divorce several times. I got so angry, so furious with her—I think that may have been my greatest mistake. I may have scared her. I know I tried to plead, to bully, to threaten, cajole, God knows I tried everything."

"And . . . ?"

"One day she just disappeared, took you and disappeared. It was a tremendous shock."

"Did you try to find us?"

"Not very hard. I think I would have killed her if I'd found her. I would have killed her for trying to leave me, for taking you away from me. I didn't trust myself, my terrible passions. Forgive me, darling, but my temper had a way of getting out of control when I was a young man. I knew that, and a voice inside my head kept warning me not to hurt her more than I already had."

He coughed nervously, then continued, his voice raspy with emotion, "You see . . . I told her one day that if she tried to leave me, I would make sure she never saw you again as long as she lived. I can still hear my voice saying that to her, I can still see her stricken face. That face haunts my dreams to this day. . . ."

Tracy stared at her father's ashen face. Her mother's words of caution came floating back to her memory: "You must never tell anyone who your father is. If you do, he will take you away from me and I'll never get to see you again." It had been the ultimate threat. Lorna had used it to keep Tracy in line, just as Tony had used it to try to keep Lorna.

She looked at her father's face, his eyes pleading for forgiveness. "She believed that, Daddy. She really believed that you would take me away from her."

They wrapped their arms around each other, their bodies convulsed in sobs.

Finally, Tony pulled away. "If there is one moment of my life that I could live over, it would be that one. You can't know how many times I've wanted to cut my tongue out for having frightened her in that way—and yet, when I said it, I meant it. I would have done anything to keep Lorna. I loved her so. . . ."

"You should have taken the two of us back to Italy, left Tamara . . ."

"Yes, I should have. But I was enjoying being the

big-shot-ambassador-in-Washington too much. Eventually, I told myself, I'll end this nightmare for Lorna, I'll take her home but she left before I did."

They walked back to the parking lot, and he took her hand. "Tanya, can you ever understand—enough to forgive me? Have you ever felt yourself in love with two men at once? Does it ever happen to a woman?"

She listened to his plea and weighed his question against her own experiences with love. *Yes*, she thought, *I can understand. If David were to arrive in Washington this afternoon and call me it would be very hard to resist, and yet Paul is the man I can begin to imagine as a companion for life. And then there's Stan—will I ever be able to stop loving Stan? Is that the way a first love affects your life?*

She smiled at him, a warm glow of love and understanding passing between them. In a quiet voice, she said, "It happens to women too. . . ."

They walked the rest of the way in silence, each lost in thought.

When they got into the car, she paused before turning the key in the ignition to ask him the question he still hadn't answered. "Daddy, why did you wait so long before you came to find me?"

"Is that why I made this trip?" He chuckled. "I thought it was to attend a symposium at the International Monetary Fund. And then of course, there was this American television star I was lusting after. . . ."

They both laughed, but Tracy's serious face told Tony that she wanted a real answer.

"I'm not sure I had the courage to come find you. I've been afraid all these years that I might do exactly what I knew was wrong. If I came looking for Lorna and my daughter Tanya, I would have taken Tanya away from Lorna. And in doing that I would have been hurting—again—the one human being in the world I loved the most. I didn't want to hurt Lorna even more deeply than I already had."

"I see." She began to turn the key.

"And there is one more thing. I was afraid of you, Tanya. I was afraid you would hate me—as you had every right to."

"Well, I'm glad it's over. For both of us, I'm glad the long wait is over."

Their wonderful month together, a month she would remember for the rest of her life, was nearly over. It was the night before he was scheduled to return to Italy. They were downstairs in the Watergate restaurant, Jean Louis.

After toasting their love with Kir Royale cocktails, Tony once more brought up a subject that was much on his mind. He had been pleading with her for two weeks to come back to Italy, claim what was hers—the Villa, the art, her grandmother's jewels —and he would give her an important job in Dandolo Enterprises if she wanted—"or you'll never have to work another day in your life."

She had resisted him, explaining that her life was here in America. She had created herself, she had become Tracy Brown, she had made herself into a major television personality, and she loved the challenge, the pressure, the fame. She loved the whole thing.

"If you ever reconsider, and decide you're tired of the rat race, the early morning hours, all the backbreaking work—you know you never have to work another day in your life. . . ."

"Neither do you, Daddy. Yet you run for political office, you work like the devil for the business— who are you to lecture me? I've just been blessed with your genes!"

"But you're a woman! Women aren't meant to work like that!"

"Daddy! Come out of the Middle Ages and into the twentieth century! Stop being a male chauvinist!"

"Look, at my age you can't expect me to change my ideas!"

"Daddy, you are as bad as Rosina. She constantly lectures me on getting married. And my friend Kristy—"

"They are both right."

"Oh, so now you've joined them! Traitor! God, I'd be so bored without my work. I can't even imagine my life without my work. Besides, I like the independence."

"Where does Paul fit in your scheme of things?"

"If I marry anyone, it will be Paul. But I don't know . . . ."

"Are you afraid?"

"Well, look at what happened to my mother and father."

"But at least we had the courage to try. Perhaps that's what you don't have. You have plenty of courage to get in front of those cameras. I realize that. But do you have the courage to let yourself really love a man, to even try?"

"I was thinking about that the other day. I can't think of one woman who has successfully combined a daily television show with marriage and motherhood—and lasted for more than ten years. Something has to give."

"Wouldn't there be a way of altering your career, but still keeping your foot in—a show once a month, something like that?"

"Look, Daddy, when the desire to get married is strong enough, I'll be willing to consider compromises in my career. Until that time . . ."

"When will you visit? I hope before Christmas."

She grinned at him, teasing, "I always spend Christmas with Rosina and Manuel."

"I'll send them two round-trip tickets. They'd probably love an all-expense-paid trip to Italy. By the way, I'm establishing a trust for them, to thank them for everything."

"Oh, Daddy, I love you! You are wonderful." Impulsively, she kissed his cheek, oblivious to stares by other diners.

Chapter Thirty

FLORENCE, ITALY—JANUARY, 1985

Once again she was a guest in the blue-and-coral bedroom—"the bedroom your mother stayed in the first time she visited the Villa"—Tony had told her as he and Tamara led her into the flower-filled guest bedroom. "And Paul has the room I had as a boy."

For Rosina and Manuel, the nicest guest room on the third floor had been reserved. They, along with several dozen friends and relatives of Paul's family, had come to Italy for the New Year's festivities, and more importantly, for the wedding of American television star Tracy Brown to Senator Paul Benson. The wedding would take place in the second-floor library, a private ceremony for only the closest relatives and friends, to be followed by a reception for four hundred of Tony's "closest friends" in the first-floor ballroom.

After the wedding, Paul and Tracy would journey

to northern Italy to Cortina d'Ampezzo, to spend the first week of their married life skiing down the same mountain slopes where her parents had skied exactly thirty-five years before. They would be staying in Tony's villa, sleeping in the same bed he and Lorna had—even as Tony had made their plans for them, Tracy had wondered at the weird symbolism. Was she tempting fate, or was she communicating with her mother in some mystic way?

She had told Paul her conflicting feelings—and he had forced her to talk them out. She told him everything these days, everything that crossed her mind. She teased him that he had become her psychotherapist, and he had responded that nothing made him more confident of her love than her new-found ability to confide in him. He wanted to help her confront all the ghosts of her past and conquer them. Perhaps then she would find the elusive serenity which seemed lurking just around the bend.

The appointed hour had arrived for her to dress for the grand occasion. She asked Kristy and Rosina to keep her company, for they had been her salvation through happy and sad days, they had shared her anxieties and victories, and now she wanted them with her as her moment of commitment arrived. Valentino knocked, came in and checked to see if the confection of white silk faille and re-embroidered lace was perfect. Satisfied, he kissed her good luck, and left her with Carita, the hairdresser who had flown in from Rome that morning. Finally, Tracy was ready, but too nervous to sit down. And there were still fifteen minutes to go.

Rosina had been weeping for the past hour,

weeping between smiles and exclamations. At last, it was time for her to take her place next to Manuel in the library. She stood on tiptoe to kiss Tracy. "God bless you." She turned away, then with her handkerchief ready to dab her tears, she added, "Your mother would be so proud of you today!" Then she fled from the room. Kristy once more began fussing with her eyeshadow, and Tracy tried to still her nerves by concentrating on the swans floating across the sparkling lake.

There was a knock at the door, then it opened. "It's me!" Tony beamed, as he walked in carrying a silver tray with three glasses of champagne and a large velvet jewelry box. "I thought we ought to loosen up a bit!" he said as he offered Kristy a glass of bubbly.

Kristy, realizing this was to be a private moment, accepted the glass and excused herself, pleading that she had to see Kevin for a moment.

"I have a special favor to ask, my dear."

What now? thought Tracy, as she remembered all the compromises she had made with her father so that this wedding would be what he wanted it to be. She had rationalized that this was his way of telling all his relatives and friends that he had recovered his daughter—only to lose her to another man!

"I took your grandmother Catarina's jewels out of the safe yesterday and picked out these earrings and this necklace. They were her favorites and she always said she was going to give them to you on your wedding day. Well, she left you everything, as you know, and I think she will weep with joy up in heaven if you wear them today."

Tracy stared at the earrings and matching pendant. Each earring was composed of two diamonds—a small round diamond attached to a huge pear-shaped diamond. The pendant was a matching, larger pear-shaped diamond suspended from a collar of round diamonds. "My God! I've never seen such diamonds!"

"Magnificent, aren't they? Three of the finest diamonds ever mined. The pear-shaped stones in the earrings are thirteen carats each and the pendant is twenty-two carats. Bulgari claims they are the finest pieces he's ever handled."

"But Daddy, a senator's wife can't wear jewelry like this! It would be a scandal!"

"I'm sure that when the Rockefellers and the Fords and the Vanderbilts attend parties at the White House, they wear jewelry like this. When Paul is elected President, I want my daughter to be equally well-dressed!"

"Daddy, you really are incorrigible!"

"Which reminds me—that friend of yours, Kristy, is really something!"

"Yes, and she's very much married! Hands off!"

"You know I'm only kidding."

"I'm never sure about you. I understand there was an American television star you tried to seduce not too long ago."

"Yeah, but she's getting married to an ambitious Senator later today."

"Daddy, I love you so much. Thank you . . . for finding me, for this wedding . . ."

"As your father, I'm entitled to give one last piece of advice. And I have to start by saying 'don't do as I do, do as I say.' The concept of family is Italy's great contribution to the world. The family is our only shelter against a cold, cruel world. Love your husband, trust him, bring tolerance and flexibility into your relationship. And have children, my darling—they will be your greatest source of happiness as the years move on. I know. I have you and I have Alberto, and I would give up everything I've ever had or owned if necessary to keep the love of the two of you. Your respect and love mean more to me than anything else in the world. I want you to have that same joy someday, the joy of loving your adult children. It's the greatest gift God gives us."

He pulled a handkerchief out of his pocket, wiped his eyes, and then gruffly commanded her to put her jewelry on. "Our guests are waiting. Your man is waiting."

Then, after one last look in the mirror, the two of them walked down the hall toward the library. Tony led his Tanya down the aisle toward Paul. He kissed her on both cheeks, then surrendered her to her lover, whispering "Go, with God's love."